THE

MONSTER'S

DAUGHTER

A NOVEL

MICHELLE PRETORIUS

MELVILLE HOUSE
BROOKLYN • LONDON

THE MONSTER'S DAUGHTER

Copyright © 2016 by Michelle Pretorius
First Melville House Hardcover Printing: July 2016
First Melville House Paperback Printing: July 2017

Melville House Publishing   8 Blackstock Mews
        46 John Street   and   Islington
     Brooklyn, NY 11201   London N4 2BT

mhpbooks.com   facebook.com/mhpbooks   @melvillehouse

Library of Congress Cataloging-in-Publication Data
Names: Pretorius, Michelle.
Title: The monster's daughter : a novel / Michelle Pretorius.
Description: Brooklyn : Melville House, [2016]
Identifiers: LCCN 2016006383| ISBN 9781612195384 (hardback) |
    ISBN 9781612195391 (ebook)
Subjects: LCSH: Policewomen—Fiction. | Young women—Crimes
    against—Fiction. | South Africa—Race relations—Fiction. |
    Apartheid—South Africa—Fiction. | BISAC: FICTION /
    Mystery & Detective / Women Sleuths. | GSAFD: Mystery fiction.
    | Suspense fiction.
Classification: LCC PS3616.R4923 M66 2016 | DDC 813/.6—dc23
LC record available at http://lccn.loc.gov/2016006383

Design by Marina Drukman

ISBN: 978-1-61219-622-0

Printed in the United States of America
1 3 5 7 9 10 8 6 4 2

For Steve

THE

MONSTER'S

DAUGHTER

1

To get to Unie from Johannesburg, take the N1 highway to Cape Town and veer onto the N12 Southwest. The road is little more than a faded line in the savannah, pockmarked with cracks and potholes, heat rising off it in undulating wisps. Black women walk on the red dirt shoulder from farm to shantytown, babies tied to their backs in bright blankets, while children, some barely able to walk, clutch at their mothers' wide skirts. Sleek cars fitted with radar detectors thunder past them at irregular intervals, stirring dead air in their wake.

Ten kilometers past the exit, traffic came to an abrupt halt, discordant horns provoking others in response. A BMW had flipped on its side, the front crumpled like silver wrapping paper on Christmas morning. Shattered glass sparkled on the blacktop. A middle-aged man lay in the road, clutching his head between his hands, his cropped blond hair streaked with blood that seeped through his fingers, staining the cuffs of his dress shirt. The old semi the BMW had collided with stood unscathed a few meters away, Nigerian rap blaring from its speakers.

Constable Alet Berg had seen this scene many times since she'd transferred to Unie. From the skid marks it was obvious the BMW had been going at one hell of a speed. Stuck behind the semi, his view of oncoming traffic obscured, the driver had probably decided to overtake on the left, going onto the shoulder of the road. Only after he pulled out did he see the people walking there, their lives teetering on his next move. He hit the brakes, jerked the wheel, prayed he'd avoid hitting the truck. But, he didn't.

Alet knelt down next to the man lying in the road. "Sir, can you hear me? *Meneer?*" His shoulders jerked in response, a sob escaping his lips, his gaze fixed on where Sergeant Johannes Mathebe crouched next to the wreck.

Mathebe's droopy brown eyes scanned the interior. "There are people in the car." He strained to open the door. The bent frame of the BMW resisted his efforts.

"Are they . . . ?"

Mathebe looked back at Alet, slowly shaking his head. The semi driver yelled into his cell above the rap music, gesturing wildly with his free hand.

"Turn that off," Mathebe yelled.

A rapid exchange followed between the two men in a language Alet didn't understand. Xhosa? Maybe Zulu? She forgot which Mathebe was. The semi driver swept both arms through the air, shooing Mathebe away and climbed into the cab. Distant sirens replaced the heavy bass. Only an hour after the accident was called in, a record speed for that time of year.

Alet turned her attention to the man on the blacktop. "What is your name, sir?"

"Schutte," came the muted reply.

"Who was in the car with you, Mr. Schutte?"

Tears mixed with blood, running down his face in diluted crimson rivulets. "My wife. The baby, Hentie." Schutte tried to push himself off the ground. "They're okay, hey?"

Alet bit the inside of her cheek. "Stay still, Mr. Schutte. We're doing what we can."

An onslaught of sirens and horns overpowered her words. Cars, trucks, and a donkey cart lazily moved onto the skirt of the road to make way for the ambulance. Alet and Mathebe were pushed out of the way as the emergency services descended like locusts. The police were reduced to coaxing traffic past the accident. The corpses of Schutte's wife and son were laid out on the blacktop, covered with a sheet, while men in dark uniforms barked instructions. They lifted the still-crying Schutte onto a gurney. As if crying would help.

Alet's eyes lingered on the small bundle in the road as sirens faded, the ambulance taking the turnoff to George, the nearest town with a hospital.

Heat rose through the soles of Alet's boots as they waited for a tow truck to remove the wreck. An African taxi, an old Volkswagen combi filled with paying passengers, honked at the people in its way, then stopped abruptly to squeeze in a few more before speeding past. Gawkers hung out of sedan windows, straining to get a look at the carnage. At their destinations they would tell friends and lovers about what they'd seen, reveling in the excitement of gazing upon the dead.

The air inside the white police van was oppressive. Dark stains showed under Alet's arms and down the back of her police uniform. She rolled the window down, the reflection of her round face disappearing by degrees.

"I've been here six months now, right?"

Mathebe nodded as he got into the driver's seat. He kept one hand on the steering wheel, stubby fingers gripping tightly, the other hand taking a handkerchief out of his pocket to wipe his forehead.

"So when are they going to fix the *fokken* air-conditioning?"

Mathebe shot her a disapproving look, his nostrils flaring. He opened his mouth to speak, but changed his mind, shifting in his seat. The man had the soul of a Calvinist minister. They drove in silence, avoiding the fraught two-step of political correctness that seemed to mire most of their interactions. Alet stared at the barren earth and dry bushes bleeding into monotony, as repetitive as the days since she was transferred here from Johannesburg. Unie was what she imagined purgatory would be like. Not that she believed in that sort of thing, but still.

A kilometer after the turnoff, the road snaked up into the mountains. Mathebe handled the sharp curves with the expertise of a lifetime in the Western Cape, his muscular limbs performing a coordinated dance as the speedometer stayed above 120 kilometers an hour. Unie appeared in the expanse below. Where nothing and *fokol* got together and grew six feet high, Alet thought. Though it was surrounded by mountains, the town itself was flat and dusty, with only two tarred roads. One side of town was populated by white buildings with thatched roofs and spacious yards, the other side with the pink, blue, and lime-green walls of the tightly packed *location*. "Quaint" was the best description one travel website could muster. Unie had one bank, a farmers' co-op, two churches, and four liquor stores. At least they had their priorities straight.

Mathebe turned onto Kerk Street and pulled up to the police station. A group of black teenagers huddled in front of the convenience store across the street, music droning from a boom box on the ground among them. One of the girls looked up as Alet got out of the van. Her eyes were dull, her lips smeared with red lipstick. On the brick wall behind her hung a faded poster demanding STOP VIOLENCE AGAINST WOMEN AND CHILDREN. The national campaign against gender-based violence, now in its last throes, had kicked off with great pomp and circumstance fifteen days earlier, local school children marching in the street carrying placards hand-painted with shaky exclamations. The town had settled back into banality by evening.

Young boys leaned against the store, watching with big eyes as older kids smoked. A white pickup truck pulled up, shifting their attention. They swarmed the white faces that got out. "Please, *Mies*. Please, *Baas*," the chorus echoed, holding out cupped hands. "I'm hungry." The farmer threw them loose change. The boys fought among themselves, grabbing and shoving, the little ones crying when they were left with nothing. The victors would buy sweets. Nobody ever shared.

Alet turned to Mathebe. "So, who's writing this one up?"

"It is your turn," Mathebe said as he walked up the station's stone steps. It was a small, single-story building in the area's Cape Dutch style, its ornate rounded gables and curlicues compensating for its modesty. A South African flag hung limp from a pole in front of the station, its Y-shaped pattern sun-bleached.

Alet contemplated the stagnant heat inside the station, air circulated only by a single fan on the charge desk. "I'll go get lunch first," she said. "Want anything?"

Mathebe hesitated in the doorway, then shook his head slowly before going inside.

"Can I have some service here?" Alet sat down on one of the wrought iron stools that lined the bar at Zebra House, Unie's only guesthouse.

6

A tabby jumped off the pine countertop and disappeared into the back. The place was empty, tables set up with silverware and condiments in garland-lined buckets, snowmen-adorned specials menus stuck beneath the clear plastic tablecloths. Alet picked up a Cape Town newspaper from the bar. The headlines announced corruption allegations against local municipal officials, tourists attacked while hiking up Table Mountain, and two murders during a home invasion in Simonstown. The paper already carried a tally of road deaths for the holidays and Christmas was still weeks away. Page five showcased a special interview to wrap up the gender violence campaign. There was a picture of a young woman, fair and pink-cheeked, pointing to a patch of trees on the university campus. Her attacker had tried to strangle her, but was scared off by a security guard. There was a sidebar with bullet points on safety, most of which required some sort of male presence and conservative habits. Alet tossed the paper aside.

"Haaaaai." Tilly Pienaar, Zebra House's manager, appeared at the kitchen entrance carrying a case of Black Label beers, her back arched to balance the weight. She got onto the tips of her toes to set the case down on the counter, her cheeks flushing from the effort. Alet rented a flat from Tilly's mom, Trudie. The rent was cheap and, for the most part, Trudie kept to herself, although Alet often caught her peeping through the main house's curtains, which inevitably led to pursed lips and high-horse platitudes when their paths crossed in the garden.

Tilly ducked under the bar, and Alet grabbed one of the cans before Tilly could pop up on the other side.

Tilly raised an eyebrow. *"Jissis.* Don't you think it's a little early?"

"It's five o'clock somewhere."

Tilly set the case on the ground to stock the bar fridge. Alet only saw the top of her chin-length chestnut hair as she moved back and forth. Tilly dumped the cardboard packaging in an overfilled trash bin, her whole body straining as she pushed it down.

"You want food?" Tilly looked back over her shoulder. "You look like shit, by the way."

Alet's reflection fought for a place between the bottles of brandy and cane that lined the bar's big mirrored panels, the words "soft" and "ineffectual" suddenly creeping into her consciousness. Her hazel eyes were shadowed by purplish half-moons, the product of little sleep and too much junk food from the corner chip shop. The sunburn on her pale cheeks spread all the way to her clavicles, interrupted only by the collar of her shirt. Her long dark hair was pasted in a sweaty mess against her scalp, a visible indent at the edges where her uniform cap had sat.

Alet grunted and put the cap back on. "What do you mean? It takes work to look this good."

Tilly smiled, the skin around her eyes scrunching up. "What happened?"

"Accident out on the highway. Guy hit a truck." Alet burped.

"Don't they have a rule about drinking in uniform?"

"You're going to tell Mathebe?"

Tilly raised a thin plucked eyebrow. "You know we are like this." She held up her left hand, crossing her middle and index fingers.

"He was only upholding the law, you know," Alet said with a straight face. She imitated Mathebe's hound dog expression and thick accent. "Ouwa jop is verry serrious."

"He stopped me for speeding on an empty road!" Tilly raised her voice in indignation. "Threatened to arrest me. Twice. It's persecution, I'm telling you."

Mathebe never patronized Zebra House and Tilly crossed the street whenever she saw him walking in her direction. This had all happened before Alet transferred to Unie, before she even knew the place existed. At the time, she'd been up in Jo'burg, training for the Special Task Force, trying to prove that she could be one of the elite. That turned out to be a misguided venture. She'd been caught with her pants down, so to speak, demoted for an "indiscretion with a superior." Instead of dealing with urban hostage situations or protecting foreign dignitaries, she was forced to live in this small town, dealing with stupid little feuds in the middle of nowhere. An elite *fokop*. Alet wondered if Mathebe knew why she'd been transferred to Unie. The thought that anyone might judge her disgrace really pissed her off.

Alet tipped her head back, emptying the beer can. "Well, if you're not going to report me, you might as well hand me another."

Tilly reached down into the fridge. "They're all warm."

"Doesn't matter. And the Thursday special."

"Maria is only in at four today. It's *saamies* or nothing till then."

"Fine. Toasted cheese, then."

Tilly ducked out under the bar and disappeared through the kitchen doorway. Froth spurted out as soon as Alet pulled the tab on her second beer. She licked it off her index finger. Somewhere in the guesthouse, a phone rang. Tilly's muffled voice mechanically recited the standard greeting. There was a short pause, followed by a curt, "Please hold." She marched back into the bar and held out the cordless. "For you."

Alet took the handset. "*Ja?*"

"Constable Berg. You are needed at the station." Even though Mathebe had a precise, pedantic way of pronouncing his words when he spoke English, Alet still had trouble understanding him over the phone.

"Johannes, I told you I'm knocking off for lunch. I'll get the report done before I book off. Promise, hey." Alet winked at Tilly and took a sip from the can. There was a brief silence on the line. She imagined Mathebe closing his eyes, the way he always did when she said something that frustrated him, as if he was praying for deliverance before answering.

"A call came in, Constable."

"I'm sure whatever it is can wait for a half hour, Sergeant."

Another silence. "A body was found on the Terblanche farm."

Boet and Jana Terblanche's farm was about thirty kilometers west of Unie, off a misanthropic dirt road that cut through the mountain range, high rock faces on one side, sheer drops on the other. The GPS was useless. It didn't even register that they were on a road. Alet could navigate the area from memory now, but in the beginning she only had directions involving trees and gate-counting. The valley below them, caught between jagged black mountains enveloped by fog, stretched out to where blue sky and green earth were separated by a thin line of nothing. At the foot of the cliffs, brown workers picked peaches in orchards, led sheep to pasture, and tilled the red dirt. Their barefoot children hugged the side of the road when they heard the police van approach. Thin arms waved as it sped past, excited chatter and speculation among the smiling faces.

On her weekly community outreach patrol, Alet usually approached the boulders and turns in the road at a snail's pace, feeling a hostility radiating from the landscape. But Mathebe sped along the narrow road, only slowing down when they approached a blind curve, honking the horn in warning. The van's wheels sprayed gravel over the road's edge. Baboons scattered in the trees below.

"When were you last here, Constable?" Dark pearls of sweat beaded on Mathebe's forehead. New sweat on old.

"Day before yesterday. Everything was fine."

Unie had a low crime rate compared to the rest of the country, but the farms were isolated. Cattle thieves abounded, the farmers easy targets. An elderly farmer and his wife were attacked the year before. The attackers took everything they could lay their hands on, after assaulting the couple and tying them up. It was days before neighbors found them. The wife barely survived. Her husband had a heart condition and hadn't been so lucky.

"And the workers?" Mathebe kept right at a fork in the road.

"Nobody mentioned anything."

They passed a row of small brick houses with beautifully tended gardens, flowers wilting in the summer heat. An old woman sat outside one of the buildings on an upturned milk crate, her deeply wrinkled face framed by a long white scarf wrapped tight around her hair. Not long ago, one of the coloured women had told her that they refused to speak English because it was the language of the Antichrist. It was the prevailing sentiment in the valley. Mathebe's Afrikaans wasn't good, so Alet patrolled the farms by herself. She didn't mind it. The most serious thing she had to deal with was domestic disturbances on payday, when farmhands bought liter bottles of cheap booze off the back of the smuggler's pickup. Every farmhouse she stopped at usually had tea and baked goods waiting for her. No wonder she had gained weight.

"It's the next gate," Alet said as they approached a cattle encampment. Bonsmara hides glistened red in the sun as the animals gathered around the feed.

"I know." Mathebe stopped in front of the wire gate designating the Terblanche property. Alet got out, unhooked the rusted pin and swung the gate open. There was no point getting back into the van, it was hotter than hell either way, so she walked alongside as it crawled over rocky terrain to the next gate.

Boet Terblanche met them up the road. He leaned against his white pickup, his broad shoulders hunched, his tanned arms crossed over his chest, brown hair falling in his face, long and unkempt. His olive-green sweatshirt was full of holes, the sleeves pushed past his forearms, grass stains on the knees of his cargo pants. Jakob, his coloured foreman, sat on the back of the truck, his blue coveralls' arms tied around his waist, his head resting in his hands, barely looking up as the police van approached.

Boet nodded in their direction and got into his pickup. Alet and Mathebe followed, slowly traversing the rocky mountainside. Jakob jumped off the truck to open and close gates, his sinewy body moving fast for his fifty-odd years. Abandoned ruins were scattered along the path, their roofless white walls patched with brown stains, broken windows like unblinking eyes staring out over the valley. Alet wondered how people lived all the way up there back in the day, without running water or electricity. Even the squatter camps had satellite dishes nowadays.

Boet's truck came to a stop where the road dead-ended at the bottom of a rise, cordoned off by an ancient wire fence. He got out and pointed to a small ruin in the middle of an open patch of dry grass and rocks, forlorn trees perched on the edge.

"On the other side."

Jakob huddled quietly on the back of the pickup. Alet wondered why he wasn't making a nuisance of himself. The foreman was a boisterous character, full of talk about the way he saw things and the gossip of the valley. Alet had had to lock him up for public intoxication a few weeks before, but he was generally a good bloke, always ready with a smile and a story.

Alet took the camera out of the glove box and followed Mathebe, climbing over heaps of discarded furniture, rusted oil drums and inner tubes—junk left behind by a string of unwelcome transients. Strange smells intertwined, acrid and sweet, growing stronger as they walked past the house, burned rubber and something she couldn't put her finger on right away, something comforting, familiar even. It was the smell of lazy Sunday afternoons, trying to forget your troubles, beer in hand, men talking about rugby and politics and children chasing each other around the yard, as steaks and *boerewors* grilled on an open fire.

Alet's stomach turned when she saw it. The body lay curled in a fetal position, its hands balled into fists in front of its face, like a boxer readying for a fight. It had been burned, the flesh so charred that it looked as if the slightest breeze might lift the ashes into the air and destroy its integrity. Blackened skin split across the corpse's abdomen exposing charred bowels. A brown flaky substance extruded from the skull. Its jaw hung open, mouth agape in a silent scream. Wire hoops, clearly the remnants of a tire, encircled its shoulders.

"A necklacing?" Alet felt jittery. She had read the case files. Members of the ANC had used necklacings in the mid-eighties to keep dissidents in check. The practice disappeared after the party won South Africa's first multiracial election in '94. But after years of escalating violent crime, necklacings were resurfacing. An old black woman had been attacked in her home in the Eastern Cape the previous year. Two men had raped her and killed her son, then fled with her valuables. During their crime spree, men in the community caught them and dragged them to the town square, where people took turns beating the offenders with planks and throwing rocks at them. Tires filled with petrol were forced around their shoulders and set on fire. The whole community watched them die. And nobody saw a thing.

"It appears that way." Mathebe laid a measuring stick next to the body. He stepped aside.

Alet focused the camera. "A vigilante killing?" She snapped a photograph of the body.

"Not here." Mathebe was right. Necklacings happened in high-crime areas, not in towns like Unie.

"Nobody's been reported missing in Unie in the past month." Alet changed the angle of the shot. "Maybe there were some violent offenders that walked in from George or Oudtshoorn."

Mathebe made a sweeping motion with his upturned palm. "But look where we are."

Alet's eyes trailed the movement of his hand over the valley below. God's country, she thought wryly. She turned back to Mathebe. "So?"

"Necklacing is a warning not to step out of line, Constable. It happens where everyone can see."

"It would have been a hell of a job to get a crowd up here."

Mathebe went down on his haunches next to the body. "Nobody here to see," he muttered.

"So, the killer burned the body to get rid of evidence? Made it look like a necklacing to throw us off?"

"He perhaps saw the old tires over there and said, yes, this is how I become invisible."

"Well, that's a bitch."

Mathebe closed his eyes.

"I mean, the evidence is burned to a crisp."

"We will do the best we can."

Mathebe's stoicism frustrated Alet. He followed procedure like a robot, even at moments like this. She, meanwhile, wanted to punch something, feeling sick, angry, and yet curiously excited, something long dormant in her stirring. "I'll go see if Oosthuizen got lost," she said.

Dr. Oosthuizen was the only local doctor. He ran a clinic near the *location*, treating minor injuries and venereal diseases, doing double duty as mortician. The white farmers only went to him if it was an emergency, preferring the two-hour drive to Oudtshoorn or George.

"Radio April," Mathebe called after her. "We need help searching the area."

Boet Terblanche sat in his truck, his arm resting on the open window, staring off into the distance. He barely took notice of Alet as she walked over.

"Hey, Boet."

"Alet." His green eyes were wary, tired. He smelled of earth and animal.

"What time did you find it?"

Boet cleared his throat, his voice hoarse when he spoke. "Jakob saw smoke during morning meeting. Six, six-thirty maybe."

Alet looked up at the back of the pickup. "Is that right, Jakob?"

"*Ja, Mies.*" Jakob peered at her between the guardrails. The flesh around his left eye was bruised and swollen.

"And you told *Baas* Boet right away?"

"*Ja, Mies.* The *baas*, he always says to be on the lookout."

"The river's low," Boet interjected. "No way to get water up here if a fire gets out of hand." He ran his thick fingers through his hair. His fingernails were dirty.

"Did you touch anything?"

"No." Boet watched Mathebe walk into the ruin. "We drove to the house, to call you people, but they said nobody could come out right away. So we waited."

"I'll need a full statement. From Jana too."

"I told you everything," Boet snapped.

Alet touched his forearm. "Are you okay?"

"I have a farm to run, Alet." Boet looked away. "I don't have time for this. And Jana is almost due . . ."

Alet withdrew her hand. "I need to talk to Jakob, then."

Boet sighed and crossed his arms.

"Jakob?"

"*Ja, Mies?*"

"Come with me."

The foreman climbed down from the back of the pickup and followed Alet to the police van.

"What happened this morning, Jakob?"

Jakob looked at Alet as if she was stupid, the slits of his brown eyes almost closed, a frown deepening the grooves in his leathery face. "We found the body, *Mies.*"

Alet smiled. Patience, she reminded herself. "*Ja*, I know, Jakob. Tell me what you saw when you got here."

"It looks like a man or a flat-chested woman to me, *Mies.* I can't say." Jakob's gaze drifted back to where the body lay, his eyes glassy. "All curled up like. *Mies*, you know, like a baby. Like it doesn't want to show its privates or something. You then saw it with your own eyes."

Alet nodded. "Did anything else happen?"

"We waited for you, *Mies.*"

"And that shiner? Looks fresh to me."

The foreman fixed his gaze on the ground. "*Ag*, it's nothing, *Mies.*"

"Jakob, I'm not in the mood for this. Tell me what happened. If not, I'll take you to the station and ask there. *Baas* Boet won't like it. And you'll lose the day's wages."

"*Ai* no, *Mies.* That's not right."

"Then tell me."

Jakob glanced over at Boet before he spoke, his voice low. "I *checked* the smoke, *Mies.* I'm old but my eyes are sharp-sharp. None of the others saw, just me." Jakob's tongue dashed between his missing front teeth. "So I tell the *baas* and he says it's *skollies* and that we have to go chase them before they steal cattle. But when we get here, there's nobody. Just that black thing, still smoking. I went over to it and *Baas* Boet, he looks sick, but I couldn't take my eyes off it. It looked like the wings of a million black butterflies. Like if I touch it, they will all *chaile* and the thing will vanish."

"Okay. So you found the body. Then what?"

"I'm sorry for it, *Mies. Ag* shame, I think. *Ag* shame." Jakob folded his hands.

"You still haven't told me why your eye looks like that, Jakob."

"*Mies*, I'm coming to that, see? I reached to touch it. I didn't mean anything or nothing, honest. But *Baas* Boet, he goes ape, yelling at me." He shook his head. "So I go back to the truck, but the *baas* he says no, I gotta stay."

Jakob reached for the half-smoked cigarette behind his ear, rolled it nervously between his thumb and forefinger. "*Mies*, right then I get scared. I don't want to be alone with that thing, hey. And the *baas* he says we cannot just leave it there. But me stay alone and that black thing checking me? No ways! It's bad, *Mies.* I feel it. The *baas*, he feels it too, that's why he wants to get away. So I say, "No, *Baas*, man, not that. I go with you." Then the *baas* hits me, see? Square in the eye. *Baas* Boet, he's a big man. It was like my eyeball went poosh! Like there's too many things trying to be in my head and there's no room no more."

"*Baas* Boet hit you?" Alet frowned. This didn't meld with the Boet Terblanche she knew.

"*Ja, Mies*, like I said, but don't tell him I told you. I don't want no trouble."

"Has he done this before?"

"No ways. Never did the *baas* hit anybody that I know of, *Mies.* Maybe when he was a small *boytjie* did he rumble with the other *laaities.* Boys do that you know, but not when he got to be boss. He's okay. Just had a fright. I don't want no trouble with him." Jakob pulled a book of matches from his pocket and lit his cigarette with a shaky hand.

"And then?"

Jakob hesitated, as if he had forgotten. "My eye hurt like *mampoer* on a raw sore, *Mies*, but I run till I get on the truck. I say, I'm sorry, *Baas*. I'm sorry, my *Basie*. I just say it over and over again until the *baas* starts driving and then I feel better. 'Cause I'm away from that thing, see? That thing lying there, bad, dead, like a hole in the world." Jakob looked back at the body again, his eyes wet.

"And you waited at the bottom. You didn't come back up here, right?"

"*Ja, Mies.*"

Jakob ran to the pickup as soon as Alet told him it was okay to go. He huddled in the back, clinging to the guardrails, shaken about by the truck backing up and turning around. He lifted a weathered palm to her as the pickup descended, no bigger than a child's toy in the distance.

1901

Andrew

Pritchard sprawled sideways over the train tracks, black lines of ants pulsating across his pale face like throbbing veins. His khaki helmet lay next to him, useless against the bullet hole in his forehead. Large curved tree branches, piled in as levers to dislodge the rails, stuck in the air like the ribs of an animal carcass.

"Maundin is going to have a *bleddie* fit, *ja*," Jooste, one of the joiners, shouted from down the line, his English crippled by a thick Dutch accent. He was a big brute with yellow hair, eyes that sat too close together, and a ruddy complexion. He kicked at one of the erect branches, trying to dislodge it. The sound rolled across the dry open veld.

Andrew noticed the ghost of a smile on Jooste's lips. He wondered again if they had been wise to trust the man. Jooste was too slick, too easily converted to their side, too eager to participate without a hint of guilt when he sabotaged his own people. But he knew the land and spoke the language, making him a valuable asset to the British forces. And they were desperate. After two years, they were still stuck in this Godforsaken country, the easy victory promised to them made elusive by the Boers' guerrilla tactics.

Andrew dusted the red dirt from his knees. "I don't envy you, then, Mr. Jooste."

"What do you say, hey?" Jooste walked closer to Andrew, dragging one of the tree branches, a snakelike trail waking the dirt behind him.

"You have to go report to the lieutenant. Oudtshoorn needs to be notified that the tracks are out before the supply run."

"Why don't you do it?" Jooste looked back at the damaged track, his distaste for the task at hand clear. Andrew felt a whisper of satisfaction at seeing his distress.

"It's an order, Mr. Jooste."

The corner of Jooste's mouth lifted, exposing crooked teeth. "Sir." He unzipped his pants. "After this, *ja*." His eyes challenged Andrew as he started relieving himself.

"You could do that behind a tree, Mr. Jooste." Andrew looked away.

"I don't waste time, sir."

The disdain with which Jooste pronounced "Sir" boiled Andrew's blood. He pretended to survey the veld. There was nothing but dry grass stirring on the plain in the biting morning breeze, but that didn't mean that they weren't being watched. Jooste finished his business and walked away without a word, starting the hour-long journey to camp with a languid stride. Andrew thought about following the joiner, but he didn't want to leave Pritchard behind. Pritchard was seventeen, had been on African soil for barely a month. He hadn't even had the time to dull his buttons and scabbard. Andrew squatted next to the body, hoping the tall grass would provide enough cover. He closed Pritchard's eyelids, the flesh cold under his fingertips, and said a silent prayer. Pritchard had family in Wales, a mother and three sisters. To his shame, Andrew felt envious at the thought of their grief. There was no one waiting for him back home.

Andrew's joints were stiff from the cold by the time Jooste came back with more men, six of them in khaki uniforms, their faces red from the sun. There was a restlessness among them, a nervous buzz of excitement barely contained by rank or protocol.

"Some action at last." Jooste had a strange light in his eyes. "I didn't join you people to patrol railway lines, *ja*?"

"What do you mean, Mr. Jooste?"

"We're going to hit the Boers where it hurts, Corporal," one of the privates chipped in, an Australian by the sound of him. He gestured toward Pritchard with bombastic bravado. "Those bastards will pay for this."

"Lieutenant Maundin gave the order?"

"Scorched Earth, sir. All the way from Lord Kitchener himself. We're going to the farms."

• • •

VERGELEGEN. The stern letters filled the breadth of the gatepost. A curving lane led to a small whitewashed farmhouse sheltered by black mountains. Andrew knocked on the door. Next to him, Lieutenant Maundin rocked on his heels, the day's dust clinging to his red beard. Andrew braced himself, dreading the anticipated shock on the women's faces, the subsequent abuse or begging, the inevitable pattern of their raids in the week since they had found Pritchard's body. His thoughts of revenge had been crushed by the devastation they were leaving behind, their column tracing a black trail through the Dutch farms.

Maundin banged on the door with his fist when there was no immediate answer. It was opened, at last, by a small girl, no older than fourteen.

"Who are you?" Maundin's words radiated contempt.

"Anna Richter." She tucked a stray strand of fair blond hair behind her ear, terror flaring in her sky-blue eyes.

"We are here in service of the Crown." Maundin pushed past her into the house.

Andrew followed, venturing an apologetic look to the girl. The front room of the house was simple, but clean. A family Bible lay next to an oil lamp on a large wooden table. The hide of some sort of small native buck covered the floor next to a rudimentary couch made from wood and woven leather thongs. A young boy with short blond hair peered around the doorway of a back room, then immediately ducked out of sight again.

Maundin turned to Anna. "Where are your parents?"

"My mother is *baie* sick," Anna said in broken English. "She is *by* the other farm."

"And your father?"

"He's gone away."

"Is that right?" Maundin sighed, catching Andrew's eye, sarcasm twisting his lips. "Your father is Christiaan Richter, a Boer commander, is he not?" He waved his hand dismissively. "Don't bother denying it."

Anna's bottom lip quivered.

"We know you aid the Boers who kill our men." Maundin spat each word out as if it was a piece of chewing tobacco. "Therefore, all

property will be seized and destroyed under order of Her Majesty."
He took a dramatic pause, his pleasure in this piece of theater not lost
on Andrew. "You have ten minutes."

Anna's eyes wandered from Maundin to Andrew, silently pleading
with him. Andrew felt embarrassed and looked away.

"Ten minutes!" Maundin shouted over his shoulder as he strode
out of the house. Anna stood dazed in the middle of the floor as if she
couldn't make sense of what just happened.

"Please. Hurry," Andrew whispered. "Take what you need and get
out." His words seemed to break her spell.

"Hansie!" Anna's voice broke as she ran to the back room.

The boy left his hiding place. He was small, too young to ride out
on commando with his *pappa*. Anna stroked his shoulders gently as
she spoke. Andrew had trouble understanding their rapid exchange,
recognizing only a few of the Dutch words. The boy nodded, tears and
snot streaming down his face as he followed Anna into the bedroom.
They returned, pushing a large wooden dowry chest into the front
room. Anna disappeared into the kitchen while Hansie held on to the
chest as if his life depended on it. The commotion in the farmyard
brought a new wave of tears to his eyes. Anna cradled dried meats,
fruit and a metal tin in her arms when she returned. She opened the
dowry chest lid and made room for the provisions among bed linens
and clothes.

Jooste barged into the house, shouting something in Dutch. He
grabbed the tin from Anna. She tried to resist, but Jooste shoved her
with his free hand, scattering the bottles of Lennon's home remedies
it held all over the floor. Anna scrambled on all fours to pick them up.
Andrew made a move to help, but soldiers swarmed into the house,
kicking the small bottles in all directions.

"Get out," Jooste shouted in a grandiose show for the others. "Your
time is finish, *ja*."

Anna pushed the big wooden box out of the house, straining to
navigate it through the doorway. Hansie cried hysterically, clutching her long gray dress. Khaki uniforms shoved past them as if they
weren't there, heavy boots kicking dust up from the dry dung floor.
Soldiers marched through the scant rooms, taking what they wanted,
smashing mirrors, stomping on toys. Clothing and shoes ended up in

tangled bundles on the ground. A rednecked soldier banged on the keys of the small house organ with the butt of his rifle, while others broke off its wood panels. As the men took turns smashing its innards to pieces, the notes that rang out sounded like wails of desperation. They dragged the fodder outside, then used it for fuel to boil water for their tea.

A couple of the soldiers used the pictures on the walls for target practice. Shots, accompanied by laughter and cheers, rang through the house as glass shattered on the ground. Once they were done, they emptied cans of paraffin, dousing the floors and walls. Jooste scraped a torch along the edges of the roof outside. Everyone looked on as flames crept along the thatch, seething, writhing, devouring. Black smoke rose, blemishing the clear winter sky. In the distance, on the nearest high ground, troops guarded against an attack from the Boers, who, even farther away, camouflaged by trees and foliage, watched the destruction helplessly.

Andrew stood before the blaze, flames licking the modest pieces of furniture on the porch—a rocking chair, a straw mattress, a baby cradle. His cheeks burned, sweat running down the side of his face. Behind him, the bleating of sheep rose to a crescendo. Soldiers sank their bayonets into the livestock, striking repeatedly until the animals fell, their white coats matted with blood. Men chased poultry in the farmyard, throwing stones and flinging themselves at chickens and ducks whose anguished squawks filled the air. Soon the farm was littered with carcasses, to be left behind to rot. Everything would be looted or destroyed, leaving no sustenance for the enemy.

Black farmworkers were rounded up, herded like cattle behind the British supply wagons, mothers clutching half-naked infants, hardened men bowing their heads. Andrew searched for the Richter children in the chaos. Anna had managed to push the dowry chest to the edge of the field, where they huddled together. How much they looked like English children, fair and healthy, Andrew thought. He prayed that Maundin and the others wouldn't notice him as he went over to them. Hansie, too distraught to watch, had buried his face in the folds of Anna's dress. A big sunbonnet lay forgotten at her feet, a *kappie*, the Dutch called it. Andrew bent down to pick it up. Dirt clung to the white cotton and he clumsily tried to dust it off.

"Your name is Anna?" Andrew held the bonnet out to her. When she didn't react, he lay it down on the chest. He noticed its craftsmanship: someone had put a lot of love into making the box, carving an intricate pastoral scene into the lid. Andrew remembered his father doing woodwork like that when he was a boy, sitting up late at night until everything was just so. Those were the happy days before his mother died, before his father succumbed to grief and liquor, the memory of a dead wife more real than the heartbeat of the son in front of him.

"I am Corporal Andrew Morgan." Andrew tried again. He knelt next to Anna. "Do you have somewhere to go?"

Anna pointed at the neighboring farmhouse, a white flag hanging from the beams on the porch, signaling that the occupants had signed an oath of neutrality and would not take part in the war.

"Go there now."

Anna's knuckles turned white on the dowry chest. "I can't carry it."

Andrew looked back at the blazing farmhouse. "Leave it."

"It's all we have left." Tears pooled on Anna's eyelashes.

"You have to go," Andrew pleaded. The first raids had been conducted with civility, but the facade soon wore thin, giving way to manic violence, the frenzy intensifying with each burning building. The faces of men Andrew knew grew distorted as they plundered the farms. Things were done to the women. Their cries banished Andrew's sleep. He couldn't live with his part in that, for allowing it to happen, for thinking, even for a moment, that it was justified, the helplessness he had felt for so many months giving over to a rage that scared him. Looking at the two children in front of him, he knew he had to help them, if only for his own salvation.

Andrew took Anna's hand, her light-blue irises boring into his soul. "It is not safe. Understand? You have to protect Hansie. And yourself."

Anna nodded, pulling her hand away from his. She picked Hansie up and hurried toward the next farm without a word. Andrew watched her go, his heart racing, praying that she wouldn't be noticed. Halfway up the hill, Anna stopped and glanced over her shoulder, like Lot's wife looking back at the carnage. Fire burst forth from the windows of the house as the panicked neighing of a horse rang out from inside the burning barn. Andrew knew he'd never forget the image of

Anna standing there, watching their barbarism, a shadow against the darkening sky. He felt ashamed.

The two small figures melted away in the twilight—safe, at least for now. Andrew pulled a small journal from his pocket. He tore a page from among the tallies of family names and seized goods. Crouching down so the others wouldn't see him, he used the chest as a writing surface, his pencil denting the paper. He slipped the note between the folds of a blanket in the chest and walked away. Leaving it was a risk, but after all he'd seen, he no longer cared if his name was found among Boer things.

Anna

The approaching storm rose like the hand of God, turning the sky vermilion. The wind lifted earth from its resting place, ripping at the bell tents of the Bloemfontein concentration camp, which were squashed together in misshapen rows like white ant heaps. A grave-yard, littered with crude markers, lay a few hundred meters from the camp. Its border had crept closer with each passing day. Emaciated figures stood next to an open grave, bracing themselves against the cold, the sound of a hymn dissipating over the veld.

Anna squinted to keep dust out of her eyes, trying to focus on the reading. There was no minister, so people looked to Aunt Kotie, the oldest person in the camp, to pray over the dead. Aunt Kotie read from the Bible, mostly from Job, and recited ill-remembered sermons. Anna wiped sweat from her upper lip. She had woken up that morning with a fever, an ache creeping through her body as the day wore on, burning slowly, her skin clammy and tender, fighting nausea with every breath she took. She wasn't sure how much longer she could hold down the sloppy porridge she'd made from the last of the ration meal, but she needed to stay strong for Hansie. She needed to see him laid to rest.

Aunt Kotie bowed her frail head and recited a prayer, her liver-spotted hands clutching the Bible. Anna peered down into the shallow grave at Hansie's small body, its outlines visible through the thread-bare sheet, the toes of his small bare foot sticking out the side. Wood was scarce, a coffin a luxury. Her mother had been wrapped in a rough gray blanket, and Anna still wondered if she had received a proper burial. She had died in an open cattle truck, too weak for the two-day journey to Bloemfontein. Anna had had to sit with the body while the other women complained about the stench, threatening to throw it over the side. The Khakis ordered her to leave her mother at the side of the tracks when they arrived in Bloemfontein. It shamed Anna that she had felt relieved to be rid of the burden.

Aunt Kotie ended the prayer with a solemn, "Amen." Her sunken eyes filled with fervor, her lips peeling back from her sparse teeth. "Have faith in the Lord, my people," she said. "For we do not know His plan for us."

Older boys shoveled dirt into the grave. Women dispersed, moving back to the camp to seek shelter. They kept their heads low, letting their eyes linger on the graves of their own loved ones, wondering how long it would be until they too lay there. In the camp, shadows flitted as children moved furtively in the twilight, helping to secure tent flaps and tie down ropes. Anna stared listlessly at Hansie's grave, her thoughts incoherently skipping over the days and weeks gone by. The Khakis and black joiners had herded Anna, Hansie and the other women the three miles from the train station to the camp that night they arrived, jeering and prodding. Anna carried Hansie when he became too tired to walk, trying to comfort him as best she could.

At the camp, they were assigned to share a tent with fat Mrs. Botha and her daughter, Hester. Hester was a year older than Anna and moved through the world with passive sloth, her gaze fixed on the ground, "*Ja, Ma*," her only words. Anna had tried to talk to her, but the girl only gave monosyllabic answers. The Bothas had money. Mrs. Botha kept it tied in a handkerchief to her underskirts and bought fresh vegetables and supplies from camp authorities, storing them in a trunk that she and Hester took turns guarding. Anna sometimes fantasized about breaking the Botha trunk open with a rock and devouring everything inside, the dried fruits, canned goods, especially the coffee. The coffee they got in their rations was undrinkable, diluted with sawdust, not even enough for two cups. But she knew her parents would have been ashamed of her for even thinking about it.

Anna had approached Mrs. Botha a few days after they arrived, her palms moist as she stated her case in stops and starts. Hansie was hungry, crying himself to sleep every night. Anna had shared her rations with him, but it wasn't enough. "My brother needs milk," she pleaded. "We'll pay you back."

Mrs. Botha's porcine eyes narrowed. "With what, my dear girl?"

"Please, Mrs. Botha. He's only little."

"Everybody here is hungry, girl. If I give to you, it won't be long till the next one comes begging." Mrs. Botha turned her back to Anna, waving her off. "Don't ask again."

The humiliation had stung. Anna knew she was in one of the "lower classes" that Mrs. Botha referred to in the letters she dictated to Hester in the afternoons, a nuisance to be tolerated, like the fleas that infested their rough straw mattresses. Anna's only solace was that the camp rendered them all equal. Mrs. Botha might have thought that she was better than them, piously reading from her Bible while she fondled her money, but she too had to endure the smell of her own excrement sunning in the overfull slop buckets. If the wind blew in the right direction, you could smell the sewage all the way to town, an inconvenient reminder to the British that the Boer women were still here, still alive.

Hansie caught fever a week later. The authorities made daily inspections of the tents, hauling the sick away. Hansie was given a bed at the camp hospital, under the care of English doctors and nurses who couldn't understand Dutch and had little sympathy for their patients. Anna wasn't allowed to visit, even though she walked the mile to the hospital tent every day to find out how he was feeling. Yesterday they'd told her she didn't need to come anymore. Anna almost hadn't recognized the skeletal body when they laid him out. She imagined his last labored breaths, a small frightened boy alone, crying for comfort. Anna hoped he had it now.

"You!" The Khaki soldier spoke Dutch. The way his big frame moved through the dust toward her sparked a memory of hope giving way to despair, sharp as a knife in her stomach. "Come here." He was one of their people, riding with the enemy. He had looked at her and Hansie with indifference that day their home burned, like they were nothing, taking what little they had and laughing about it.

"I said come here."

Anna realized that she was alone in the cemetery. She backed away from the joiner, straining against the wind, her feet giving way every few steps. The joiner lengthened his stride, closing in. Anna ran. In the distance, tents billowed like ghosts in the dark. Anna prayed that she would be lucky enough to reach them.

The dirt floor was damp beneath Anna, the smell of earth in her nostrils. A dull pain pulsed at the back of her head. She remembered the cemetery. Hansie's small foot sticking out from beneath the sheet. The joiner's hands closing around her shoulders as he tackled her to the ground.

"Get up." It was him. The one who came to Vergelegen with the Khakis. The British soldiers had called him Jooste.

A sudden kick to her stomach forced her eyes open. She gasped for breath. Light beams fell diagonally from the holes in a concrete wall. She had seen buildings like this along the train tracks when they were moved to the camp, British blockhouses, guarding against Boer attacks. The joiner grabbed her chin between his thumb and forefinger, forcing her face up. She looked into calculating gray eyes.

"Nice," Jooste said. "He'll like you, *Suster*." Jooste ran his thumb over her cheek. Anna tried to pull away. A small vein in Jooste's temple bulged. He brought his hand down across her face. The blow pulsed hot on her cheek. Anna scrambled to get away, still weak from fever. Jooste grabbed her and flung her to the ground.

"You will do as I say, *ja*?" Jooste forced her on her back and straddled her. Anna squirmed beneath him. "I see you need a little breaking in." He pushed her legs apart with his knees and kicked at her ankles. She fought for breath under his bulk as he lay down on top of her.

Anna felt him tearing at her bloomers with his free hand, paralyzed as she felt his rough hand creep under her dress. She closed her eyes, biting down as he crushed her breasts in his hands. Jooste forced his hand between her legs. Then the pain. She cried out, the movement inside her tearing, stabbing, the smell of him rancid against her face. She tried to force the reality of what was happening out, but thoughts of her home quickly regressed to burnt-out buildings and camp graves. Jooste grunted as his body went into a spasm.

"Clean yourself." Jooste pulled away. It was the first time she had seen a grown man like that. "And don't bother trying to escape, *Suster.* The nearest town is thirty kilometers away, *ja.* If the animals don't get you, the *kaffirs* will."

Imposing stone steps rolled down from a wide *stoep.* An enormous door interrupted the house's pristine white facade and rounded gables. A vision of splendor, it was almost ten times the size of Vergelegen, its windows covered with thick wood panels, British soldiers standing guard at the gate.

But the bare interior of the building offered no opulence. No sunlight penetrated the thick walls, and the hallways were cold. Polished floors reflected the light from large oil lamps, placed sporadically on the floor. The room Jooste had taken Anna to was sparsely furnished, the floors scrubbed dull, the walls unadorned. A large desk stood in the middle of the room, books piled haphazardly on top. In one corner, a bed peeked out from behind a white screen. A strange object rested on a table next to it, copper coiled around a spindle, exposed wires attached to a black box.

"Damn it all, Jooste. I told you to be careful with them." The man, who had introduced himself as Dr. Samuel Leath, dropped Anna's bruised wrists. Other than his white temples and trimmed beard, he was completely bald, dressed in a black suit with a cravat and polished black boots.

"She tried to escape, see? Had to be restrained."

"Is she intact?"

Jooste shot a warning look at Anna. "If she's not, it has nothing to do with me, *ja*? I only catch them and bring them to you."

"It's not all that important. I can still use her, as long as she's fertile."

Jooste shrugged. Leath ran his fingers over Anna's face, inspecting her like a horse, with instructions to turn and look up issued in a monotone. He took Anna's head in his hands. A shudder ran through her. Leath had been civil enough, but there was something about the way he looked at her, his deadpan expression and indifferent eyes, that made him seem soulless as a serpent.

"Keep still." Leath pulled her eyelids down with his thumbs. He bent over the desk, dipping a pen in ink and scribbling something in a leather-bound book. He pulled her lips away from her teeth with his thumbs. "Fine specimen otherwise. Where did you get her?"

"Bloemfontein."

"I have someone working that camp already."

Jooste shrugged. "It's doubled in size. Plenty to go around."

"Did you use the doctor?"

Jooste sneered. "The girls from the hospital are ill. I found this one myself."

"Will she be missed?"

Jooste shook his head. "They'll think she's run away, *ja*. A lot of them do."

"I need more." Leath returned to his desk. "But go somewhere else. Winburg, perhaps."

"It's too far."

Leath's face reddened slightly. "I am doing important work here, my good man. I don't need it compromised." His voice took on a defensive tone. "That Hobhouse woman from the Ladies' Commission is causing a racket back home after her 'charitable' visit to the camps, and nobody seems to be reining her in. We don't need women sticking their noses in men's business. And the bloody Germans think if they side with the Boers they'll be able to get their hands on the mines. Everybody grows a conscience when it suits them." He waved a finger at Jooste. "I'm not taking any chances. You'll go to Winburg or not at all."

"*Ja*, all right." Jooste yawned.

Leath closed his journal. "That will be all."

Jooste didn't move.

"Well?"

"What about the money?"

"You'll get what we agreed on." Leath clutched the book under his arm and headed to the door, his spine straight, a stiffness in his step. "Be a good chap and take her to the kitchen so Sarah can clean her up. She reeks." He disappeared into the house.

Jooste came up behind Anna, pressing into her. "Sorry to let you go, *Suster*," he said, his mouth close to her ear. Shame and fear swept through Anna in hot waves. After the night at the blockhouse, Jooste had taken her across winding game paths, staying off the main roads, traveling only at night. They had passed burnt-out farmhouses and dead things, big empty sky stretching endlessly. Sometimes Jooste repeated what he did to her in the blockhouse, right there in the veld like an animal, spending himself, his sweat dripping on her, clinging to her skin, like she was a thing to be used, nothing more. She didn't know what this Dr. Leath had in store for her, but anything was better than staying with Jooste.

"When the war is over," Anna said, her voice wavering, "the *Boere* will shoot you for what you have done to your people."

Jooste laughed. "The *Boere* are losing, *Suster*. By the time this is done, they'll be too busy making nice with the Khakis to worry about me. See I know which side my bread is buttered. Loyalty doesn't fill your stomach."

A young black woman with deep-set dark eyes, high cheekbones and a wide mouth, dressed in a rust-colored dress and white apron, stood in the kitchen doorway, her hands clasped in front of her, two lines etched between her brows. The kitchen was much warmer than the rest of the house. Tall iron pots and a stack of tin plates and mugs stood on a table, the food smells intoxicating.

"You Sarah?" Jooste shoved Anna toward the woman. "Deal with this. I'll eat in the front room."

Sarah watched Jooste walk away, her expression filled with loathing. She pointed Anna to a low chair next to a black stove. "Sit here, *Nooi*. Get warm."

Anna was unable to take her eyes off the plate of stiff maize porridge and a sloppy stew that Sarah dished and handed to her. She stuck spoonfuls of it her mouth, barely chewing. The meat was fresh, the meal salted. She was sure it was the best thing she had ever tasted.

"Slow down. You'll get sick and I'm not cleaning it up."

Anna only looked up for a moment before she scraped the drops of sauce up with her fingers, sticking them in her mouth. Sarah shook her head. She dished more plates, placing them in a row on the table before ringing a brass bell mounted on the wall. A petite young woman appeared at the door. She had light-blond hair, partially hidden under a black *kappie*, and wore a simple black dress that didn't disguise her bulging stomach. She looked at Anna with little more than passing interest before taking a plate from Sarah.

Another woman appeared. She had sad blue eyes and sandy hair tied in a bun. The rounding under the black dress wasn't as far along as the first woman's, but she moved uncomfortably, her lower back curved, her breasts heavy. She stared at Anna. "Another?"

Sarah nodded. She handed the woman a plate. "Go on now."

Yet another girl appeared, very fair with light freckles dusting her turned-up nose. She was followed by a girl with greasy blond curls.

"Hester?" Anna rushed to the familiar face.

Hester looked up, shocked out of her daze. "Anna?" Her face contracted. She wiped her eyes with the sleeve of her dress. "Is my *ma* all right?"

"I don't know. When did you . . . ?"

"I got sick and they took me to the hospital. Yesterday. Maybe before that." Hester wiped her eyes again. "The Englishman he—"

"Enough." Sarah stepped closer.

Anna held on to Hester. "What's going on?"

"In the room. He—"

Sarah forced Anna and Hester apart. "I said, enough. Come with me." She grabbed Anna by the wrist.

"Wait."

"You listen to me now before there is trouble." Sarah dragged Anna to a small room with boarded-up windows. Against the far wall lay a mattress with a thick blanket, a chamber pot next to it.

"What is this place?"

"This is where you sleep." Sarah backed out of the room and shut the door.

Panic thickened in Anna's throat. "Please! Don't leave me alone."

A key turned in the lock. Sarah's muted voice came from the other side. "Be quiet now. The doctor doesn't like noise."

Anna jerked awake the next morning when the key turned again, confused when she didn't find dirty straw under her. Her mind felt thick, her body stiff. The door opened and Sarah carried a porcelain basin of water into the room and set it on the floor. She lit a candle.

"The doctor wants to see you." Sarah took soap and a rough brush out of her apron pocket and held them out to Anna. "Be thorough. There too." She motioned to the place between Anna's legs.

Anna gripped Sarah's arm as she turned to go. "What does he want with me?"

"You saw the others." Sarah freed herself from Anna's grip. "Don't keep him waiting."

Anna held the pink soap to her face. It smelled like the flower garden her mother had kept at the back of the house. "There is little enough pleasure in the world, Anna," her mother used to say. "You have to make your own." Her father was different. He only believed in work and the Bible. A flower garden was a waste of time to him. There were more important things that needed tending on a farm. Anna wondered if he was still fighting in the veld, or if he was being held prisoner in Ceylon. She refused to let her mind wander to the third option. She prayed to God that he would never know of her shame. She broke out in goose bumps as the cold water touched her body, her pale skin flushing as she ran the rough bristles of the scrub brush over it. She pressed harder, wishing she could wash off everything that had happened, leave it with the stink and filth in the water, to be tossed out and forgotten.

The door swung open. Dr. Leath stepped into the room. Anna reached for her dress so she could cover herself.

"That is only fit for burning. Put this on." Leath handed her a black dress. "I'll wait." He stayed there while she turned her back to him and dressed, her skin damp under the thick black cloth, her hair dripping down her back. "Come." He led her back to the room from the previous day and gestured to the bed as he closed the door behind her. "Lie down."

Anna had to get on her toes to get on top of the bed. The thin mattress was covered in starched sheets that crackled when she moved. She lay down and crossed her arms.

"Let's start with base measurements." Leath took her temperature and pulse, noting everything in his book. Then he lifted her dress.

"No," Anna pleaded. She pushed the skirt back down, tears welling.

Leath pursed his lips. "I have no use for you if you don't cooperate." He clutched his hands behind his back. "Would you prefer to go back to the camp?"

What could he do to her that hasn't already been done? Anna thought. In the camp there were men like Jooste, and there was hunger, and filth, and the constant stench of death. Here she had a bed, warmth, food that wasn't rancid. She had thought many times of dying, but the Bible said it was her duty to stay alive until God took the decision out of her hands. Maybe then He would forgive her for doing this. Anna gathered the skirt of dress and lifted it slowly, exposing herself from the waist down.

A smile played at the corners of Leath's mouth.

After that first day, Anna's life became a dependable routine. Two meals a day, interspersed with a morning visit to Leath's room, which he called his surgery. There she would receive "treatment." Leath always draped a sheet over her, covering her face so she couldn't see what he was doing. His touch was cold, but he never did what Jooste had done. She sometimes felt him move something inside her. A dull soreness would linger after. Leath showed little sympathy for her discomfort, obsessively noting everything he did in his book. She had to stand very still in front of the machine every day. It didn't hurt. Leath said he could see the baby in her with it, but he never showed her anything. Before she was allowed to leave, Leath gave her a mug of milk that he called "nutrients." It tasted strange, metallic.

Once a day she could go outside with the others for an hour. The girls were all young, some barely thirteen. There were a couple of older ones, around twenty, whose husbands had been captured and sent away. They always led the Bible reading and prayers. There was a lot of talk about revenge against the British, of how they would be made to pay one day. Anna sometimes thought of Andrew. Every time the women asked God to smite their enemy, Anna silently asked that Andrew be spared. One by one, their number diminished as they went into confinement. Only Leath and Sarah were allowed in the rooms. Anna knew her time would come soon. The child's kicking grew stronger, pains waking her up at odd hours as the skin on her stomach grew taut, marred by red lines.

Away from her mother, Hester became talkative, animated. She gained weight on potatoes and fatty meat, her cheeks rounding out, her body becoming soft. She was kind to Anna. They always sat together in the courtyard, talking about life before the war and what they were going to do once it was over. They sometimes talked idly about escaping, but there was nowhere to go. The farm was near a British stronghold and soldiers regularly crossed the property. Hester had a young man, Theunis, and they were going to get married once the war was over. But Anna noticed that as Hester's stomach grew she talked less and less about Theunis, the hope she had clung to devoured by the unborn child. Anna tried to cheer Hester up, but she too knew that kind of sadness. It sometimes threatened to swallow her and there were days when she couldn't leave her dark room. The latest talk among the women frightened her. About babies that never drew a breath, mothers taken away at night by soldiers, heads of the deformed monsters that came from their wombs smashed open against the walls of the house by Leath himself, so that nobody would know of his failures. Anna didn't want to listen to such things. She remembered how one of the ewes on their farm had given birth to a lamb without front legs. Her father had killed it right away, bashing its head in as it struggled for life. Maybe that was what grew inside her. Something only God would pity.

Sarah carried a tray into Anna's room, set it down on the bed, and took the baby from her. "She's fat, the little one." She swaddled the girl in a blanket and put her down in the crib next to Anna's bed, running her hand over the girl's wispy white hair. The baby fought with sleep, her strange silver eyes losing the battle by degrees. Anna couldn't remember ever seeing Sarah smile before.

Since giving birth, Anna had been locked in her room. Sarah brought her food and emptied the slop bucket and Leath came twice a day. He seemed tense these days, irritable, barely noting her presence in the room as he examined the child. Anna dreaded Leath touching the baby, but there was little she could do to prevent it. The thought that the child might lose its life on the whim of this madman scared her. She had thought of naming her daughter after her mother, but a name would make a loss unbearable, so she just called the child Baby.

Sarah handed Anna a tin mug off the tray. "The doctor says you have to drink this before you eat."

"He's back?" Sarah nodded. Leath hadn't been to Anna's room in two days, and she had heard him argue with Sarah outside her door the day before he'd left.

"The commanders, they . . ." Sarah pressed her lips together. "Finish all of that," she said, folding her hands, waiting until Anna had swallowed the last of the thick white liquid. It tasted different than the nutrients she had had before Baby was born, like bitter almonds.

Anna met Sarah's eyes as she handed back the mug. "It's true, then? About the inquiry? That they'll—"

"What do you know of that?"

Anna felt a flicker of hope. She glanced at the crib. "If they come, maybe she'll live."

"Do not concern yourself. Your baby is healthy." Sarah turned to go.

"Why are you helping him?" An indignant hysteria welled in Anna's chest. She was overwhelmed by her own powerlessness, her inability to protect her child. "Why did you turn against your people?"

Sarah turned back from the door. "My people?" A perplexed frown crept over her brow.

"The *Boere* that once owned this farm. The family who fed you and gave you a place to sleep."

"My people." Sarah scoffed. "Let me tell you about how it was before, *Nooi*, before the doctor came here. About how the *baas* owns you, not just your labor, but your body too if you want to feed your family and keep a roof over your head. How he whipped me and my brother when we were only little children and forced himself on my mother at night. How sometimes he made us watch. How it became my turn when I was barely old enough to be thought of as a woman. How his wife and children thought it their birthright to humiliate us every opportunity they got." A hardness had settled into Sarah's face. "One white man is as good as another to me, even if the language they speak is different.

"The day the Khakis rode in here, they tied us to the back of the ox wagon the white family rode in. Old people and small children all had to keep up, there was no mercy. I know what happens in the black camps. Native people are treated worse than animals. At least when you're white the Khakis think twice. The doctor said he'd keep me out of the camps as long as I work for him. I can do nothing about what he does here. If it wasn't me, it would be someone else. They would be safe instead of me. My mother, my family, they're all gone, but I am alive. That is good enough for me. Death is not beautiful or peaceful, that much I know from working for the doctor. Death is ugly, and terrifying, and empty, and it means nothing—"

A scream of raw anguish interrupted Sarah. Her anger dissipated, her eyes suddenly wide and scared. "I have to go."

"Is it Hester? Her time is near."

Sarah nodded. "She is having trouble." She rushed off, closing the door behind her.

Anna didn't hear the key turn in the lock. She shifted to the edge of the bed, still sore from the birth, her legs weak, the floorboards rough under her bare feet. The door opened without resistance, the hallway empty, Hester's screams the only sound. In her long white nightdress and cap, her long blond hair falling past her pale face, Anna cut a ghostly figure in the dark as she slowly made her way toward Hester's room. The rooms she passed were stripped bare, the smell of lye thick, memories of the girls that occupied them only weeks ago scrubbed away.

A baby's first screams cut through the quiet hallway. Anna froze at the sight that greeted her as she turned the corner. Sarah stood in front of Hester's open door, her hands covering her mouth, her expression one of horror. Leath emerged, his sleeves rolled up, carrying a wriggling newborn in his bloodied hands. Sarah held her hands out to take the child, but Leath ignored her.

"A male. This one must survive." Leath headed down the hall.

Anna pressed her back against the wall, slinking into the nearest empty room.

"What about the girl, Doctor?" Sarah called after Leath. He stopped for a moment outside the room where Anna hid. She was sure that he would hear her frantic heartbeat.

"She is not needed. Do what must be done."

Anna waited until Leath's footfalls disappeared before she left her hiding place. Sweat broke out on her brow as she made her way toward Hester's room. Sarah looked up from where she stood next to Hester, her expression when she saw Anna one of dismay rather than anger. A deep gash ran across Hester's naked abdomen, her chest rising infrequently. Anna felt dizzy. She grabbed hold of the bed to steady herself, her hand sinking into warm wet, red seeping between her fingers. A crimson drop separated from the edge of the saturated wool blanket and fell in slow motion, spreading onto the wooden floor, its edges disintegrating. Hester turned her head slowly, recognition in her glassy eyes. She opened her mouth. A final breath escaped and she was still.

"No!"

"Shhh." Sarah knelt down next to Anna, tears brimming in her large eyes. "You have to go. He might come back."

"Hester, she . . ." The room suddenly swam around Anna, nausea rising from the pit of her stomach.

Sarah held Anna close, her brown dress full of cooking smells, a faint odor of spirits lingering on her sleeve. "There is nothing you can do."

Waves of nausea rippled through Anna. She tried to stand, but her legs wouldn't hold her. "What's wrong with me?"

Sarah averted her eyes. "The doctor told me to pack everything when he came back from town. He says the ones in charge don't understand his work. They are sending soldiers."

Sarah wrapped both arms around Anna's waist and lifted her off the ground. She forced Anna out of the room and back down the hallway. Anna's heart pounded, each short step paid for in agony. Edges became soft, colors blending, the house suddenly unfamiliar. Faces of girls peered from the corners, their hands reaching, trying to hold her back. Sarah dragged Anna the last few steps. Crippling pain ripped through Anna's stomach as she doubled over on the bed. The baby cried, distressed by the commotion around her.

Anna grabbed Sarah's wrist. "He's going to kill Baby too." Sarah tried to pull away, but Anna held on with all her strength. "You have to save her."

"*Aikona.*" Sarah struggled against Anna.

Pain rippled through Anna's body. She fought against the darkness pulling at her. "Take her to the Khakis."

Sarah stared uncomprehendingly at her. "They will be here tomorrow."

"No. There is a soldier. He was stationed near George. He will help."

"Why would he? The Khakis are not your people."

"Ask for him. Tell them she is his."

"It's been a long time, *Nooi.*" Sarah's voice softened as she freed herself from Anna's weakening grip. "He won't be there anymore."

"You have to try. Please . . ."

Sarah could barely hear Anna's plea, the lights rapidly fading from her eyes. She backed away. Leave these white people to themselves, she thought. They brought this war, soaking the land in blood. All this suffering for the love of yellow metal. Boer or Brit, no matter, they cared about little else. She had to get away before the troops arrived. She had siphoned money and supplies from the household over the past two years, enough to get her to the border. But with a white child? Never. They would shoot her on the spot.

"She's done nothing." Anna reached for a torn page under her pillow, her movements painful to watch. "Andrew Morgan. Give him this. He was kind to me once. Maybe he will be again." Anna's words slurred, her tongue thick. "Ask him to remember Anna Richter of Vergelegen." Her body slackened against the pillows, the page still clutched in her hand. Her crusted lips had a bluish tint, her eyes staring at nothing, as if she was surprised to find it there at the end of her days. The baby cried, somehow understanding that there was no hope for comfort left to her, her face turning red, her limbs fretting loose from the blankets.

Sarah reached for the child.

The figure of a woman merged with the shadows of vines and trees, enveloped by night, a complicit friend, a small bundle tied in a blanket to her back. She stayed away from the road, her movements furtive, only stopping once she had crossed the river that bordered the property. Daylight sauntered steadily over the hills ahead, where shelter lay in hidden places, only known to people who lived on this land long before any white faces forged their way in blood. Only once she was far enough away from the house did Sarah dare to look back. The thick white walls betrayed no sign of the turmoil inside, but in the distance, the dust of approaching horses billowed. Sarah wondered what the soldiers would make of the things they found within those staid walls, the earth mounds among the grapevines, the bloodstains between the floorboards that no amount of scrubbing could remove.

Sarah touched the front of her dress, comforted by the piece of paper hidden next to her skin. She had read the sparse words scrawled on it over and over, struggling with her decision, while the baby cried against her chest.

Dear Anna, it read in thick lines, *I will pray every night that you can one day forgive me for what has been done to you and yours.* It was signed *Lance Corporal Andrew J. Morgan.*

In the end, Sarah had known that leaving the child behind would haunt her forever. She adjusted the bundle on her back before continuing her journey. For the first time in her life she felt like she had power—to change something, to choose.

2

Thursday
DECEMBER 9, 2010

"There you are." Captain Mynhardt stood in the archive doorway, coffee mug in hand.

Alet turned, knocking her pen off the desk. "What is it, Captain?"

"I forgot to tell you, a call came in this morning." Mynhardt bent down to pick up the pen. He studied the silver engraving for a moment: *To Alet from Pa.*

"Graduation present." Alet took the pen from him.

"You made the old boy proud when you decided to follow in his footsteps, you know."

Alet bit her lip. "*Ja.* I know."

"I sent him the parade photos I took. There's a few good ones of you with the children."

"Thanks." Alet wasn't sure what pictures of a parade would do to mend her relationship with her father, but it was kind of Mynhardt to try.

"Ansie and I are heading to Port Elizabeth early Saturday. You need a ride?"

Until she transferred to Unie, Alet didn't even know that her father knew Captain Mynhardt, never mind well enough for Mynhardt to get an invitation to his wedding. She imagined the uncomfortable conversation in the car on the way to PE, arriving early, dealing with the faffing women and the tipsy old men, being forced to stick around at the reception, making small talk with strangers about how she fit into the new family dynamic. "Thanks, Captain," she said. "But I'm on shift till noon. I'll drive myself."

"Don't be late, hear. He doesn't tolerate that *kak*, not even from you."
Alet nodded. "You said there was a call?"

"*Ja*. Right. Teacher from the farm school. Something about a girl saying the Thokoloshe came to her house. Nonnie Kok. Her mother is the local working girl."

Alet sighed. The Thokoloshe was a myth, a tiny evil sprite possessed of a voracious sexual appetite. The older black people still raised their beds on bricks so he couldn't assault them at night. Kids talking about the Thokoloshe visiting was usually a sure sign that something bad was going on at home. None of the men at the station wanted to deal with domestic cases, especially if abuse was suspected, so they always got relegated to her.

"Shouldn't social services deal with it, Captain?"

"We don't need another child in the system unless we're sure there's really a problem. Go pay the mother a visit tomorrow. Feel things out. But go home now. There's no overtime in the budget."

"I'm just finishing up." Alet pushed her chair out from the desk.

"What's this?" Mynhardt stepped closer, squinting at the computer screen.

Alet felt like she had been caught with her hand in the till. "I thought I'd go through missing persons, Captain," she said nonchalantly. "See if we can identify the victim on the mountain."

"This isn't your case, girlie. You're still on probation." Mynhardt had chronic halitosis. His lunch of stale coffee and sausage pie had made it worse.

"It happened in my patrol area, Captain. I know the people." Alet balled her fists in her lap, wondering how long she would have to do penance with traffic duty before she would be trusted with real police work again. She needed to get the hell out of Unie, get her career, her life, back on track. Solving a murder could be her ticket to a transfer.

"You think the coloureds up there will give you anything?" Mynhardt put his coffee cup down on the desk. "Let me tell you something, my girl. You're an outsider, white police, and a woman. They will lie to your face and sort things for themselves."

"They won't talk to Mathebe, you know that. Please, Captain. I already spent the whole bloody day on that mountain bagging evidence. I might as well work the case."

"Find anything useful?" Mynhardt sat down on the desk, the grip of the Rap 401 on his hip disappearing beneath a fold of flesh.

"Rubbish. Bags full. It'll take days to sort through it all."

"Catalog that if you want to help, then."

"Give me a chance, Captain. I did the detective training, I can handle this."

Deep lines formed a fleshy M between Mynhardt's eyes. "When I started in the force there was no detective training at college, girlie. You learned the job by doing the *kak* work like fingerprints and worked your way up to robberies and the serious stuff. That's how your dad and I did it. The old-fashioned way. The right way. Don't think you're too good for it."

"*Ja*, but—"

"These days you young *laaities* want to start at the top. Think you know everything because you read it in a manual. You know nothing. You don't understand about seeing evidence for what it is, sniffing out witnesses and working them. No book teaches you that."

"How am I supposed to—"

"Evening, Captain." Sergeant Hein Strijdom stood at the door. He was a sturdy middle-aged man with a buzz cut, a thick, boorish face, and a permanent scowl.

"*Naand*, Hein."

Strijdom briefly looked in Alet's direction and dipped his head slightly before returning his attention to Mynhardt. "April books off at five. We're waiting for briefing and parade."

"*Ja*. Right." Mynhardt picked up his coffee cup, leaving a wet ring on the desk.

"Captain?" Alet smiled, aware that Strijdom was watching them. "Think about it?"

"It's better that you stay on traffic duty for the time being, Alet. Sergeant Mathebe is CID. He'll request your help if he needs it." Mynhardt patted her shoulder. "You're doing okay here, girlie. Don't mess it up, see?"

Strijdom lingered in the doorway after Mynhardt left. "Too good for traffic duty, hey?" He crossed his arms. "You're not special here, Berg. No matter who your *pappie* is. Remember that."

Alet stifled her anger as he walked away. Strijdom was in charge of road operations. She had pulled shift with him in her first month, saw him taking a bribe from a truck driver. Strijdom had caught her looking as he palmed the money and had been on edge around her ever since. He tried his best to get to her, implying that she was incompetent during parade, and getting her stuck on service desk duty. She had thought about going to Mynhardt, or the Hawks, but it was her word against Strijdom's. Anyway, getting a senior officer suspended or fired would not win her any friends.

Alet got her backpack from her locker and checked her cell. One missed call, no message. Boet Terblanche's number appeared on the monochrome screen. Alet stepped out the station's back door and sank into one of the faded plastic chairs in the backyard. Half-smoked cigarettes lined a rusted coffee can on the ground next to her. She stared at the can for a moment before reaching in and retrieving the longest butt, dusting the sand off, and pinching it between her lips. A squad car pulled into the yard, Mathebe behind the wheel. Alet quickly flicked the butt into the grass.

Mathebe was dressed in a clean office uniform, pressed long-sleeved white shirt, dark blue tie and pants, navy peaked cap with the yellow eight-point star emblem of the SAPS on the front. He'd probably gone home to shower and change after they transported the body to the clinic. Layers of stink and filth itched Alet's skin. She couldn't wait to go home and soak in the tub until her fingertips shriveled.

Mathebe headed for the station entrance, a manila envelope under his arm. "Good evening, Constable Berg," he said curtly as he passed her.

"You know you can call me Alet, right, Johannes?"

Mathebe nodded and kept walking.

"Johannes, wait a second."

"Constable?"

"Listen, I spoke to the captain. I mean, I'd like to help with the case since I know the farmers and the area."

Mathebe seemed to clutch the envelope a bit tighter, shifting his weight onto the balls of his feet. "Captain Mynhardt approved this?"

"He assigned the crime scene evidence to me. And you're going to need help canvassing the area too, right?"

Mathebe nodded. "I will talk to the captain about this."

"It's just that they're busy with parade right now, hey. But sure, check with him when they're done. No worries." Alet glanced at the back door. "Look, I was just about to knock off. How about we go get a drink and you can catch me up on the case?"

Mathebe studied her for a moment. "We can do it here." He sat down on the plastic chair, his back preacher-straight. He took a file out of the envelope and held it on his lap.

"You sure you don't want to get a drink?"

"No. Thank you."

Alet pulled up a chair next to him. "So what's new?"

"I have the preliminary autopsy report from Dr. Oosthuizen."

Alet held her hand out. "Can I see?"

"The victim is female, approximately one-point-five meters tall, weighing forty-three kilograms." Mathebe recited the facts without opening the file. "Estimated age of fifteen."

A soft grunt escaped Alet's lips. She tried to remember herself at fifteen, barely knowing up from down, meeting her father, her mother's death. Even though it felt like everything was falling apart, there was still the promise of time, of a life ahead of her. Fifteen was too young to die, much less to die like that.

Mathebe paused briefly, his expression taut. "The time of death is estimated between twenty-three hundred and oh-two-hundred. From the preliminary examination, the victim appears to have suffered extensive fourth-degree burns. Probable cause of death, asphyxiation due to inhalation of smoke and subsequent thermal burns."

"Is there anything to identify her by? I didn't find any fifteen-year-old girls in missing persons."

Mathebe's features briefly betrayed annoyance. "Dr. Oosthuizen took an X-ray of the victim's teeth. We will search for a match."

"No race, hair color, nothing? No offense to Oosthuizen, but he probably treats HIV with beetroot and African potato. Isn't there anyone else we can call in? Maybe someone in Oudtshoorn?"

"Dr. Oosthuizen is qualified."

Alet hid her frustration. "Must be one of the worker kids, you think? Why else would she have been on the mountain?"

"We will go door-to-door at the Terblanche farm in the morning."

"It's going to be a hell of a job getting to everyone, Johannes. It's

Friday tomorrow. Most of them knock off early for the weekend. Even if we split up it's still—"

Mathebe stood up. "No. We stay together."

Alet smiled. "Whatever you say, Boss. Pick you up at seven?"

"Askies, Mies." Maria's voice rose an octave above the din in Zebra House's packed dining room. Alet stepped aside. The woman sidled past her with a tray laden with plates, a whiff of curried lamb rising from the spread. Alet's stomach growled. She lifted one of the plates off the tray.

"Looks *lekker. Dankie!*"

"Aikona! It is not for you. I will get you your own, now-now."

"Put it on the bar with a brandy and coke and you have a deal," Alet said. She put the plate back on the tray. Maria walked away, her enormous bottom canting back and forth like two pit bulls fighting in a bag. She stopped at the table of an unfamiliar couple. The woman was mousy and pale, the man had dark hair and glasses. Snippets of an American accent carried above the din in the room as they thanked Maria. Tourists. They probably thought Unie would be an authentic place to stop on the way to Cape Town and expected more than they got. Join the club.

Alet scanned the room. The tables were packed with locals. Boet Terblanche sat at the bar, talking to Petrus Brink, who ran the farmers' co-op. Boet's arms were crossed, his attention focused on Petrus, who gestured with puffy hands, two empty beer cans lined up next to a huge glass stein. Boet wore a crisp button-down shirt, a tan line visible just below the rolled-up sleeves. Alet remembered his pale skin from the neck down and the elbow up and looked away.

"Hey, sexy!" Joey Joubert suddenly stood beside her. Joey was the local theater-degree dropout. He managed Joyboys, a coffee shop nestled in the old vestry of the Dutch Reform Church. Alet had spent many entertaining lunchtimes there, catching up on local gossip. Nobody in town could *poep* without Joey knowing something about it. Plus he made the best iced coffee she had ever had.

Joey kissed her on the cheek. "You clean up nice." They almost bumped heads. Alet could never remember if one or both cheeks was the fashion now. At least Joey didn't insist on kissing her on the mouth like the older people did.

"The uniform doesn't do much for my social life, hey."

"I don't know that dressing up is going to work for you here, doll," Joey said. "Only old farts around."

"*Ja*, well . . ." Alet shrugged, uncomfortable in her low-cut blouse. It was the only thing in her closet that didn't feel too tight at the moment.

Joey tapped her on the arm. "So, I hear you found a body?"

"How do you know about that?"

Joey rolled his eyes. "Please. Everyone knows. It's the most exciting thing that's happened here since Petrus's wife ran off with that educated coloured from Grahamstown. So? Who died?"

Alet recognized the pleasure in Joey's voice, the way he leaned in, his big-eyed anticipation. She felt off balance, strangely protective, as if discussing the girl's death would violate some secret bond they had. "Don't know yet," she said, trying to sound nonchalant. "Nobody has been reported missing."

"Well, that's no surprise. The blacks have so many snot-noses running around, I don't think they'd even notice if one was gone." Joey glanced around the restaurant and waved at someone. "Listen, I'm meeting my dad to discuss the Church bazaar. They want to get someone to perform at Joyboys for a fund-raiser. You want to come sit by us for a drink?"

At a table in the back, *Dominee* Joubert, the Dutch Reform Church's minister, sat talking with a middle-aged man, a half-empty bottle of red wine between them. The elder Joubert gave Alet a curt "*Goeienaand*" through tight lips. She sighed inwardly. Her lack of any effort to attend church since moving here was clearly frowned upon. She had always thought of God as a dirty, voyeuristic old man, who seemed to watch her every move. She kept this thought to herself in Unie, though. Here, Sundays were devoted to stiff necks and hypocrisy, led with perverse pleasure from the pulpit by the esteemed *Dominee*.

"Neels Burger. I'm a deacon," the other man at the table volunteered. "I organize the school's participation in the bazaar."

Alet wondered why he felt the need to explain his presence. "You teach high school, right?"

"History, grades three through seven. And I'm hostel master."

"So you know all the kids?"

Neels nodded, a sudden air of authority lifting his sad-sack expression. "The whole lot."

"Did any of the girls not show up this week?"

"Alet's investigating the murder, you know," Joey said.

Minister Joubert looked up from studying the wine in his glass. "Terrible thing," he said in a monotone. "We will pray for her soul."

"Rather pray that we get the guy who did this," Alet said.

Minister Joubert pursed his lips, a look passing between him and Joey.

"It's hard to tell." Neels fingered his silverware. "You know, if there isn't enough money to pay for a ride into town, the farm kids don't show up for the week. And then there's the ones who drop out because fruit-picking pays better than going to school. They don't let us know, they just don't show up one day."

Alet got impatient. Neels was obviously slow on the uptake. "I need to know if anybody didn't show up today."

Neels paused. "Two girls from the hostel, I think."

"How old?"

"One is twelve, the other sixteen. The twelve-year-old is white, though."

Alet wondered why everyone assumed the victim was black. "What about the non-boarders?"

"I'd have to check attendance records."

"I'll come by the school in the morning. And I need the names and addresses of the missing girls."

"I'm sure everyone in town will do their best to help, Alet," *Dominee* Joubert said. "Wine for you?"

The wine tasted like vinegar. Alet took labored sips while Joey proposed André du Plessis, an Afrikaans folk singer from Oudtshoorn, for the bazaar fund-raiser.

"I've not heard of him," Minister Joubert said.

"He's famous, *Pa*. Got quite a following among the younger crowd."

Alet's eyes wandered to the bar. Boet was gone, a R50 note wedged under his glass. An unfamiliar barrel-chested man with gray hair had taken his seat.

"Who's that?" Alet asked when Joey paused for breath.

"Where?" Joey looked over his shoulder. "Oh, you mean the pink version of the Hulk?" He smirked. "That is Jeff Wexler."

"The owner?" Alet had never met the British ex-pat who owned Zebra House. According to Tilly, he had bought the place as something to do in retirement, but only stopped by a few times a year.

Joey lowered his voice. "Rumor has it he used to be a soccer hooligan, like on TV."

"*Ja?* Whose rumor is that?"

Joey raised his eyebrows and tilted his head to the side. "*Ag*, you know. People like to talk."

"There are all sorts around these days," *Dominee* Joubert said. He smiled at Alet. "No way to keep them out, I'm afraid."

Alet had stayed as long as a thin pretense at politeness required. "Hey, listen, Joey," she said. "I've got food coming to the bar. I'll leave you to it." She pushed her chair out. "Thanks for the drink."

"Bye, doll," Joey said. "Come tell us when you catch the bad guy, mmm? Milk tart and *koeksisters* on me."

Alet made brief eye contact with Jeffrey Wexler before she took a seat next to him. Lukas, the bartender, placed a brandy and coke in front of her without a word.

Wexler ran his eyes over her. "A regular, luv?"

Alet smiled. "I don't recall you sleeping with me or handing me a paycheck. So don't call me 'luv.'"

"A paycheck, huh? Is that all it takes?"

"You have to draw the line somewhere."

"A sense of humor. How refreshing." Wexler took a sip from his drink. Alet noticed the small broken capillaries on the flattened bridge of his nose. "So what should I call you, then? Miss . . . ? Or is it Missus?"

"Constable Berg."

"The law." He eyed her with renewed interest. "I don't remember you."

"I've been here a few months."

"I'm Jeff." He extended his oversize hand, then squeezed too hard.

"Wexler, right?" Alet gritted her teeth.

"Brilliant deduction, Constable." Wexler let go of Alet's hand, the pressure still lingering. She felt like dipping it in the ice bucket behind the bar, but she wasn't about to give him the satisfaction. "A tire-biter with a brain."

"News travels here."

"So it does."

"You arrived today, Jeff?"

"Landed in Jo'burg this morning and drove down."

"That's an eleven-hour drive."

"For some. I don't dawdle, Constable." Wexler had a faint look of pride about him.

"In for the holidays, then?"

"I try not to make firm plans." Wexler lingered on Alet's cleavage a beat too long before he met her eyes. "But if something catches my interest . . ."

"Jeff, I—" Tilly walked up to the bar. She looked startled to see Alet, a brief look of concern, or was that panic, on her face. "I can't seem to get rid of you today, Alet," she said awkwardly. Her smile didn't reach her eyes.

Alet lifted her glass. "It's so nice to be missed at your favorite bar."

"Your only bar."

"True, *ja*. But also my favorite. Must be 'cause you're here."

"Well, this is cozy, innit?" Wexler interrupted.

Tilly's shoulders sank slightly. "Sorry, Jeff. This is Alet."

"Ahhh-let," Wexler repeated with a note of condescension. "Yeah, we met." He pushed his empty glass across the bar. "I'm going upstairs, Mathilda. Go ahead and finish what we discussed earlier." He stood up. He was nearly a foot taller than Tilly. "Constable. I'm sure I'll see you again." Alet held Wexler's gaze. His innuendo clung like an oil slick even after he'd lumbered out the door.

Tilly sat down next to Alet. "You shot out of here this morning without finishing your beer. Or paying, mind you."

"There was a body on Boet's farm."

Tilly dipped her chin. "Don't tell me he finally lost it with Jana's mood swings."

Alet burst out laughing, in spite of herself. "Jana's alive and well, as far as I know."

"Who was it, then?"

"Don't know. It was burned beyond recognition."

Tilly grimaced, drawing her breath in. "Shame, man."

"So when did Jeff get here?"

"He was here when I got back from the co-op this afternoon. Why?"

"Just asking. You didn't mention that he was coming."

Tilly shrugged. "He does that. Bastard likes to keep us on our toes. Are you eating?"

Alet considered her options. Eating alone at a bar while the whole town looked on suddenly felt pathetic. "Know what, it's late and I'm tired." She turned to the bartender. "Lukas, can you ask Maria to put my Bobotie in a doggie bag?"

Lukas nodded and disappeared into the kitchen.

Tilly leaned on the bar, straightening the coasters so they lined up. "You should do something about those bags under your eyes. Cucumber slices work wonders."

"Why are you on my case today?"

"I'm just trying to help. You have to look better than the bride on Saturday, you know. I think it's a rule."

"Well, she is older than me by like . . . twelve seconds. Shouldn't be too much of a problem."

"Can't wait to hear all about it. Come for a walk with me Sunday?"

"I plan on being appropriately hungover, thanks. Tell your ma not to make so much noise with that sprayer."

"You tell her. She's not talking to me."

"Again?"

Tilly nodded. "I used a swear-word in front of her. Now the world is ending because nobody has any respect anymore."

"How old are you?"

"I know." Tilly held her hands up in exasperation. "The older I get, the more she treats me like a child. Be glad you weren't around when she went through her you-should-be-ashamed-of-not-knowing-your-own-history phase. I used to fall asleep sitting upright at the dinner table."

Lukas reappeared with a Styrofoam container and put it down in front of Alet. She drained her glass, ice bouncing on her lip. "And that's that."

"Get some sleep." Tilly stood up and disappeared into the back office.

Alet made her way out of the restaurant and down the polished steps. Outside, a sliver of moon held court over bright stars. Back in Jo'burg she was barely able to see stars through the smog. They shone even brighter on the farms. Had the girl seen them as she was dying? Once the thought crept into Alet's mind, she couldn't stop. Was the girl conscious? Did she struggle as her flesh burned? Alet imagined herself lying on the ground as a dark figure doused her with liquid, the image so real that she could smell the petrol, feel her stomach contracting at the thought of a match being lit. Stop it, she told herself, unease settling in her bones. She turned full circle in the middle of the street, unable to shake the feeling that someone was watching her.

Sparse streetlamps cast shadows as she walked past the skeletons of guesthouses that had popped up along the main road in anticipation of the soccer World Cup earlier that year, going out of business almost as fast as Bafana Bafana lost. Alet lengthened her stride, her sandal straps digging painfully into her flesh, relieved when Trudie Pienaar's house came into view up the street. She lifted the latch of the front gate, but changed her mind. The gate always made a hell of a noise. She couldn't stand the thought of another lecture on consideration from the old cow. No wonder her daughter lived at work.

Alet decided to climb over the fence, then almost fell down when her blouse caught on one of the iron spikes. Her heels sank into the freshly watered flower bed on the other side. Dammit. Trudie was bound to bang on her door in the morning now, demanding an explanation for the state of her garden. It was the only thing she seemed to enjoy, and she tended to it religiously, water restrictions be damned. Trudie was always there, eyes hiding behind dark glasses, tilling away at the crack of dawn, planting this or pruning that, her rubber gloves and straw hat covering the pale skin her loose cotton dresses didn't.

Peach trees lined the path to the back of the house where Alet's flat stood. It was a small two-room building that had once been the maid's quarters, but had been enlarged to include a kitchen and a bathtub. Alet felt her way in the dark, negotiating between her dinner and her purse as she searched for her keys. A dark figure stepped into the path in front of her. She froze, her pulse racing, dark demons still occupying her thoughts.

"Alet?"

"Boet." Alet fought the instinct to throw her Bobotie at him and run.

"I couldn't get you alone at Zebra, so I thought—"

Anger replaced fear. "You scared the *kak* out of me, man."

"Sorry, I—"

"What the *fok* do you think you are playing at?" Alet stormed past him to her flat. She unlocked the security gate. The hinges of the glass door behind it protested as she jerked it open.

"Can I come in?"

Alet looked back at him, unsure of what her answer should be.

"Not for long. Promise." Boet looked like a lost puppy.

Alet flipped the light switch. A low hum preceded flickering fluorescent bulbs. Harsh white light washed over the flat. A small kitchen area with cheap brown cabinets lined the left wall. A secondhand blue couch divided the room. Behind it, a messy bed stood unmade. Alet felt self-conscious about the clothes and underwear she had left strewn everywhere, vacillating between clearing the mess and ignoring it.

Boet walked to the fridge. He took a beer out of the case she kept on the bottom shelf. "Want one?" He opened the can and handed it to her.

Alet put the beer down on the large trunk that doubled as a coffee table. "It's late, Boet."

Boet sat down on the couch. "Please. Sit for a bit."

Alet leaned against the door frame and crossed her arms.

"Did you find out anything?" Boet stared down at his boots, his beer suspended between his palms, his hair falling in soft brown curls around his face. "About the body, I mean."

"Not yet."

"What happened . . . when I saw it this morning, you know, I got scared. I wanted to drive as far away as the diesel in the tank would take me and never go back." He took a sip of beer. "And then, you showed up."

Alet clenched her jaw when she met his pleading, deep-set green eyes. "*Jissis*. What?"

"I just want to talk to you."

"Talk, then."

Boet inched to the edge of the couch and reached out, his fingers cold, briefly touching her hand.

Alet pulled away. "Don't."

"Sorry." There was a dark shadow on Boet's face. Alet imagined the roughness of his cheek under her fingertips. Longing formed in the pit of her stomach.

"Listen, Boet. It's been a hell of a day. Just tell me what you want."

Boet nodded. "I hope we're okay?"

"What do you mean?"

"I haven't seen you for a while. I just . . ."

"Ah, I see. You're scared I might open my big mouth over Rooibos tea at your house. Mrs. Terblanche, did you know the victim? Oh, and by the way, your husband and I *steeked*, but that's long done, so don't worry, hey. *Ja*, I'll have a biscuit with that, *dankie*."

"It was a mistake."

"Something we agree on."

Boet stood up. He leaned against the kitchen cabinet close to her. "Please understand. It's not just about me and Jana anymore. There's going to be a baby."

"I noticed." Alet hated the burning sensation behind her eyes. "Would've been nice if you mentioned it at the time."

"I didn't know."

"Right." Alet forced a smile. "Look, don't worry, hey." She rested her hand on the door handle.

Boet's limbs seemed awkward, his breathing loud in the silence between them. "Well, good night, then." He squeezed past her, turning around on the *stoep*. "Thank you."

Alet closed the security gate behind him, slamming it too hard, numbness settling over her. In the main house, a light went on.

1910

Tessa

Tessa crept from between Andrew and Sarah where they napped together on the bed, their usual Sunday-afternoon ritual. Tessa hated taking naps. She closed her eyes and pretended, but instead she thought of all the things she could be doing instead, reading, playing outside, everything except chores. Sarah said that young ladies had to learn to knit and mend clothes and bake bread and preserve fruit and dry meat and sing their psalms in the morning and say their prayers at night. Being a young lady was awfully boring, especially during the rainy season when she had to stay cooped inside. Just before she made it to the door, she turned back. Sarah turned on her side, her jaw hanging slack, her lips parted by shallow breathing. Without opening his eyes, Andrew moved closer to her, his arm circling her waist. Tessa only saw them touch like that when they were alone, when the doors were locked and the curtains drawn.

Tessa opened the farmhouse door as quietly as she could. Green valley and black mountains greeted her outside, a low-lying sun casting brilliant pinks and yellows against patchy clouds. Tessa liked it much better here than the small house in Oudtshoorn, where they lived while Andrew worked for the British. Tessa didn't like Oudtshoorn. Strangers called Andrew a *kaffir*-loving redneck to his face, and after the first time it happened, Sarah refused to go out with them. But here, in the mountains, they rarely saw anyone but the farmworkers. They could make a life here, Andrew said, put down roots and be a family.

They had hiked up the mountain that morning, the first day of sunshine after a week of constant downpours. Andrew had knocked on the door of each of the small white houses they passed, checking in on the workers, handing them a Christmas box full of *beskuit* and jam that Tessa had helped Sarah make. Tessa had heard some of the coloured workers talk about Sarah, disdainful of a black living in the big house with the white man and his daughter, but she hadn't told Andrew. The workers still called Andrew "New *Baas*," even though he had bought the farm almost five years ago. Their house was the only one in the district that hadn't been burned down in the war. The workers said it had belonged to a joiner, who betrayed his friends so he could take their land. They said that his ghost still walked the farm, his guilt too heavy for him to ever rest. Tessa didn't know if this was true, but she always felt uneasy when she was alone in the house, especially when she looked out the window at the burned-out ruin of the small farmhouse in the distance, convinced that she could see someone there, especially at twilight. Andrew said it was her imagination, that ghosts didn't exist. There was only the Holy Ghost, and he would never harm her.

Every night they lit a candle so Andrew could read out loud from the Bible. He had taught Tessa how to read a long time ago and she could recite every word. She didn't know how she did it, but things seemed to stick in her memory like small insects to a spider's web. When she closed her eyes, she could even remember the color of the blanket Sarah had wrapped her in as she carried Tessa to the British camp. Sarah's heart had beat frantically against Tessa's ear as the soldiers interrogated her before they sent for Andrew. Sarah now recalled it as a happy day, but Tessa only remembered the fear.

Tessa also had an easy time learning languages. Sarah spoke Sotho to her, and Andrew spoke English, and the workers on the farm spoke that Dutch language they sometimes called Afrikaans. She understood all three. Tessa didn't know what the people in town spoke, though. Andrew had never taken her or Sarah along when he went to buy supplies or sell sheep. He said it'd be better for them to stay on the farm. But Tessa was curious. She wondered if there were children like her in town, or anywhere for that matter.

The river was still flooded, so Tessa ventured down the dirt path that hugged the mountain and into the underbrush, trying to decide what she was going to do with her afternoon of freedom. She had never ventured up the mountain by herself. Andrew sometimes took her out with him on the farm if she was good. He once showed her how to make coffee in a tin can in the veld with dam water so you didn't get sick, and another time, he'd pointed out which berries were good to eat. Recently, when it was almost time to go home, he showed her an old lookout in the mountain, all grown over with branches, the red walls crumbling in places. Andrew said it was used in the war and that the British stuck their guns through the tiny windows to fire on the Boers. Tessa had heard him speak proudly of glory days and battles before, but his voice grew soft that day as he talked. "You're old enough to know the truth," he said.

Andrew explained to her that the British invaded because they wanted the country's gold. He also told her about the Boers shooting their own people if they thought they were traitors, how pride made them refuse to give up, how many women and children died in camps from disease and starvation, and how black people like Sarah suffered, treated badly by both the British and the Boers. He had dropped his head in shame as he talked about what people were capable of doing to each other. "Remember, Theresa, we all have bad and good in us. Don't only surround yourself with people who think like you. Listen to everybody before you decide what is right."

Tessa ventured farther up the mountain, wondering if she could find the lookout again. Small moths and other insects flew up as her steps disturbed their hiding places. There was a faint smell of smoke, which grew stronger as the workers' wives started cooking evening meals. Tessa's own stomach rumbled in response. She climbed on top of an enormous tree trunk that blocked the path, taking note of the scorched parts at the base where it had snapped. Lightning was common in the mountains, the spring storms particularly bad. Her foot caught as she jumped down the other side, propelling her face-first into the mud. Tessa opened her mouth to cry, tears already blurring her vision. Her Sunday dress was ruined. Sarah would be so mad.

"Hey you, *sharrap*." The urgent whisper came from close by.

Tessa blinked hard to clear her vision, the high-pitched distress call halted mid-vowel. On the other side of the trunk crouched two brown children, a boy and a girl, maybe six or seven years old. They both had sullen dark eyes, the boy's hair cropped close to his head, the girl's tied with a white bow. They both wore pants with suspenders and shirts made from meal sacks, patched in various places. Tessa immediately felt envious. Their clothes were much better for running around in than a stupid dress. The boy held one index finger to his mouth, pointing into the distance with the other. Tessa turned her head, clamping both hands over her mouth when she saw what he was pointing at.

A leopard moved languidly through the underbrush ahead, swaying gracefully with each step. It seemed to float from tree to tree, its lower body disappearing in the tall grass. Tessa wondered at its thick muscled neck and legs, its big head, the way its spotted hide glistened in the afternoon sun. She had never seen anything as beautiful before in her life. For a moment the beast looked right at her. Tessa felt her heart skip a beat, time disappearing until the two of them were the only living things in the world. She ached to know the creature, feel what it was feeling, live inside its skin, if only for a moment. As fast as it appeared, the mirage disappeared into the underbrush.

"It's watching us," the boy said. "They do that before they jump you."

The girl's eyes grew wide. "What do we do, hey Poena?"

"We move slow, Grietjie. No running, hear? Otherwise it will chase us."

Tessa pulled herself up. "It doesn't matter. It's gone now."

"What do you know?" Grietjie's chin jutted out defiantly. A knowing glance passed between the siblings.

Their hostility confused Tessa. "Can't you see?" She pointed in the distance. "It crossed to the other side of the mountain."

"You're lying," Poena said. "Nobody can see that far."

"*Ja*, nobody," Grietjie echoed, her nostrils flaring. "Besides, we go to school, you don't, so we're smarter."

Tessa had asked Andrew if she could go to the farm school down the road, but he said she wasn't old enough. Tessa was almost nine, but her body was short and pudgy. She had watched the coloured women with their babies from afar, had noticed the babies growing older, growing bigger. Every time she asked Andrew or Sarah why her body didn't change the same way, they answered that she was growing exactly the way God wanted her to. Tessa wondered why God didn't just make everybody the same. This would solve so many problems.

The two siblings turned in unison and retreated with comical slowness, their walk exaggerated into huge steps, their faces knotted in concentration.

"Can I come with you?" Tessa called after them.

"You go to your own house," Grietjie fired snippily. "You *mos* live in the big house with the *baas* and that *meit* that thinks she's so grand."

"*Ma* doesn't think that."

"You think she's your *ma*?" Grietjie looked at her brother and rolled her eyes. She put her hands in her sides, her body issuing a challenge. "You're thick, hey. She's a black."

Tessa felt a pang. She had a memory, the first one, of a woman with blond hair and sad eyes. But Sarah had raised her, loved her. "Come home with me, then," Tessa said. She desperately wanted Poena and Grietjie to like her, to meet Sarah and see that she was good.

"My *pa* will *bliksem* us if we set foot in the *baas*'s house," Poena said.

"Why?"

Poena's eyes narrowed. "You just don't. We live in our house and the *baas* lives in his. White people eat with white people. Coloured people eat with coloured people. That's how it works."

Grietjie's face scrunched into a scowl. "My *pa* said there's something wrong with you. That we should stay away from you."

Poena and Grietjie stared at Tessa as if she was something dirty. They know I'm not like them, Tessa thought. The idea that they could hate her that much just because she didn't look like them seemed so unfair. She turned and ran from them before they could say anything else, tears of hurt and anger blurring her vision. She wished the leopard would come back and eat Poena and Grietjie and their *pa* for dinner. The world away from Andrew and Sarah suddenly felt cold and hostile, full of people who hated for stupid reasons.

Tessa stumbled a few times as she descended the narrow path into the valley, her shoes scuffing against the rocks, but she barely noticed. In the distance she could see the house, a white dot in a blanket of green. As she drew closer, she saw Andrew in the doorway, talking to a short man in black clothes. A warning flashed in Andrew's eyes as Tessa approached. The man turned around and looked straight at her, a snarl deforming his lips. He had a big head and his nose was a different color than the rest of his face, as if it belonged to someone else.

"Theresa." Andrew put himself between her and the man. "Where were you?" He picked her up, carrying her on his hip back into the house.

"I saw a leopard, *Pa*," Tessa's excitement burst. "It was so big." She held her hand above her chest, fingers brought together, pointing up, the way Sarah had taught her.

"Mr. Morgan." The man's voice sounded like thunder rolling over the mountains. "This is a serious matter."

"*Dominee*, I can assure you that nothing immoral happens in this house."

"Witnesses have come forward."

"Witnesses? Trespassers with designs on my land, you mean. You can tell them all that I will never sell." Andrew's expression was stern, but Tessa felt the quivering in his body. She had only seen him that mad once before, when baboons had destroyed his vegetable patch. They had spent a whole afternoon after that stringing cans together to make noise and scare the mischief-makers off.

"Cutting yourself off from the church and hiding in your house won't protect you from your sins, Mr. Morgan," said the man in black. "God sees all. Your type will never be welcome among good people."

Andrew's grip on Tessa grew uncomfortably tight. "Get off my property, sir."

"This is not done." The man's face turned red. He raised a shaky finger in the air. "There will be consequences to your debauchery. And the child—"

"Go now, *Dominee*, or I will help you do so with my rifle." Andrew's narrow face was white, his teeth exposed beneath his trimmed mustache.

"It is against God's law, Mr. Morgan, fornicating outside your kind," the man yelled as Andrew closed the door. "It is unnatural. We cannot allow this to go on in our midst."

Tessa wriggled loose from Andrew's grip. Fear had written itself on Sarah's face as she stepped out of the dark bedroom. She took Tessa from Andrew and hugged her close, her tears wetting Tessa's cheeks.

"We were worried sick, Theresa," Andrew said, the anger still in his voice. "Don't ever go off like that again. These people—"

"He'll be back," Sarah interrupted. She looked pleadingly at Andrew. "He'll bring others with him."

Andrew nodded. He sank down on a chair, his head in his hands. "I'll leave. They'll stop if I'm not here."

"No." Andrew grabbed Sarah's hand. "This is our land, our home. They can't force us off."

"Don't go, *Ma*." Tessa started crying, feeling as if someone had inexplicably blown a candle out in her life without asking and she was sitting alone in the dark. "Don't leave me."

"It's all right, little one." Sarah kissed her on the cheek. "Maybe it will only be for a little while."

"It's not only you," Andrew said. A meaningful look passed between him and Sarah, an unspoken secret Tessa wasn't supposed to understand, though she did.

Andrew stood up, his body straight and resolute again, like long ago when he had confidently marched into battle. "We leave tonight. Together."

"Andrew, no." Sarah held a hand up in protest. Andrew grabbed it with both of his.

"I don't see another way, darling." Andrew encircled both of them in his arms. "We can start over, go where nobody knows us." He patted Tessa's back. "It will be all right."

"But this is our home." Tessa hiccupped the words.

"It is only a house, Theresa. Only things. You understand, don't you?"

Tessa nodded even though she didn't. She wondered where they would go. Perhaps to the lookout. It was a good hiding place.

"There's a man on the next farm over, Terblanche. He was interested in leasing the orchards." Andrew put his hat on his head. "Take only what we can carry. If we leave by midnight we'll be well on the road by morning."

Sarah looked around the room. "This is too sudden. Can't we wait a few days? See if—"

Andrew shook his head. "The sooner we go, the better."

They left in a donkey cart under the cover of darkness. Tessa tried to remember everything she could about the farm: the smell of the thatch on their house, the greenish-brown color of the duck pond, the sounds of baboons calling in the hills. Andrew had once told her that land binds you to a place. He had bought the farm, he said, so there would be a place she could always come home to. But if she didn't belong here anymore, would she belong anywhere?

Benjamin

As far back as he could remember, Benjamin had slept in *Saal* 1 on a steel cot with chipped paint. But he wasn't a baby anymore. *Matrone* Jansen fetched him one morning and told him that he was moving to *Saal* 3, and that was that. She picked him up in her bony arms and carried him down the hall. Benjamin held on to his blankie and his brown teddy bear. The bear had been donated by the Ladies' Church Group, who came every Christmas with gifts and treats and always said what a shame it was as they held their hands over their mouths. Benjamin wasn't so sure what they meant by that, but he liked the funny hats they made everybody wear, so he always smiled back.

Saal 3 was down two corridors and to the left. *Matrone* Jansen had put Benjamin down on a thin blue mattress in the corner of *Saal* 3 and told him that it was his bed now. The whitecoat, Pieter, had complained that he had enough work already, but *Matrone* Jansen gave him one of the scary looks she gave when you were really in trouble. Everyone knew better than to say something back after *Matrone* Jansen gave you that look.

Saal 3 smelled the same as the rest of the hospital, thick and sweet. The air refused to move through the barred windows in summer and the older nurses all walked around fanning themselves with books and sheets of paper. In winter, the sun's heat didn't penetrate the thick stone walls and *Matrone* Jansen gave him a pair of extra socks to keep his feet warm. The walls in *Saal* 3 were a shiny yellow. But not yellow like the crayon Benjamin used to draw the sun, more like the yellow of the inside half of the small round squash they served at the hospital for Sunday lunch. It was easy to wipe blood off those shiny yellow walls. He knew that because he'd seen the whitecoats and nurses do it many times.

Benjamin had asked *Matrone* Jansen why she didn't take him to *Saal* 2. Two came after one and before three, *Matrone* Jansen had taught him that. *Matrone* Jansen said he didn't belong in *Saal* 2. It was for the children that didn't look like the rest of them. The whitecoats called them defects and monsters, making strange faces and walking funny with their arms close to their bodies and their tongues hanging out whenever they talked about *Saal* 2. Benjamin wondered why they allowed monsters to live in the hospital. He worried that they would escape from *Saal* 2 and come after him.

Benjamin learned to do everything Pieter said, otherwise Pieter would *bliksem* him. Pieter had done it a few times after Benjamin had moved to *Saal* 3, but never when any of the nurses or *Matrone* Jansen were around. Pieter's light beard and pockmarked cheeks always deformed in a lopsided smile whenever he saw nurses walking by. Then he would disappear for a long time. At that point, the other children in *Saal* 3 began to make noise, like monkeys, Benjamin thought, though he'd never heard a monkey. Some of the children cried when the lights went off at night too. Benjamin couldn't understand that. Noises scared him, but he liked the dark. He'd learned, in *Saal* 1F, that grown-ups couldn't see in the dark, not like him. When it was dark the whitecoats and nurses would stay away. In the dark, it was always safe.

Sometimes nurses came to sit with Pieter in *Saal* 3. They'd talk about how South Africa would one day be a Union, with a proper prime minister, and it wouldn't be long before Afrikaners got rid of the Englishman. "Englishman" sounded like a bad word, Benjamin thought, especially because Pieter's voice became all hard and angry when he talked about the English. Pieter never looked at Benjamin and the other children while he talked, only at the pretty nurses. Sometimes he'd touch a nurse's arm or her leg. Some of them didn't like it, but Pieter always said that there were plenty of fish in the sea, the war had seen to that. Benjamin didn't understand what fish had to do with nurses. Pieter sometimes talked to Benjamin about grown-up things, which were confusing. Pieter said Benjamin would never have to worry about these things, and Benjamin was glad about that. Grown-up things did not sound fun.

Benjamin had one friend in *Saal* 3. He didn't know his name but he called him Jo-jo, because that was the sound he sometimes made when he got upset. Jo-jo slept on the mattress next to Benjamin, and had bulging eyes. Spit would drip from his mouth in a steady stream and sometimes he just rocked back and forth all day. Mostly Jo-jo would stare at the ceiling, but when Benjamin made a funny face, or jumped up and down, Jo-jo would smile. Benjamin told Jo-jo everything that he remembered, which was a lot. About *Matrone* Jansen telling Benjamin that he was special and how the library where she took him smelled funny and made Benjamin's nose itch, but he didn't mind because he liked looking at pictures in books while *Matrone* Jansen taught him to read. Reading was hard. Benjamin tried holding the page close to his face, but he'd still get it wrong and then he got nervous, and his mouth wouldn't obey what his brain was thinking, and the harder he tried, the more the sound would get stuck in his mouth. T-t-tr-train. B-b-boat.

"D-d-d-dummy," *Matrone* Jansen would sigh and tap her heel on the ground. "Stupid retard, I shouldn't have bothered."

Benjamin didn't like when she called him that. He wasn't sure what a retard was, but he knew it was a bad thing, like an Englishman maybe. He didn't remember anything about the time before he came to the hospital, but he thought about it a lot. *Matrone* Jansen said he was too little to remember. She said he was a war orphan. Orphan meant he didn't have a mother or father, that they were dead or gave him away. *Matrone* Jansen never lied about anything, so her story had to be true. *Matrone* Jansen said lying was a sin, and so was not obeying grown-ups, taking things that didn't belong to you, and saying the Lord's name when you weren't praying. That last one was really, really bad. You went to Hell for that.

When he read well, *Matrone* Jansen gave him fudge. Benjamin really liked fudge. She also gave him something she called coconut ice, which he liked even more. Once, his tummy hurt when he ate too much coconut ice and he couldn't sit still even though he tried his best, so Pieter gave him a punch which made his tummy hurt even more than before.

Jo-jo never said anything when Benjamin told him these things. That meant he was good at keeping secrets. Benjamin had a secret he knew he wasn't supposed to tell, but it bounced around his insides.

Benjamin knew he wasn't three years old like *Matrone* Jansen told the doctors he was. That she changed things in his chart every time a new doctor came to work at the hospital. She said he'd be taken away if anyone knew how special he was and then he'd be locked in a tiny room and never get fudge again. Benjamin wasn't three years old, but he wasn't a grown-up either. *Matrone* Jansen said that was because he wasn't growing right and didn't look like normal children. Benjamin had a pale face with cheeks that were thin and hollow, not round like babies' cheeks. His eyes hid under his white eyebrows and they turned up a little in the outside corners and were almost the color of thin clouds on winter days. That was another secret *Matrone* Jansen had told him. She had said that God only gave special eyes like that to His chosen ones. Jesus surely had eyes like that, she said. But Benjamin didn't want to hang on a cross one day like Jesus did, no matter what *Matrone* Jansen said. He wondered if you could get off the cross to go to the bathroom. Peeing in your pants was not allowed at the hospital, even if it was an accident.

Every day, the black women came to *Saal* 3 to kneel on the floor and polish the tiles. Pieter usually went outside then, to talk to the new nurse with the pink cheeks. He said this one was special, more than the others, and that he might make her his girl. Benjamin always joked around when Pieter wasn't there, to make Jo-jo smile. He walked fast in his socks, just a little, and stopped suddenly, bending his knees, so he slid across the polished floor. He liked the way this felt, so he did it again, only faster this time, flailing his arms, looking back to see if Jo-jo was watching. But one day he felt someone push him, and his feet disappeared right out from under him. His body was suspended in air, not touching anything. Free. First it felt good, a jumble of gray ceiling and chair legs and blue mattresses. Then it felt like a giant hiccup, a cracking sound in his head, and he screamed because it hurt very very much.

Pieter towered over him. "If you don't want to listen, you must feel," he said. "That's the only remedy for a little *kak* like you."

Benjamin kept screaming as his head throbbed, not caring what Pieter did to him. He heard *Matrone* Jansen's thick heels clack down the hall long before her thin body appeared in the doorway. Her white cap dangled from her stiff brown hair by a single hairpin, her white apron flapping like the morning wings of the small brown birds in the tree outside as she rushed to him.

"What is going on?" The vein over the bony bump on *Matrone* Jansen's forehead bulged when she yelled.

"He did it to himself. I told him to stay on his mat, *Matrone*," Pieter stumbled defensively. "I can't help it if these dum-dums don't listen."

"You are supposed to be watching them." *Matrone* Jansen crouched over Benjamin, her hands sliding under his armpits and lifting him to his feet. "You should do as you're told, son," she whispered. "Otherwise we'll have to visit with the Angel."

The Angel was the strap *Matrone* Jansen kept in her desk drawer, a thick leather belt cut in half and nailed to a plank. She called it the Angel, because it was a warrior of God, like the Archangel Michael, and would beat Satan out of you any day. When she swung her arm, the belt part made a loud "fwhop," and licked your bottom till it felt like it was on fire. Sometimes, when she was really angry, *Matrone* Jansen would use the plank side. She said it was for Benjamin's own good, that it would save his eternal soul.

"Stop crying, boy." Pieter grabbed Benjamin's arm, his face swollen.

Benjamin closed his eyes and held his hands to his face, waiting for the slap to come, but *Matrone* Jansen stepped in front of Pieter. She pushed Benjamin's head down, her thumbs parting his hair. "No blood, just a bump. Lucky for you, Mr. Smuts."

"It wasn't my fault, *Matrone*—"

"I'll see you in my office." *Matrone* Jansen turned and walked away, her body a straight gray line.

"Witch," Pieter muttered when she was out of earshot. He shoved Benjamin. "You stay in the corner the rest of the week for that, hear?" He turned to the rest of the room. "And nobody talks to him." He was greeted by dull eyes blinking listlessly. Jo-jo continued his perpetual rock, his head flopping as if his neck was made of jelly. Pieter smirked.

On Sundays, *Matrone* Jansen took Benjamin to church with her. He sat very still during services, so that *Matrone* Jansen would be proud of him. Benjamin didn't like church much. The *Dominee* stood behind a box and always spoke in an angry voice. He had slicked-back hair and wore a long black dress. *Matrone* Jansen said that when it was a man of God, they didn't call it a dress, they called it something else.

The *Dominee* said that their nation was chosen by God, because He led them to this land in dark Africa, and gave it to them, and it was their sacred mission to guard their Christian heritage here. The *Dominee* talked about God testing His people in the war. Some of the older women would wipe their eyes then and the men would cross their arms and stare at the floor. The *Dominee* said their suffering would be rewarded. If they truly believed, God would avenge His people. That made everyone happy again and they said, "Amen."

After the service, *Matrone* Jansen always took him into the storeroom at the back of her office, where shelves ran from the floor to the ceiling filled with sheets and cleaning supplies and extra kerosene. *Matrone* Jansen used the storeroom to drive demons out. The other children had many demons, making them act up and yell and shake and not understand. That was why they were in the hospital, because of the demons, *Matrone* Jansen said. "I command you, Devil be gone!" she would shout, lifting her arms in the air. When *Matrone* Jansen drove the demons out, her mouth stuck to the edges of her face, so Benjamin could see all her teeth, even the ones in the back. He sometimes imagined that they were as pointy as her fingernails and that she bit demons in half as they flew out of the children. He didn't think *Matrone* Jansen was very good at driving demons out, because the children would just stay the same, but he didn't tell her that. He knew that would mean there was a demon in him and that *Matrone* Jansen would have to drive it out and wouldn't believe he was special anymore. That scared him more than anything, so he tried to remember Sunday sermons as best he could to please her. *Matrone* Jansen would lock the door once they were in the storeroom. It was so small in there that Benjamin's nose almost touched the shiny seams on *Matrone* Jansen dress.

"Who is your savior, Benjamin?" *Matrone* Jansen would always ask.

"The Lord Jesus Christ, *Matrone*." That one was easy.

"And what happened to our Lord, Benjamin?"

"He died, *Matrone*."

"*Ja*, but why did he die?"

"The Jews asked the Romans to crucify him, *Matrone*."

"That's how. I asked why."

He got it wrong. A lump bulged in his throat. "F-for my s-s-s . . ." He closed his eyes anticipating the blow. "S-sins."

"Stop that." *Matrone* Jansen tapped her heel. "What can you do to be free from sin?"

"I have to b-b-beg f-for f-f-forgiveness. I have to f-f-ollow the rules."

"Commandments."

Benjamin nodded. He didn't want to talk anymore. *Matrone* Jansen put her hand on Benjamin's head, her long fingers squeezing his skull. "Beg, then, Benjamin. Beg for forgiveness, so that when His fiery wrath comes, you may be saved."

And he did, panicked thoughts jaggedly confessing things the minister said were bad, words he didn't know the meaning of, a liturgy of wrong, professing a legacy bestowed on him, the son of a man, birthed from the loins of a woman, the offal of the world, the product of lust and greed. When he couldn't think of anything anymore, *Matrone* Jansen would make her voice soft and say, "He is the servant of God, to execute his wrath on the wrongdoer. Amen." And then it was over and Benjamin was glad.

"You must never tell what we do here, Bennie." *Matrone* Jansen smiled, the skin on her face pushing into deep grooves, like there wasn't enough room for it.

He always promised, because then *Matrone* Jansen would give him fudge and call him a good boy. *Matrone* Jansen made the fudge at her home. Benjamin once asked what her house looked like, if the walls were glossy yellow too and if she had a family that had kept her. *Matrone* Jansen had laughed. She told him that she lived alone and that her parents were dead. She was an orphan, like him.

The Sunday night that everything changed, a white flash woke Benjamin. He couldn't see Pieter anywhere. Only a single kerosene lamp stood on the shift table, bathing everything around it in a soft light circle. Outside the sky raged, making breathing sounds, growling like the caretaker's dog when he saw black people. An invisible giant stomped on the trees, setting the sky on fire. It was the wrath of God, like *Matrone* Jansen had said. Benjamin panicked. What if God was there to take him? Something banged against the window above Benjamin's head, over and over again. God was knocking, demanding to be let in.

There was another flash of lightning. Rain scraped on the glass like

Lucifer's talons on the souls of sinners. The room stirred, the sounds of the others drowned by the voice of God. Small bodies on blue mattresses squirmed, their movement growing like a sea-wave. Next to Benjamin, Jo-jo thrashed wildly. His tongue protruded from a slack mouth, saliva dripping onto his blanket. They would all go to Heaven, Jo-jo and the others, because they weren't twelve yet, that's what the *Dominees* had said. But Benjamin was different and nobody could fool God. Something banged outside. Jo-jo screamed, his body tightening into a ball. This set the others off.

Benjamin crawled over to Jo-jo, his mouth dry, his skin hot and clammy. "Stop. Quiet, Jo-jo. God's going to find us."

Jo-jo's arms wriggled wild. Benjamin put his hand on Jo-jo's head, trying to stop it from moving. The boy squirmed, kicking, rolling away from Benjamin, falling off the mattress onto the floor. A barrage of gut-wrenching shrieks followed. Benjamin put his hand over Jo-jo's mouth, but it was too late. The sky exploded, lighting the distorted faces around him. Benjamin's breath stuck in his throat, refusing to let go. He had to get away. He had to get to the light, like *Matrone* Jansen always said. The light would save them all. He crawled to the shift table, his hands leaving wet prints on the red tiles. His stomach retched, his dinner spilling onto the floor, a sickly yellow of squash and fudge that burned his throat. Pieter didn't like cleaning throw-up. He would *bliksem* Benjamin now for sure. Benjamin struggled to straighten up, holding on to the side of the table. He jabbed at the lamp, slowly pushing it to the edge of the table. He stood on the tips of his toes, gripping the lamp's copper base between his small pudgy hands. He would bring the light. God would see that he was in the light. That he was a good boy. The lamp perched, suspended between table and nothing. Benjamin reached up to grab its handle, but it was heavy, too heavy for him to hold, and it fell.

Flames somersaulted over shattered glass, bounding up, clasping the tablecloth. Benjamin tried to get up, get away, kerosene wet on his nightshirt. He tried to push himself up. A sharp pain shot up from his palm. When he looked, he saw a shard of glass that stuck out of his hand, reflecting the fire, as if it was growing out of him, as if he was the fire. He stared at it, mesmerized, as blood spiraled down his arm in thick black vines. Heat radiated from his left foot where the fire gnawed on it. He became the light as flames crawled up his left leg. Benjamin tried to stand up, to show the others, but his lungs burned, the pain suddenly excruciating. He didn't want to be the light. "Make it stop make it stop make it stop," he screamed. There was a commotion somewhere far off. Someone ran toward him and covered him with something rough and heavy, bearing down on his body, and suddenly he existed in in a world of nothing.

"Bennie?" *Matrone* Jansen sat at his bedside, her hands clutching the rails. "You're awake." Her lip quivered, her eyes shining in a way Benjamin had never seen before. He fought the numbness, the fog pushing against raw pain.

Two rows of beds lined the long colorless room. Grown-up heads with cotton-candy hair peeked above starched sheets, few of them showing any signs of life. A nurse pushed a steel cart down the middle, stopping at all the beds, forcing something down every occupant's throat.

"It's time to change your bandage." *Matrone* Jansen pulled the sheets back, exposing Benjamin's thin body, amber pus seeping through a thick bandage on his leg. He felt something hollow and tingling in his tummy when he looked at it.

"You are a brave boy." *Matrone* Jansen unwound the gauze, revealing raw flesh. She ripped at the last piece of gauze.

"*Eina!*"

"There, now. The worst is over. God has spared you."

Benjamin's eyes teared up. He whispered the words he had been thinking. "I didn't want Him to."

Matrone Jansen wrapped her hard bony hands around his face, bringing it close to hers until their foreheads almost touched. "It is not for you to decide, son. Earthly pain is nothing. Your soul will burn like this for eternity if you refuse Him." She let go. "And if you keep talking like that, I can't look after you anymore. I'll never see you again. Is that what you want?"

Benjamin felt a pain worse than his legs in his insides.

"You should rejoice, Bennie. You have been purified with fire. You are His now."

Benjamin didn't understand God, didn't understand why God had chosen him or burned him. To Benjamin, God was even scarier than Satan.

Matrone Jansen ran her hand over his hair. She resumed changing his bandage, her mood lifted, jovial even. "I have talked to the new administrator. He said, when you are better, you can come with me to my house. Maybe for a while."

Benjamin stared silently at her, not trusting his words.

Matrone Jansen stopped fussing with his bandage. She looked unsure of herself. "You would like that, wouldn't you?"

Benjamin nodded. *Matrone* Jansen kissed him on the forehead. He felt warm inside, light. He wondered if this was why people did all these things for God, so they could maybe get to go to an eternal home in Heaven.

3

Alet canvassed the Terblanche farm with Mathebe glued to her side. He demanded clarification for every colloquialism, taking copious notes in careful block letters. The process was cumbersome. They had to leave the van parked on the side of the road and hike up narrow footpaths to get to the houses, knocking on weather-weary doors, questioning glassy-eyed men and wary women. News of the murder had spread, and it was hard to ferret out useful information between rumor and imagination. Nobody knew anything about a missing girl.

"The workers will show up here for their wages at four," Alet said as they neared the main gate of the Terblanche farm.

"You know the family, Constable."

"*Ja*, but maybe Boet will tell you things that he doesn't want me to know if you're by yourself. You know. Man stuff. Besides, I still have to look into that call from the school."

Mathebe nodded. He stopped the van at the Terblanche farm gate. "We will meet at the main house in two hours," he said and got out.

Magda Kok's house was half a kilometer inside the farm border, where the distance between the small houses grew larger as the road followed the rise of the mountain. Alet pulled to the side of the road, partially blocking a dirt walkway that led to a small rectangular building with a red zinc roof and narrow windows. Water stains crawled down painted brick. An outhouse leaned against the outer wall of the house like a cancerous growth, its slanted metal door rusty, an air hole gaping above the frame. A brown mutt with a white chest was tied to a post in front of the door. The dog growled, its chest heaving with punctuating barks. He bared his teeth, his short muscular legs straining.

A young coloured woman leaned against the door frame, perched on one leg, her hands behind her back. She wore a short black dress, her droopy breasts visible through its keyhole. Her shiny round face peeked out from under a floppy yellow hat. Alet only knew Magda Kok by reputation. The women of the valley talked about her as if she was a necessary evil, rather than competition for their husbands' affection. Amid the moral condemnations, Alet had often heard notes of sympathy.

Alet got out of the van. "Magda?" She had to raise her voice to be heard above the barking.

Magda nodded. "*Miesies.*"

"I'm Constable Berg. I need to talk to you for a bit, okay?" Alet took a step closer. The dog lurched forward suddenly, pulled back in midair by its chain. Magda didn't move. Alet smiled at her. "You think you can get the dog?"

Magda looked at Alet with hooded brown eyes. "Hey, Voetsek! *Sharrap* man!" The dog quieted down, pacing as far as its chain would allow, keeping small black eyes trained on Alet.

"Can we talk inside?"

"I don't know, *Mies.*"

"Just talk. I promise."

Magda grabbed the dog's collar behind his neck and pressed his hindquarters down, crouching beside him. The animal's body shivered with a low growl. She nodded in the direction of the door. "You can go now."

Alet stayed close to the wall as she slipped into the house. Sparse furniture lined the front room: a worn couch, a low, rickety table, a vase with red plastic roses on top of a boom box. A faded rug with a paisley pattern partially covered the rough concrete floor. In the corner, an old baby cradle was covered in blankets and clothes. Panels of thick net curtains covered the doorways that led to the other rooms of the house. A single silver garland, intertwined with fairy lights, draped over two nails on the wall.

"You're getting ready for Christmas, hey," Alet said when Magda walked in behind her.

Magda's eyes scrunched to slits, her mouth opening to expose the gap where her two front teeth used to be. She covered her smile with her right hand. "It's for the little one, *Mies*."

"Nonnie, right? That's her name?"

Magda's smile faded. "*Ja*." She eyed Alet suspiciously.

"I'm sure it's very pretty when you turn the lights on."

Magda nodded, her hand still over her mouth. She bent down in front of the garland and flipped the plug's switch, a slight tremor in her hand. The fairy lights flickered on, their reflection dancing in the silver of the garland. "Like they do in the stores."

"It's beautiful, hey."

"Every night we put it on and sing a *Krismis* song. Nonnie teaches me the ones she learns in school."

Alet imagined the intimate scene, mother and daughter sitting together under the lights, talking about their day. "Is Nonnie home?"

Magda's body tensed, her fingers digging into her fleshy upper arms. "Just now, *Mies*. She goes to a friend's house after school for a bit, see?"

"Magda, the school called us. They said Nonnie was talking about the Thokoloshe coming here."

"*Ai!*" Magda shook her head. "That child!"

"What was she talking about?"

Magda's eyes trailed to the doorway. "I don't know, *Mies*."

Alet sighed. "Magda, I need you to be honest with me, okay? I know what you do here."

Magda backed away from Alet, waving her hands emphatically in front of her. "It's not true. Those bitches in the valley, they all lie."

"It's all right, Magda. I told you, no trouble. I just want to know if Nonnie is here when you do it. When the men come."

Magda dropped her head. After a moment she shook it slowly. "Never when Nonnie is here, *Mies*. Never."

"They only come in the day?"

Magda looked at the doorway again. "*Ja, Mies*."

"You're sure?"

"Nonnie goes on sleepover to her *ouma* on Saturdays. Sometimes then."

"Nonnie has never seen the men? She's never been here when they come around?"

"They know not to come then."

"Have there been ones who you don't know? New men?"

"No. Only if I know them. Too much trouble otherwise." Magda's eyes started to water.

Alet clenched her hands. "No, don't cry."

Magda drew one of the curtains aside and went into a small kitchen area. Alet followed her. Magda reached for a box of tissues perched between mismatched plates. Clippings from the local paper were taped to the door of an oversize old fridge. Alet stepped closer to take a look.

"That one. That's Nonnie." Magda wiped her eyes with a tissue. She pointed at one of the faces in the picture. "She was in the papers for the school play." A thin girl of about seven stood in a staggered line with other kids in the photograph, all of them dressed in what looked like puffy white sacks. "She was a snowflake. I helped make the costume with *Miesies* Terblanche and the other teachers."

Alet smiled. "Very cute."

"Nonnie is clever, *Mies*. Not like me. Just the other day she got a gold star for recital. She's going to go to hostel. I'm saving."

The farm school only went to the fifth grade. The children who wanted to go to high school had to go to Unie. It was too far to walk, and most of the workers couldn't afford the hostel fees. Some kids paid for a ride into town on the back of a smuggler's pickup, but most of them stayed behind, earning money by working on the farm, getting pregnant when they were still children themselves. On one of her patrols, Alet had found a ten-year-old boy in the orchards. When she'd asked him why he wasn't in school, he'd shrugged his shoulders. "What's the point in finishing, *Mies*?" he had said, the skin of his abdomen visible through a tear in his shirt. "*Pa* says you don't need school to pick peaches."

Magda touched Nonnie's face in the paper clipping with her index finger. "Nonnie, she's gotta learn, so she gets a good job one day." She threw the crumpled tissue in a plastic bucket that served as a trash can. "Do you want coffee, *Mies*?"

"Thank you, Magda. I'd like that." Alet pulled one of the green

Formica chairs out and sat at the kitchen table as Magda turned the kettle on and scooped teaspoons of instant coffee into mugs. The condensed milk Magda put out formed a congealed bubble on Alet's teaspoon before she dunked it in her cup. Alet remembered punching two holes in a tin of condensed milk when she was a kid, sucking the sweet liquid through them until the tin made a hollow gurgling sound. Voetsek started barking.

"Mamma?" A child's voice strained to be heard above the din.

"It's Nonnie. I have to go get Voetsek," Magda said apologetically. The people who gave him to me weren't nice people. That's why he's so *bedonnerd*. He doesn't let anybody come near him but me."

"Aren't you scared he's going to bite Nonnie?"

"No, *Mies*. He protects us, see?"

Alet followed Magda to the living room and watched through the open door as she dragged Voetsek to a wire cage, the dog digging his hind legs into the dirt. Magda returned, holding a young girl's hand. Nonnie wore a black pinafore and a plain white shirt, her hair tied in a thin braid with pink baubles at both ends. Almond eyes stared up at Alet. Nonnie had the same round face as her mother, but with honey-colored skin. Sharp cheekbones and full lips gave her an unusual look, straddling the world between white and black.

"*Haai*, Nonnie." Alet smiled at the child, feeling like she was imitating people who knew how to deal with children.

"The *Mies* is here to talk to you, so you be good, hear?"

Nonnie looked at her mother, rebellion threatening in her scrunched-up eyes. "I didn't do anything."

"You told stories at school. I told you, don't do that." A stern tone had crept into Magda's voice. Nonnie shook her head and looked down at the ground, her bottom lip bulging out slightly.

"It's okay." Alet got down on her haunches in front of Nonnie, hoping she could calm everyone down, but Nonnie bounded past her into the bedroom.

"Come back here, right now." Magda marched to the doorway, pulling the net curtain aside. She turned to Alet. "She's a good girl, *Mies*. I don't know what's gotten into her."

"There's no problem, Magda."

"But you come here, *Mies*. The police only come because of trouble. I do what I can. I don't drink. I don't buy things for me or get my hair done in the salon. I give that girl everything I can."

"Nobody is accusing you of anything."

"Then why did you come here? The last time people came to talk they wanted to take her away." Hysteria brimmed in the woman's dark eyes. Alet followed Magda's gaze. Nonnie's whole body was hidden under the blanket of a twin-size bed, separated by a low table from an identical one on the other side of the bedroom.

"You can be right here while I talk to Nonnie, Magda. Then we can finish our coffee, okay?"

Magda searched Alet's face, her body deflating. "*Ja, Mies.*" She sagged down on the couch in the front room, her arms crossed, her head low.

Alet sat down on the foot end of Nonnie's bed. Afternoon sunlight squeezed through a narrow window. In the distance, the looming mountain peak cast long shadows over the valley. Nonnie peered over the edge of the faded blanket, quickly pulling it over her head again when she caught Alet's eye.

"My name is Alet, Nonnie. It's nice to meet you."

Nonnie stirred under the blanket. On the brick wall beside the bed, clothes hung from long nails, a Sunday-best dress, a school uniform and the snowflake costume.

"I saw your picture in the paper," Alet said. "I wish I could have seen the concert."

Two almond eyes appeared gradually above the blanket. "Why didn't you?"

Alet was at a loss for a moment. "Well, I was living far away."

"How far?"

"All the way up in Jo'burg."

"Why?"

"Because that's where I learned to be a police officer."

"Mamma says I should stay away from police. They are troubles."

"Mmm. The police can help too, you know."

"How?"

"Well, we catch bad guys, for one thing. Bad guys that try to hurt you."

Nonnie sat up in the bed, keeping the blanket over her nose. "But you're a girl!"

"Girls can catch bad guys." Alet feigned indignation.

Nonnie looked perplexed. "Can I be a police too?"

"I think you would make a really good policewoman."

Nonnie giggled, holding her hands to her mouth the way her mother did.

"Nonnie, can I ask you something?"

The girl scrunched up her eyes, then nodded.

"You told people at school that you saw the Thokoloshe. That he was here at the house."

Nonnie pressed her lips together. Her hands fisted over the blanket.

"Is it true?" Alet felt a sense of dread as Nonnie averted her eyes. "You see, he's a bad guy."

Something flickered in Nonnie's face. "Will you catch him so he doesn't take children?"

"*Ja.* Will you help me?"

Nonnie hesitated for a moment, then wiggled out from under the blanket. She sat down, pressing close to Alet. Alet held her breath for a moment, scared she might break the spell.

"When did the Thokoloshe come here, Nonnie?"

"Wednesday."

"Are you sure?"

"*Juffrou* Jana gave us Afrikaans homework then." Nonnie jumped down from the bed. She grabbed her book bag and lifted it onto the bed. It was the same kind Alet had had in the first grade. A rectangular case made of sturdy brown cardboard that closed with a spring-loaded lock. Nonnie took a ruled exercise book out of the case. A photocopied sheet was pasted onto one of the pages. She pointed at the top of the sheet where the date was written in big uneven letters. "See?"

"I believe you."

"I got a gold star."

"I'm sure you get a lot of gold stars."

Nonnie nodded.

"Can you remember what time you saw the Thokoloshe? Was it day or night?"

"Night."

"Was your Mamma here?"

Nonnie pointed to the living room. "Out there."

"And where was the Thokoloshe?"

Nonnie turned her pointing finger to the bedroom window. "Out there."

"In your garden?"

"In the road. He took his friend away."

"He has a friend?"

Nonnie nodded.

"Did he come into your room at all?"

"No. He just wanted his friend."

Alet felt relieved. Nonnie probably just saw some of the neighbor boys messing around after dark.

"If you want to catch him you have to go high."

Alet followed Nonnie's gesture at the window to the jagged rock of the mountain peak. "Up the mountain?"

"That's where he was going."

"Can you tell me what he looks like?"

"Everyone knows what the Thokoloshe looks like." Nonnie threw up her hands and rolled her eyes for effect, probably copying her mother or another adult.

"*Ja*, but remember, I'm from Jo'burg, hey. The Thokoloshe doesn't go to the city."

"He's this big." Nonnie held her arm out slightly above her head, the fingers of her hand scrunched together, pointing up at the ceiling. Alet hadn't seen the gesture since she was a child and her own nanny used it. Blacks used it to indicate someone's height, believing that the European gesture of a flat hand, palm facing down, impeded the spirit's growth.

"And his friend?"

Nonnie shrugged. She flipped through her school book, her interest in the conversation suddenly lost. Alet hated interviewing children. If you tried to intimidate or scare them into cooperating there would be a parent or social worker on your back in no time. She took a deep breath. "Okay. Did you hear them saying anything?"

Nonnie shook her head. Magda leaned in the doorway. Alet smiled reassuringly at her.

"Is there anything else you remember, Nonnie? It would really help me to find the Thokoloshe."

"I drew a picture." Nonnie took a rudimentary sketch in colored pencil out of the folds of the book. "You can have it for a present." She held the drawing out to Alet, the edge of the white page wrinkling in her grip.

A huge thorn tree provided respite from the heat as Alet waited for Mathebe. At the end of the driveway, three short cement steps led down to a sunken vegetable garden at the back door of Boet and Jana's house. Mathebe was taking his time, probably sitting at the big wooden table in the kitchen as he took Boet's statement. People just naturally ended up there, even though the living room with the old beat-up leather couch, mismatched green recliners and springbok hides covering the worn floorboards was more comfortable.

Mathebe appeared at the back door a few minutes later, followed by Boet and Jana, her camisole taut over the rounding of her stomach. The two men shook hands.

Alet pretended to study Nonnie's drawing in front of her. "How did it go?" she asked when Mathebe got into the van.

Mathebe shook his head as he closed the passenger door, his features more hound-like than usual. "Perhaps you should have spoken to Mr. and Mrs. Terblanche."

Alet reversed down the driveway and turned around at the gate. She waited until they were on the dirt road before she spoke. "I may have found a witness."

Mathebe turned to her. "Who?"

"I thought that might cheer you up. Nonnie Kok, our local working girl's daughter."

"The domestic call?"

"Hear me out. The Thokoloshe is small, right? She said she saw the Thokoloshe with a friend. She might have seen the victim and the killer. Look at the picture she drew."

Alet handed Nonnie's picture to Mathebe. A yellow moon and blue stars topped the page. Two wavy brown lines underscored them, forming hilltops. On the bottom left of the page was a square house with two rectangular windows and smoke coming out of the chimney. Next to the house were two stick figures in black, one with its arms around the other.

"It is a child's drawing."

"It's not much, but they live near the trail on the west side of the mountain. See that?" Alet kept her right hand on the steering wheel and pointed at the picture. "That triangular shape there?"

"Yes?"

"It looks like a rock formation that's farther up the trail. You can see it from her bedroom window. Which means that if that is our killer dragging the victim, they went up the mountain on the opposite side from where we found the body."

"That is very far to go on foot. Why would he not leave the body on that side of the mountain?"

"I don't know, but we should at least check it out. Search the area. Ask the captain if April can help."

"What is this?" Mathebe pointed at a blob of brown drawn next to the Thokoloshe's hand.

"Don't know. He probably had a bag or something with him. The girl refused to talk once the mother came into the room. I couldn't exactly tell her to leave."

Mathebe nodded. "There are a lot of murders in this country," he said thoughtfully. "A lot of people die every day."

Alet followed Mathebe's gaze out the car window. Rock face and dry bush rushed past, blurring into a hypnotic pattern. She turned her attention back to the road just in time to see a black-and-white cat dash across. She slammed on the brakes. "Dammit!" The van skidded forward, dust rising in a thick cloud. The cat froze for a moment before jumping into the bushes. Mathebe didn't react, his gaze fixed straight ahead at the horizon.

"Is there anything you're not telling me, Johannes?"

Mathebe pursed his lips before he spoke, each word measured. "I spoke to Captain Mynhardt about forensic help. He told me that we do not have the budget."

"I thought as much."

"I wonder if that would be true if the victim was white. Perhaps Mr. Terblanche would also be more cooperative, then."

This had always been there, lurking below the surface, but Alet didn't want to get into an argument about racial inequality with Mathebe. Blacks felt cheated and whites felt robbed, but it wasn't that easy pointing fingers, not anymore. The clarity of people fighting for their freedom had given way to twenty years of unchallenged government, and in that time, the lines had begun to blur.

Alet started up the van. "I don't know. I guess it's possible. Not a whole lot of precedence for white women getting necklaced, you know."

Mathebe shook his head as if clearing out a bad memory.

"Look, I know this is flimsy, but at least we have something. I have to be in PE tomorrow night for a family thing, but we can search the mountain tomorrow morning."

"Gauteng schools let out for the holidays today." Mathebe had returned to his robotic self. "Everybody is on traffic duty."

Alet tried not to sound disappointed. "I'll drive back tomorrow night, then. We can start early Sunday." She hoped that by then, there would still be something left for them to find.

1918

Tessa

I AM A DONKEY.

The chalk snapped in two on the black slate. Mrs. Berman's mouth set in a stern grimace as she dusted off her hands and attached a piece of twine to the board. Sebastian stood in front of the class, his knobby knees trembling under threadbare shorts. Tessa felt a sense of satisfaction. Sebastian always pulled her hair and called her a white rat when Mrs. Berman wasn't looking. He deserved what was coming.

"What is the first rule?" Mrs. Berman ran her eyes over the first-graders in front of her, resting on Tessa. "Tell us, Theresa."

Tessa held her breath. Mrs. Berman scared her. She had once broken a ruler on Gisela De Klerk's behind because her nails were too long. The girl was forced to stand in the corner for the rest of the day. Tessa stood up, careful to lift her chair and not scrape it along the floor, otherwise *she* might end up in front of the class with a board around her neck.

"Well?" Mrs. Berman's raisin eyes didn't budge from Tessa's face.

Tessa almost felt sorry for Sebastian, but then she remembered the nasty thing he said in Afrikaans when she'd caught him stealing her sandwich that morning. "We only speak English, Mrs. Berman." Tessa felt a sense of power as she looked at Sebastian. "Dutch is for donkeys."

"Exactly." Mrs. Berman hung the board around Sebastian's neck. "You will wear this for the rest of the day, Sebastian. If you take it off, you'll get ten lashes."

Sebastian took his seat next to Tessa. "You'll pay for this you, you English," he muttered under his breath when Mrs. Berman turned her back to write on the big chalkboard.

Tessa was glad Sebastian's English was poor, otherwise his insults might have been a lot more elaborate. Her Afrikaans was fluent, even if she wouldn't be caught dead using it. Tessa had picked up Xhosa, Zulu, some Chinese and a little bit of Portuguese from listening to all the different people in Johannesburg. Her favorite was Sotho, which she spoke with Sarah. It glided through your mouth and dripped off the tongue. Xhosa was great fun with all its different clicks and was so close to Zulu that you almost couldn't speak one without knowing the other. When you stripped away all the different words though, people sounded very much alike, Tessa thought. Even though there was a big difference in how they were treated.

Sebastian kicked her feet under their shared desk. "Keep on your side."

Tessa made herself small, her momentary victory forgotten. She moved her chair to the edge of the desk. In the front of the class, Mrs. Berman droned on, making the students copy three-letter words she wrote on the board. B-A-T. C-A-T. Next week they would advance to four letters. Tessa sighed. She had begged Andrew to send her to school. He would have nothing of it, citing the dangers involved if anyone found out that she was different. "Special," is what he called her, but Tessa wasn't so sure. All she knew were lonely, static hours, locked up in the house with Sarah and Andrew, hiding, always hiding, while the world outside her window changed. She wanted to be part of that world, talk to its people, the longing physically painful. She made every promise she could think of to counter Andrew's objections. When that didn't work, she ran away.

Tessa had snuck out, hiding in the back of Andrew's car as he drove to the mines in the early hours. It took half a day for someone to find her. One of the miners noticed her among the mine heaps on his way back to the hostel after his shift. The bosses were called. Andrew had to face uncomfortable questions, his mood dour as he delivered Tessa to a frantic Sarah. They'd had no choice. Either they had to move again, or send Tessa to school. They began the charade.

The prospect of meeting other children and having friends had made Tessa feel giddy, despite Andrew's admonitions. She should have realized that it could never live up to her expectations, especially after the day Sarah took her to town to buy a school uniform. A saleslady had thundered up to Tessa and Sarah moments after they entered the store, putting her plump frame directly in their path, her lips curling with distaste. "Yes? Can I help?"

"Askies, Miesies. The little *mies* needs to get a uniform. For the school."

Tessa had felt confused by the sudden shift in Sarah's speech and manner. She was subservient, dumbed down, unfamiliar.

The saleslady glared at Sarah over her horn-rimmed glasses. "Why are *you* here?"

"The *baas* sent me, *Miesies.* He can't come."

"Wait outside, then."

Sarah didn't protest. She touched Tessa's shoulder, a look passing between them, and went to stand outside the store, her hands folded in front of her, her eyes trained on the ground. Tessa suddenly hated the saleslady, with her tight gray hair and stupid fat face, fidgeting and measuring, pulling at the uniform, talking to Tessa in a proprietary tone.

"Why isn't your mother here, girl?"

"She died." Tessa delivered the coached words with a deadpan expression.

The saleslady didn't miss a beat. "You tell your *ousie* that she has to shorten the hem. We don't stock anything smaller than this."

Tessa nodded and took the package from her. The woman shorted her on the change, probably thinking that a six-year-old and a black woman would be too stupid to realize that they'd been cheated. Tessa didn't care, she wanted to get out of there. She grabbed the money from the woman's hand and ran out of the store, ignoring the loud comment about how this is what happens when *kaffirs* and *meide* raise white children.

There was some kind of law now that said black people had to live outside the city limits. Even though Sarah lived with them in the house, they had to call her a domestic in front of people and pretend that she slept in the servant quarters outside. Mrs. Berman said that black people had to stay on the reserves at night because races being separate is what God intended by making people different from each other. The refrain was becoming sickeningly repetitive as with everything Tessa was taught at school. In a matter of days, she had grown bored with the simplicity of Mrs. Berman's lessons and the childish ideas of her fellow students. Instead of making friends, like she desperately wanted, shunned by the girls and teased by the boys. Sometimes she thought she saw pure hatred in their eyes, as if they knew, instinctively, that she wasn't like them.

Sebastian followed Tessa during break, the board thumping against his knees with each step. He kicked at her heels. "Rat! White rat!"

"Leave me alone, Sebastian." Tessa walked faster.

"Or what? You rat again?" He shoved her from behind.

Tessa turned around, her hands balled into fists. "You are smelly and dirty," she yelled out of frustration. "A stupid Dutchman."

Sebastian's face contorted in a snarl. He took the board off and flung it at her. It caught her under her eye with such force that blotches of light assaulted her. Tessa let out a primal scream and lunged at Sebastian. He turned to run, suddenly not so confident that he could fend off this girl, half his size. Tessa landed on top of him in the dirt. He rolled over, his bony elbow digging into her side, and threw a punch. Tessa bit down on Sebastian's arm. He balled his fist in the air, but was suddenly yanked away. The vice-principal, Mr. Els, held on to Sebastian by the scruff of his neck.

"She called me stupid!" Sebastian squirmed.

"He kicked me and stole my sandwich!" Tessa yelled back. Her eyes watered and her face was covered in dirt.

"Quiet. You are both going to the office. Right now."

Tessa pulled her dress down and made a weak attempt at dusting herself off. "I didn't do anything. He—"

"Not another word, Theresa Morgan."

Tessa followed meekly behind Mr. Els and Sebastian. Mr. Els spoke to Sebastian in barely a whisper, but Tessa knew he was speaking Afrikaans.

Andrew

He came up behind Sarah where she stood washing dishes at the table and kissed her neck, his hands reaching for her breasts, his hips pushing against her buttocks. In the lamplight her skin was a molten brown, her huge eyes soft and inviting as she looked back at him, telling him the news, unable to hide her joy. A child of their own after all these years. Andrew pushed the nagging concerns aside. They would find a way.

"Remember when we met?" He ran his hands over her shoulders and down her arms, stopping at the cuff of her blouse, gripping her wrist and taking her wet hands away from their task.

"You said you couldn't take care of a child." Sarah laughed as he turned her around, pulling at her rust-colored head scarf, running his fingers through her hair.

"When I looked at you, I knew everything would work out all right."

"Is that so?" Sarah laughed.

Andrew searched for her mouth, her lips soft against his, the taste of cinnamon lingering. When Sarah had shown up at the British camp she hadn't said a word. She simply showed him a note in his own handwriting—a note he had tucked into a dowry chest almost a year before. Then she told him everything about Dr. Leath and the women, barely able to verbalize the things she had seen. It had sent a chill through him. He had sworn that he would keep them safe, but the outside world was not so obliging. After the war ended, he had gone back to Vergelegen in search of Tessa's family. Nobody had returned. The farm was for sale.

Andrew had already decided to stay in South Africa when the end of the war came. The British were in charge and there were opportunities for men like him. After he, Sarah, and Tessa had fled their farm in Unie, the Great War had extended its reach to South Africa. Andrew was called up again to help suppress an Afrikaner rebellion. Even though the South African government decided to fight on the side of Britain, many Afrikaners remembered German sympathies during the Boer War and resisted the decision. The Ossewabrandwag rebellion was easily quelled, and with his service record, Andrew could get a job at almost any British-run company. That was how he ended up in Johannesburg, in the mines. The city was a good place to become invisible, keep secrets. Andrew had helped resolve a strike and the owners liked him, so they made him a boss, overseeing the influx of workers, some of them still draped in tribal blankets when they arrived at the site.

"*Ma?*" Tessa stood in the doorway of the bedroom, her white hair tangled in a wild mess, her long nightdress creased. A nasty purple bruise had taken up residence under her left eye.

Sarah pushed Andrew away and refastened the knot he had loosened on her scarf.

"Theresa, why aren't you in bed?" There was warning in Andrew's voice. He was a patient man, but he had been short with her since she came home from school, bloodied and bruised, handing him a letter from the principal.

"My eye hurts." Tessa walked over to the table and pulled out the chair next to his, struggling clumsily with her short legs to get onto it. Sarah stepped forward to help, but Andrew signaled her to stop. Tessa was sixteen; girls her age were being married off already. The day's events had brought the stark realization that he wouldn't be able to mend fences for her all her life.

Andrew lit his pipe. "I have an appointment with your principal tomorrow."

"I'm not going back." Tessa crossed her arms for emphasis.

"And what about your friends?"

Tessa shrugged. "I already know everything they teach, *Pa*."

"Don't run away because of this boy."

"Please, *Pa*. You can teach me at home again."

"You'll need to learn more than what is written in a book, Theresa. More than you can find between four walls. I didn't understand that before."

Tessa crossed her arms, her chin raised in a challenge. "Like what?"

"For one thing, you need to learn that there is a reason why other people act the way they do. Sebastian's parents are poor. That sandwich is probably the only meal he'll have today. He's being taught in a language he doesn't speak at home and he probably doesn't understand a lot of what is being said. How would you feel if—"

There was a knock at the door. Andrew put his pipe down. It was after eight. Nobody was supposed to come around this late. A second knock, more insistent this time.

"Go see," Sarah said when he didn't move.

"Hold on, I heard you," Andrew yelled. He tucked his shirt into his pants and pulled his suspenders over his shoulders. He gestured to Sarah. "Go."

Sarah took Tessa into the bedroom and locked the door. Andrew parted a slither of the curtains with his index finger. Two English lads from the mine stood outside, their clothes disheveled.

"James?" Andrew addressed the taller of the two as he opened the door.

"It's Selborne Hall, sir. There's trouble."

"What trouble?"

"Those National Party Dutchmen tore down the Union Jack, sir. Pat saw 'em do it."

The man next to James nodded. "The boys are gathering outside, waiting for them to come out. More than a thousand of them. There's going to be a right good buggering. We thought that maybe you could organize the mine boys . . ."

Andrew clenched his jaw. Things had been smoldering under the surface for years now. With the Afrikaners blaming the British for their poverty and the Natives striking at the mines, he had his hands full trying to keep the men off each other. "Wait. I'll be out in a minute." He closed and locked the door. At the bedroom door he hesitated. "Sarah? There's trouble at the Republican meeting. I have to go."

Sarah's face appeared in the slit of the opened door. "The police can—"

"The police won't be able to handle that many men. I'm a boss. Maybe they'll listen to me." He pecked her on the forehead.

"Don't go. You can't change anything." Tessa looked at him in that unnerving way she had, old eyes peering from a child's pink-cheeked face.

"I have to try, Tessa." Andrew grabbed his jacket. "Don't go out, no matter what, hear?"

Andrew got into the cab of a beat-up truck with the two lads, the street lights growing denser as they approached the city center, houses giving way to squatter camps and mine dormitories where the black men slept, packed in rows of bunk beds. They pulled into a side street, a few blocks from Selborne Hall. The two lads jumped out.

"It started already," James shouted as he took off.

A brand-new Morris burned in front of the hall, its innards blazing beneath a smoke column. A throng of men had gathered outside the hall, singing *Tipperary* over and over again, their voices taunting the

Afrikaners inside. James and Pat became one with the fray. Suddenly, the hall's doors flung open and a couple hundred burly Afrikaners burst through, raging with fists against the mob outside. Bodies flailed, slumped, fell, the mob reacting in a wave of fervid violence. Andrew noticed a small group of men watching from the balcony above, their expressions inscrutable. He weaved through the throng, dodging stray blows, finding it impossible to tell who was on which side. He had to talk some sense into the men in charge, try to stop this before it became a bloodbath. According to the papers, the National Party leader, Dr. Malan, was a Dutch Reform minister. Surely he had to see reason.

Andrew waded through the crowd to the building, still dodging blows. Once inside, he weaved through corridors to get to the main hall. *Dominee* Malan was onstage, conferring with a group of men. None of them was older than thirty-five, shreds of the Union Jack under their feet. Andrew made his way toward them. He had almost reached the stage when he was stopped short by a sudden blow to the stomach.

"It's a Redneck!" A knee connected with his head.

Andrew looked up at his attacker, whose voice he recognized all too quickly. The man had aged. His beard was more white than yellow now, his skin marred by deep grooves, but it was definitely the joiner, Jooste. Somebody kicked Andrew from behind, sending him sprawling.

"What you doing here, *Rooinek*? You come spy on decent people?"

Andrew gasped for air. He held his hand out toward Malan on stage. "Please. We have to stop this."

"Afraid you're going to lose, huh?" Jooste's fist caught Andrew in the jaw. He addressed the men around them. "He burned farms in the war. I saw him do it."

Andrew opened his mouth to speak, but Jooste's boot made contact with his face. Blood filled his mouth. Blows came from everywhere now in a confusion of pain. He tried not to swallow the broken tooth in his mouth.

"*Broeders*, our cause is just. We have suffered enough injustice, our rights, violated by his kind. It is time an example is made." Another boot made contact with Andrew's head, then another, until the uniform roar of male voices blurred into silence.

• • •

Jooste watched Andrew's hospital room from the hallway, waiting for the right opportunity. He would make sure that Andrew never got a chance to talk. A small girl came out of Andrew's room and headed down the hall. Jooste found himself staring at her, unable to believe what he was seeing. Could he trust his eyes? He had thought that the boy was the only one of them to have survived, but there she was, same pale eyes, same high cheekbones, same white hair, the resemblance unmistakable. He followed her out of the hospital, careful not to be noticed.

Jooste had had some hard years after the war. Ignored by the British and despised by the Boers, he'd had to scrape by. But memories faded quickly. He was moving up in the world again, one of Malan's trusted men. It still amazed him how little it took to pull the wool over people's eyes when there was a cause to rally behind. It made them blind to all else. Jooste found causes fluid, his own always trumping any other.

The British, for all their ingratitude, had paid Jooste well to clean things up at the farmhouse after Leath was marched away and shipped back to England. The dear doctor had been quite an embarrassment for some of the higher-ups in the British forces, everybody eager to sweep the whole thing under the rug, especially once they started discovering the bodies, women and mutilated infants, buried between grapevines. Jooste had discovered Leath's journals under the floorboards in the study and snuck them out. He had thought about burning them, afraid he might be implicated, but the chance that they might be valuable was great. Curiosity, more than anything else, made him pore over the rants about human imperfection and strange formulas and correspondence with a man named Röntgen. The good doctor wanted to strengthen the stock, as it were; create a better human. The depravity the journals described fueled a strange fascination for Jooste, his obsession growing by degrees. He tracked the baby boy they had found that day at the farm to a mental hospital in Bloemfontein. Jooste had bribed one of the staff, a man named Smuts, to get access to the boy. What he found unnerved him, a scrawny little thing, his eyes all strange and too large for his head, staring at Jooste as if he knew what he was thinking. Smuts said the boy was severely retarded, that's why he was put there. Jooste wasn't so sure.

Jooste stayed within arm's length of the girl, but hung back when she exited the hospital. He watched her from the doorway as she crossed the road. A black woman waited for her on the edge of the park, across the road. Jooste recognized Sarah immediately.

"So that's what you did, my pretty? Stole yourself a white baby," Jooste muttered. He followed the pair down the street, weaving between people, trying not to be noticed. The *meit* and the girl ambled toward the suburbs, unable to board a bus together, their faces contracted in serious conversation. Jooste watched from a distance as they entered a working-class house with a low roof and a small garden, a smile spreading on his face.

Andrew stirred. His skin was still sallow and bruised, but at least the swelling in his face had gone down. Tessa shifted closer to his hospital bed and reached for his hand. She remembered how strong it had been the night he left, deep grooves lining the palms, dirt lodged permanently under the cuticles no matter how much he scrubbed them. He tightened his grip. Spasm or reflex, she didn't know, but the doctors looked at her dubiously when she told them about it, condescendingly calling it a little girl's imagination. She'd often felt hampered by her body, but this was the first time it had really mattered. When Tessa looked up again, Andrew's eyes were open, looking at her as if he couldn't remember who she was.

"*Pa?*"

"T . . . T . . ." Andrew struggled to get the sound out.

Tessa leaned closer. "Shhh, *Pa*. I'm here."

"Sa . . . ?"

Tessa glanced over at Mr. Visagie, the old man who shared a room with Andrew. He glared at her, snorting when she caught him watching, and turned around in bed, the back of his striped pajamas riding up into his bottom.

"She is good, *Pa*."

"Where?"

"They wouldn't allow her into the hospital."

"Quiet!" Visagie's head snapped back in their direction. "There shouldn't be children in this ward." He started mumbling. "Rules are only good for some people. Others do whatever they want."

"Oh, shut it." Tessa put her hand in front of her mouth, but it was too late.

Visagie look at her strangely. "How dare you talk to me like that, you little twit. My *pa* would give me a good whipping if I talked to him so. God-fearing man, he was. Knew how to keep his children on the narrow road."

Tessa turned her back to Visagie. She put her lips close to Andrew's ear. "You can't do that again, *Pa*. You hear?"

Andrew's eyes were teary. "I had to try. They needed . . ."

Tessa touched his face. "*We* need you. If you're gone, we can't survive. They'll take me from *Ma*. The landlord doesn't want a black woman alone in the house. *Ma* had to take work cleaning white people's houses while you're in here. They have her scrubbing floors on her hands and knees. They leave her plate and cup next to the dog's kennel. They won't even let her eat in their house."

"What are you whispering about?"

Tessa tried to block out the old man's whining. "They call *Ma* lazy when she gets tired because of the baby." Her voice broke, helplessness spilling over. "So no more of this, hear. Not ever."

Andrew averted his eyes. "I'm so sorry," he whispered.

Tessa had the strangest sensation of doing a grown-up thing, of being the one that made the rules for the first time in her life instead of being swept up in other people's choices. "A man came to the house yesterday, a Dutchman. *Ma* recognized him. He knocked for a long time. We didn't open the door for him. She said I should tell you it's one of the men who brought the girls to the doctor. What does that mean, *Pa*?"

A frown had lodged between Andrew's thick dark eyebrows. "It means we have to leave."

"Why?"

"Have to trust me." Sweat formed on his pale forehead. "There's money in the tea-box. Tell Sarah to take everything and come get me tonight."

"You're in no condition to—"

Andrew grabbed her hand, pulling her closer to him. "It's important, Tessa."

• • •

Tessa found a distressed Sarah at their normal meeting place next to the park. She took Sarah's hand, trying to reassure her. *"Pa said we need to go to the next town on the list, Ma."*

Sarah glanced back at the hospital, weighing her desire to see Andrew against the consequences. "Is he . . . ?"

"Tell me what's going on, *Ma*." Tessa heard the demanding tone in her own voice again. Its effect fascinated Tessa as Sarah acquiesced, the power of her own will becoming more real. She let Sarah pick her up, feeling a sudden weariness penetrate her bones as she listened to Sarah's truth.

Johannesburg hazed like a gray dream in the late afternoon, a smoky mirage. Around them, lines of color divided the masses of people trying to eat, breathe, and live, going home to separate areas. Would it fall one day, this city of Gomorrah? Would she alone be standing at the end, eternally a child, and know the truth about misery and the consequence of hate? See the result of their toils, of their poverty, of their greed, while they lived only for what today offered? The loneliness of that future ripped at her. She would go on, she decided, for Sarah and Andrew. But when the time came, when they were gone, she would know what to do. No hell she could imagine would be worse than bearing that kind of knowledge alone in the world.

4

The bride bopped on the dance floor like a rhythm-challenged stripper, her legs spread wide, the long white train clutched between fuchsia-taloned fingers. The hem of her dress rose with every step, exposing spray-tanned thighs between layers of sequins and chiffon.

From where she sat at the bar, Alet could see Frieda's garter as she hopped around with her bridesmaids, her hips canting back and forth like a marula-drunk elephant. Even a couple of the older aunts and uncles had joined in the fray, flocking up from their tables the moment the DJ started the song.

"Sheep," Alet muttered under her breath.

"What?" The uncle of the bride had planted himself next to Alet. He had patchy dark eyebrows and a tic in his left eye that punctuated every third word. It was hotter than hell and he was wearing a leather jacket, zipped up to his throat.

"Nothing." Alet tilted her glass back.

He leaned in, bringing his ear against her nose. "Sorry? You said something?"

The effort of remaining civil with a stranger over the noise drained Alet. She pushed her glass toward the edge of the bar and made a circle above it with her finger as soon as she caught the young bartender's eye, probably the bride's underaged brother employed for the evening to keep him out of trouble. He came over, gin bottle in hand, smiling.

"Another?"

Alet winked at him. "You're my savior."

"So what were you saying, huh?" The uncle stepped even closer, rank body odor escaping from his jacket collar. Alet shook her head, turning to see the dance floor doing a grapevine in unison before "Go low!" had them all squatting down, like synchronized idiots.

The uncle tapped her on her shoulder. Alet shook his hand off. "What?"

"What did you say?"

Alet sighed, wondering what it would take to get rid of him. "I said, people love to be told what to do. Like sheep."

"It's fun." He smiled, genuine delight on his face.

"*Ja?*"

He nodded, his big head moving in slow motion.

"You like to be told what to do?"

He was quiet for a moment, thoughts trickling like molasses. Alet noticed a patch of hair on the side of his bald head that he'd missed while shaving.

"Listen, I'm just not into this, okay?" Alet took a large sip of her fresh gin. "Go play with someone else."

The bartender boy leaned over the bar, his freckles a tie-dye brown. "My uncle's a bit not *lekker*," he shouted in her ear. "Slow. It's not his fault. You don't have to be ugly."

Ah, *fok*. Alet was already having trouble with the new in-laws and her dad hadn't been married three hours. On top of that she was now out of favor with the bartender. It was time to quit the party. She drained her glass and pushed her seat away from the bar, sucking her stomach in before standing up. The black velvet cocktail dress had fit ten kilograms ago when she wore it to her graduation party. Her patent leather heels were also doing a number on her, the balls of her feet throbbing in rhythm with the cha-cha. Her hair fell forward, covering her face, as she crouched over her bag to try to find her keys. Alet lost her equilibrium for a moment.

"You're not thinking of driving like that, are you?" Her father, Adriaan Berg, put a firm grip on her arm.

"I'm fine, *Pa*." Alet pulled her arm away. "Lovely wedding, but duty calls."

Adriaan's lips moved to the side of his face, a sure sign that he was pissed off.

"By the way, does your new father-in-law know he's now family with police? I saw kids over there nipping schnapps. Underage drinking and so on." Alet shook her head gravely.

Adriaan's expression remained unchanged. Alet wondered if her father had any sense of humor at all. He was a man who didn't tolerate insubordination. Even now he probably wasn't above making the wedding guests drop and do push-ups if any of them stepped out of line. The thought made Alet giggle.

"Auntie Mattie said you can have the couch. I'll drive you over."

"You can't leave the blushing bride alone on your wedding day. I won't have it."

"Stay here." Adriaan walked over to Frieda, interrupting her mid-hop, her blond-streaked hair falling in ringlets from beneath her rhinestone tiara. She shot Alet a look of disdain.

"Who the *fok* still wears a tiara?" Alet muttered as she waved at Frieda.

Frieda turned her back to Alet and kissed Adriaan passionately on the mouth, her newly ringed hand on his cheek. Alet made a loud wolf-whistle. Embarrassed glances shot in her direction.

"Come." Adriaan marched past her without waiting to see if she'd follow. Outside, some of the groomsmen had already begun to deface his Mercedes with white shoe-shine, singing "For he's a jolly good fellow," as they saw him approach.

"Dammit, Greeff!" Adriaan shouted at one of the men. "I need a car that doesn't look like a black taxi." The men stopped singing abruptly.

"Take mine, Boss." Greeff, a balding, bulbous-nosed drill sergeant who Alet remembered from back in basic training, fidgeted with his hands in his pockets, finally producing a set of car keys. "Sorry, hey. It's just a little fun, see?"

Adriaan didn't respond. He took Greeff's keys, dragged Alet over to a white sedan, and opened the passenger-side door for her. "Put your seat belt on."

"What about my car?"

"Come get it in the morning."

"This isn't necessary. I'm fine to drive."

A muscle in Adriaan's temple jumped. "I don't need you in a drunken accident. You've been enough of an embarrassment."

"Sorry." Alet slid down in her seat, her head resting against the back, a surge of self-loathing washing over her. Adriaan was ashamed of her for more than just misbehaving at his wedding. She had been late for the ceremony and made no effort to be sociable during the reception, offering labored words of congratulations to Frieda. She looked over at Adriaan in his dark suit with the pink carnation on the lapel. His dark hair and trimmed mustache had always been frosted with silver, which had launched ever more aggressive invasions as the years passed. She suddenly wondered if she would ever have a wedding day where he would give her away.

Alet had met her father for the first time shortly after her mother, Gerda, announced that she had been diagnosed with cancer. Adriaan had been an enigma to her before then. She had disparate memories of him from when she was little, fragments of him picking her up from her grandmother's apartment for a custody visit, her mother scrubbing her clean, tying her hair in a tight braid, laying out her best dress, the one with the pink polka dots, and telling her to behave. Her grandmother faffed nervously, gathering toys for her to take along in the pink plastic handbag with Cinderella on the front. They stood in a line in the living room, her mother, her grandmother and Alet, waiting for the doorbell to ring at eight a.m. sharp. Even at four years old, Alet could sense the tension in the room when her father walked in, her mother's words measured, her posture stiff and unyielding. Her dad was a tall man. He always wore a neatly pressed white shirt with dark jeans and brown leather shoes. It was his off-duty uniform. On duty he was a policeman, something important, her mother had told her.

Gerda didn't want Adriaan in their lives after the divorce. She seemed genuinely scared of him. She later married an Englishman, Rob Turner, and they moved far away from Jo'burg, far enough that regular visits with Alet's dad became impractical. Alet had always wondered if her mother had done it on purpose. Gerda kept suing for more child support, and Adriaan agreed to give up custody without much of an argument. Alet remembered how Gerda had coached her for the phone call, her dad's voice curt on the other end of the line, a stranger asking her if she wanted him or Rob to be her dad.

"Rob." Alet had answered, the way Gerda had taught her.

"Are you sure?"

Alet had looked at Gerda, who stood next to the telephone, a cigarette clasped between her fingers. Gerda had nodded slowly, pressing her lips together in a tight smile before taking a drag.

"*Ja*."

"You want Rob Turner to be your *pa*." An emotionless statement of fact from Adriaan.

"*Ja*." Alet wished it would be over. She wanted to go back outside and ride her new bike.

"Tell your mother to come talk to me."

Alet never heard from Adriaan again. She later daydreamed about her real father rescuing her, showing up one day and telling her that she could come live with him, especially when her mother and stepfather were having a go at each other. She imagined Adriaan giving her all the attention Rob never did. Rob was nice enough, but his demeanor made her understand that she wasn't his. Then, just after she turned fifteen, Rob got a job in Kempton Park, a suburb next to the Jo'burg airport. Four months after they moved, Adriaan Berg sent her a letter in the mail, simply requesting that they meet.

"You look like your mother," was the first thing Adriaan had said to her. He was late picking her up after school, their agreed-upon meeting point. She was on the verge of walking home, trying not to cry, when the Mercedes pulled up.

"She says I look like you." Alet feigned nonchalance as her heart beat furiously.

Adriaan shrugged. "Is the Spur okay for you?"

Alet nodded and got into the car. Once they were seated at the restaurant, it was Alet who broke the awkward silence. "So, what now?" Her anxiousness had diminished as she studied his face. Adriaan wasn't the god she had always thought him to be. He was just a man in a white button-down shirt and dark-blue jeans, the way she remembered, only the lines in his face were deeper, his eyes sunken and wary as if he too spent his nights lying awake.

"I thought we might get to know each other." Adriaan's words were quiet, measured. "You're almost an adult now. We can talk."

"I'm not going to call you *Pa*, if that's what you're after."

"I don't expect it." Adriaan crossed his arms, his look inscrutable. "It wasn't my choice to be out of your life."

"Whose was it, then?"

"I called. You said—"

"I remember."

"My own child said she didn't want me in her life."

Alet's temper flared, her temples pulsing. "I was six. I hadn't seen you in two years and all that time *Ma* talked about you as if you were some kind of . . ." She balled her fists under the table, trying to hide her hurt in a veil of resentment. "Don't you dare blame me. You were the adult."

"You're right." A hardness had suddenly crept into Adriaan's voice, his mouth set sternly under the peppered mustache. That would be the Adriaan Berg she would know from then on, distant, in charge. "But I knew exactly where you were, Alet. Always."

"You kept tabs?" Alet's anger was momentarily knocked out of her.

"You are my only child."

As if that was an explanation, or an excuse. Yet Alet was desperate to hold on to anything that might indicate he cared about her. She felt a reckless stubbornness, asking the question she had been mulling over all her life. "Why did you leave?"

Adriaan studied her for a moment. "You're old enough to know the truth, I suppose." He looked away. "I was no good at domestic life," he said at last. "My work got in the way. Your mother—"

"She says you hit her."

Adriaan sighed wearily. "I lost control once. Only once." And with that, the subject was closed. The rest of the lunch felt like an interrogation. Alet answered Adriaan's questions with reserve. Gerda had started intensive chemo, the prognosis wasn't good. Rob couldn't hold on to money and regularly uprooted the family because of some scheme that went sour. Some days were harder than others, but she didn't have a bad childhood, she told him.

"I have to go," Alet had said during a drawn-out silence. "I have a test tomorrow."

"Look," Adriaan had said as they got up, "this didn't go well."

"Really?"

"Sarcasm." Adriaan curled his lips in disapproval.

"Can we go, please?"

"I have a pool."

"What?" Alet was about to congratulate him, but the vulnerable look on Adriaan's face made her bite her tongue.

"We can *braai* and watch the game this weekend."

Alet still wasn't sure if she wanted Adriaan to become a part of her life. She definitely wasn't going to pretend to like rugby for him. But perhaps he was trying. Perhaps she should too. "*Ja.* Okay," she said quickly before she could change her mind.

They regularly spent time together after that, though this occasionally meant vacations with the latest in a succession of young bleach-blond girlfriends. He bought her a secondhand motorbike when she turned sixteen so she could get around, performing the maintenance himself. When her mother started losing the battle, his house became a refuge. It was the first time in her life that Alet had felt taken care of. In spite of herself, she looked up to him. She loved listening to the stories he told of his days as a detective in Brixton Murder and Robbery. It turned out that he was something of a celebrity, known for solving almost every case that had landed on his desk, his picture regularly appearing in the paper in connection with some high-profile case. He was later transferred to John Vorster Square, but he always missed Brixton, he said. By the time Alet matriculated, she was enamored of the life he described. She decided to enroll at the police college in Pretoria.

Some people became police officers because they couldn't find other work, some were just glorified bullies, but Alet knew she fit into the third category, the ones who had it in their DNA. All of her life, she had felt like she was pulling the wool over people's eyes, but the very first day she set foot on the police college campus, she knew that she was going to be good at it. She flew through Basic and in-field training, graduating top of her class. By the time she started in-service training, she couldn't imagine doing anything else. She loved the look of pride in Adriaan's eyes, especially when she told him that she had applied for Special Task Force training. There were no women in the unit, but Colonel Adriaan Berg's daughter would be the first if any woman was.

Adriaan pulled into the driveway of a red brick house in a suburb of Port Elizabeth, stopping in front of the enormous security gate. Barbed wire ran across the top of the fence. Aunt Mattie's dressing-gowned figure waddled past the barred living-room window of the house and the *stoep* light went on.

"Our flight for Mauritius leaves at eight." Adriaan left the car idling. "I'll ask someone to come pick you up."

"I'll call a taxi."

Adriaan nodded. Alet noticed the edge of a scratch mark protruding from his dress shirt collar. She imagined Frieda digging her talons in passionately while screaming in ecstasy, then cursed herself for the image. If that was the kind of kink they were into, she really didn't need to know.

"How are things? You've gained some weight." Adriaan's voice had a strained gravity.

"Don't worry, I'm not pregnant. I'm just fat."

Adriaan pursed his lips for a moment, but let it go. "Are you getting along in Unie?" It was the first time since she'd been kicked out of Special Task Force training that he had shown any interest in her life. She grabbed the opportunity.

"I'm on a murder investigation."

"Oh?" Adriaan looked puzzled. "Tokkie didn't mention anything."

It didn't surprise Alet that her dad discussed her with Captain Mynhardt. He was probably the only reason she was still on the force, calling in favors from friends to keep her there after the affair with her superior came to light. She had the sudden urge to tell him about everything, how sorry she was for failing, for disappointing him. How scared she was of doing it again. How she hated small-town life and small-town people and arrogant assholes trying to kill each other on the N12 every day. How people like Strijdom held out their palms and turned their heads the other way and made her wonder why she even bothered doing the right thing. But if there was one thing Adriaan Berg had taught her, it's that what happens on shift stays there. It had nothing to do with the outside world. Nothing.

"You shouldn't jeopardize your probation." Adriaan spoke in measured tones without looking at her. "If you mess up this investigation . . ."

Alet bristled. "I've uncovered most of the leads we have so far."

"I'm sure you've contributed."

"We don't have money for decent forensics and the labs are slow." She forged ahead, remembering the stories he'd told her from the old days. "You said you sometimes consulted with a forensics guy at the university when you were in homicide. He helped you catch that strangler guy when you had no leads. Maybe he can help."

"Koch?" Adriaan had a look of distaste. "I don't think so, Alet. Let the investigating officer handle this. Is he experienced?"

"Mathebe is okay. He's—"

"You don't need outside help. Just do as he tells you." Adriaan's words had bite.

Alet felt sure that she would burst into tears if she stayed in the car another moment. "Well, have fun on your honeymoon." She got out and closed the car door before Adriaan could respond.

Alet snuck out, as soon as Aunt Mattie said good night and the lights went out. The velvet dress felt sticky and unglamorous against her skin, Cinderella after the clock struck twelve. The taxi she had ordered idled in the street, the driver surly, at the end of his shift, the smell of stale cigarettes and coffee permeating the upholstery. Her Toyota was parked in the lot among the last stragglers from the wedding. Alet fished the keys out of her bag, grateful that her father didn't get it into his head to take them. She exchanged her heels for a pair of old trainers she kept in the trunk before she took off, following the signs to the N2. A drowsiness hung over Port Elizabeth's abandoned streets, ghosts of the normal bustle illuminated by solitary streetlights. Shantytowns slumbered in the late hours, an occasional fire still smoking in a drum, the homeless crouching around it. Alet exited onto the R62 and the road opened up, illuminated only by the crisp white of her high beams, the speedometer wavering at 120 km/h.

Alet's head was pounding, every approaching headlight waging war on her optic nerves. She almost didn't see it, the feeble attempt of a thin arm to wave her down, the woman lying on the side of the road, pale breasts protruding from her torn blouse. It took Alet a moment to process the image, doubting her sanity even as she slammed on the brakes. The sedan strained, skidding on gravel before coming to a stop. Alet's purse fell off the passenger seat.

Oh, God. Alet's hands trembled as she fumbled for her purse. She squinted at the rearview mirror, barely making out the human form on the ground. She found her phone between old tissues and lipstick, almost dropping it again as she dialed 112, relieved when the call connected.

"This is Constable Alet Berg from the Unie Police. I'm about twenty kilometers outside Joubertina. I have Tracker installed. Toyota, license plate CA 893–919." Alet pushed the tracker's panic button. "There is an injured female lying on the side of the road. Send an ambulance right away."

Alet reached for her holster under her seat while she waited for the operator's confirmation, the butt of the 9mm sliding into her palm. She flipped the safety off and got out. Her eyes had trouble adjusting to the dark. She took a few steps forward, barely able to distinguish shapes. The picnic rest stop had a concrete table and bench next to a row of scraggly trees. The woman on the ground in front of it whimpered like an injured dog.

"Hallo?" The world around Alet held its breath.

The woman's right arm lifted a few inches off the ground, dropped back as if it were encased in lead. Alet realized that the whimpers were gasps for air. *Fok.* She ran to the woman.

"Help is on the way." Alet prayed it was true.

The woman's eyes were wide with terror, her mouth opening and closing, a shrill, labored treble the only thing escaping. Dark patches of blood soaked the front of her cap-sleeved blouse. Her pinched face looked familiar, but Alet didn't allow herself to think about why. She knelt down, peeling back what remained of the fabric. A long gash ran unevenly down the woman's chest, as if the attacker had tried to trace a line with multiple stabs. Alet couldn't tell how deep the wounds were, only that the woman was bleeding profusely, the bone of her sternum visible in places.

"Stay calm." It sounded ridiculous even as Alet said it.

The woman's eyes darted to the right. Alet turned her head in time to see a branch coming down. What would have been a blow to the back of her head caught her on her nose. A searing pain shot through her skull. She fell on her side, the 9mm pinned under her body. Something took over, instinct, or maybe it was training, but she immediately rolled onto her back. A shoe connected with her side as she lifted her gun. She pulled the trigger anyway.

The deafening pop had the desired effect. Footsteps crunched in the gravel as her attacker ran. Alet pushed herself off the ground with effort. She had trouble focusing her eyes. She aimed the gun in the direction of the footsteps. Pop. Again, aim. Pop. She tasted blood. Aim. Pop. *Ah for* fok*'s sake.* The man was still running. *You're never going to get him like this, Berg.*

A car door slammed. "Shit." Alet had left her keys in the ignition and the *fokker* was stealing her car. She got off the ground, raw rage propelling her. She had almost reached the Toyota when the car's engine started up, tires spinning, kicking up dust.

If you're going to do it, you should stop fucking around and do it right. Alet planted her legs shoulder-width apart, wrapped her hands over the butt of the gun, extended both arms and took a deep breath. She squeezed off two rapid rounds on the exhale. The car swerved, the back window blowing out. It didn't slow down. Alet aimed. Her ears were ringing. Pop. The car veered to the side, hitting the lip on the other side of the road. It slid down the shallow embankment, wheels spinning as it flipped onto its side. Alet followed the car down, adrenaline coursing through her veins, blinding her judgment.

The Toyota had come to a stop against an old telephone pole edged by wire fencing. In the field behind it, sheep startled by the noise scattered. Alet opened the Toyota's passenger door. A black man lay with his bloodied head against the driver-side window, his eyes closed, his chest rising and falling in shallow breaths, the blood from a wound at his collarbone spreading down his T-shirt.

"*Fokker!*" Alet's voice bordered on hysteria. "I got you." Her index finger tightened around the trigger.

Yellow and blue lights caught her eye. A lone flying squad vehicle rounded a bend in the road, a siren's wail breaking the silence. Alet lowered her gun. She reached into the car to turn the Toyota's hazards on. The man stirred. Alet scrambled back, hitting her head on the car door. She trained the gun on him again with shaky hands. When he didn't move, she slammed her free hand against the door. "I got you."

1938

Tessa

"I can't wait any longer, Theresa." Mrs. Uys stood at the classroom door, keys in hand. "I have a choir to coach." Tessa took the sheet music to "Für Elise" off the stand and tucked it between the schoolbooks in her satchel. It had been a trying lesson. Throughout the whole ordeal, Tessa had tried not to stare at the music teacher's chin, where a thick, gray wire sprouted from a brown mole the size of one of Flippie's marbles.

She wondered how old Mrs. Uys was. Her own age? Perhaps. It fascinated her to think that she should have looked like that by now. Tessa's body carried only the hint of adolescence, her skin unblemished and smooth, her white curls still downy. Her mind was a different matter though, memories of every moment of her existence always there, years of knowledge crowding her thoughts. She had come to resent the way these so-called adults treated her, as if something as negligible as age earned them rights over her. It was getting harder to take their arbitrary abuses, harder not to correct the fallacies in their insipid ideologies.

"You should tell your *pa* that *boy* is no good," Mrs. Uys said. "It's not decent for him to hang around a white girl. Why does he let a black come pick you up?"

The question seemed easy, but, as with most things, once Tessa started thinking about what it really meant, she got tripped up. She obsessed about the details and nuanced variations, the language she used, what would be socially acceptable versus what she really thought and felt, the reaction of her teachers and her peers. She lost herself in a maze of possibilities too infinite to encompass in a simple answer.

"Honestly. You'd think I was talking to a wall. The good Lord gave you a tongue, girl."

"*Pa* works late, Mrs. Uys." Tessa recited the rote answer, the least interesting of the lot. Her Afrikaans was marred with soft consonants. The language felt wrong in her mouth, rigid and stiff, like the people who spoke it. But here, in the Free State, people frowned if you spoke English, calling you a redneck or a traitor behind your back.

Mrs. Uys fiddled with her keys. "What about your *ma?*"

"She died." Tessa felt physical pain as she said it. It was the answer Andrew had coached her into giving all her life if anyone asked, but now that Sarah was gone, it wasn't a lie any longer. Her mind drifted to Sarah's frail body struggling into the back of a black man's taxi for her weekly hospital visits. Flippie, his eyes fixed on the ground, gently squeezed in beside her as if he was scared she would break. Tessa and Andrew had had to stay behind. Whites weren't allowed in the *location*, and a black would never be allowed through a white hospital's doors. On their return, Sarah would beg Andrew not to make her go again. Tessa knew that Sarah braved that hospital in the *location* for Andrew's sake. And then, one day, only Flippie climbed back out of that black man's taxi. Tessa pressed her lips together, fighting back the sudden wave of emotion.

Mrs. Uys's buggy eyes softened for a moment. "I hope you have someone to help you get your costume ready. The wagons pass through on Friday."

"*Ja*, Mrs. Uys." It embarrassed Tessa to admit that there was no-body. She had taken care of the monstrosity herself, sewing with clumsy fingers by candlelight to the specifications given by the home economics teacher after she handed uniform cloth out to the girls. Bloemfontein was a conservative, model Afrikaner town, the fourth (or was that fifth?) place they had lived since leaving Johannesburg, and it was buzzing in anticipation of the Big Trek Centennial. Everyone was participating in the celebrations in full costume. They practiced traditional dances during early-morning assemblies at school, and even though Tessa was new, she was forced into the fray, clumsily copying the other girls in their militaristic skirt-swishing and partner-swapping, her feet several steps behind as she did her best to avoid eye contact.

Tessa followed Mrs. Uys out of the music room and waited until she locked the door. Children from the orphanage played in the street outside the school gate. You could always tell them apart by their hand-me-down uniforms and greasy hair. Most of the town parents didn't want their children to be friends with them, so they mainly stuck together, huddling at the edge of the school grounds, always up to no good. All of them belonged to the *Voortrekkers*, the Afrikaner answer to the Hitler Youth, meant to emulate and promote the culture of their forefathers who'd trekked inland to escape the British-ruled Cape Colony.

"Afternoon, Mrs. Uys," Mr. Hugo said as he passed them on his way from coaching the rugby team, tie undone, hair wet with sweat. Tessa noticed the beginnings of a beard on his square jaw. All the men around town were suddenly sprouting facial hair in anticipation of the ox-wagons that were following the *trek* route up from the Cape to Pretoria.

"Good afternoon, Mr. Hugo." A blush spread over Mrs. Uys's cheeks, her eyes lingering on his back. Old goat longing for a young leaf, Tessa thought. All the girls in school had crushes on Mr. Hugo. Tessa silently mocked them as she listened to their nervous twitter during recess, the wishful thinking of guppies. She refused to admit that she too sometimes felt a rush of something inexplicable when he called on her during history lessons, and that she worked extra hard to impress him.

These days, they had to forgo the Renaissance in favor of their Afrikaner ancestors, the original *Voortrekkers*. Everybody sang *volk* songs and learned how to make stick dolls and cook in anthills. Tessa found it unbearable, even under the guidance of Mr. Hugo, who seemed to relay the folklore with a bemused smile. The other teachers took it more seriously, treating the stories like gospel, the *Voortrekkers* gods from Greek mythology.

Mrs. Uys turned her attention back to Tessa as Mr. Hugo disappeared behind one of the asbestos classrooms. "Your scales are no good," she said. "I can tell you don't practice."

"*Ja*, Mrs. Uys." Tessa had taken to music as easily as to any other language, but her hands were too small to reach the notes on the piano. She would have liked to switch to the violin, but she didn't want to ask Andrew for one. The only job he could find in Bloemfontein was road-building, so money was tight.

Mrs. Uys plodded down to the main gate, where her husband waited in his Chevy. She looked out of the window of the car as they drove off, a kind of sadness on her face. Tessa scanned the road, hoping to see Flippie appear among the low buildings now that she was gone. He should have been there half an hour ago, but he didn't like having to call her "*Mies*" in front of her teachers and other white people. She couldn't blame him for that, but even so, he was acting strange lately, as if graduating from high school made him too important to talk to his own sister, treating her like a leper when Andrew wasn't around.

Tessa kicked a pebble out of frustration. A billow of red dust rose up from the dry ground, dulling her new school shoes and socks. It was only a couple of miles to their *plot*, and it wasn't as if she didn't know the way. Andrew would have a fit if he found out, though. He had forbidden her to go anywhere alone, and they both had to be home by six, at which point nobody opened the door until Andrew got home from work. Flippie wasn't a child anymore. There would be trouble if he was discovered in the white areas after dark.

Tessa hated her child's body, hated having to depend on either of them. Whenever Tessa had had questions about why she wasn't growing like other children, neither Sarah nor Andrew could answer her. Last night, when she brought it up again, Andrew had called it a gift, citing God's mysterious ways, which had only made her angry. Tessa suddenly felt sorry for the way she had behaved, for yelling at him and calling him a liar. Andrew just sat there with hunched shoulders while she vented, saying nothing. Perhaps he really didn't know. In Tessa's mind she was sure she was damned, like Cain. Or perhaps she was immortal, like the Titans, only she would be a child for all eternity. But that wasn't right either. Her body was changing, even if the process was painfully slow. The hint of inchoate mounds had recently appeared on her chest. Tessa hoped that the charade of childhood might at last be coming to an end. She wondered whether she'd be too embarrassed to talk to Andrew about getting a bra.

Tessa sat down on one of the concrete steps that led down to the street, hugging her schoolbag in her lap, watching the teenage boys coming from their *Voortrekker* scout meeting and showing off for the girls by picking on the orphans. Boys had never shown off for her, not in any of the schools in any of the towns. For the most part they ignored her or made fun of her. She touched her chest absentmindedly, wondering if that would change now.

Tessa didn't notice the old man until he was right next to her, his weathered face as brown as his stained clothing.

"*Kleinmies*, why are you sitting alone?" He glanced around the schoolyard as he spoke to her. "Are you waiting for someone?"

"What do you want? I don't have money." Tessa was surprised by the disdainful authority of her own voice. The old man looked as if she had slapped him, a sad, disappointed look sagging his face farther. Tessa suddenly felt ashamed. People talked down to blacks, made snide remarks and jokes and treated them like dimwits. She was supposed to know better. She dropped her head, studying the dust on her shoes, not sure how to make amends.

The man sat down next to her on the step. "How old are you?"

"Twelve," Tessa hoped he would go away, before someone saw him and caused trouble.

"There was a *kleinmies* on the farm where I used to work," the man said. "She was as old as you." He shook his head mournfully. "But the *baas* he didn't want me there anymore."

"Why not?"

"I was good friends with the *kleinmies*, see? It wasn't like here in town. Here they are all so greedy, greedy, greedy. The *kleinmies* was my friend." The man rubbed his head, his white hair sticking up like down. "Will you give me a hug?" He inched closer to Tessa. She was intensely aware of the rank smoke smell on his clothes. "The *kleinmies* on the farm always hugged me. Or do you hate an old man like the others?"

"I am not like them." Tessa held her arms out, desperate to prove the point.

The man pulled her toward him. She could feel his bony ribs through the rough cloth of his clothes. She tried to push away, a wrong feeling clenching her stomach. The man held on to her, holding her head against him, his chest rising and falling heavily, his heart beating next to her ear. His right hand suddenly slipped under the schoolbag on her lap. His fingers gripped her thigh over her school dress, forcing the fabric back.

"No!"

"You promised a hug. This is the same."

Tessa struggled, trying to get away from him, a shrill, desperate sound escaping her lips. The man let go of her thigh and pushed his palm against her mouth. His arm wrapped around her torso, pinning her arms. He lifted her onto her feet and dragged her toward the school buildings. Tessa kicked into air, her petite frame struggling against his sinewy strength.

"Hey! What you doing, *kaffir*?" A boy's voice came from far away.

Tessa bit the man's palm and screamed for help when he let go. She fell on gravel, small pebbles digging into her palms and knees.

"Hey! Get him."

Footsteps, young men running, a garble of voices passing by. Three burly teenagers gave chase, joined suddenly by Mr. Hugo. "Come here, *boy*!" one of them shouted. "I'll beat the *kak* out of you!" The *Voortrekker* scouts in their brown-and-khaki uniforms were suddenly there too, faces crowding to see Tessa.

"What did you do?" One of the older girls accused. "A *kaffir boy*? *Sies*, man." They were all staring as if she had grown horns.

Tessa got up on shaky legs. "I didn't do anything. He . . ." She realized the futility of trying to convince them of anything as she looked from one face to the next. She pushed past the gaping girls. All she could think about was getting away from their leering. Tomorrow the story would be all over the school grounds. They would snigger and point. She would be the girl that had been seen with, been touched by, a black. As if his essence had rubbed off and made her as dark and rank as he was, something foul and shameful. The teachers would discuss it over tea. Andrew would be called to school. She wished she could disappear, go where Sarah was, let it all be over.

"Hey, wait. Come back." Someone was following Tessa, a gangly boy. She ran faster, but he kept up. "Your b——. Your b——. Wait."

Tessa was halfway up the street before she dared to look at him. The boy was almost a foot taller than she was, his white hair shaved close to his scalp with cowlicks in strange places. His pale eyebrows seemed to disappear against porcelain skin that was tightly wrapped over the sculpted contours of his face. She started when she noticed his pale silver eyes, their almost imperceptible slant giving him a strangely graceful air, belied by the sharp angles in his body and the awkward way he moved. It was like looking at a memory of herself, familiar, but different.

"You l-l-left it." The boy's stutter was jarring.

Tessa realized that he was hugging her schoolbag. "Give it here," she said.

The boy dropped the bag on the ground and took a step back. "I d-didn't s-s-." His face contracted as he tried to get the word out. He took a breath. "S-steal it."

Tessa grabbed her bag, holding it in front of her like a shield. "I didn't say you did."

The boy's pale eyes followed her every move. "Did the b-black hurt you?"

Tessa had to think about it. The rush of adrenaline, the others staring at her, it was over so fast, it felt unreal, like a nightmare confusing reality. "I'm fine," she said tersely.

"I s-saw you at s-school." He frowned. "You s-sit al-lone."

"We just moved here." Tessa felt defensive.

"I'm B-Benjamin. I can s-sit with you."

"I don't need to sit with anyone." Tessa turned and started walking away, not sure why she felt scared of him.

Benjamin followed. "Nobody s-s-sits with m-me either."

Tessa glanced over at the hole in the big toe of his shoe and the shiny well-ironed lines of his brown shorts. "Doesn't mean we have to be friends."

"I've n-never had a f-friend." Benjamin sighed despondently. "I-I was in a h-hospital f-for a l-long time. B-because I d-didn't grow."

Tessa stopped. Sarah had said the other babies like her had all died, but she'd always hoped that it wasn't true. "How old are you?" Her eyes narrowed, issuing a challenge.

Color rose to Benjamin's cheeks under her scrutiny. "*M-matrone* said I should say I'm el-leven last year when I came to this s-school."

"Who is *Matrone*?"

"I l-live with her."

"She's your mom?"

Benjamin shook his head.

Tessa thought for a moment. "When is your birthday?"

Benjamin shrugged. "*Matrone* s-said they aren't imp-portant, only

J-jesus's b-birthday, so I count those. I've counted more years than t-twelve." He looked down at the ground, his voice growing soft. "More than t-twice as many. M-maybe three t-times."

Could it be true? Was Benjamin really like her? Tessa had spent so many years denying what she was to people that she didn't know if she should trust him. "I'm thirty-six," she ventured. "I was born in March . . . 1902." If he turned on her, she would deny everything, pretend that it was a joke. She had learned long ago that people only believed things that fit their views of the world, brushing aside or ignoring anomalies. She knew that was also the reason Andrew insisted that they move when someone noticed that she was different. Once people started believing that the improbable was true, there was no way to talk them out of it. She watched Benjamin's reaction closely.

"M-maybe me too?" Benjamin looked at Tessa in anticipation. "We could be—"

"Maybe."

Benjamin's brow knotted. "I r-remember everything f-from every d-day. F-fr-from the t-time I was l-little."

Tessa dropped her guard. "I see better than other people in the dark," she blurted before she could stop herself.

Benjamin nodded, his eyes wide. "And I understand the Bantu l-languages."

Tessa felt a strange wonder looking at him. She reached out and touched his face, pale skin like hers, eyes like hers, the world suddenly opening up. Benjamin touched her hand, wordless understanding passing between them. They alone lived in that moment, sealed together in secret knowledge. Tessa suddenly wrapped her arms around him. His body jerked in response, but she refused to let go. She held him close, scared that he might not be real.

"I'm Tessa Morgan," she whispered into his ear.

"I kn-know."

"Will I see you at school tomorrow, Ben?"

"*J-ja.*" Benjamin's breath came in an airy rattle, his body relaxing in her arms.

"Then we'll sit together?"

"*J-ja.*"

Tessa pecked him on the cheek, her limbs tingling with excitement. She wanted to tell him everything Sarah had told her, about the doctor, and the other babies, but he looked so happy that she stopped herself. It could wait until another time. They had nothing but time now. She kissed him again, leaving him in the middle of the road as she ran home to tell Flippie and Andrew that she'd found someone like her, that she wasn't the only one. She turned off the asphalt road onto gravel, her steps light, a smile lingering on her lips. The twilight disappeared, her feeling of elation heightening as darkness wrapped its tender arms around her.

Tessa closed the back door behind her and found Flippie at the kitchen table, reading. He could have been a young version of Andrew as he sat there in the candlelight, his European features betraying the expectations of his dark skin. Intelligent eyes moved across the pamphlet in front of him, the page resting lightly between the thumb and forefinger of his slender hands. When Flippie refused to acknowledge her, Tessa slammed her bag down on the table.

"You weren't at school, Flippie."

"You got here just the same." Flippie calmly turned the page.

"I was waiting for you and then there was this man . . ." Tears welled in Tessa's eyes, more from his neglect than the actual trauma of the event.

Flippie glanced sideways at her, agitation infecting his angular face. "What now?"

"Why didn't you come for me, Flippie?"

"I forgot." His tone was dismissive, his indifference scathing.

"I'm telling *Pa*."

Flippie folded the pamphlet and stood up, his eyes almost black. "You'd better not. You know how he gets. And then it will be all your fault." He walked out of the kitchen with the candle, a fleeting silhouette in the doorway. A door slammed down the hall moments later.

Tessa's eyes burned. Even thoughts of Benjamin couldn't drive away her loneliness. She moved around the kitchen in the dark. Flippie had left some lukewarm maize pap on the stove. She dished everything for Andrew, then covered the plate carefully and set it aside for when he came home. She got into bed without bothering to brush her teeth or do her homework, wishing that morning would never come. Her light sleep was interrupted an hour later by dissonant male voices as Andrew's modulated baritone intertwined with Flippie's staccato anger.

"—a telephone call. The principal. I asked you to look after her."

"I'm not her nanny."

"We're not discussing this again."

"I have to hide or pretend to be the garden *boy* and mind Tessa like a lackey. Only *Ma* cared about what happened to me."

"Phillip."

"It's true." Flippie's voice broke.

"We've done all right, old man," Andrew said after a long silence. "We've managed."

"I need things too, *Pa*. All I have to look forward to is saying *Ja, Mies, Ja, Baas*, for the rest of my life. That isn't a life."

Tessa crept out from under the blankets and shuffled toward the dim line of light under the door. She slowly turned the knob and peeked through the crack. Flippie had his arms crossed, his head down. Andrew sat at the table, hollow and ragged. His shoulders were always drooping now, his hair completely gray. Sarah had been the glue, wordlessly bearing the insults and insinuations so they could be together. Now their tenuous bond threatened to disintegrate, each of them wandering around aimlessly through the house.

"You can study, son. Make something of yourself." Even Andrew didn't sound convinced.

"A *kaffir* college?" Flippie seethed. "So I can learn to be what? An educated slave? You know what that National Party's stance is. Their own man, Le Roux, said it beautifully." He deepened his voice, reciting in a mockingly officious tone. "We should not give the Natives any academic education. If we do, who is going to do the manual labor in the community?"

"Things will change."

"Things are changing, *Pa*. But not the way you think. There is hate in this country for anyone who isn't white, and it's getting worse. Have you heard the talk about the *trek*? They say there's going to be a revolt. That they'll refuse to sing *God Save the King*, once they get to Pretoria and try to take over the government."

"It's talk, nothing more. The Afrikaners will never stand together. We still control—"

"You are blind if you don't see what's happening, *Pa*. My people, the African National Congress is fighting for the black man to have a say in his own land—"

"We are your people, Phillip, not the ANC. I'm your father. Tessa's your sister."

"She's not my sister. Look at her."

Andrew sighed, the circles under his eyes looked even darker in the candlelight. "We only have each other, son. Don't throw that away. Your mom wouldn't have wanted that."

Flippie's hands clenched at his side. "Did they catch him? The man who grabbed Tessa?"

Andrew nodded. "We should be thankful that she wasn't harmed." He got up from the table and touched Flippie's shoulder. "I'm sorry this is so hard." His hand fell away when Flippie showed no reaction.

Tessa scurried back to her mattress and burrowed under the covers, closing her eyes as Andrew's footsteps approached. Light danced on her eyelids as he opened the door to check in on her, disappearing moments later. She waited until she heard him close his bedroom door, the sound of his movements quieting down. Slipping out of bed, she trod lightly, avoiding the spots where the old planks creaked under the weathered carpet as she made her way down the hall.

"Flippie?" Tessa slowly opened his door.

"Go away, Tessa."

Tessa slipped inside his room and closed the door behind her. "Flippie, why are you being ugly to me? I didn't tell *Pa*, promise."

"I know."

Tessa stood quietly in the dark, watching him curl up in a ball on his mattress.

"Can I sleep with you tonight?"

"You have your own bed."

"I don't want to be alone. *Ag*, please, Flippie?"

"Go sleep by *Pa*, then."

"He snores. Pretty please, man."

"Stop talking like that. You sound like one of those stupid Dutchmen."

"Sorry." Tessa shrugged it off in the dark, forgetting that he couldn't see her. She'd spent so much time copying her classmates, pretending she was like them, that she didn't even realize she was doing it anymore. There was a rustle as Flippie opened the covers.

"This is the last time, hear? And I don't want to feel your rough heels anywhere near me. Stay on your side or I'll kick you out."

Tessa scooted to the edge of the mattress. "Hey, Flippie?" She hesitated, not sure if she should broach the subject. "Where were you today?"

"None of your business."

"*Ag*, tell me."

Flippie sighed. "There are people, Tess. They talk about the way things are. About what we can do to change them, you know?"

"Like what?"

"Like black people taking back their rightful place. Not being treated like children."

"What are they going to do?"

"I don't know. Take a stand. Fight against the oppressor." Anger sputtered through his words, his body tensing beside her.

Tessa sat up. "Are you angry at me?"

"No."

"You are."

Flippie turned his back to her. "You won't understand. You're white. White women have a vote, a say. Blacks have nothing."

"Do you think I don't know what it feels like to be treated like a child?" Tessa's cheeks burned hot with indignation. "I'm older than you, but you forget that. I'm older than some of my teachers and I have to act like they're better and smarter than me. Like I'm *dof* and don't know what's going on."

"At least you have freedom."

"What freedom? All they care about at school is that my uniform's hem isn't too short, and that I act like a lady. Learning anything useful is only important if you're a boy. The only freedom I have is to choose between becoming a teacher or a nurse. What if I don't want to be either of those things? Or do you mean I have the freedom to go and get a husband and become a housewife like Nienie Prinsloo from next door who quit Teachers' College after a month because she had a ring on her finger? So even if I can vote someday, it doesn't matter. Men control everything anyway."

"It's not the same."

"Yes, it is."

"You don't know what you're talking about, so just shut up before you wake *Pa*."

Tessa clutched the pillow. She had been bursting to tell Flippie about Ben, but she was too angry now. Her mind flitted from one thing to the next, listening to him breathe in the dark. "They don't hate you, you know? The whites, I mean. They don't mix with black people. How can they hate you if they don't know you? I think what's really going on is that they're scared."

"What are you talking about?" Flippie sat up in bed, pulling the covers open.

Tessa tugged at the sheets, drawing them over her against the cold. "There are a lot of black people, coloured people, Indians, you know? Many more than the whites. If you didn't know them, wouldn't you be scared?"

"I already am, Tess." Flippie sighed. "Go to sleep now, please?"

Tessa turned over. Sounds and images overlapped into a haze of dreams, interrupted too soon by gray light creeping through the thin curtains, and a rooster announcing the day on a neighboring *plot*. Her body jerked alert at the click of a latch trying not to be heard. She realized that Flippie wasn't next to her anymore. She found him in the kitchen, his schoolbag open on the floor, his two good shirts folded neatly inside, a half bag of maize meal and dried fruit piled on top. His clothes looked too big for him, as if his suspenders were the only thing that kept his pants up. Tessa stood still in the doorway. He caught sight of her as he turned around, his expression immediately changing to a scowl.

"What do you want, Tessa?"

"What are you doing, Flippie?"

"Keep your voice down." He tore a chunk of bread from a loaf on the table and tucked it away in his schoolbag, like a secret. Tessa noticed a small pouch with a check pattern. She had made the pouch for him in her second-grade sewing class. He always kept his best marbles in it.

"Are you going to look for work?"

"I'm leaving for a while."

"Don't, Flippie. *Pa* will find you a good job. Just wait. You won't have to be a garden boy or a trash man."

"It's not that simple, Tessa." A distant hurt lodged behind Flippie's eyes. Tessa knew that it had been there for a long time, but it still surprised her, like when she sometimes realized for herself why something worked a certain way, even though her teacher had made her recite the lesson about it with the rest of the class many times before. It was all just words, until it connected with something real in her mind.

"Are you coming back?"

Flippie closed his bag. "I don't know."

"I'm getting *Pa*."

Flippie grabbed Tessa by the arm as she dashed for the door. He put his hand over her mouth when she tried to yell. The violent memory of a black hand over her face rushed at her, fear sour and irrational in her stomach. The eyes of the old man peered at her from Flippie's face, and she bit his hand.

"*Eina!* Dammit, Tessa." Flippie looked at her in disbelief, slowly shaking his head. He grabbed his bag without a word, hesitating briefly at the back door before disappearing.

Tessa leaned against the wall, trying to catch her breath. She wasn't sure what exactly had happened. She marched to Andrew's room, a fist poised in the air, inches from the door, but it dropped to her side. She pressed her ear against the wood. No sound came from the room. She wouldn't bother him now, she thought. Andrew needed his sleep, and even if she did manage to stop Flippie, he'd just leave again another day. She went to her room and shut the door.

Benjamin

"Bennie?" The shrill voice drifted from the bedroom as soon as he walked into the apartment. Benjamin quickly locked the door behind him. The kitchen was dark, no smell of food to indicate that there would be a meal tonight. Headache-powder wrappers lay strewn on the floor. Cigarette butts spilled over the sides of a saucer perched on the armrest of a worn couch. A melancholic Afrikaans ballad blared from the radio, too loud for the late hour. Benjamin turned it off, freezing the female voice mid-vowel.

"Bennie, where are you?"

The smell of camphor assaulted his senses as he opened the bedroom door. Twin beds with gray-white bedspreads stood against the wall, divided by a small nightstand covered in liniments and bottles of drops. *Matrone* Jansen's bony, shriveled figure lay in the twin bed closest to the door, her hair hidden under a scarf, a sliver of her parchment neck visible above the top button of her faded yellow nightdress. Benjamin opened the curtains and reached for the window catch.

"Don't."

"A l-little f-fresh air?"

"You know my lungs don't like cold, son. I'll be up all night."

Benjamin sat down on the empty bed, his hands folded together in his lap.

"You did not sleep in the room last night." *Matrone*'s words were an accusation, demanding a defense.

"I had h-homew-work. It was l-late. I didn't want to w-wake you."

"The couch is not big enough. You have to sleep in here, with me." She pushed herself into a sitting position with effort, pain distorting her face, and held out her hand, motioning him to come closer. "A good boy." *Matrone* Jansen ran the back of her hand over his cheek. "Such a good boy." Benjamin noticed a long cut running from her index finger across her palm, yellow pus drying on the edges. This had been happening a lot lately. More often than not, he'd come home and find that she had injured herself, a burn on her forearm, bruises from a fall in the tub.

"You h-hurt yourself?" He took her hand in his, trying to examine the cut.

She bristled. "Leave it."

Benjamin's stomach rumbled. "Is there s-something t-to eat, *Matrone*?" His cheeks flushed.

Matrone Jansen looked distraught, her eyes watery. "My hand made me forget to go to the pension office." She pushed the cover aside and tried to get up. "I'll go now."

"No, *M-Matrone*." Benjamin stopped her. "It's n-night, see? They're closed. If you w-write a letter again, I can—"

"No!" She slapped him suddenly, a ringing noise starting in his left ear. "Devil. I know what you did last time. Thought I wouldn't notice two rand missing? I'll call the police."

"No, p-please. I t-told you, I used it to buy b-bread." Benjamin held her at arm's length, her hands clawing at his face. She had called the police before and accused him of stealing. They had taken him to the station. There was no court or jail for juveniles, only corporal punishment. And who would believe that he was a man if they saw his smooth cheeks and scrawny body? A constable he remembered, a brute who had barely graduated from high school the year before, whipped him with a *sjambok* until there were thick lines over his back and it hurt too much to go to school the next day.

"I won't let you do that again," Benjamin said, his voice wavering.

Matrone Jansen's face flushed crimson. "Honor thy father and mother, for anyone who curses his father or mother must be put to death."

"No, *Matrone*. I'm a g-good b-boy, remember?"

Matrone Jansen looked at him with unseeing eyes, something changing in her expression. She stopped suddenly as if remembering something and looked around the room, an embedded groove between her gray eyebrows. "Bennie? You're home?"

"*Ja, M-Matrone.*"

"My hand hurts. Why must it hurt?"

"God t-tests us in m-many ways, *Matrone*. We have to s-stay s-strong. B-believe. The sufferings of this present time are not worth comparing with the glory that is to be revealed to us." Benjamin recited. He knew that the familiarity of the words would calm her down, make her feel safe, even if they had lost real meaning. *Matrone* Jansen sank back onto the bed, confusion on her face.

"S-shall I rub salve on your h-hand?" Benjamin took her hand in his, uttering soothing sounds when she winced. He gently covered the open wound with the camphor before wrapping it in a bandage. He covered her with the blanket, hoping that tonight would be an easy night as he watched her head loll to one side.

"Don't go, Bennie." She reached for him as he tried to steal away.

"I have to do h-homework, *Matrone*."

"No. Sit a little while." She looked like she would cry, her mood threatening to turn again.

Benjamin acquiesced, perching on the edge of her bed, taking her rough hands in his. As long as she needed him, as long as he could do something for her, he was wanted. Tessa's image danced before him, inescapable since the moment she had touched him. Maybe she would need him too. He dared to utter the thing on his mind. "D-do you think there are other people l-like m-me, *Matrone*?"

Matrone's eyes stared glassily past him. He wondered if she had understood the question, or if she was willfully ignoring him. Some days she was better than others. When she spoke again, her lucidity surprised him. "There was a boy long ago. They brought him after the war, but he was a monster. Full of demons. You could feel it when you got close to him." She lowered her voice. "Evil." The word escaped in a whimper. "They called him Apie, the nurses. He cried so much. He had no hands, no ears, face all wrong. Horrible, horrible. But his eyes . . ." *Matrone* became lost in the memory, her hands drifting to Benjamin's face, caressing his cheek.

"What happened to him?"

"Don't bother yourself with him, Bennie. He was from the other place. Not like you. He couldn't stay here, see? He had to go back." She looked around the room, confused, a smile forming on her cracked lips when she looked back at him. "My feet." She said, meek as a schoolgirl. "They ache so much tonight."

"Tell me about Apie, *Matrone*. Please."

She shook her head. "My feet."

Benjamin knew that was the end of it. His prodding would only make her obstinate. He opened the covers at the foot of the bed and gently removed her thick socks, revealing feet gnarled from arthritis and years of abuse.

"For the creation . . ." *Matrone* looked expectantly at him.

Benjamin nodded. "For the creation was subjected to futility . . ." Romans flowed from memory with ease, her favorite verse. He rubbed *Matrone*'s feet, warming up the muscles, softening the knots. Her body relaxed, her jaw slack against the pillow. He lowered his voice. "The creation itself will be set free from its bondage to decay and will obtain the freedom of the glory of the children of God."

Benjamin allowed his mind to wander to Tessa. Beautiful Tessa. The thought of her made him feel strange, intense effervescent joy prickling his scalp when he remembered her eyes mirroring his longing. Her touch that afternoon had inexplicably changed him. A tightness inside him had let go. He willed his thoughts to the moment of her lips on his cheek, the sense memory vivid as the rose soap smell on her skin and the feel of her small breasts against his chest. *Matrone's* breathing morphed into a snore next to him, but he didn't notice. He replayed the moment again, as if it was a record, Tessa's arms around him, her lips on his cheek. As soon as the scene played itself out, Tessa turning away, he went all the way back to the beginning, to the moment of revelation, when she truly saw him.

Nobody had ever looked at him that way. The children at school dismissed him, didn't allow their thoughts to linger on him for more than a moment. Even the teachers kept their distance, sparing the rod unless there was no other way. When he was called to bend over, the punishment was disproportionate to the crime, a warning that he should keep his distance in the future, lest they were forced to deal with him again. Yes, he had suffered. He had wandered in the desert, alone and afraid always. But God rewards his faithful, Benjamin thought as he replayed the memory again. God rewards his chosen ones.

Tessa

The dress itched. Tessa kept stepping on the hem. She didn't know how the *Voortrekker* women made it across the Drankensberg in these outfits. It would have been easier to do it naked. Even the *kappie* was like a tent on her head, threatening to blow away with the slightest breeze. She refastened the bow under her chin, tightening the knot until it was hard to move her jaw.

All along the newly named Eeufees Road, hundreds, maybe thousands of *kappies* and bearded men in felt hats lined up to see the procession. Their excitement sizzled like a dynamite fuse. They had flocked in from the farms and nearby towns, some following the wagons since they'd left Cape Town. A murmur went through the crowd, erupting in cheers as the first wagon appeared, a speck in the distance, accompanied on both sides by costumed men on horseback. A second wagon followed. All around them women wept, while men bellowed, lifting their sons onto their shoulders.

Tessa caught a glimpse of the wagon through the forest of bodies. Young men in the brown *Voortrekker* uniforms were at the yoke, drawing the wagons. She turned to Ben, who had donned his own *Voortrekker* uniform for the occasion. "Why aren't there oxen?"

"To s-show Mr. P-prophet he can s-stuff it." Ben raised his chin proudly.

Tessa thought of the unassuming mayor of Bloemfontein. "Why?"

"He's n-not an Afrikaner." Ben said it as if it explained everything. He craned his neck. "He didn't w-want to s-support the celebrations. D-didn't w-want to change the s-street names or n-nothing."

"What's that got to do with drawing a wagon?"

"The *t-trekkers* get n-new oxen at every t-town. Now the *Voortrekker* boys are pulling the wagon to show the m-mayor we d-don't need him."

"Why aren't you there, then?"

"They d-d-didn't choose me." Benjamin looked away, his thin arms crossed. Tessa looked over at the young men pulling the wagon, all thick-necked masses of muscle. She felt sorry for asking.

An old woman stepped out from the sidelines, hunched over a cane, and lay her hand on one of the wagons as it drew near, tears streaming over her cheeks, her body shaking. Another woman stepped forward to do the same. Soon, bodies crammed close to touch the wagons, guiding them forward. Tessa stumbled as the crowd heaved around her, a confusion of long skirts and suspenders. Her breath came in short panicked puffs as she realized that they were trampling her, knees and elbows dealing blows to her body. A hand closed around her wrist. Ben pulled her up in one motion, setting her back on her feet.

"I don't like this." Tessa tried to move to the edge of the stampede, but Ben held on to her.

Ben fixed his gaze on the wagons. "It is an imp-portant m-moment in history of the *v-volk*. Don't you see? We can t-tell our children and their children."

The wagons rolled through the center of town, past the big two-steeple church. More people joined the procession. The Women's

War Memorial, a thirty-five-meter obelisk with a semicircle wing on each side, rose up to meet them. At its base, a large bronze statue of two women stood on display, one sitting with a dead child in her lap, the other staring off into the distance, her face partially covered by a *kappie*. The models could have been any of the women in the procession. Tessa felt relieved as the stampede around them eased, people scrambling to find a good vantage point. She looked down, reading the engraved rose-colored stone at her feet.

WINBURG
Persons 15 years and younger   355
Persons older than 15   132
Total   487
"How long, Lord, must I call for help, but you do not listen?
Or cry out to you, violence! But you do not save." (Hab 1:2)

Long rows of similar stones lined both sides of the walkway. Each bore the name of a town where a concentration camp was located, with the total deaths, most of them women and children, a whole generation decimated. Could this be what had happened to the frail woman with the blond hair that once held her? The memory was sheer, clinging on through the abyss of time. Overwhelming sadness suddenly took hold of Tessa.

The crowd suddenly hushed, a church-like reverence descending over them as the *trekkers* lighted the relay torches. Some of the women scorched the edges of their handkerchiefs in the flames and tucked them away next to their breasts as mementoes.

A platform had been erected next to the monument for the choir, which was comprised of singers from all the schools of the district. Their footsteps were the only sound as they arranged themselves. Mrs. Uys gave the note. The power of hundreds of voices united in singing "My Sarie Marais." It sent an involuntary shiver through Tessa. She found herself drawn into the drama around her. Her mind reeled with an unfamiliar sense of belonging, pride and indignation at what had been done to people she never knew. She didn't know what to make of this thing that felt and moved together, faces blurring among the sameness of *kappies* and beards. Ben seemed to disappear, his eyes burning with a fervid passion, mirroring the expression of everyone around them. It scared Tessa.

As the sun set, the mood seemed to calm down. A traditional Boer orchestra with concertinas and accordions accompanied school groups and adults going through their dance steps on the grass. Tessa and Benjamin joined in under Mrs. Uys's glare, mechanically going through the steps they had rehearsed, Benjamin's face twisted in painful concentration, his awkwardness excruciating. Tessa felt his discomfort deep in her own core, the connection between them palpable. As the last notes died down, they assembled at the base of the monument, where the *trekkers* conversed with town officials, frowns marring almost every brow.

The *trek* leader, a short man with an unkempt beard, held a Bible in front of his chest. "*Broeders en Susters.*" He bellowed. "Brothers and Sisters. Bloemfontein is a proud Afrikaner city, a place where our forefathers deemed it fit to raise their children as faithful Christians. Your hearts are warm, but the Orange Free State has been a cold place for us. Why should an Afrikaner like myself feel like a stranger in his own city?" A murmur rippled through the people. "Therefore, before we have our reading and prayer for the evening, I would like to request that Mr. Prophet leave the proceedings." A violent cheer burst from the subdued crowd, all eyes focused on a blushing man in a dark suit. He looked around nervously, his hands clutched in front of him. Tessa felt sorry for the mayor as two *trekkers* escorted him off the stage.

The *trek* leader held up his hands again once the mayor was out of sight. "We are welcomed in slums, but men like Mr. Prophet deny us here, in a place we rightly belong!" The murmurs turned to jeers. Eyes rested upon those present who were known to be English—businessmen, politicians, neighbors. The *trek* leader nodded his head, the corners of his mouth drooping in disgust. Behind him, town officials in suits and slicked-back hair stood expressionless.

"While the Afrikaner works with a pick and shovel, the Stranger occupies the offices of this land. There are monuments to men who gave their lives to foreign countries, but where are monuments of our Afrikaner heroes?" He pointed to the heavens with his right index finger. "We will erect those monuments in the cities they belong. Cities like this. Today I plead with you to stand together, my Brothers, my

Sisters. The time is here for the Afrikaner to demand an Afrikaans government, bone of our bone, flesh of our flesh. To inspire us, bind us together in unity and power as God destined it. Join me, for we will no longer be strangers in this land, a land paid for by the blood of our ancestors." He took his hat off, his tenor almost inaudible above the crowd's cheers as he began to sing. *"Uit die blou van onse Hemel . . ."*

One by one voices joined, singing the song by the poet, Langenhoven, "Die Stem van Suid-Afrika." The Voice of South Africa.

There was an eerie silence as the last note died down. Tessa touched Ben's arm. He jumped, relaxing as their eyes met.

"I'm hungry, Ben."

He looked away. "I d-don't have any food." There was an apology in his voice.

"I have some money," Tessa smiled. "You like fat cakes and mince?"

Tessa bought them food from the stall at the back of the monument, where women worked feverishly to feed the crowd. They sat on the ground, watching the bonfire as they ate. Sugar syrup seeped from the dough of Ben's *koeksister*, running down the side of his mouth, pure joy on his face as he licked his fingers. It made Tessa happy to think that she was the cause. With Ben there were no lies, no hiding. She had tried to tell Andrew about him, but a chasm had opened up between them after Flippie left. Andrew came home later than usual now, and barely talked to her, his mood desultory. He didn't even say anything when she appeared in the kitchen that morning wearing her costume. Though it was ugly, the accomplishment of making it herself had given her a sense of pride, but Andrew barely looked up before going back to his paper. Tessa knew at that moment that he blamed her for everything.

Tessa reached to wipe syrup off Ben's cheek, his whole face sticky. "I'm glad I found you."

Ben smiled, hesitantly placing his hand over hers. "Me too."

"We found each other." She thought of what Sarah had told her. "There must be others like us."

Ben frowned. "God will reveal them, if that is His plan."

Tessa shifted. "You believe that?"

"Don't you?"

Tessa shrugged. She had always read the Bible the way she read

Homer or the Brothers Grimm. "The Greeks and Romans had gods, and even Arabs have their own Bible. How do you know which one is real?"

"Those are false gods." Ben had an absoluteness in his voice. "The Bible warns us about them. There is only one true God. He created man in His image. The Devil is making you doubt, Tessa. You should pray that God sends him away."

Tessa tried to silence the voice of rebellion in her. Ben believed. So did everybody else. Andrew prayed on Sundays, and even Flippie when he thought nobody was looking. She felt jealous of everyone's conviction.

"Tessa?" Ben's eyes were fixed on the toe-hole in his shoe.

"*Ja*, Ben?"

"We're together now. For always, right? Will you promise?" Ben looked up when she didn't answer right away, his eyes mirroring a longing she knew intimately.

"For always." Tessa leaned over and kissed him on his forehead. "I promise."

5

Sunday
DECEMBER 12, 2010

"There will be an attempted-murder inquiry," Captain Groenewald said. He had graying temples, leathery skin, and thick bags under his eyes; a decent type, just worn down by many years on the job.

"I should bloody well hope so." Alet sat down in the chair in front of Groenewald's desk. The Joubertina police station was even smaller than Unie's. Groenewald's office was directly behind the station's service desk, and you could see the shadow of a constable hugging the frosted glass of the door.

Groenewald took his wire-rimmed glasses off and pressed the bridge of his nose between his cracked thumb and forefinger. "Against you."

Incredulity burst through Alet's thin veneer of calm. "What? He attacked me."

"Be that as it may, Constable Berg, you can't fire at people just because they're running away. We also didn't find a weapon."

"That woman didn't stab herself, I can tell you that much."

"It's procedure. We have no proof that your bloke was the one who stabbed her." Groenewald put his glasses back on. "Look, between you and me, I think you did the right thing."

It was a small consolation. There would be an investigation, hearings. Usually police shootings were justified, but the fact that the suspect wasn't carrying a gun made things complicated.

"How is she, Captain?" Alet asked, fairly sure that she knew the answer.

"Ambulance took over an hour to get there. She was gone by the time they . . ." Groenewald let out a sigh. "There was a second body, a man, behind the picnic table. Looks like a carjacking. There was another set of tire tracks, but we don't know for sure if it was part of this." He shook his head. "Bloody tourists come here and think they can act like they do at home. Their rules don't apply here."

"Tourists?"

"We found American currency. No ID on either of them, though. If you hadn't come along we would have had two dead foreign nationals and no suspects."

"Do you have a picture of them?"

Groenewald handed her the crime-scene photographs. Alet tried not to react, imagining the faces without the blood and bruising. "There's a possibility they were in Unie on Thursday night. I thought I recognized her."

"This is going to cause a *kak* storm." Groenewald shook his head. "I've been here since '03. Not a single carjacking in this area on record. It's not like up north in the cities. There are some cruel bastards up there. I came back to the *platteland* to get away from that stuff. There's still some decency here. Some respect for life." Groenewald held up his hands in resignation. "I'm required to offer you counseling. Do you want someone from EAS to debrief you?"

"So I have to drive to Oudtshoorn once a month for a mandatory cry to a fresh-out-of-university shrink and a sleeping-tablet prescription? No thanks."

Groenewald gave her a knowing smile. "Your choice." He pushed his chair away from the desk.

"I want to sit in when you question the guy."

"Can't do that. That bastard will be lawyered up before he opens his eyes and they'll accuse you of trying to kill him. They know their rights well enough, those people." Groenewald locked eyes with Alet. "You're staying away, understand?" He waited for her to nod. His tone shifted, almost cheerful. "What I can do for you though, is get you a shower and some clean clothes." He held open his office door. "Don't worry," he said, lowering his voice, tension settling back in his shoulders. "We'll work on the bastard when we get the chance."

The medic at the scene had winced when he first saw Alet. She had a black eye and swollen cheekbone. Now her nose was obscured by thick white gauze. Groenewald's plump wife took Alet's appearance in stride, as if the captain regularly brought home strays. She fortified Alet with tea and homemade milk tart and armed her with fresh towels before sending her off to the bathroom.

Alet's dress was pasted against her by dried blood. She gingerly peeled it off, then abandoned it in the waste bin. Rust-colored water mixed with white foam, pooling on the shower tiles, as she rinsed her hair. Her muscles felt stiff and sore. Bending over to wash her legs made her woozy. As she reached out to steady herself, she bumped her nose against the side of the narrow stall, blades of pain shooting into her skull.

"Eina, moer!"

Tears burned behind her eyes. She tried to swallow them back, repeating the police mantra, cowboys don't cry, but she couldn't control the swelling panic in her chest. She stayed in the stall until she felt in control of herself again.

Groenewald had given her an old office uniform to wear. The white shirt was tight across her shoulders and the regulation calf-length blue skirt fell just below her knees, but it was clean. Alet usually avoided wearing the office uniform. It looked matronly, and she couldn't chase a suspect in the skirt and thick-heeled grandma shoes. That was one thing about the special task force. Everyone looked the same. As long as you got the job done, got the bad guys, rescued the innocents, nothing else mattered.

A Joubertina constable dropped Alet off in Unie around one o'clock that afternoon. Her flat seemed desolate. She tried to take a nap on the couch, but her thoughts kept bouncing between the woman lying on the side of the road and the burned body on the mountain. In desperation, she walked over to the main house and knocked on Trudie's door to see if she needed anything from the store. After several attempts, Alet realized that it was Sunday. Trudie usually drove off by herself in the early afternoon and only came home late. She suddenly wondered where Trudie went on her weekly outings.

Alet decided to walk to the station. The charge office was empty, April on duty at the service desk. April was a cheerful coloured bloke, fresh out of police college. He looked up from his paperwork when she walked in, a mock expression of shock on his face.

"*Eish* Kwagga! Is going to be hard to find yourself a man looking like that, hey."

Alet held her hand up. "*Ja, ja*, I know. But you should see the other guy."

April laughed. "I thought you were booked off."

"You don't like my company?"

"No, it's sharp, hey. But I'd be knocking back a few brews and putting my feet up if I was you."

"Can't." She pointed at her face. "Pain meds."

April made a grimacing face, drawing air in through his teeth.

"So, I see you're working yourself to death." Alet leaned on the counter. "What's going on?"

"Not much. Hit and run. Couple of domestics."

"Anything on the Terblanche farm?"

"No. There was a double whammy on the highway this morning and we got called out."

Alet shook her head in commiseration. "Is Mathebe here?"

"Knocked off at noon."

A thin middle-aged black woman walked into the station clutching a blue plastic shopping bag with both hands. Her clothes were varying shades of worn, but clean. She had a sense of urgency about her, hesitating just inside the doorway.

April turned his attention to her. "Afternoon. Can I help?"

The woman walked up to the service desk. She took a stiff new green ID book out of the bag and placed it on the counter in front of April. "My daughter, she did not come home," she said in broken English.

April looked at the front page of the ID. "She's sixteen?"

The woman nodded.

"When was the last time you saw her?" Alet chipped in, her heart beating a little faster. The woman squinted at her.

"She's police, don't worry," April said. "Do you know?"

The woman took a moment to think. "Lunchtime. Yesterday."

"You're sure?" Alet tried to hide her disappointment.

The woman nodded. "She made mess, that girl. Always made mess. Always running around."

April turned the page to open a new docket, copying the name from the ID.

"Hey, April?" Alet tried to get his attention. "You think I can take the patrol car?"

"Sorry, Madam, "April said to the woman. "One second." He looked over at Alet, his brows lifted in a question.

"My car is buggered up, man. In the shop till next week."

"Sharp-sharp, Letta. But it's for official business if anyone asks, right?"

Alet winked at April. "Of course, *ja.*"

The woman put her finger on the small photograph in the ID book. "She a good girl. She run around but she never not come home."

April nodded. "I understand."

Alet cleared her throat. "Keys?"

April reached under the desk for the keys and tossed them at her. "Get it back before the captain rocks up, okay?"

The woman shoved the ID book in front of April's face. "You find her."

April took it from her and returned to the docket. "We'll try, Madam."

Alet parked the patrol car near Magda Kok's house and hiked up the mountain. The sandy path rose over rocks and dipped between boulders, the climb tougher than it seemed from below. Trees clumped together at the base of the apex, their leaves varying shades of green and brown. Alet took photographs of the area, scouring the dry grass and hardened bushes for anything that might be useful. Her progress was slow, but the task had the blissful side effect of taking her mind off the early morning's events.

Alet sat down in the shade after an hour, taking a break from the relentless afternoon sun. Resting her back against a boulder, she steadied her camera on her knee and took a shot of the valley below. She could just make out the hill that cast its shadow over Unie in the distance. Alet zoomed in on the words "Unie 4 Jesus" laid out in painted white rocks. The Dutch Reformed Church had raised money to erect a lighted cross next to it. It could be seen from miles away at night. "So you can always find your way," *Dominee* Joubert had told her solemnly. She had to fight a gag reflex.

Alet moved the camera's focal point up the snaking mountain path, noticing a straight edge between the branches of a tree. She zoomed in. From the path, trees and foliage had obscured it, but here from above she could make the outlines of something man-made in the rock face. High bushes scraped her bare legs as she retraced her steps and veered off the path. A wide vertical crack marred the otherwise smooth surface of the rock, leading up to what looked to be an old war lookout. Alet slung the camera over her back, found a secure foothold in the crack, and hoisted herself up, grabbing a jagged outcrop. On STF exercises, Alet always outran and outclimbed the beefcakes in her unit, their sheer bulk putting them at a disadvantage on rugged terrain. This climb was a piece of cake in comparison to some of the obstacle courses she'd had to face. Despite being out of shape, she reached the ledge with little effort, her foot only slipping once as she struggled for a decent foothold. She clung to foliage that hung down the side of the shale as she inched her way forward, noticing the broken branches and roots where other people had climbed up before.

Mazelike turns led her to the dim interior of the lookout. The small holes in the red stone wall must have been used by the British to fire on approaching Boers. Or maybe it was the other way around? Besides the Big Trek and the concentration camps, she remembered little from high school history. Judging by the trash on the ground, the lookout was a regular haunt for vagrants and teenagers. Alet took a twig and dug through the pile, finding strips of singed newspaper, chips packets, beer cans and cigarette butts.

Alet turned the camera flash on and took a picture. Bright white light bounced off the walls, momentarily filling the claustrophobic space. A dark patch on the wall caught her eye. Alet lifted the camera and reviewed the picture on the digital screen. What looked like an indent or a shadow on the dark wall had flattened out into a reddish stain. She moved closer, her pulse quickening as she focused the camera on the area. The glare of the flash illuminated the stain again. It was blood.

Dr. Oosthuizen stood squinting in the doorway for an uncomfortable few seconds before inviting Alet in. He lived next to the Unie clinic, a stone's throw away from the invisible border between town and *location*. Oosthuizen was a lanky man in his mid-sixties with gray, greasy hair and a patchy beard. He always looked like he had just woken up from a nap.

"Please, sit," Oosthuizen said. The ramshackle living room of his four-room house was littered with medical magazines, files and dirty teacups. He pointed to a couch camouflaged with underwear and socks. He scooped clothes and files onto the floor. "It's clean. Laundry day, you know."

Alet chose not to speculate on the source of the brown stains on the couch's armrests. Oosthuizen's wife had died a few years earlier and he obviously had not adjusted to keeping house for himself.

"Tea? Coffee? I have a box of biscuits in the kitchen still."

"No, thank you." Alet turned the camera on, forwarding the display to the picture. "I need you to take a look at this, Doctor."

Oosthuizen leaned in, his bony limbs barely disturbing the seat next to her. Alet handed him a small evidence bag into which she had scraped some of the brown substance on the rock.

"I think it's blood."

"There is a simple test."

"Would you be able to match it to the victim?"

Oosthuizen shook his head. "I don't have the equipment for that sort of thing."

Alet sank back in her seat. "Give me something, Doctor. We still have no ID on the victim."

"Off the record?" Oosthuizen played with one of the hairs of his scraggly eyebrows. "Her morphology doesn't match that of a black woman."

"What does that mean?"

"The bones. As far as I can tell from the X-rays, the nasal bridge is high and pinched, not low and broad like with negroids. The nasal cavity is also tear-shaped, not rounded and wide."

"She was white?"

"Of European descent."

"So, not black?"

"Caucasian or mixed race, with Caucasian features at best. It's not a foolproof indicator."

"How do I find out for sure?"

"DNA testing. Also the only way to positively match this scraping with your victim. I have to warn you, though, labs are slow over the holidays—some of them close until January. Even if they were working at full capacity, it's going to take time."

"I might have a way to get it done faster." Alet didn't want to tell him about the half-baked idea that she had been nursing since she spoke to her dad. Pulling it off depended on a lot of bullshitting and half-truths. She studied the scraping from the lookout, hoping that her hunch would be confirmed. "Did you find any evidence that the victim was wounded before she was burned?"

"Well, it's hard to find signs of tissue damage." Oosthuizen said apologetically. "The blood and marrow boil in the skull and form an epidural hematoma. That's the brown substance. I can't tell if there was bleeding antemortem, but there were fractures of the femur and tibia."

"She hurt her legs?" Alet was surprised at Oosthuizen's knowledge. He had always struck her as the type that stayed in Unie because he couldn't find work anywhere else.

"No signs of remodeling. It could have happened just before she died." He sighed, an air of weariness settling over him. "I don't know for sure, though, Alet. I'm sorry."

Oosthuizen led the way to the front door. He hesitated before unlocking the security gate. "It is a horrible way to die, you know. We have our problems around here, I don't deny it. But things like this . . . It's unthinkable that people do that to each other."

Alet pitied Oosthuizen and the people like him who had been ignoring what was happening in the rest of the country for all these years, sure that their sheltered existence would go on indefinitely. The killer had brought a lot more than a murder to Unie. He was the harbinger of fear, ringing in an era of change.

"Don't talk to anyone about the case, please, Doctor," Alet said. "We don't know what we're dealing with yet."

"I understand."

Alet drove the patrol car back to the station, formulating a plan. She had to access the database and needed to make a few phone calls. No matter how much pleading it was going to take, she had to sell Mynhardt on the idea of getting help from outside.

1948

Benjamin

"Few days, *okes!*" The call echoed through the Tempe barracks. "*Min dae!* Hey, Jam-man! Few days!" The private—Frank Massyn was his name—planted himself on the bed next to Benjamin. Massyn was a crude oaf, his main ambition in life drinking. He always lagged behind and messed up during drills, no pride, no sense of duty. Massyn had survived conscription by latching on to people with influence or rank. He'd be a liability if there ever was a war again.

Benjamin folded the letter from Tessa, annoyed at the intrusion. It was his favorite, the one where she told him about her first day at the university, her excitement palpable on the page. It always made him smile to imagine her rushing home so she could write to him about her day. Benjamin had kept all her letters, written on whisper-thin blue pages, always with a dried Joseph's Coat leaf from her garden in its thin folds.

"I'm over this *kak, bra.*" Massyn ran his hands over the dark stubble on his head.

"*Ja?*" Benjamin put Tessa's letter in its envelope, tucking it into an old biscuit tin with the others. He had wanted to stay on in the army. It provided structure and discipline, and everyone was treated the same. Army pay was good too, good enough to support a wife and family, the life he wanted with Tessa. But the permanent force would not accept him, claimed there was a problem with his eyes, so his days in the army were at an end.

Massyn leaned in. "I told my missus I'm only getting out next Monday. When they hand me my last paycheck on Friday, I'm gonna have myself a whole weekend of freedom. Get me to a bar and ladies watch out!" He moved his hips suggestively. "You in?"

Benjamin shook his head.

"*Isit?* That chick of yours got you on a leash, I say." Massyn laughed. "Poor bugger. She's gonna want a ring soon. Then your life is over. Trust me."

Benjamin didn't want to talk about Tessa with Massyn, didn't want the slimy worm to even mention her. He looked wordlessly at Massyn until the man gave a nervous laugh, his hands fidgeting under his pillow.

"Hey, Jam-man, look at this." Massyn produced a magazine. He flipped it open to the picture of a blond woman fastening her stockings with suspenders, her naked breasts drooping down. "Nice, hey?"

Benjamin felt himself stir. He turned his face away, ashamed at his reaction to that filth.

"You never seen a woman? How old are you?" Massyn's mocking had a hint of genuine sympathy.

"Put it away before I report you."

"Okay, okay." Massyn studied Benjamin for a moment. "Hey look, I need a favor, *bra*." He rolled onto his back. "My old lady's *pa* is driving her in this afternoon for visitation. Could you show him the grounds or something?"

"Why?"

"Don't get me wrong, but you're his type. Me and Essie get no alone time. A man just sometimes wants to feel up his wife, hey."

Benjamin shrugged, hoping that would be enough of a response.

"Look, I need to stay in his good books. When he keels over, Essie gets it all. The old boy is high up in the government, has big bucks. So I make nice." Massyn sat up. "Help a bloke out?"

"Tessa might come." Benjamin tried to convince himself more than Massyn of the possibility. On her last visit, over a month ago, tension had distorted her lips as she told him about Andrew's cancer spreading, the pain he was in. It was a matter of weeks, the doctors had said. Tessa had stopped going to class, her days devoted to taking care of Andrew.

Massyn gave an awkward smile. "*Ja*, well, if she doesn't show up, hey?"

By three o'clock there was still nobody for Benjamin in the visitor's room. At the call box he waited in the queue for almost an hour to get a turn. Tessa answered the phone, her voice tired, irritable. Andrew had relapsed. She couldn't leave him now. Benjamin wanted to comfort her, but there were men behind him and he spoke self-consciously in staccato monosyllables. He felt a physical disconnection from Tessa when he put the receiver down, as if he had failed her.

Massyn stopped him in the corridor, a petite woman with round cheeks and a matronly air next to him. "Jam-man!" Massyn waved him over. "This is my wife, Essie." He turned to a big man of around seventy with brutish features. "And this is her father, Mr. Jooste."

"Private De Beer." Jooste gripped Benjamin's hand firmly, a harshness about him that was absent in Essie's doe-eyed puffiness.

"Ben said he'd show you around the base, *Pa*. Like you asked." Massyn sounded like he was offering his father-in-law the fatted calf. Essie looked expectantly at her father, her body as tense as Massyn's.

Mr. Jooste eyed Massyn with contempt, then spoke to his daughter over Massyn's head. "Be ready to go at five, Estelle."

"*Ja, Pa.*"

It was one of the last glorious days of a lingering summer that would soon be conquered by the dreary Free State winter. On the parade ground, new recruits were being put through drills, their feet moving in unison. Even the sweat stains on their shirts spread in the same places. Jooste followed Benjamin around, mumbling a disinterested, "*Ja*," or, "Is that so?" whenever Benjamin mentioned facts about the base. Benjamin caught the man's gaze a few times, unable to shake the feeling that Jooste was studying him. Part of the army base's property included the site of the Boer concentration camps. Benjamin walked to where the Dam of Tears rose during the rainy months. He stopped at the site of the graveyard where the women and children were buried.

Jooste lit a cigarette. "I've seen it." He narrowed his sunken, calculating eyes as he exhaled. "Where can we get a drink?"

"Sir, I'm not—"

"We'll go to the officers' rec room, *ja*. I have friends on base I'd like to see." Jooste held his hand up when Benjamin tried to protest. "Take me there." A plume of smoke escaped Jooste's lips as he talked.

The rec room was at the back of the single-officer quarters, packed with off-duty sergeants and captains getting drunk while listening to a rugby match over a radio perched on the bar.

Benjamin stopped short of the door. "It's officers only."

"Suit yourself."

Indignant eyes followed Jooste as he walked into the room. One of the drill sergeants opened his mouth to say something, but he immediately shut up when Major Daniels walked over to Jooste and shook his hand.

"Mr. Jooste." The major lowered his voice as they did a strange handshake. "*Broeder.* What can I do for you, sir?"

"A couple of Klipdrifts for me and the private, *ja?*"

Daniels looked over at Benjamin. Benjamin felt a sense of trepidation under his scrutiny, sure that he would be sent away, punished later for having the audacity to cross the threshold.

"I'm sure you can accommodate us." Jooste smiled, his gaze fixed meaningfully on Major Daniels.

"*Ja.*" Major Daniels looked flustered. "Of course."

A table was cleared and two brandies appeared. Benjamin sat down next to Jooste, self-conscious about the eyes on them.

"Rules are arbitrary, see?" Jooste lifted his glass, his brandy diminishing by half after the first sip. "There's always a way around them if you know the right people, if you have power." He turned his attention to Benjamin. "You get out with Frank, right?"

"Yes, sir."

"Then what?"

"Get married." Benjamin uttered the secret wish as if doing so too forcefully might shatter hope. Tessa was something fragile and dear in his mind, something that wasn't for sharing.

"That's incidental. What do you want to do with your life?"

Benjamin's discomfort grew. "Find work, sir, I suppose. I thought I'd ask in town."

Jooste tossed his brandy back and held his glass in the air, signaling the bartender for another. "Many men would kill to have your gift, do something extraordinary, but you want to waste it with mundane things like a woman and a job."

"I'm sorry, sir?"

"Let's do away with pretense, *ja?* I know who you are." A sardonic smile settled on Jooste's lips. "Kept an eye on both you and Tessa Morgan. From the beginning, you might say."

Alarm hollowed Benjamin's stomach at the mention of Tessa. "I don't know—"

"How old are you now? Fifty, must be."

Words stuck in Benjamin's throat. He wasn't prepared for this, certainly not from this stranger. "H-how?"

"Still got that speech impediment, *ja*?" Jooste's condescending tone had a familiar sting. "I know all about you, son. Like how the police gave you a good hiding when you tried to run away from that old nurse. And then how you collected her pension long after she kicked the bucket."

Benjamin looked away from Jooste's stare, his heart racing. He had tried to be invisible all his life. The fact that this man was aware of so much scared him. Benjamin knew what happened when people noticed him, noticed that he wasn't like them. They could sense it, the way a buck senses a lion in the dark. And when people got scared that way, they tried to destroy him. He remembered too well what people like Pieter had done to him behind closed doors. He didn't have the luxury of forgetting any of it. Only with Tessa did he feel like he could breathe normally, that he dared think of more than survival.

Jooste lit another cigarette. "I have something that might interest you, boy." The sport commentator's voice rose, a distant crowd's cheers fortified by those of the officers crowding around the radio on the bar. The Orange Free State was winning. Jooste raised his voice to be heard above the din. "The story of how you came to be what you are." He smiled.

Under the table, Benjamin's fingertips dug into his clammy palms. His instincts told him to get away from Jooste. An even stronger need to find out what the old man knew made him hesitate.

"I'll need something in return, of course." Jooste looked around the room at the drunk men, the right corner of his mouth raised in a sneer. "There's a doctor that works for me. He's doing important work, proving the superiority of our *volk*. He'd like to take a look at you."

Benjamin crossed his arms. "Why are you involved, sir?"

"Call it a mandate."

"Is that all?"

Jooste sighed. "A man has to have a legacy, see? I never thought that would worry me." He flicked his ash onto the floor, staring past Benjamin at the drunk young officers. "Estelle has been a disappointment, stupid, like her mother. I have no hopes for the snot-noses she and Frank Massyn will produce. So that leaves Tessa Morgan." He leaned in, his elbows on the table. "She's mine, you know? I'm her father." He reached into his jacket pocket, producing an old leather-bound journal. He slid the volume across the table. "It's all in here. Proof."

Benjamin's fingertips ran over the journal's cracked surface. The answers of where he came from, what he was, questions that had haunted him since he could remember, might lie between its covers.

"You do this and I will open doors for you, boy. Whatever you want. You'll have power over your very long future. You and the girl. And my bloodline will be part of the new super *volk*."

Benjamin let go of the journal. Jooste wasn't interested in Tessa because she was his daughter. They were both just *things* to him, laboratory rats. He wouldn't allow Jooste to hurt her. "I'm sorry," he said. He got up to go.

"I'm disappointed, boy." Jooste's nostrils flared, his irritation clear. "Wait," he said when Benjamin started to walk away. He held the journal out to Benjamin. "Take it. There's more if you decide to change your mind."

The rec room burst out in an earsplitting cacophony. The final touchdown. More beers were opened. The barman delivered Jooste's brandy.

"Well?"

Benjamin snatched the journal.

"My number is inside the cover," Jooste called after him. "Don't make me wait too long."

Benjamin had hoped that Tessa would be the first thing he saw as he exited the Tempe gates the following Friday. He waited around for an hour, hoping that she might still show up, though he knew she probably wouldn't. Andrew was dying and Benjamin felt relieved at the thought. Andrew had tolerated him for Tessa's sake, but from the moment they'd first met, Benjamin had felt a quiet animosity from the man. Tessa said it was nothing, but Benjamin knew better. His suspicions were confirmed when he went looking for Tessa one day. She was out, had gone to the shops.

Andrew had stood inside the *plot* door without inviting Benjamin in. He looked haggard, a grayish hue dusting his hollow cheeks. "What do you want with Tessa?"

The question had taken Benjamin by surprise. "We're . . . friends."

"I'm going to be honest with you, Benjamin. I'd appreciate it if you kept this conversation to yourself."

Benjamin nodded, afraid to speak.

"I have looked after Tessa, protected her as much as I could. So know that I only have her interests at heart." Andrew dropped his head for a moment before looking Benjamin in the eyes. "You have to stay away from her."

The words sent a shock through Benjamin, empty stabbing fear suddenly forming in the pit of his stomach. He couldn't be without Tessa. He had only just found her. His mouth was dry, the feeling rejection overwhelming. "W-why?" was all he could manage.

"I know you care for her."

Benjamin tried to stifle his anger. "You t-think I'm n-not g-good enough for her?"

Andrew shook his head. "I've known men like you."

"I d-don't understand."

"I think you do. You hide it well, but there is something broken in you. I beg you, walk away from my girl."

Benjamin could feel his pulse rise, his ears getting warm. "I would n-never hurt her."

Defeat deepened Andrew's scored features. "Please?"

Benjamin shook his head, biting back his hurt, a deep-seated fear taking root. He would never give Tessa up, not for anything. From then on, he avoided being alone with Andrew, working almost ten years for approval that never came. Once he was gone, Benjamin would have Tessa to himself.

Benjamin waited a bit longer, but no luck. He was the only soldier remaining, his legs stiff, a simmering panic rising. He tried to remember when this distance between them started. When had he stopped being everything to her, like she was to him? He should never have left her side, but he'd had no choice. Conscription could not be avoided unless you went to university, and for that you needed good grades and money.

Benjamin hoisted his army duffel bag over his shoulder, the edges of the journal that Jooste had given him digging into his back. He had spent every waking moment he had going over the pages, committing them to memory. There were names, first names only, and descriptions, as if Leath had been describing livestock. The notations and symbols mocked him, a language he did not understand. Knowledge of the past, of himself, intertwined with the faded loops and twirls of the claustrophobic scrawl on the brittle pages. Benjamin had liked science in school, loved to tussle with math problems and chemical equations, but after *Matrone* died, his priorities changed. School seemed unimportant when all he could think about was how to survive another day. Tessa was the only reason he managed to pass his exams. She coached him through long nights and made excuses for classes he missed as he stood in line at the pension office, praying that they would accept his forged letter one more time. But the journal had woken a dormant need to know what he was. What he and Tessa were.

Benjamin stuck his thumb into the air. Most people had sons or grandsons in the army, so hitching a ride was easy. The car that stopped already had a soldier in the back. Benjamin crammed in, his duffel bag stuck halfway out the car window to fit. The other soldier answered the inane questions of the elderly couple in the front, while Benjamin pretended to fall asleep. *Matrone*'s words echoed in his mind. "You're special, Benjamin. Chosen." She had repeated it till her last breath. And then there was Hester, the name tied to the only live male birth in the journal. He felt anger knot his insides. He was the product of suffering, of depravity. God's work distorted by the hand of man. If the woman who was his mother had lived, would she have even wanted to look at him? A need running deeper than his shame drove him back to the journal night after night, turning the pages even as the ground gave way beneath him. He had to find out why God had allowed him to be.

Buildings and people crammed together as they approached the city center, houses giving way to offices, apartment buildings and stores. The couple dropped them off in the town square, Preller Plein, where they lined up at the whites only sign to wait for buses. On the opposite side of the square, black men and women crowded for transportation to the *location*.

The noise and bustle of the city ground on Benjamin's nerves, the feelings of self-loathing churning his mind. All these people around him were happy in the little self-knowledge they possessed, while he was living with a truth that would shake them to the core. He was an abomination, created by evil, a dark thing to scare children with. Jooste had called it a gift, something of value. What value did a long life have if you had no art for living? The fear and loneliness of his childhood crawled out of the recesses of his mind. The burn scar on his leg itched, the skin thick and strange to the touch. Benjamin grabbed his duffel and started walking. He had to be alone with his thoughts.

Benjamin found the spare key in the old chicken coop in the back of the house and let himself in. The musty, sticky smell of illness clung to the air inside. The milk in the refrigerator was sour and the old stray cat that Andrew had adopted toward the end was begging for food. In Tessa's room, he found her silver necklace on the nightstand. He hooked the chain around his middle and index fingers, clutching the small cross in his palm. He had bought it for her with his first army paycheck, and she promised to always wear it. He felt uneasy, out of sorts. He lay down on her bed, clutching the pillow, comforted by the lingering smell of her.

The noise of a car pulling up to the house woke him. He crept through the dark to the kitchen. The large clock on the wall had just gone eleven. Benjamin slipped out the back door and clung to the shadows. In front of the house, a black man sat behind the wheel of an old pickup. Tessa hunched in the passenger seat, her eyes swollen, her cheeks wet. She wiped her face with the sleeve of her dress. The black talked to her, his eyes trained in front of him. Tessa leaned over and hugged the man, holding his head between her hands, kissing him. Benjamin clenched his fists. As Tessa got out of the pickup, their eyes met. A strange look froze her features, as if she was disappointed that it was him standing there. The black couldn't see Benjamin and started backing up. Tessa's silhouette, illuminated in the headlights, threw a shifty shadow against the house's brick walls as the pickup turned back to the main road.

"Ben." Almost a whisper, marred with something he imagined to be guilt.

"I got out today."

"*Pa*, he . . ." Tessa bit her lip. There was the stink of sweat and disease on her. *Matrone* Jansen had smelled like that the day she gave her last breath.

Pity softened his anger. "When?"

"Last night."

"You didn't call."

"I needed to be alone."

"With a black man?" Fear and anger cracked through the veneer. It always lingered so close to the surface.

Tessa crossed her arms. "Don't."

"There are laws, Tessa. You kissed him. Both of you can be locked up."

"It wasn't like that."

"Then what?"

"Ben, please." She hung her head.

"Who is he? Answer me."

Tessa sighed. "That was Andrew's son. My brother, Phillip."

Benjamin's lungs filled again. "You never told me."

"He left. A long time ago. When *Pa* got sick I went looking for him. I found the deed for land *Pa* owned—"

"Blacks can't own property. He can't take it from you."

"That's not what it's about. For God's sake, Ben."

"Don't use the Lord's name."

Tessa frowned. "Sorry."

"It's late. Where were you?"

"There's no phone in the *location*. I had to let him know that *Pa* was gone." She turned to go into the house, but Benjamin blocked her way.

"Ben, please. I'm tired and it's cold." Her spirit seemed gone, the hardship of the past few months too much to bear. Benjamin longed for her to look at him the way she used to.

Tessa suddenly reached for him, her hand resting on his. "I don't want to fight." She stepped closer. "Please. Hold me."

Benjamin wrapped his arms stiffly around her. He felt foolish for doubting her. Things would get better now, he was sure of it. "I'm sorry about your *pa*," he said. She needed him, and he would take care of her. Soon she would be his Tessa again. They would be happy.

Tessa kissed him on the cheek, her face wet against his. She held on to him, her lips searching for his, her left hand rubbing the back of his neck. It always calmed him, this simple gesture. He kissed her, a tenderness between them. Tessa unbuttoned his uniform's buttons, running her hands over his clavicles and down to his chest, her touch awakening every nerve ending in his body. They'd experimented with these things before, always with restraint, aware of the line that shouldn't be crossed, but something now felt different.

"Tessa, don't." Benjamin pushed her hands away, fighting the raw gnawing need, his skin clammy, his heart racing. He had always walked God's path, followed the rules. It had taken every ounce of his willpower never to let things go further, but it had to be right when they went before the altar, both of them pure, their union blessed.

Tessa stepped away from him, vulnerable, her eyes pale as the moon, pain lodged so deep that he suddenly doubted whether he would ever be able to bring her back. She walked away from him, disappearing into the house.

"I'm sorry," he said when he caught up to her. "When we're married . . ."

Tessa's slight frame was outlined by the soft light falling through the kitchen window. Her hands fumbled behind her back and Benjamin heard the sound of her zipper. Benjamin wished the dark would mask the truth for him, just like it did for everybody else, but when her dress fell to the ground, he didn't look away. She was beautiful, her body lean and pale. He knew he'd be able to circle her waist with his hands if he tried. The thought of touching her skin woke a desire so strong that he panicked.

"Put your clothes back on." The words came out harsher than he intended.

"For one night, can't we just be human, Ben?" Tessa's voice pleaded, quiet, desperate. She searched his face, tears flowing down her cheeks.

She unhooked the clasp of her bra and let it fall to the floor, revealing full breasts that before now he'd only ever guiltily imagined. She slid her stockings down and stepped out of her underwear. He could sense the heat of her body, his own rising in turn.

Tessa stepped closer. She took his hands and cupped them over her breasts. "Please." Her lip quivered. "I need you." Her hands guided him, running them over her softness, guiding him inside her until his will succumbed to hers, his body banishing his mind as they came together, the same being, one, before God.

Tessa

Tessa ran her eyes over the pews as she walked out of the church. Nobody had come to mourn Andrew. He had spent his life hiding her from people and ended up hiding from the world himself. Flippie had stayed away, but he had no choice, there would probably have been a scene if he had tried to enter a white church. She had been alone with Andrew when he died, having watched his body struggle for months, losing by measures, death robbing him of his quiet dignity. He hadn't even known she was there in his last hours. She had said goodbye as he fought for his last, rattling breath, her lips on his weathered palms.

"Ready?" Ben held the Chevy door for her. He was lean enough to fit into one of Andrew's suits, but had grown almost six inches while in the army. She had let out the seams as much as possible, but he still looked like a teenager in borrowed clothes.

"Tessa?" Mrs. Uys stood outside the church in her Sunday best, her hair speckled with silver, her figure crumpled. "I saw the obituary in the paper. I'm so sorry for your loss."

"Thank you." Tessa wondered why the woman had come to gawk at her suffering.

"Every dark day is always followed by a brighter one," Mrs. Uys smiled, looking at Benjamin. "I'm sure funeral bells will be replaced by wedding bells." Ben smiled shyly.

Tessa clenched her fists. "I'm sorry, but we have to go."

"You're in my prayers," Mrs. Uys said.

Tessa didn't answer her. "Wedding bells," she muttered under her breath as they drove away.

"We have to decide on a date." Ben turned onto the main road.

A possessiveness had crept into the way Ben talked to her since Andrew's death. He had taken charge of the funeral and other arrangements with an air of authority she hadn't thought him capable of. He now refused to let her out of his sight, wouldn't even leave her alone to grieve. It was suffocating. Tessa had always believed that it was her destiny to be with Ben. Finding him had meant that she wasn't alone anymore, that there was one person she could be completely honest with, a person who would be able to walk life's journey with her. He had always been like a lost child, eager to please, clinging to her like she was his salvation. And she had always felt that it was her responsibility to make up for the bad he had been through in his life, a life she had been spared because of Andrew. Perhaps she had mistaken that responsibility for love. After their night together, Tessa had realized the truth. She didn't love him, at least not the way that he wanted her to.

"I think we should wait," she said. She knew she was a coward, but she didn't have the energy for a fight.

Ben glanced over at her, his boyish face contracting in an adult frown. "We have waited, Tessa. It's time we make it right."

"I don't want to get married, Ben." Tessa felt relief as soon as the words left her mouth.

Ben kept his eyes trained on the road. In the sunlight coming through the windshield, his high cheekbones cast dark shadows, making him look gaunt, hollow.

"Did you hear me?" Tessa searched his face for any sign of emotion, relief turning to feelings of guilt. "Ben?"

"We already are one before God, Tessa. The rest is a piece of paper for the scrutiny of men, a matter of formality."

Tessa stared at him in disbelief. "I don't want to. Don't you understand?"

Ben turned into the *plot*'s driveway and parked the car. He got out and opened the door for her.

"Ben! Are you listening to me?" Tessa got out. Her childhood friend was gone. Before her stood a stranger, a man who was demanding a lifelong obligation. "I need time alone," she said. "To figure things out."

"We'll figure them out together, Tessa. We're together now, like we always talked about." He was close to her now, his arms around her. "You're all that matters. I won't let you go." He had grown strong in the army, his embrace unforgiving. He put his hand behind her head, weaving his fingers through her hair, pulling painfully at the roots. "Tell me for always. Like you promised, Tessa." He touched the silver cross around her neck with his free hand, caressing it tenderly. "Promise. For always." His grip tightened forcefully when she didn't respond.

Tessa gasped, fear opening her eyes. "For always, Ben," she whispered.

Benjamin

Benjamin threw the covers off, the predawn cold creeping on his bare skin. "Tessa?" He touched the indentation in the pillow next to him. Her clothes were draped over her desk chair, her shoes kicked into the corner, where she'd left them the night before. He got up and pulled a sweater on. "Tessa!"

He stumbled through the house, room by room. The kitchen was cold, empty, as was the living room. Tessa's toothbrush lay on the sink in the bathroom, her towel damp on the rack. He glanced out the window, feeling somewhat relieved when he saw the Chevy still parked under the awning. She had probably gone for a walk. He decided to go join her. But Benjamin hesitated outside Andrew's bedroom, a nagging feeling taking hold of him. Tessa hadn't cleaned out the old man's things yet. The thick curtains were drawn, the dank air inside the room stifling. He opened the closet. Next to Andrew's two pairs of shoes, one for work and one for church, gaped a space where an old leather suitcase was usually kept.

Benjamin ran back to Tessa's room. He frantically opened the top drawer of her dresser. Conspicuous rearrangements camouflaged the spaces where her favorite things used to be—a baby-blue cardigan, a cream scarf, a pair of stockings. He opened the next drawer. Her brown skirt, her sun hat, the small jewelry box. He turned all the drawers over, clothes piling on the floor. Her shoes with the kitten heels, her flower-print dress. Something sharp dug into his bare left foot. Tessa's silver cross lay on the ground, entangled with a sock. The realization hit home with such force that Benjamin thought his heart had stopped. Tessa had left him. He sunk down on the floor, reeling from the pain in his chest. Shadows flooded his mind. He was a boy again, never telling what happened in storerooms or in hospital bathrooms. He tried to breathe but the air held no oxygen. He knew now that he deserved that punishment, that shame. Not even Tessa could love him. How could he go on without her?

"I'll do anything you want, God," Benjamin murmured. He repeated the words, his body shivering on the cold floor. "Give her back to me. I'll do anything." Light had overpowered darkness and succumbed again by the time His answer came.

Benjamin slowly pushed himself off the floor. His limbs felt strange, alien, reborn. He took a few trembling steps, feeling the flutter of renewed strength awakening inside him. He would find Tessa, no matter what it took. God had promised to show him the way.

The Maitland Hotel was doused in opulence, the gilded mirrors lining walls that reflected crystal chandeliers and dark oaks, vulgar and obscene as the jewels and gowns that walked past Benjamin. Condescending glances rested momentarily on the disheveled intruder in the ill-fitting suit. *It would be easier for a camel to pass through the eye of a needle.* Benjamin glared back at them with disdain as he walked through the marbled lobby, the emptiness inside him trumping any pride.

Jooste waited at the hotel bar, a brandy in front of him. He looked at ease in these surroundings, as if the smoky haze were an extension of himself, a stench that infiltrated the cracks and crevices of the room, clinging to every person there who, in turn, carried it out with them into the world.

"So you've changed your mind," Jooste said as Benjamin sat down on the stool next to him. The bartender poured another brandy without asking and placed it in front of Benjamin.

Jooste nodded at a man walking by. He turned his attention back to Benjamin. "Well?"

Benjamin took a sip of his brandy, swallowing caution with the burning liquid. "I need things," he said when he emerged from the numbness.

"What are we talking about?"

"All the journals."

"*Ja?*"

Benjamin didn't take his eyes off his glass. "I want to join the Broederbond."

Jooste paled slightly. "What do you know about the Bond, boy?"

"That being a member opens those doors you talked about. Gets you access to work, an education, information." Benjamin had frantically searched for Tessa for days, not sleeping, barely eating. He had even gone to the *location* to try to find the black she had been with. She had simply disappeared. Members of the Broederbond had connections, reach, a network of eyes that stretched across the country. They could find her for him.

"We are a cultural organization, no more. I don't know what you think—"

"I know what you are, Mr. Jooste. Cultural organizations don't need to operate in secret."

"The Bond is an organization of leaders. We've united the Afrikaners, raised them up economically, spiritually, politically. To do that, we need to operate without scrutiny." Jooste gave Benjamin a calculating look. "What could you possibly offer us? You're nobody."

Barely contained anger tickled Benjamin's extremities. He clenched his jaw, keeping his voice low. "You and the *Broeders* plan to make the Afrikaners a superior race."

"I never said—"

"You want to play God, Mr. Jooste? You'll need His monster. That makes me somebody."

Jooste eyed Benjamin, his drink poised in the air. "The girl—"

"She's gone."

Jooste narrowed his eyes, the thin flesh folding over shallow veins. "What do you mean?"

"You might be her father, Mr. Jooste, but know this, she belongs to me. If you go near her, I will kill you." As Benjamin said this, he knew he meant every word.

"I'm not scared of idle threats, *ja*." Jooste took his hat off the counter. He downed the rest of his drink. "You have no idea who you're dealing with, boy."

"Do we have a deal?"

Jooste hovered for a moment, a tug of war between desires in his expression. "I may have underestimated you," he said at last. "You have more backbone than Frank said you did." He asked the bartender for a pen and scribbled an address on a piece of paper. "Be here in the morning."

"Be strong!" Benjamin called after him, mocking the Broeder-bond motto. Jooste didn't look back. Benjamin emptied his brandy and ordered another on the old man's tab.

6

Professor Koch's large desk loomed in front of Alet. Behind it, a wall of books lined the windowless office, arranged alphabetically. Everything about the room indicated a careful, methodical mind, but Koch was not at all what Alet had expected while talking to him on the phone. She had envisioned a man not unlike her father, stern and studious. In real life, Koch reminded her of a rubber ball with too much bounce, short and round and always fidgeting, a lisp sidling into his speech when he got excited. He had a full head of gray hair, a scraggly goatee, and porcine eyes obscured by heavy glasses, the frames at least ten years out of date.

Koch squinted over the rim of the case file. "I need to examine the body."

Alet shifted, uncomfortable in the straight-backed wooden chair. "I have to check with my captain about a transfer."

"Never mind that." Koch waved his hand, his short fat fingers blurring together. "I'm not new at dealing with the police. It'll take a month of paperwork. By that time, the evidence will have been compromised by some nincompoop who thinks he knows what he's doing. I'll come to you." He jumped out of his seat as if he was ready to start the journey right away.

Alet suddenly felt sorry for Dr. Oosthuizen. "As I explained on the phone, Professor, we don't really have a budget to pay your consultation fee. I was hoping that—"

"I suspected as much. Don't worry. The university administration smiles on my cooperation with the SAPS. Helps with fund-raising."

Koch curled the corners of his mouth in distaste. "Justifies their existence, come review time."

Koch dialed a three-digit extension on his office phone. "Mike? Could you pick up some samples? This has priority." He put the phone down and lifted Oosthuizen's preliminary autopsy report to his face again.

"Thanks for agreeing to this, Professor."

"Well, you did drop Adriaan Berg's name." There was a note of hostility in Koch's voice. "And since you brought your father into the conversation, I don't mind telling you that I am not one of his lackeys."

"I didn't think—"

Koch held up his hand to silence her. "Under normal circumstances I would have put the phone down, but you had the good sense to identify your purpose first. I will give this case my full attention, but any sign of Adriaan Berg getting involved and I will leave you to your own devices. Understand?"

"I understand." Alet tried to hide her nervousness with a smile. It had taken a few phone calls, but she had tracked Professor Koch down at the University of Cape Town. Convincing Mynhardt that they should bring an outsider in on the case was a lot harder. He only relented when she hinted that it might have been her father's idea, playing up the high-profile cases her dad and Koch had solved together. If this led nowhere, she would be on traffic duty for the rest of her life.

There was a knock at the door. A slender man in his mid-thirties stepped into the room. Sandy hair encroached on his shirt collar. He had a full beard, neatly trimmed, masking sculpted features, his eyes framed by thick black-rimmed glasses.

"Constable Berg, this is my colleague, Mike Engelman. Mike, this is Constable Berg from Unie Police."

Mike's gaze lingered momentarily on Alet's bruised face before he extended his hand. His grip was firm, his hands not as soft as one would expect from a typical academic. "Nice to meet you, Constable."

"You too, Mr. Engelman."

"Actually it's Dr. Engelman," Koch interrupted.

"Call me Mike."

"Alet."

"Mike has done some very interesting research on DNA mutations in viruses. Maybe you've read about it?" Koch looked at her expectantly.

Alet smiled apologetically.

"Unie Police requested a homicide consult." Koch spoke to Mike as if Alet had disappeared from the room. "I'm on my way there to do the autopsy."

"Do you need me to come along?"

"No need to disrupt both our lives. One would hope the local coroner is able to assist. Would you mind running DNA on these, though? Seems we're the only two people in this department interested in working in December." He picked up the evidence bags Alet had brought. Alet had included cigarette butts she'd found at the war lookout as well as the blood scraping and samples of the victim's tissue for comparison.

"And there I hoped I would be let out of my cage." Mike smiled at Alet, a dimple forming in his right cheek.

"Tell your coroner to have the body ready, Constable Berg," Koch said. "I'll be there by six."

"Why don't you wait till morning, Nico? Perhaps Alet would like some lunch. She could fill us in on the case?"

"No need to talk about it." Koch's irritation was clear. "Evidence speaks for itself. The less I know, the better." He dipped frantically into supply closets, cramming instruments into a steel case. "Case details are not our concern."

Mike opened the office door. "I'll walk you out, Alet. This place is a maze." Most men were nervous around her when she was in uniform, but Mike spoke to her with relaxed charm as he guided her through the building's corridors. "So how about lunch?" They had come to the building's main entrance. "There's a nice curry place around the corner."

"I have another appointment. Sorry." Alet was surprised that she meant it. Mike had asked pointed, interesting questions about the case, and it felt good to be able to talk about it with someone who knew what he was doing. It also felt good to be taken seriously.

"Maybe some other time, then?"

"*Ja.*" Alet returned his smile.

"This is my cell." Mike scribbled his number on a card. "In case you have questions."

"*Dankie.*" Alet took the card from him, wondering if this could be more than an offer for lunch. Mike extended his hand formally, and she pushed the thought out of her mind. She was here to solve a crime.

She was greeted by the misty Cape morning as she exited the building. Roman pillars and gables adorned every building on the beautiful old campus, a reminder of the colonial Dutch who had settled here in the 1600s. Alet made her way to the university's main entrance, down a long stone staircase that led to the street. A man sat on the bottom step, leaning against the ivy-covered walls, his blue dress shirt tight over his broad back and muscled arms. Fine water droplets from the morning drizzle clung to his black buzz cut. Alet almost reached out to brush them off, but stopped herself. The last time she'd seen Theo van Niekerk, they were both standing in front of a police disciplinary committee, Theo relaying the facts of their affair with a deadpan expression, admitting guilt without argument. She had felt betrayed, and she'd left Johannesburg without speaking to him again. She'd heard from mutual friends that Theo had taken a position at the University of Cape Town's criminology department.

Theo turned, his face breaking into a smile when he saw her. "Alet." She knew there would be a crease in his dress pants, ironed in with military precision, even before he got up. Theo kissed her on the cheek, his hands on her shoulders in an easy gesture.

"Thanks for meeting me, Theo."

"No worries. I'm just up the block a bit." Theo gestured at the campus behind them, which was sheltered by the back side of Table Mountain, its peak obscured by thick clouds. Once, when she was little, Alet and her father had taken the cable-car ride up on a day like this. Everything around her had been white, the world simply disappearing. At the top, Adriaan had let go of her hand. He had taken a few steps away from her, and the white swallowed him up completely. Alet remembered crying hysterically because she could not find him. Adriaan stepped out of the mist as easily as he had disappeared. He picked her up and pressed his lips close to her ears. "Don't you know that nobody can see you here?" he smiled. Alet had trouble understanding why this had made him happy.

Alet stepped out of Theo's embrace. "You look good." There was a relaxed air about him that Alet had never seen before, settling in his dark almond-shaped eyes and smoothing out his brow.

Theo patted his stomach. "A little more padding, I think. But look at you! What's with the . . ." He gestured at her bruises.

"Slammed my face into a suspect's shoe a few times. I'm thinking of starting a trend."

Theo laughed. "You always look beautiful." The remark hung awkwardly between them.

"I hear there's a good curry place nearby," Alet said, choosing to ignore the comment.

"You heard right. Aggie's Kitchen has the best fish curry this side of the mountain. Shall we?"

Like an old habit, a memory of lazy evenings, Alet fell in step with Theo. He had been in the middle of a nasty divorce and custody battle when she started STF training. They both knew what would happen if anyone found out about them, so they tucked their relationship into weekends and secret nights, playing the role of instructor and student during the daytime. It had been exciting, skulking around in the shadows of the forbidden. Alet often wondered what would have happened if they hadn't been caught.

Aggie's Kitchen was a bright little hole-in-the wall with yellow tablecloths and plastic chairs. Theo ordered for them, rattling off more dishes than Alet thought they could finish.

"So . . . to what do I owe this pleasure?" Theo laced his fingers together, resting his chin on his hands.

"I was in the area. I thought we could catch up."

"Don't get me wrong, it's good to see you, but months of silence and then a call out of the blue?"

"Before . . . it was all . . ." Alet searched for the right words. "Too much."

"*Ja.*" Theo looked away.

"So, you're teaching, huh?"

Theo leaned back. "At least nobody gets killed if something goes wrong, hey."

Alet nodded. She felt guilty. Theo had loved his work in STF. At least she'd gotten to stay on the police force, even if it was in the middle of nowhere.

"How about you? Must be quite a change of pace over there in Unie. Lowest crime in the Western Cape, according to statistics."

"You looked it up?"

"Research is most of what I do these days." Theo cracked his interlaced fingers. "I'm connected, you might say."

Alet laughed. "It's not that bad. I'm investigating a murder at the moment. That's why I'm in Cape Town. We're collaborating with Professor Koch on forensics. Do you know him?"

"Only by reputation."

"He really doesn't like my dad."

Theo shrugged. "It's Adriaan Berg, what do you expect?"

"I know he's not an easy person, but there's something else going on between them."

"Interesting."

"I hate it when you do that."

"What?"

"The way you say 'interesting,' when you know something I don't." The corners of Theo's mouth spread, warming his whole face.

"*Ja?*" she went on.

"It's rumors, mostly. Which is why I won't repeat them." The quotation marks between Theo's eyes deepened. "If you want, I can look into it."

Alet hesitated. Policemen all did things that they weren't proud of in the apartheid era, and these days old misdeeds had a nasty way of coming to light at the worst possible time. If she was going to work with Koch, she needed to know who she was dealing with before it buggered up her case come court day. "*Ja.*" she said. "If you can, that would be great."

A plump woman with Malay features came over to their table. She had an array of plates and small dishes balanced on each arm. Fish curry, yellow rice, *waterblommetjie* stew, sambals, and fruit chutneys threatened to spill over the edge of the table by the time she had unloaded her burden. Theo bowed his head for a second, his lips moving quietly before he picked up his fork.

"I'm in trouble, Theo." Alet hadn't planned on bringing up the subject, least of all to Theo, but she needed someone to talk to. Theo knew what it was like to be on the wrong side of the SAPS.

He finished his first bite of curry. "Man, that's *lekker*." He put his fork down. "So now we come to the real reason you're here."

"You know what, never mind."

"Sorry." Theo reached for her arm. "Tell me."

Alet took a deep breath. "I shot a hijacker."

"Is he dead?"

"Not last time I checked."

Theo withdrew his hand and picked up his fork. "You're okay, then."

"He wasn't an immediate threat, see? That, and my demotion, all in under a year . . ." She bit her lip.

"With all the corruption going on in the police? It takes more than that, believe me. This job has opened my eyes. We get to research all the cases, put them in a spreadsheet for statistics. Superintendents taking bribes, dockets disappearing. One day a guy is under investigation, the next, he gets promoted. Can't say I blame them for trying to make extra cash, though. You know that working here, at the university, it's the first time that I don't have to choose between child support and a decent place to live."

Alet felt her mood souring. "*Ja*, but I'm pigmentally challenged, see? They'll go after me to set an example."

Theo's eyes grew hard with the same deadpan expression he'd worn at their hearing. Alet wished that she had bitten her tongue. Theo's mother was coloured, his white father a lowlife who had skipped town the moment he'd found out she was pregnant. Theo had had to fight both poverty and stereotypes all his life.

"I'm sure your dad can call in a few favors, make the docket disappear," Theo said.

"What?"

Theo shrugged. "I got kicked out. You got to stay." He pushed his food around on his plate. "It doesn't take a genius to figure out the difference between us."

Alet knew she was foolish to have contacted Theo, to try to confide in him as if nothing had happened. She pushed her chair out. "You know what, I have to go."

"You haven't even tasted your curry yet." Theo spoke with a measured joviality that barely masked his anger. Alet knew all too well the way he shut down.

"I have to get back to Unie," she said. "Get things ready for Koch."

"Suit yourself."

Just outside the door Alet looked back at him. Theo didn't notice, didn't look up from his food. There was that pressure behind her eyes again, but she refused to give in.

Professor Koch removed the victim's charred bowels from the abdominal cavity. He ran his gloved hand along the large intestine, like he was stuffing *boerewors*. The stench penetrated the Vicks VapoRub that Alet had smeared under her nostrils earlier. Mathebe seemed unfazed as he scribbled in his notebook, his neck stiff, his expression stony. He had hardly spoken to her since she'd gotten back, nodding curtly when she told him about Koch's impending visit.

On the exam table, a Y-shaped gash sliced through the corpse's chest cavity, running from both shoulders down the center of the body to its pubic bone. Organs, tongue still attached to esophagus and lungs, were spread on a stainless-steel tray. It reminded Alet of the offal her grandmother used to cook for Sunday lunch when she felt nostalgic for the farm life of her childhood. Gerda would usually treat Alet to a well-done burger at the Wimpy after.

Koch muttered an occasional, "Can't conclusively determine," and other medical terminology into a small microphone, his tongue lingering on his teeth, producing muddled sibilant sounds. He seemed unaware of their presence, only acknowledging Oosthuizen when he needed information on the "damage" he had done with his earlier handling of the corpse. Oosthuizen answered questions patiently, unfazed by Koch's remarks. Yes, he took the X-rays of the body while it was still in the body bag. No, the right arm had detached during removal from the crime scene. Yes, soil samples were taken from the surrounding area to examine the melted body fat. He quietly handed Koch forceps, pruning shears and something that looked very much like a bread knife, taking photographs and measurements of the brain, body parts and organs when instructed to do so.

"Well, I think that's it," Koch said, peeling his gloves off and dumping them in a bio-waste container. "I'll leave you to close her up while I compile the report."

Oosthuizen took the primary position next to the table, methodically sealing the bowels and intestines in a plastic bag before returning them to the body cavity. Koch washed his hands at the sink, scrubbing his nails with a small brush. Alet followed him and Mathebe out of the room, relieved when Mathebe suggested that they conduct the interview at the station the next morning. Koch, however, wasn't as pleased.

"You may not realize this, but I do have other responsibilities."

"Please, Professor." Alet tried her best to calm him down. "Captain Mynhardt wants to sit in. It's late and I'm sure you're tired. We'll be much more productive in the morning."

Koch waved his puffy hand as if he was swatting flies. "Just as well. It might take till morning to explain all your man's mistakes." He waddled to his car. As soon as he got in, he bounced out again. "I don't know if I can find the guesthouse again."

"You really can't get lost here. I can ride along with you," Alet offered. Tilly would be closing Zebra House's bar in the next fifteen minutes; perhaps she could make last call.

"I need to discuss a few details of the case with Constable Berg, Professor," Mathebe said before she could get into Koch's car. "You can follow this street to the main tar road. Turn right and then left when you reach the big stone church. Zebra House is up the block."

Koch's sedan disappeared down the road, dust billowing in its wake. Mathebe headed for the police van without a word. He waited until Alet had closed the passenger side door before he spoke.

"Professor Koch's assistance will be valuable." Mathebe didn't make eye contact.

"Lucky break, hey." Alet hoped this wouldn't take long.

Mathebe took a deep breath. "I have shown you respect since you joined the Unie police service, Constable Berg. Have I not?"

"*Ja.*" A dull headache suddenly flared behind Alet's eyes.

"I do my best to show respect to all, because I believe it is the only way to move forward. Things were not fair in the past, but no matter what was done to me or how I was treated, I cannot hold anyone but the person who did those things responsible. I keep my feelings here," he brought the fingertips of his right hand together and touched them to his chest, "and my actions here." He touched his forehead.

"Very healthy of you."

"Then why do you feel that I should not be respected in return, Constable Berg?"

"What are you talking about?"

"Captain Mynhardt appointed me to lead this investigation. I trust that he believed I could do the job."

"Look, Johannes—"

Mathebe held his hand up. "Please give me the opportunity to finish what I have to say."

Pressure built at Alet's temples.

"You did not feel it was necessary to involve me in recruiting Professor Koch. You withheld your findings from searching the path and lookout. You neglected to mention Doctor Oosthuizen's findings about the race of the victim. You did not come to me with any of this information. Instead, you went to Captain Mynhardt."

"I had to get permission from the captain to involve Koch."

"You did not include me in the investigation of which I am in charge. Is this not true?"

"Dammit, Johannes. We only got Koch because of me. It wasn't as if I was taking anything away from you. Besides, you would have stopped me before I even picked up the phone."

Mathebe pursed his lips. "You still do not understand."

"Explain it to me, then, because it seems that the only progress in this case happened because of me."

"That is the way you see it."

"There's no other way to see it." Alet stared out the windshield of the van. The clinic was dark, except for the bright fluorescents in the makeshift autopsy room. Oosthuizen was alone with the body, touching its charred fragile exterior, stitching it back together. She shuddered.

"I thank you for your help in this investigation, Constable Berg, but I do not believe that your continued presence will be a benefit in solving this case."

It took a moment for Mathebe's words to sink in. "You're kicking me off?"

"I will discuss the situation with Captain Mynhardt in the morning."

The sudden rush of blood to Alet's face augmented the hammers in her skull. "This is *kak*. You hear me?"

Mathebe closed his eyes.

"And stop doing that. It's getting old." Alet got out, slammed the door and started walking to Kerk Street. Mathebe started the engine and drove away.

Zebra House was dark by the time Alet reached it. She went around the back to see if Tilly was still there. The kitchen door was unlocked and she felt her way to the hallway. A slither of light snuck out from under the door of the management office. Muffled voices entwined in a heated discussion.

". . . let me talk to him, sort things." A man. Jeff Wexler, if Alet was not mistaken.

"What if he doesn't?" Tilly's strained reply.

"Dear child, I'm not hiding anything from you."

"Wouldn't be the first time."

"You're being paranoid. Make the call."

The door opened before Alet had time to step back into the kitchen. Wexler stopped short, a peculiar look on his face when he saw her. "What are you doing here?"

Alet smiled. "I was looking for Tilly."

Wexler's initial surprise morphed into practiced charm. "She's just finishing up, Constable." He looked back into the office.

Tilly's head appeared in the door behind him. She looked tired, her mascara lightly smeared, forming asymmetrical black lines in the corners of her eyes.

"Hey, Till. You up for a drink?"

"I'll be there now-now," Tilly said. "Give me a minute."

"I'm afraid I've kept you from your plans, Mathilda."

"No, I didn't—"

Wexler turned to Alet. "Why don't I pour you a nightcap, Constable?"

"*Ja* . . . Thanks." Alet followed Wexler to the bar, wondering what exactly she had overheard.

"Can you appreciate a good scotch, Constable Berg?" Wexler reached under the bar and produced a bottle. "I hide this from the plebeians."

"I drink whiskey."

"Prepare to be delighted, then." Wexler set out two short glasses and poured a healthy measure into each. It was smoother than anything Unie had to offer, subtle layers of flavor dancing on Alet's tongue.

"You might be spoiling me for rotgut, Mr. Wexler."

Wexler laughed. "Life's too short to drink bad liquor, my dear." He took another sip. "Were you waiting long? Outside the office, I mean."

"No." Alet buried her nose in the glass. There was a tenseness in Wexler's charm, a wariness that made him seem all the more suspicious.

Tilly appeared in the doorway. "I'm sorry, Alet. Would you mind if we do this some other time? It's late and I have to make a supply run to Oudtshoorn in the morning."

"*Ja.* No worries." Alet pushed her chair away from the bar. "Hey, maybe I'll come with you? I have to go to Oudtshoorn anyway. We can catch up on the way." A brief look passed between Tilly and Wexler.

"I suppose that's okay," Tilly said.

Alet drained her glass. "Thanks for the drink, Mr. Wexler."

Wexler's fixed smile listed to the right. "Pleasure, Constable."

Alet felt strangely alert as she descended Zebra House's steps. Something was off and Wexler was involved, that much she was sure of. The fact that he had suddenly appeared in Unie the day of the murder was suspicious. And he had looked positively spooked when he thought that she had overheard his conversation with Tilly.

Without knowing the identity of the victim, there was no way to tie Wexler or anyone else to the murder. Alet desperately needed to put a name and a face to the charred remains. To do that, she had to find out what was in Koch's report before Mathebe got her kicked off the case.

1955

Flippie

The tension in Sophiatown's narrow streets was palpable as Flippie stepped off the bus. He walked over to a group of people gathered in front of an eviction notice, which had come three days earlier than the government had initially scheduled it. Flippie read over the converging heads, the words banal, the message clear. Vacate your homes and leave for Meadowlands by six a.m. Or else. Policemen armed with Sten guns and knobkerries drove by and the crowd dispersed, skulking back to their shacks.

The Odin Theater's lights were out as Flippie walked past, as if it too had given up. He had been a mere child, scared and troubled, when he first sat in its seats, wondering if he had made a mistake in coming to Johannesburg. He had followed an ANC man there from Bloemfontein. There was the promise of meaningful work, of getting an education, of the party looking after its own. But few were truly trusted. His fortune had changed when, on a lark, he submitted a satire about life in the township to *African Drum* magazine. He was offered a regular gig. The moment he had walked into the *Drum* offices, he forgot that he was a second-class citizen.

The sound of jazz ghosted in Flippie's mind, memories of the greats that had performed on the Odin's stage, Hugh Masekela blasting his trumpet, Miriam Makeba, her voice like a mournful call from God, he saw them all. And the parties, the rallies, black and white and coloured and Indian mixed in those seats, defiant of laws and regulations, bringing to life a world that could have been, everybody blissfully ignoring the precipice they were on. But the government was not blind to the dangers it posed. The government had introduced the Native Resettlement Bill, and Sophiatown was next.

The Odin's stage became host to political meetings, everyone eager to resist the Western Areas removal scheme. Through all the chanting, fists in the air, spirits high on skokiaan, they adhered to the policy of passive resistance. Some, like Mandela, brought up the possibility of violence, but the leaders put an end to such talk. They had resisted, and they had lost. That was all there was to it.

As he passed through Bertha Street, Flippie let his eyes rest on an enormous oak tree. Two souls had hanged themselves from its branches in protest some weeks before. Flippie had known one of the men from the 39 Steps, his favorite shebeen. Drunk on his own importance, Flippie had once accused him of being a police informant simply because the man didn't agree with Dr. Xuma's leadership. He now envied the man his conviction. But then again, what did the death of a black man prove to white men who wouldn't even share a bus seat for fear that they would catch the disease of colour?

Flippie needed a drink, to hear *mbaqanga* one last time, before it was silenced forever in Sophiatown. He drifted through the familiar streets, past the neat brick houses and the one-room shacks, walls with WE WONT MOVE painted on them in crude letters. He walked by the Jewish and Chinese shops on Good Street, gang members still hiding in dark corners, as if the notices were a bluff meant to deprive them of their fiefdoms. At the top of the rickety staircase he was greeted by silence. The shebeen door would not give, locked and bolted, as if Fatty had cared that someone might loot her establishment before it got bulldozed.

"Hey, you! *Sy's weg.* Gone yesterday *al.* You missed a *lekker* party." In the street below, a young boy waved at Flippie. He was a baby, no more than eight or nine, with scared eyes too big for his face. "You looking for *dop?*" The boy looked around for a moment as if asking permission from the shadows before answering. "Gestapo." He pointed at himself. "I fix you good."

Flippie laughed. "You're in a gang, hey? So where's this place?" He leaned on the railing. "This place I can get a *dop.*"

"Last shebeen standing in Sophiatown, *Baba.*" The boy looked around nervously. "Sell you by the bottle. You like you some whiskey? Gin? How 'bout some Barberton, hey? You give me two bob, I go get it for you. Cheap-cheap."

"Two bob? Sheesh!" Flippie sauntered down the stairs. Close up, he noticed the old flat cap on the boy's head, probably scavenged off the streets where people's unwanted things piled up as the time of leaving approached. "You think I'm stupid, hey? I give you my money, I never see your face again. You bring that *dop* here, then we talk."

The boy looked like he might cry, his scheme unraveling with the slightest resistance. Flippie reached out to touch his shoulder, meant as an apology for not being gullible. He was rewarded with a swift kick to the shin.

"Hey, you little *kak*!"

The boy took off, suddenly accompanied, out of nowhere, by a dog with a ratty coat. The pair disappeared down the street, into the confusion of people milling around in a resigned stupor.

Toby Street was lined with furniture and boxes. Children chased each other between the piles and made forts under chair legs. At number fifteen, Mamma Day backed out of her front door, clinging to a plank-backed wardrobe. She stood on her tiptoes, her hefty curves squished against the side as she tried to lift it.

"*Haai nee*, Philemon. Watch what you do. You going to drop it! Stupid man."

"Sorry, sorry, Mamma." Only Philemon's fingertips and the top of his fedora were visible behind the wardrobe. The two did a comical two-step, grunting and shuffling, negotiating their way down the front steps and into the street, Mamma Day cursing and Philemon apologizing.

"You need help, Mamma?" Flippie folded his jacket on top of the Sunlight Soap boxes that were tied with twine and piled high next to the couch. The whole scene was surreal, the cozy living room transported into the open air, as if somebody had erased the walls of Mamma Day's boardinghouse.

"Now you ask, you good-for-nothing." Mamma Day fell onto the sofa, its seams exploding with a poof. She used the tip of her head scarf to tap at sweat running down her face. "Where you been all day, *hê*?"

"Man's gotta earn a living, Mamma."

"You call that work? All you do is write stories and party. Not a scratch on your Florsheims."

"Is good work, Mamma. You then also read *Drum*."

"To make sure you can pay rent!"

Flippie laughed, but Mamma Day's eyes welled up. Tomorrow there would be no more boardinghouse, no more rent to collect. He sat down next to her, wrapping his arms around her soft shoulders.

"Hey now, Mamma. Hey. It's going to be all right."

Mamma shook her head, her voice a high-pitched wail struggling between sobs. "When I was a girl we lived in a shack by the mines. Police kicked us out. We moved, all the time. One squatter camp to the next. So I said to myself, save your money, Doris. No movies, no parties. I bought this house, here, with everything I had. When I moved that big coffin in, I thought, I'll never have to move it out again. This place is mine and nobody can make me go again."

Flippie took the handkerchief from his breast pocket and gave it to Mamma Day. She melted into him, blowing her nose without modesty, white cloth disappearing up her nostrils.

"You know what they are going to call it? The new name when the whites move in?"

Flippie nodded. Triomf. The whites' triumph over the likes of them.

"They won," Mamma Day said. She turned to look Flippie in the eye, her hand on his. "You promise me."

"What, Mamma?"

"Finish those classes at the university. So you become a big man. Help your people."

"I don't know, Mamma." Flippie looked away. He had finished his second year of law school, correspondence classes, but it was a futile dream. Black lawyers couldn't even defend their own people in court, and working for *Drum* offered easy money and good times.

"You're a smart boy, Phillip. Don't be a nothing. You promise!" She clutched him tighter.

"Okay, Mamma, okay. Don't cry."

Mamma Day pulled away. "This house isn't going to pack itself." She was her down-to-business self again, refusing to look at him. "I still have to clean everything."

"Mamma, don't do that."

"Nobody is going to look in these rooms and say I was a dirty *meit*, hear? You go now. Go pack. The lorries won't wait."

Flippie walked through the eerily empty rooms of number fifteen.

Mamma Day's bright batiks were gone, only their outlines visible on discolored walls. He pulled a battered suitcase out from under his bed and piled everything he owned into it. Travel light. Never put down roots, never be more than a suitcase away from leaving. Rules his father had lived by, drilled into him and Tessa. It had prepared him well for this day. He allowed himself only a moment to linger on the memories of his childhood.

Flippie helped Philemon carry his bed and the small dresser outside with the other things that were bound for a shack rented from the government. The water taps and outhouses would be communal because the government had decided that indoor plumbing was a luxury they didn't need. When he went back in to get his bag, Mamma Day was already going through his room with a broom.

"I'm going now, Mamma."

She paused, eying the suitcase in his hand.

Flippie suddenly felt guilty. "You know I can't come with you."

His skin was dark, his mother a black, so he was officially classified black, even though his father was white. Mamma Day was a coloured, descended from a long line of mixed blood, from the original Dutch colonists to the Malay and Chinese indentured laborers. For this distinction, a shade of brown, he had to go to Meadowlands and she to Eldorado Park. The government did tests when they weren't sure which category you fell into. The color of your eyes and the flatness of your nose were all measured. If a comb went smoothly through your hair, you were classified a coloured; if not, you were black.

"You take care of yourself," Mamma Day said without stopping her labor.

Flippie put his fedora on his head. "I will, Mamma."

Fear distorted the faces of the people he passed outside. Flippie pulled out the Mycro camera he had borrowed from one of his *Drum* colleagues. The picture quality wasn't great, but the camera was small and could be hidden easily. Small children sat on piles of debris, forlorn women in their Sunday best huddled near their possessions while men stood helplessly beside them. They all tried to smile when the flash went off, but mustered only looks of dazed bewilderment. The world had to see, this day had to be remembered, Flippie thought as he walked through the chaos.

The rumble of lorries rolled along the edge of day as two thousand policemen descended on the township. Resistance was met with practiced violence, a blow with a *sjambok*, the barrel of a gun pointed at the transgressor's head. Women clutched blankets around their shoulders, a last barrier between them and the invaders, as they waited their turn to be herded onto the backs of the trucks. Bulldozers flattened shacks minutes after their occupants walked out.

A commotion of angry male voices and a woman's screams drew Flippie's attention to the end of the block. Two white policemen raised their guns at the crowd of people that surrounded them. A third one held a small boy by the neck. Flippie recognized the little swindler from the night before. His dog lay at his feet, blood running from its mouth. The animal wasn't dead yet. It whimpered pitifully, its sides heaving. The boy struggled against the policeman, his arms flailing, tears running down his cheeks.

The policeman raised the *kierie* and brought it down on the boy's back, his face reddening from the strain. "That'll teach you, *boytjie!*" As he lifted his arm again, the boy looked over at Flippie, cowering in anticipation. A young woman stifled a scream as the blow fell, her hands cupped over her mouth.

"Officer!" Flippie ran toward them, not sure what he was going to do.

A sneer of contempt crossed the policeman's face. "Stay back, or you're next, *kaffir.*"

Flippie smiled, his shaking body belying his bravado. "I'm a reporter for *Drum*, sir. Could we have a picture?" He revealed the Mycro under his coat.

The policeman looked at this colleagues in a moment of indecision. It was enough to distract them. The boy broke loose and ran. The policeman pulled out a gun.

"*Nee*, Willem!" one of the other policemen shouted. He inclined his head toward Flippie.

The policeman trained his gun on the dog in frustration and fired. The animal's body jerked, the head wound ending its suffering. The panicked crowd scattered. He trained his gun on Flippie. "Give me that!" He stormed over to Flippie and knocked the camera out of his hands. The Mycro landed in the dirt and the policeman kicked it, stomping on what remained.

"You're done, okay?" The barrel of the gun remained trained on Flippie.

"*Ja, Baas.*" Flippie kept his eyes on the ground, aware of the animal fear clawing at his insides, commanding him to run. A sudden blow stung his cheek and he fell back. The policeman called Willem stared him down, daring him to retaliate. Flippie stayed down. He stared at the policeman's polished boots, wondering if this was how it all ended. His eyes stayed trained on those boots as they backed away, going back to loading the lorries. Flippie heard them shouting at people above the din.

"Are you all right, sir?" The young woman who had been so distressed stood before him. She was tall and slender, carrying herself with a grace that belied her worn dress.

Flippie nodded. He quickly looked away from her big eyes, knowing he'd break down if he stayed there one more moment.

"You're hurt." She touched her cheek.

Flippie became aware of a searing pain in the mirroring spot on his own cheek.

"Don't," she said as he lifted his hand.

"*Eina!*" His touch sparked a raw explosion, his fingers red with blood.

"It looks bad." She glanced around helplessly. "The clinic's been bulldozed. I can see to that once we get to Meadowlands."

"I'm all right," Flippie said. He struggled to get up, ignoring her outstretched hand. "Don't worry yourself, *Ousie.*"

"Prudence."

Flippie nodded. "Prudence."

"You were brave. My brother, Zweli, he . . ." Prudence put her hand to her mouth again. It took her a moment to speak. "I will help you." There was a quiet dignity about her, her words a statement of purpose. It was a faint flash, a vision of a future Flippie had never thought about, her life alongside his. He had accepted being alone as his fate, but he suddenly saw this woman, the possibility of more than himself, more than loneliness in a country that had pushed him to the margins. Flippie watched as Prudence walked toward the lorries, then he picked up his suitcase and followed her to Meadowlands.

Tessa

"I would like to bring a final motion to the floor, ladies."

Tessa sighed as the Free State Women's Agricultural Union's representative from Verkeerdevlei stood up. She was a hawkish woman, her lips permanently pursed, her hips too narrow to bear normal-size children. Tessa glanced at the enormous clock on the wall. It was three already. She'd never have enough time to run her errands.

Being in Bloemfontein brought back too many memories. As Tessa drove into town early that morning, she wondered what had happened to the *plot*, resisting the temptation to drive by it. She had left, what was it, seven years ago now? The realization shocked her. The passage of time seemed so irrelevant while you were living it. Only in hindsight did it become monstrous. She had had to steal away from her home like a thief, waiting on the platform all night, taking the first train out, getting off in Bethlehem. Two days later, she was employed as a housekeeper by a farmer named Booysen, a cantankerous widower. It was Booysen who had asked her to attend the annual meeting. "Women interfering with men's business," he had said. "Go listen what they are yammering about." As far as Tessa could tell, he was right about the yammering. Every motion was a charade of self-delusion and frivolous absurdity.

"We will hear the motion," the chairwoman said.

The representative from Verkeerdevlei folded her hands in front of her. She tilted her head to the left, her eyes looking up at the ceiling while she spoke. "Apartheid has been our way of life for some time now. Yet our dairies still accept milk and cream from Native farmers and mix it with those of Europeans. If we are to maintain apartheid in all spheres of life, I move that Native milk and cream be kept separate from those of white farmers and be designated strictly for Native use."

Next to Tessa, a bullfrog of a woman nodded her head vigorously.

"Mrs. Nel brings up a valid point," the chairwoman said. "We will open the floor to discussion."

"I second the motion." A plump woman with stiff hair and big hands stood up in the second row. "Nettie van der Spuy. Parys district." The woman turned to the assembly. "Separation is in the Bible.

God's plan. If we are to follow His will completely, then it is only right that we separate our food as well."

A round of applause followed.

"This is a waste of time." Tessa bounced up before she could stop herself. Heads turned in her direction.

"Please identify your district, missus?" The chairwoman raised her thin eyebrows. In her pink suit, she looked like a newborn rat.

"Miss Theresa Morgan, representing the Booysen farm, Bethlehem district."

Tessa's neighbor looked up at her, disapproval written in the folds of her face.

"Proceed."

"I would just like to point out to the representatives from Verkeerdevlei and Parys that the milking on dairy farms is certainly not done by the farmer or his wife. It is done by Native farmworkers. Do the representatives object to black hands touching the milk, or merely to ownership? And if it is the former, would they wish to do the milking themselves, or do they perhaps employ white farmworkers? If that is the case, I think they should share with the rest of the room how they manage to keep labor costs so low."

The chairwoman's hand covered her mouth in slow motion. There was complete silence in the room. The representative from Verkeerdevlei looked mortified, a crimson hue creeping up over the high collar of her dress, climbing up to her cheeks until her whole face was aflame. Whether it was from anger or embarrassment, Tessa didn't know. And she didn't care. She had sat all afternoon listening to motions, one more absurd than the next.

The chairwoman cleared her throat. "Miss Morgan certainly brings up a valid point." She paused, waiting for a response from the ladies. When none came, she turned to the representative of Verkeerdevlei, a placating smile on her lips. "I believe it might be premature to put this to a vote. I move that we discuss it with our men first and put it on the agenda for next time. And now, if Mrs. Nel would please lead us in a closing prayer?"

By "Amen," Tessa was already heading for her car. She had almost reached it when the representative from Verkeerdevlei stepped in front of her.

"You call yourself a Christian, Miss Morgan?"

"That is certainly none of your business, Mrs. . . . ?"

"Heyns. Well, I thought not." The woman lifted her nose in the air. If she hadn't been so annoyed, Tessa might have burst out laughing. She walked around the woman.

"So you live alone with a man on the farm?" The remark was full of innuendo.

Tessa turned around. "Jan Booysen is as old as the gates of Hell, Mrs. Heyns. I keep house and cook for him, that's all. I'm sorry you feel the need to insinuate something unseemly."

Mrs. Heyns looked ready to explode, her lips pursed so tight that new lines formed on top of the wrinkles around her mouth. "You have no respect."

"I have yet to find anyone here who warrants my respect, Mrs. Heyns. Good day."

Mrs. Heyns took a sharp breath. Tessa didn't wait for her to recover. She got into her car and drove off, leaving Mrs. Heyns in the dust of the show grounds, her mouth opening and closing like that of a fish on dry land.

Tessa drove into the city center. Booysen needed new overalls and she wanted to pick up a few things for herself. Bloemfontein had almost doubled in size since the last time she'd seen it. A big haberdashery had opened next to the pharmacy, with a sweet shop and a new department store just up the street. Tessa felt like a child again as she walked into the Woolworths, examining everything, stopping by a perfume counter and letting the saleslady dab a musky odor on her wrist. She selected new stockings and a hat for church, worrying that its blue flowers and wide rim might be too extravagant for Bethlehem.

"Tessa."

Tessa turned around. It was Ben. For the last seven years she had tried not to dwell on the past, but he had been on her mind since Booysen had asked her to come to Bloemfontein. For a moment she wondered if he was real. He was dressed in a gray suit, his pale-blond hair slicked back under his hat. No longer a boy, he carried himself with an air of authority. There was a maturity in his face that she hadn't remembered.

"Ben," she stumbled, clutching her packages in front of her. "I . . ." She wished she could see his eyes behind the dark glasses.

Ben's full lips curled into a generous smile. "I'm so happy to see you." His voice was a relaxed, honeyed bass. He leaned in and kissed her formally on the cheek.

"How have you been?" Tessa managed. She suddenly realized that she had missed him. You couldn't spend that many years sharing a secret with somebody without it altering you.

"Well . . . quite well." He looked around the store. "Still living on the *plot*. I hope you don't mind. I had nowhere else to go. If you need me to leave . . ."

"No, it's—"

"I kept up with the payments."

"I guess it's yours, then."

"I always thought it would be ours." He looked vulnerable, like the boy that had brought her back her schoolbag. "Perhaps we could talk? Tea at the hotel," he said quickly when Tessa hesitated, "that's all I ask." He smiled reassuringly.

Tessa nodded.

The restaurant bustled with women in hoopskirts and men in smart suits. Tessa pulled at her cardigan, feeling underdressed and self-conscious. Life on the farm didn't call for keeping up with the latest fashions. Ben pulled a chair out for her before sitting down on the other side of the table, his slender hands folded on top of the white linen tablecloth, an excited glint in his eyes. "Shall I order wine?"

It struck Tessa that she had never had alcohol in a public place before. Not only had she looked too young, but there was never money for that sort of thing. "Rooibos for me," she said apologetically.

"*Ja*. Of course." Ben looked put out.

"How have you been?" Tessa tried.

"I'm at the university now." Ben said it as if asking for approval, or perhaps waiting for praise. "Degree in biology." There was a light in his eyes. "I want to study this molecule that's been discovered. It's very exciting. It encodes our genetic instructions, see? They call it deoxyribonucleic acid. My professor says it could be the secret to what we are."

"I don't . . ." Tessa was unsure of where he was going with this.

"We always wondered why we were different." There was a tremor in Benjamin's hand. "I have the journals, Tessa. Of the man who caused us to be this way. Dr. Leath. I'm working to find what he did. How we began."

Tessa took in her breath at the mention of Leath. He was a dark creator, casting a shadow across time from the recesses of her imagination. What he did to her mother, to Sarah, was the work of madness, and she was his creation. She had watched people around her being born, blooming and withering in the blink of an eye. She should have been an old woman by now, yet she still wore the blush of youth.

Ben studied her face. "You knew about this?"

"My *ma* told me."

"You never told me." A frown spread across Ben's brow. He crossed his arms. "How could you keep something that important from me? You . . . you're a liar, Tessa. You always lie." His words held a mixture of regret and menace. It made the hairs at the back of Tessa's neck stand on end.

"I'm sorry, I don't think I can stay."

"No. Please listen to me." The intensity of Ben's gaze scared her. Tessa hovered on the edge of her seat. "I wanted to die when you left, Tessa." His words took on a frantic quality. "I didn't know how to go on without you."

"I'm sorry, Ben, I—"

"I wanted to end it, be rid of you in my head forever. I just couldn't . . . but then God spoke to me, see? It changed everything. I love you, Tessa. God help me, I still do after what you did to me. And seeing you today . . ."

"Ben, I—" Tessa looked away, seeking refuge in the faces of others.

"You are the only thing that makes me believe that our kind is not destined for Hell."

Tessa searched for the right thing to say, to calm him down. "God creates everything, right? So maybe He allowed for us to happen. Evolution."

Ben brought his fist down on the table. People glanced in their direction.

"I need to go," Tessa said, getting up.

"Sit down, Tessa." He put his hands in the air. "I'm sorry. Please, sit down."

"I know your life has been hard, Ben, and that I didn't make it easier."

Ben's eyes softened. "I think God will spare us if I do as He commands. He meant for us to be together."

"Ben, I can't."

"Give me a chance, Tessa." His eyes bored into hers. "The house is ready for you. I have some money. We'll be comfortable."

Tessa felt that familiar pity, the need to make things right for him, but she shook it off. "I have a different life now, Ben."

"Playing maid on a farm?" Ben sneered, his eyes suddenly hard. "Is this what you wanted your life to be?"

"How . . . ?" Tessa's mouth felt dry.

"I've known where you were all along, Tessa. I know the right people now. There's nowhere you can go that I won't find you." The way he said it terrified her.

"I need to use the ladies' room." Tessa managed a weak smile. She got up and walked away, vaguely aware that Ben was calling her name.

It was dark outside, the streets quiet after the day's bustle. Tessa crossed Preller Plein as a late bus to the *location* pulled away from the stop, leaving the square deserted. She didn't need to look back to know that Ben was following her. His presence lurched in the shadows, reached out to her, chilling her to the bone like the Free State winter. Booysen's truck was parked two blocks away. Tessa lengthened her stride.

"You can't run from me, Tessa." Ben rammed her against the side of the car.

Tessa screamed. Ben lifted her off the ground like a rag doll. Tessa kicked against the side of the car as her feet left the ground, pushing him back, catching him off-balance. Ben loosened his grip for a moment. Tessa tore away from him and ran back to the town center, to the safety of people. She heard Ben's footsteps behind her. He could always outrun her.

Ben grabbed her hair from behind, pulling her back. He spun her around. "For always, Tessa. Remember? Always."

Tessa scratched at his face. Ben let out a low grunt and his palm made contact with her cheek. Tessa felt disoriented. He threw her down, suddenly on top of her, straddling her, his bulk crushing her, his hands on her throat. She kicked, her legs wild. He was too big, too strong. Tessa's movements weakened to ineffectual flutters. Her lungs burned, the pain in her throat like a hot poker. Was this how it ended? She had thought of life as protracted misery, her gift of time a punishment. But now that it was being taken away from her, she would sacrifice anything to keep it.

Tessa looked up at Ben. She found a hatred in his eyes that could only have come from something that had once been love. Desperate, she mouthed the words. "I love you."

Confusion crept into Ben's features. He relaxed his grip just enough for oxygen to seep into her lungs. Tears blinded her. Violent cough spasms ripped through her body. His weight was suddenly gone. Tessa rolled onto her side, struggling to clear her throat.

"*Miesies?* Are you all right?" A black man in a waiter's uniform hovered at the end of the alley. "Do you want me to go get someone, *Miesies?*" He stepped closer, but suddenly realized the position he was in and backed off.

"No. Don't go," Tessa pleaded hoarsely. She couldn't see Ben anywhere, but she could still feel his presence.

The man looked around nervously, his eyes darting back at the street.

"Please help me get up. No trouble. I promise."

The man came to her side. She leaned heavily on him as he helped her stand.

"Could you please stay with me? Walk with me to my car?"

"*Ja, Mies.*"

"*Dankie.*" Tessa held on to him all the way across Preller Plein. As soon as she locked the door behind her, he darted away, putting as much distance as he could between them. Tessa suspected she owed her life to him. And he was fearing for his because of a good deed.

Tessa reached the end of Eeufees Road without remembering how she got there. The highway turnoff loomed in front of her. She pulled onto the side of the road to think. She couldn't go back to Booysen's farm. Ben would come after her, finish what he started. Flippie had gone to Johannesburg, to make a difference, he had said. The city had sheltered her once before; maybe enough time had passed that she could get lost among the faces again. Perhaps they'd make her invisible.

She would start over. One more time, just one more time. Tessa put the car into gear and turned north on the highway.

Benjamin

He receded into the night as the black man helped Tessa to her car. He watched her drive away until the red taillights disappeared in the distance. Longing and self-hatred burned his stomach. She had looked at him as if he was a stranger, delusional, out of his mind. Stupid, stupid Benjamin. How could he have expected her to carry the burden of God's plan when it was his alone to bear?

Leath's journals cataloged almost forty women. Many miscarried, and perhaps there were more like Apie, but other children must have survived too, walking the earth like him and Tessa, not truly understanding what they were. As Tessa's life ebbed under his hands, God had spoken to Benjamin, revealing His command, His promise. Tessa would be his. He alone would have her love, for as long as they both lived. But he had to earn her first.

A policeman stopped the black waiter as he crossed the street, and barked something at him. The waiter dug around in his pockets and produced his passbook, stating where he worked and that he had permission to be in town after dark. The black cowered, letting the policeman search the bag he was carrying. As he watched the familiar scene play out, Benjamin realized that he'd gotten it wrong. It was the police who had real power in South Africa, not the academics or political bulldogs. Nobody questioned their authority. A smile broke out on Benjamin's lips. Yet again God had shown him the way. With his connections in the Broederbond and a police badge on his chest, he would find the others. He would rid the world of the abominations. Then God would bestow his reward.

7

Tuesday
DECEMBER 14, 2010

Maria had just opened the dining room for breakfast service when Alet walked into Zebra House. She ordered a cup of coffee and waited at the bar. At seven sharp, Koch came down from his room, trailing a small suitcase behind him.

"Professor. Nice to see you."

"Constable Berg." Koch didn't look pleased with the ambush.

"I was about to have breakfast. Want to join me?"

Koch consented reluctantly and followed Alet to a table. Maria filled their coffee cups and disappeared into the kitchen.

"Did you sleep well?"

Koch heaped three teaspoons of sugar into his cup before answering. "Why are you here, Constable?"

Alet didn't let her smile slip. "I was hoping we could discuss your findings."

"I'm meeting with your captain in an hour. You couldn't wait till then?"

"We're a little shorthanded at the moment, Professor, so I won't be there. I was hoping you could fill me in on the important stuff yourself."

Koch eyed her suspiciously. "Your father always felt that he deserved special treatment. Didn't ask for permission or follow protocol. Could it be that the apple didn't fall far from the tree?"

"Look, Professor, don't hold my father against me. I'm only trying to find a killer."

"I suppose it won't matter either way." Koch added another spoon of sugar to his coffee. Alet felt her own teeth decaying as she watched him slurp it down. "The victim was an adult female. Somewhere between her late thirties and early fifties. It's hard to be more accurate than that."

"It wasn't a child?"

"Heat makes a body contract. That's why it looked small." Koch rearranged the silverware in front of him so it lined up at right angles. "That wasn't the only part Dr. Oosthuizen got wrong."

"He thought that she might be white."

Koch turned to her in surprise. "Yes, the skull suggests that, but it is not definitive. We have to wait for the DNA results. I take it you have tried to match dental records?"

"We have to contact all the dentists in the area. It takes time."

The smell of fried onions and bacon drifted into the room. Koch unfolded his napkin and placed it on his lap.

"What about the fractures of her legs?"

"Extreme heat chars the muscle and soft tissue, resulting in exposure of the underlying bones to heat, which in turn causes fractures. You can see this on the skull too, on the temporal bones."

"How do you know the killer didn't hit her over the head?"

Koch gave Alet a pitying smile. "The fractured edges are ragged and cross suture lines. Antemortem fractures usually terminate at suture lines."

"So the cause of death was fire."

Someone dropped something heavy on the floor of the guest room directly above the restaurant. Koch looked up at the ceiling. "Noisy place. I got no sleep from all the comings and goings last night. You'd expect the countryside to be quiet." He sighed. "No. To answer your question. Cause of death was not fire or smoke inhalation."

"Dr. Oosthuizen said—"

"Never mind what Dr. Oosthuizen said. There was no soot on the back of the tongue or trachea. The victim was definitely dead by the time she was set on fire."

"Then what killed her?"

Koch took a dramatic pause. Alet half expected him to tap his teaspoon against his coffee cup for attention before answering.

"The hyoid bone had a clean break."

A middle-aged couple entered the restaurant. The man was skinny with enormous protruding ears. The woman, presumably his wife, was twice his width. Maria almost bumped into them as she exited the kitchen with a tray full of plates.

"*Môre*."

"Morning," the woman said stiffly in a European accent that Alet couldn't place. The woman glared at her husband. He seemed to shrink back before also muttering a greeting.

"Any place you like," Maria said. "I'll bring coffee now-now." She navigated her way around the couple, the man obviously waiting on the woman's decision as to where they would be sitting. Maria unloaded her tray at Alet and Koch's table. Bacon, fried eggs and *boerewors* for Koch, oatmeal for Alet.

Alet waited until Maria was out of earshot before she turned to Koch, who was already scooping egg into his mouth, bits of yolk accumulating at the corners. "What does it mean, the broken hyoid bone?"

Koch washed his food down with coffee before answering. "The hyoid is a small bone over here." He held his hand to his throat. "If it's broken, it usually means the victim was either in a car accident, or died from some form of strangulation."

"You're sure about this?"

Koch looked at her in astonishment. "I wouldn't have said it if I wasn't."

"I'm putting you on administrative leave pending the ICD investigation, Constable."

Mynhardt had called Alet into his office the moment she walked through the station door with Koch. The captain spoke in short, curt sentences, his easy demeanor gone, his face redder than usual.

Alet took her cap off. "Please, Captain. I know Johannes and I don't agree on everything, but I've helped this investigation."

"I don't like this either, Constable. We need all the help we can get right now."

"Then let me stay on."

"I can't ignore everything that's been going on here, my girl. I took a risk taking you on."

"And I'm grateful, Captain. Let me work the charge office, at least."

"You have a complaint of excessive force against you, my girl, and Sergeant Mathebe has voiced doubts about your ability to conduct yourself."

"That's bullshit."

Mynhardt half raised himself off his chair, leaning his arms on the desk. "Now, listen here, Constable." He dropped his voice, speaking through tight lips, low and urgent. "My *gat* is on the line here. Out there is a shithouse full of blacks who are the boss of you and me and can't wait to boot me out. I'm not losing my job because of you. Understand?" Alet nodded. Mynhardt sat back in his chair, pushing paperwork over to her. "Sign here."

Alet glanced over the incident report, the role of perpetrator leaving a strangeness on her skin, sticky, like oil on a bird's wings. The pen dented the paper's surface as she signed. She pushed it back across the desk, glad to be rid of it.

"Captain Groenewald from Joubertina called me this morning." Mynhardt said, his composure restored.

Alet's palms were moist against the wooden armrest of her chair. "Did he talk to the suspect?"

"He denies involvement in the murders."

"Of course he does."

"Says he found the two victims like that and panicked when you stopped. Thought he might be framed for what happened."

"So he attacks me and steals my car. Sure sounds like he's innocent. I don't know what I was thinking."

Mynhardt's lips tightened across his teeth. "I know this is hard, believe me. But the law is on his side."

"I risk my neck every day for the law. When will it be on my side?" Alet looked away, crossing her arms. "What's his name, this innocent bystander?"

Mynhardt pulled a file out from under his computer's keyboard, scanning the first page. "One Joseph Ngwenya. Seems he ran with a gang that is well known in the area. Petty crime, drugs, nothing violent."

"In other words, he could walk away." Alet tried to keep her voice steady. "What happens now?"

"Now, you go home and wait until you hear from me."

● ● ●

"You're going in uniform?"

Alet got in the passenger seat of Tilly's red pickup with the Zebra House decals on the side. "I'm on official business."

"Put your seat belt on."

"*Ja, Ma.*"

Tilly's chestnut curls cascaded from a ponytail high on her head. Combined with her pearl-buttoned blouse, she looked uncharacteristically girly.

"Is that lipstick?"

"*Ja.* So?"

"Just wondering if you have a *skelmpie* in Oudtshoorn I don't know about."

"You jealous?" Tilly flipped the air-conditioning dial to high.

"Been thinking of becoming a nun, actually."

Tilly gave her a look.

"Don't ask. Just drive."

Tilly pulled away from the curb. The dirt road's bumpy drone quieted down as they took the exit to the highway. Tilly turned the radio on to an Afrikaans station that played hits from the eighties and nineties, reporting on local events with bits of national news thrown in between the weather forecast and Pick n Pay ads. Alet put her cap on the dashboard and played with her braid, humming along to a Roxette song she used to like in high school.

"Sorry about bursting in last night." Alet tried to sound casual.

Tilly bit her bottom lip, the burned-orange lipstick staining her teeth. "No worries." She moved onto the skirt of the road, pebbles crunching under the wheels of the pickup, as a red Hyundai streaked past, its hazards flashing twice. Tilly made a smooth return to the tarred road, picking up speed, following the car closely. A-ha faded in with "The Sun Always Shines on TV."

"Sounded like you and Jeff were going at it." Alet sensed a shift in Tilly's demeanor, a subtle hostility as she leaned forward, her shoulders hunching over the wheel.

"Don't remember," Tilly said. She turned the volume up on the radio. A woman droned the news in Afrikaans. Government corruption, as usual, AIDS infecting one in six, robberies, assaults, almost five hundred dead on the roads already this month. The usual buzzwords losing their ability to shock, understanding numbed by too much going wrong and too little being done about it. Everybody called for the government, the police, to take control, when the truth was that nobody had control over anything.

The red Hyundai was doing close to 135 kilometers an hour in front of them, Tilly's pickup not too far behind. Green road signs flashed by, counting down kilometers to Oudtshoorn's city limits. The morning DJ chatted to a caller about her family's holiday plans.

"Shit." Tilly slammed on the brakes.

Alet's kneecaps hit the dash hard. Ahead of them the Hyundai's brake lights flared. She saw Strijdom down the road, his arms extended, signaling the Hyundai to pull over. She released her seat belt in one swoop and ducked her head down.

"Mind telling me what you're doing?" Tilly slowed the pickup to a crawl, pressing the window button, opening it halfway.

"Don't let him see me."

Tilly stopped the truck and leaned over Alet, sticking her face out the window, her elbow digging into Alet's side. "Hi Hein!"

Strijdom shouted a distant reply.

"Tilly, I swear . . ." Alet whispered.

Tilly pressed her elbow harder into Alet's side. "We have Peri-Peri chicken on special this weekend. You and Sussie should stop by. I'll stick you for pudding." Strijdom's muffled "Will do" had Tilly back in her seat and shifting gears again moments later.

Alet straightened out, venturing a glance through the rear window. Strijdom had his arm on the Hyundai's roof, his attention on the driver. "Bribe much?"

"You haven't answered my question, Alet."

Alet sank back in the seat, crossing her arms. "Technically, I'm not supposed to be working."

"Technically?"

"Okay." Alet sighed. "I'm in deep shit if they catch me."

"Then why am I driving you to Oudtshoorn?"

"Because I don't like being told what I can and can't do."

Tilly sniggered. "Obsess much?"

Alet fought the urge to bite the hangnail on her thumb. "I'm not sitting at home."

An OUDTSHOORN 10KM sign flashed by. Billboards with advertisements for ostrich farms and tours of the Kango Caves proliferated as they neared the city limits. Alet slouched in her seat, her head leaning against the backrest, her long legs crunched against the dashboard. She closed her eyes for a moment. *What the hell are you doing, Berg?* She would lose everything if she was caught. There was a fluttering sensation in her stomach, butterflies some would call it. *The wings of a million black butterflies.*

"Where do you want me to drop you?" Tilly looked expectantly at Alet.

Alet hesitated for only a moment before the lights changed. "The police station."

The officer behind the Oudtshoorn service desk didn't look up from the occurrence book when Alet cut to the front of the line. Her name badge read CONST. DLAMINI. Alet stared at the top of her blue porkpie hat for a full minute. "Excuse me?"

Constable Dlamini eyed Alet, boredom in her expression. "Yes?"

"I'm Constable Berg from Unie Police. Is Sergeant Maree in?"

Constable Dlamini pointed with her pen to a door on the opposite side of the charge office. "Through there, on the left."

Maree's door was open. He sat at his desk, eating a sandwich, a half cup of tea at his elbow, a mustard stain on his tie. Alet had only dealt with him over the phone before, but he had always been friendly and helpful. She hoped that she could count on that today.

"We weren't expecting you," he said when she introduced herself. "We're a little overwhelmed at the moment."

"It's just that I couldn't find enough on the national database, and it's urgent. A murder," she added for effect. "I need information on necklacings in the area. Possibly going back a few years."

"How far?"

"I'm not sure. Ten, twenty years? Maybe more. We need to rule out the possibility of a repeat offender." Alet smiled, hoping to put him at ease. "Look, point me to a computer. I can find what I need myself."

"That won't work." Maree's eyes lingered on his sandwich. "I barely keep up with the new cases coming in. There's just no time to digitize the old stuff, see?"

Alet had known it was going to be a long shot.

"I can show you the archives," Maree said. "If you don't mind digging."

Alet followed Maree through the station. He took a right at the other end of the charge office and went down a flight of stairs to a room, marked ARGIEF in gold letters. Filing cabinets lined the windowless office. A single bulb illuminated linoleum flooring that probably hadn't seen a mop since the eighties.

"The oldest ones are in this corner," Maree pointed. "1928, I think, and they run from left to right, top to bottom by case number. Eighties should be around here." He walked to a row of cabinets to the right side of the room, pulled one of the top drawers open, and ran his fingers along the faded brown folders. "*Ja*, here. See? 'Seventy-seven, so maybe a couple drawers down."

"I'll manage," Alet smiled. "*Dankie.*" Her smile faded as Maree left. No keywords, no quick searches. She opened drawers until she found files around the date of the first known necklacing. March 23, 1985. It happened somewhere near Uitenhage, less than an hour from PE. Nowhere near Oudtshoorn or Unie. But 672 people were necklaced in the country in a matter of two years. There had to have been local cases. The killer knew what he was doing. It definitely wasn't his first time.

It took Alet over an hour to work her way to 1987, carefully going through each necklacing case's pathology report to look for victims who had been strangled. Nothing in the files followed that pattern. This was probably a wild-goose chase. Or she was thinking about it wrong. It was easy for crimes to get misidentified, especially back then. The only reason they had found out that the woman on the mountain was strangled was because they had an expert like Koch. Her body had been burned to get rid of evidence. "Dammit." Alet clenched her fists, irritated by the time she had wasted. She started over, pulling files that involved people killed by fire, or whose bodies were burned, a short stack building next to her. There were no discernible links between the victims or methods as far as she could tell.

1988, 1989. Nothing. She checked her watch. She was supposed to meet Tilly in an hour at the shopping center across the street. She decided to work her way back from 1985, just in case. An unsolved case from 1976 caught her attention. Strangulation. A local schoolteacher's body was set on fire and abandoned in an isolated area. No suspects. Alet went back further. Another case in 1972. Strangulation and the partially burned body of a secretary in a cornfield. Alet paused. Both victims were female, both blond. If it was the same guy and he was, say, in his teens, during the '72 murder, he would be in his fifties now, maybe even older. She thought of Wexler. He could easily have carried a woman up that mountain.

Alet took the two files and made her way back to Maree's office. She found him hunched over his keyboard, a stack of SAP 5's next to him. She put the two files on his desk, her eyes briefly resting on his name tag, and smiled. "I know you're busy, Kallie, but I need your help." She leaned on the desk. "I'd really appreciate it."

Maree nodded. A light pink hue spread across his youthful cheeks. "What do you need?"

"Could you let me know if you happen to come across any cases that are similar to these?"

Maree studied the case files she placed in front of him, making flustered eye contact.

"I need to ask one more favor. I feel so stupid." Alet peered at him from beneath her lashes. "Thing is, I'm also in town to follow up on a lead. You won't believe this, but I forgot the file and I need to go over something quickly. My captain will *kak* himself if I have to come back again."

"*Ja.* Sure, hey." Maree's blush extended all the way to his ears. "What's the name?"

"Joseph Ngwenya." Alet smiled. "You're really helping me out, hey."

Maree hunched over, his fingers pounding the keyboard. "Got it."

The printer on his desk sputtered to life. Alet grabbed the warm pages as they dropped into the tray. "I owe you a drink, Kallie."

Alet scanned the red tables of the Wimpy, finding only averted eyes or the undisguised stares of children between cardboard cutouts of burgers and milk shakes. She sat down at an open table near the door and ordered a sandwich and coffee. Ngwenya's file only confirmed what Mynhardt had told her. Drug running, gang activity. Hijacking and murder would have been an escalation. She flipped the page stopping on the known-associates list. There were a few interesting names among Ngwenya's friends, one of them, a Gareth Skosana, with a rap sheet as long as her arm.

"Get what you came for?" Tilly sat down opposite her.

"Maybe."

Tilly reached for Alet's coffee and poured milk in.

"That's mine and I like it black."

"Order another one. I can barely keep my eyes open. My bags have bags."

Alet put the file down, suddenly in a better mood. "I have a favor to ask."

"Pile it on."

"Can I borrow your pickup when we get back?"

Tilly stirred sweetener in the coffee. "Fine. I'm having an early night anyway. Fill up the tank when you're done."

"Are you going to tell me what you're doing in the wee hours instead of sleeping, or do I have to beat it out of you?"

"Ooh. Police brutality."

"What's one more charge? Talk."

"What do you want to know, Officer?"

"You and Jeff. Last night. Out with it." Tilly's shoulders rose and she opened her mouth to speak, but Alet cut her off. "Don't give me that *kak* of 'I can't remember.'"

Tilly put her coffee cup down suddenly. Liquid sloshed into the saucer. "It's private, Alet. Please, just leave it alone."

"Sorry, I—"

"I don't pry into your business. I've never asked what you did to get stuck here even though everybody's—" Tilly stopped suddenly.

Alet eyed her for a moment. "So the whole town knows. Big *fokken* surprise. Who was it? Strijdom? You know what, doesn't matter."

Tilly looked out the window. She rested her head on her hand. Alet's cell broke the uncomfortable silence, Unie Police Station's number on the screen. "Time to face the music," Alet muttered before answering. "Hallo?"

"Alet?" Mynhardt sounded apologetic. "We are looking for Mathilda Pienaar. Is she with you?"

"*Ja*. Why?"

"That's good."

Alet said nothing as Mynhardt spoke. Her eyes traced Tilly's short fingers on the red tabletop, the way her curls flattened against her other palm. She tried to remember the childlike petulance on Tilly's face, the dreamy way she looked out the window in an attempt to give Alet privacy. It would all change now, Alet thought. As soon as she put the phone down and started talking, Tilly would change forever.

"Thank you, Captain." Alet hung up.

"Do they miss you?" The playfulness was back in Tilly's voice.

Alet attempted a smile, but it turned rancid right away. "When was the last time you spoke to your *ma*?"

"Did she start a fistfight at church, or is she drunk in the bar?" Tilly raised her hands in mock exasperation. "Can't take her anywhere."

"No, I—"

"I knew it would eventually come to this." Tilly shook her head, the curl of her lips threatening to explode her mock seriousness. "She needs bail money, doesn't she?"

"Don't. Please. I need you to listen to me."

Confusion clouded Tilly's features. "Okay."

The waitress slammed a plate down in front of Alet, fries falling off the edge. She put a slip of cash register paper next to it. "You pay with me."

"Come back," Alet said. The waitress clicked her tongue and walked away. Alet pushed the plate of food away.

Across the table, Tilly's frown deepened. "Why are you asking about my *ma*, Alet?"

Alet reached for Tilly's hand. "They found a match for the dental imprints of the victim, Tilly. They believe it's Trudie."

"I'm not going to ask why you're still in uniform, Alet," Mynhardt said. He looked over at where Mathebe escorted Tilly into the interrogation room. Tilly had stared into space the whole way back to Unie, her face void of emotion. Alet wished she knew what to say, but she had always been bad at that sort of thing, delivering little more than ineffectual platitudes she had heard on TV. She sank into a chair in Mynhardt's office.

"When was the last time you saw Trudie Pienaar?"

"I was late with the rent . . . the third? She was in the garden most mornings, though." Alet crouched over, resting her head in her hands. She tried to remember, but days flowed into monotonous unity. Trudie had died late Friday or early Thursday morning. Someone had dragged her up the mountain, strangled her and set her body on fire. Alet felt like she was having a vivid nightmare. "I honestly don't know, Captain."

"She's been dead for five days! You live in her backyard, Alet. Are you telling me that you didn't notice she was gone? We found her car hidden behind some bushes on the farm. You didn't notice that was gone either?"

"Trudie parked in the garage. And there was this Ngwenya *kak*. I've been a little preoccupied."

"And Mathilda?"

"This wasn't unusual. They're always at each other. Trudie was stubborn. She refused to answer the phone and—"

"You have no *kooking* clue about the shitstorm in this town when they find out it wasn't just some random black. That it was one of our own."

"I want to help. There must be something I can do?"

"Stay away from the investigation." Mynhardt frowned. "I mean it. Go home and look after your friend."

Alet drove Tilly back to Zebra House after Mathebe had finished questioning her. Tilly placidly followed Alet's instructions, taking the sleeping pill Oosthuizen prescribed and going to bed. Alet gave Maria instructions to look in on her. She considered going home, but she knew Mathebe would be there, going through Trudie's house, looking for evidence. Alet took Tilly's car keys from the coffee table. If there was one thing she hated, it was waiting around.

Voetsek was locked up in his cage, baring his teeth, emitting a barrage of barks as Alet approached, his black snout pressed up against the chicken wire. She marveled that it was strong enough to hold him. She knocked at the back door. After the third time without answer, she walked around to the back of the house to Magda and Nonnie's bedroom and banged on the window.

"*Fokof!*" a man yelled from inside. Alet recognized the voice.

"Police," Alet said.

The pink net curtains parted and Magda's face appeared. "A moment, *Mies*. Please. No trouble."

Alet waited at the back door. A flustered Petrus Brink, the head of the farmers' co-op, appeared in the doorway after a few minutes. He scowled at her, his face red, his hair and clothes disheveled. He opened his mouth to speak, but she waved him along. "Just go."

Petrus swore as he headed down the driveway. Alet hadn't seen his car when she pulled up, but most likely he'd pulled off the main road, hiding it in case anybody drove by, exactly the way the murderer might have done. She waited a couple of minutes before she went into the house, finding Magda in the bedroom, frantically straightening the bed.

"I'm not here about that."

Magda looked at Alet with wide eyes. "What, then, *Mies?* Mr. Brink, he won't come back now. He's a regular."

Alet suddenly felt sorry for barging in, her uniform a calculated move to take advantage of Magda. Nobody in town would have tolerated her still playing cop. And Petrus's money probably also went a long way to contribute to Nonnie's school fund. "I'm sorry, Magda," she said, "but I need to talk to you. What Nonnie said—"

"It was just kids' talk, *Mies*. You said so yourself."

"No it wasn't, Magda. You know it wasn't."

Magda sat down on the edge of the bed, her hands folded in her lap, her upper body slumped. "I don't know what you want, *Mies*."

"I want you to be honest with me."

Magda shrugged her shoulders.

"Do you know a man named Joseph Ngwenya?"

"No, *Mies*."

"Look." Alet held Ngwenya's photocopied mug shot up for Magda. "Is this one of your men?"

Magda shook her head.

"You sure? How about Gareth Skosana?"

Magda averted her eyes. Alet felt a stir of excitement, her hunch paying off. Skosana was the leader of the gang. Ngwenya was a small-time criminal, but Skosana was a different matter altogether.

"He sometimes does business here in the area, Magda. People call him the Thokoloshe."

Magda kept her eyes fixed on the ground.

"You know what I think? I think he is one of your boyfriends. Am I right?"

Magda pulled her cheap satin nightgown tighter around her. "He'll kill me, *Mies*."

"Is that what Nonnie meant when she said she saw the Thokoloshe? Was Skosana here that night?"

"Please, *Mies*."

"If you don't tell me the truth, I'll get Child Services in." Alet knew she was being cruel, but she didn't care. "Do you hear me? I'll tell them what I saw. I'm police, they'll believe me. They'll take Nonnie away for good."

Magda let out a sob. "Please, no."

"Then you tell me the truth."

"*Ja, Mies*. He comes here."

"And Nonnie saw him last Wednesday?"

Magda nodded. Alet shuddered at the thought of Gareth Skosana going anywhere near Nonnie. He was dangerous, his gang involved in a number of violent crimes. And he was a known associate of Joseph Ngwenya. He was in the mountains on Wednesday night, the same night Trudie was killed. The same night the American tourists were in town. It was tenuous, but then, Alet had never believed in coincidences.

1960

Benjamin

The prime minister, Dr. Hendrik Verwoerd, was a large man with a square jaw and wavy blond hair greased flat on his head. Benjamin noticed the scar on Verwoerd's ear where an assassin's .22 bullet had grazed the skin that April. The joke around town was that Verwoerd's skull was too thick to be penetrated by a .22.

Verwoerd addressed the tall man. "Is he one of yours, Van Vuuren?" He shifted his piercing gaze to Benjamin. "Looks wet behind the ears."

"He is trusted."

Verwoerd nodded. Van Vuuren's authority was never doubted. Even powerful men deferred to him. There were rumors in police offices and government hallways, nothing confirmed, of course, but Benjamin recognized something in the Security Branch chief, understood it absolutely the first time he laid eyes on the man. Van Vuuren would be a dangerous enemy to have.

"Let's get on with it, then." Verwoerd finished the last of his brandy. He lifted himself out of his seat with effort. "Have that report on my desk as soon as you're back in Pretoria."

Van Vuuren nodded. He motioned to Benjamin to open the door. Two policemen stood directly outside. The hallway had been cleared. They escorted Verwoerd to the front entrance of the building. Benjamin and his men brought up the rear. A black car waited outside, the driver one of the Security Branch men from Pretoria. Verwoerd got into the backseat.

Benjamin got into a second black car with three of Van Vuuren's men. He had been introduced to them earlier during the briefing at the station. Vossie was a burly redhead with an easy manner and Gustav could have been his porky, dish-eared cousin. A nervous guy, Stefan, was behind the wheel.

"Who did you *naai* to be in on this?"

Benjamin ignored Vossie, keeping his gaze trained on the car in front of him. He disliked these "trusted" men of Van Vuuren's. They lacked focus and alcohol seeped from their pores.

"Doesn't talk much, does he?" Gustav chipped in.

"What's important is that things go right today." Stefan ignored the traffic signals as he kept a constant distance from the prime minister's car.

The dusty Bloemfontein streets were lined with curious white faces on necks craning to see, waving vigorously as the motorcade passed. Hendrik Verwoerd, the architect of apartheid, had survived an assassination attempt by a madman at close range. He was about as popular as the risen messiah, proof that God was on their side. He was spared to lead the *volk* on a path to glory, the papers declared. It was a legend that Verwoerd was playing up. Perhaps he even believed it himself.

The fact that his would-be assassin, David Pratt, was a wealthy white farmer who disagreed with the apartheid policies was glossed over. Van Vuuren had interrogated Pratt himself, had him declared insane and committed before anyone else could get to him. Verwoerd went on British television after he recovered and denied that Pratt was a symbol of white people's mood in South Africa. Earlier that year, the Sharpeville massacre had left a scar on the country's image, another police *fokop*. Sixty-nine unarmed blacks dead, most of them shot in the back by police while they were protesting the law that required them to carry passbooks. This sparked a wave of protests throughout the country, and a state of emergency was declared. Verwoerd had tried to reassure the world that all was well, but his interview was overshadowed by the announcement that women could now take a pill and not get pregnant. Winds of change. Benjamin could feel the bedrock of control shifting.

The prime minister was an academic. He had studied German before the war, had met Hitler, was part of the Ossewabrandwag, which opposed South Africa entering the war on the British side. They supported the Nazis. Benjamin wondered if Verwoerd knew about Jooste's failed attempts to re-create Leath's experiments. That he wanted to father the perfect Afrikaner race.

The road curved. Benjamin let his eyes rest momentarily on the Oranje State Mental Hospital in the distance, the main building barely visible behind a heavy fence and enormous cypresses. Behind the thick walls, in one of the rooms that Benjamin knew intimately, David Pratt waited for a trial that would never come. A few kilometers farther they crested the bridge. The stadium came into view, orange-white-and-blue flags flying everywhere. It had rained the day before, and cars struggled through the mud as they turned off the paved road and drove through the gates.

Gustav leaned over from the backseat and patted Stefan on the shoulder. "You didn't fuck up once, girlie."

Stefan took the keys out of the ignition. "Congratulate yourself when it's over."

Bodies pulsated in waves, pushing to get a glimpse of Verwoerd. The Pretoria guys scanned the crowd, their bodies like coiled springs, ready to react at the slightest sign of trouble. The policemen made eye contact with their unit commanders. Nods passed between them. Vossie stepped aside, opening the door for Verwoerd. Applause burst forth as the prime minister got out of the car. More pushing. More shoving. Verwoerd stepped out, his shoes sinking into thick mud. He raised both arms to cheers. The conquering hero.

The stench of horse manure, *braaivleis*, and something sweet wafted through the air, weaving with the sound of distant music and a cacophony of high-pitched voices. Benjamin escorted Verwoerd up the steps and down to his seat. Huge bouquets of white balloons obscured the line of sight. A security nightmare.

A special section near the front had been cordoned off for the prime minister and other officials, sheltered by oversize parasols. A display of traditional *volk* dances was already under way, concertina music blaring over loudspeakers. Benjamin thought of Tessa in her costume during the centennial, kissing him on the cheek. A pang went through his chest, sharp as a knife. He sometimes succeeded in making himself forget, but the slightest reminder plunged him into memories so vivid that he could almost smell the sandalwood of her skin and feel her hand on his neck.

"Take position near the exit," Vossie instructed. "Don't let anyone—"

A deafening thunder interrupted him as Air Force jets flew overhead in a perfect V formation. People gasped and clapped enthusiastically at the display. It was a symbol of strength, of independence. South Africa would become a republic, shedding British rule once and for all.

A marching band streamed in from the far entrance of the stadium. Drum majorettes in tall white boots and short skirts marched in formation as the band played. Vossie and Gustav leered at hemlines and passed remarks that could not be heard above the music.

"And now, the lovely ladies of the Union of South Africa," a voice boomed over the loudspeakers. "Miss Transvaal . . ."

The first of a procession of convertibles appeared at the stadium's entrance, each with a waving beauty in an evening gown and tiara sitting in the backseat. A wide sash with her province name embroidered on it draped every girl's body. Miss Transvaal and Miss Natal rode in first. Verwoerd smiled, waving back at them.

"Miss Orange Free State, Melanie Steenkamp!"

The girl had long, almost white-blond hair, fashioned in a partial beehive that fell loosely down her back. Her features were carved in skin so fair that it seemed to bleed into the edges of her pale-pink gown. Benjamin mouthed her name, letting each consonant drip into a vowel.

". . . and Miss Union herself, Anita Erasmus!"

The crowd's rhythmic clapping rose to a crescendo as the cars circumnavigated the stadium floor, Miss Union tossing long-stemmed roses to the crowd.

"Lovely." Vossie stood next to Benjamin. "Nice childbearing hips, hey."

"Out of your league, *bra*," Gustav said in passing. He cocked his head toward Verwoerd, whose gaze was locked on the car, a hungry child eying candy. "She's not meant for the likes of you."

"Why did you leave your post?" Benjamin masked his excitement in irritability.

"He's going to give his speech. Don't want our mugs on the front page." Gustav leaned on the steel balustrade lining the stairs. "Might look like the old man is scared."

Verwoerd stepped up to the microphone. The mayor took a white fan-tail dove out of a cage at his feet and handed it to Verwoerd. The crowd hushed.

Verwoerd lifted his eyes to the sky. "We call ourselves European, but actually we represent the white men of Africa." Small beads of perspiration formed on his forehead. "The white man came to Africa, perhaps to trade, in some cases, perhaps to bring the gospel. He has remained to stay. And particularly we, in this southernmost portion of Africa, have such a stake here that this is our only land; we have nowhere else to go. We set up a country. We believe in balance, we believe in allowing opportunities to remain within the grasp of the white man who has made all this possible. In South Africa, there will be a white state, a big and strong white nation, along with various Bantu national units. How is that different from what we have in Europe? What would have happened to France, to Germany and to Britain if they had lost all their borders and their populations had become intermingled? Have those nations become intermingled, or has a multiracial state been established in Europe?"

Verwoerd paused dramatically, the dove clutched between trembling fingers. "In terms of the policy of apartheid, the white man will control his own area, whatever the difficulties might be and however hard it might be. He has the opportunity to save himself, which under a multiracial state he will not have. Leadership in a democracy is not retained by men of pious words. It depends on numbers. Must we simply allow the rest of South Africa to become mixed and in the final result to become dominated by the Bantu? With the Natives outnumbering the whites four to one?"

Verwoerd manipulated the crowd with ease, moving on to the imminent Communist threat, the black menace of the African National Congress. The recent sanctions passed by the United Nations against them made the path clear. His voice boomed, reaching the climax of his speech. "The Afrikaner would yet again pull his wagons in a *laager*, like his ancestors, this time against the rest of the world."

The mayor, gray-bearded and dressed in a three-piece suit, stepped up to the microphone and struggled to be heard above thundering applause. "And now, we will sing the national anthem while the prime minister releases a white dove as symbol of Afrikaner freedom."

A brass band started the first notes of "Die Stem van Suid Afrika."

Everybody stood at attention, their arms at their sides, their hands balled into fists. Verwoerd raised the dove high overhead. With a quick dip, he lowered the bird and flung it. The dove arced through the air.

Voices trailed off. Heads followed in unison as the dove's motionless body thumped down at Verwoerd's feet. The brass band, slow to realize what had happened, maintained an allegro tempo.

"*O fok.*" Gustav looked at Vossie in slack-jawed horror.

Verwoerd's face turned crimson, his jowls quivering. The last notes of an oblivious tuba player died down to absolute silence. The officials all stared at each other, waiting for someone else to make the first move. A murmur brewed deep in the crowd, nervous agitation threatening to build to ridicule. Benjamin broke the spell. He swooped in front of Verwoerd, grabbed the dead bird, and threw it back into the cage. Behind him, policemen sprang to life. Vossie barked orders. The mayor motioned to the bandleader and the band started the anthem's introductory notes again. Hesitant voices idled, then gained strength as the song progressed.

Benjamin grabbed a constable by the arm and handed him the cage. "Take care of this. And get the drivers."

"*Ja*, Sergeant." The young man disappeared into the torrent of bodies.

Verwoerd was still nailed to the spot, the whole stadium's eyes fixed on him while he mouthed the words to the anthem. As the last notes died down, he waved to the crowd, a strained smile on his face. A well-rehearsed pantomime followed, men moving swiftly, keeping the crowds at bay, sweeping the prime minister away. Benjamin jumped the bottom fence and walked over to the camera operators. The outside world would never see what had happened.

Melanie Steenkamp was alone in the house. Benjamin trained his binoculars on the opening between the curtains behind which she sat, her profile coming into focus. A pencil was pinched between her lips, her pale brow furrowed at the book in front of her.

"Good girl," he whispered.

She was beautiful, like a doll, with delicate molded features and porcelain skin. Benjamin had gone back to the stadium in civilian clothes after Verwoerd had been taken care of, joining the festivities, pretending to be nobody. The girls had been put on display in a large white tent with a sign that read MEET THE BEAUTIFUL LADIES OF THE UNION. Benjamin had walked right up to her, taken her hand in his, like something delicate that might shatter. He hadn't trusted himself to say more than "Hallo." Melanie had giggled at his silence, turning to the next person in line. Up close, he noticed that she didn't have Tessa's high cheekbones or full lips, but it was her eyes that betrayed her. Those impossibly light eyes. Benjamin knew in the moment he saw them what she really was.

Melanie closed the curtains and switched off the light. Benjamin eased himself out of the crook in which he had been nesting all evening. He dropped stealthily from the tree and crouched in the shadows. In the distance a dog barked, but the neighborhood around him remained placid.

Benjamin tested the handle on the back door. It moved easily. Doors were rarely locked. There was no reason to fear anything. The black threat was contained in the *location*, which was heavily guarded by police patrols. The door stuck in its frame, the wood swollen from the rain. He put his weight behind it. It inched in, accompanied by a hollow scraping sound.

"Hallo?" Melanie had heard him. The neighbors' house was close enough that they would hear her scream. "Tienie, is that you? I thought you said—"

Benjamin took a deep breath and slammed his body into the door.

"Dove Refuses to Leave Prime Minister."

The newspaper lay crumpled on Van Vuuren's desk. According to the article, the dove was so enraptured by Verwoerd's magnetism that it would rather die than leave his side.

"What do you think of this?" Van Vuuren pushed the newspaper across the desk. "It's *kak*, of course," he said when Benjamin didn't answer. "Damage control." He leaned his head on the back of his chair and stared up at the ceiling. "Maybe they'll even be stupid enough to believe it."

Benjamin wasn't sure where Van Vuuren was going with this. The presence of authority figures made him nervous. They were more malignant entities than human in his eyes.

Van Vuuren lifted his head. "I've been looking at your file, De Beer. There are some . . . issues I'd like you to explain." He opened a file on the desk, making a show of going through the pages.

Fear gripped Benjamin's mind. He was in a police station with the chief of police in front of him. If Van Vuuren cornered him now, there would be no way out.

"Seems you have a degree. Before that, military service. That would make you . . ." He ran his eyes over Benjamin's face. "Thirty-something?"

Benjamin stared straight ahead, his jaw clenched so hard his teeth hurt.

"What I don't understand is why a man with this level of education wants to be a policeman."

Benjamin tried to reach through the clutter in his mind. He had altered his birth certificate before applying to the force, but he still looked very young. It was a stretch to make people believe that he was thirty. He tried to calm himself down. "There was nothing more for me to learn, Brigadier," he said, smiling.

Van Vuuren returned the smile. He stood up and came out from behind the desk. His uniform was pristine, not a hair out of place. Benjamin admired that. He realized that he respected this man for his power, a power that forged simultaneous respect and loathing.

"Yesterday. All those stupid *fokkers* standing there with their fingers up their backsides. You took charge, De Beer. You have smarts, the way you look . . . I think we could put you to better use in Pretoria."

"I'm ready to serve, Brigadier."

"Many men are, until their mommies need them or their wives get pregnant. Then it's 'My family, I can't.'"

Benjamin looked away from the man's scrutinizing gaze. "I don't have family, sir."

"Which is why you're the right man, De Beer. But tell me, what happens when you get an itch for some wide-eyed slut and she drags you in front of a *Dominee*?"

"I . . ." Benjamin took a deep breath to steady himself. He met Van Vuuren's eyes without wavering this time. "That won't happen, sir."

Van Vuuren nodded thoughtfully. "I'm sending you for special-ops training, De Beer. Get your affairs in order. I'll expect you in Pretoria on Monday."

Benjamin walked out of the office, his thoughts careening. He had dedicated every free moment of the past five years to finding Tessa, depleting every resource in the Bond and police. Booysen's car was found in Klerksdorp. The current owner described Tessa as the blond woman who had sold it to him. There the trail ran cold. If he was part of Security Branch, he'd have room to maneuver, abandon conventional methods of investigation. Nobody would bat an eyelid, all activity sanctioned in the name of combating Communists.

"Watch it!" Warrant Officer Steyn roared, almost colliding with Benjamin as he barreled down the passage. He stopped short at the service desk. "What do you mean he isn't in?" he barked at the young constable on duty.

"Called in sick, Warrant."

"Sick my *gat*. Too much celebrating, if you ask me. I'm supposed to go off duty in ten minutes, man." Steyn looked over at Benjamin, day-old stubble on his face. "De Beer. You're coming with me. And you, Constable, get on that radio and send two cars to this address." He threw an incident report at the constable, interrupting before the youth had a chance to reply. "I don't care where you find them. They better be there."

Benjamin ran to keep up with Steyn as the warrant officer stormed out of the station to the yellow police van parked up front. He had barely shut the van's door before tires screeched on the asphalt.

"Supposed to have the day off after covering for everybody and their bloody mother," Steyn mumbled. He ignored a stop sign and a Mercedes slammed on its brakes. The driver turned red in the face, yelling something obscene. Steyn flipped the man off, stepping on the gas. "Hope you have your act together, De Beer, because I'm *fokken* tired."

Benjamin reached for his seat belt. "What happened, Warrant?"

"We're going out to the university. Seems Little Miss Free State has been murdered."

Flippie

Unforgiving heat bore down on the small brick houses and the sink-plate shacks, radiating from the dirt streets long after the sun had set. After the Sharpeville massacre, the Johannesburg police patrolled Soweto with tanks and guns, hovering on the periphery at night. Gangsters and *skollies* had resumed their roles with ease after the relocation from Sophiatown, running the shebeens, terrorizing everyone who resisted them. Community leaders tried to keep order, doing their own patrols, their own citizen's arrests, but as long as the chaos was contained, the government turned a blind eye to what happened inside township borders. The barbarians could murder each other if they wanted. It was in their nature, after all.

"The referendum is decided. It is our turn to take action." Flippie sat in the small living room of his sparsely furnished house. Coffee mugs and full ashtrays were scattered on the floor and the low wooden table in the center of the room. Six men occupied the available seats, the others sat on the hand-pulled rug, legs crossed under them.

"This is madness." Albert, a middle-aged man, threw his hands in the air. "I can't have anything to do with it. The ANC is banned. If they catch us, we'll be hanged for treason. I have a family."

As if on cue, a baby started crying in the back room of the house. Prudence rushed out of the kitchen, the telltale belly of a new mother bulging under her tight skirt. She shot a meaningful glance at Flippie before disappearing down the hallway.

"Our backs are against the wall, Albert," Flippie tried to reason. "They have left us no means of legal protest. If the country becomes a republic, independent from the Commonwealth, things will get worse."

"Maybe it will not be so bad."

Guffaws rose from the other men. Albert shook his head.

"You are blind, my friend." Flippie leaned forward in his seat. "Twenty thousand stood in the rain last night in Natal. To demand that basic human rights be included in the constitution. Do you think it did them any good?"

"We're organizing strikes."

Flippie shook his head. "It won't be enough. Peaceful resistance has gotten us nowhere."

"So you want to start a war, Phillip?"

"It's already a war, Albert. And they are winning." Flippie ran his hands over his face. "Can't you see? They've forced us onto reserves that can't possibly house everybody because they claim blacks are not citizens of this country. Our children have to go to Bantu schools and we have to sit on Bantu buses and shit in Bantu toilets. They provide one water tap for a whole block of houses, then complain that we stink. Our men are crammed into mining compounds away from their families, our women have to work as servants if they want to work at all. And for what? A wage that barely feeds us after we pay them bus transport into their cities because they won't allow us to live there. The pigs get fat off our labor. How much worse does it need to get before we fight back?"

"But bombs? Guns?" Albert's face contracted. "*Aikona.*"

"*They* have guns."

"You have a son. Think of that before you do this."

"I think of nothing but Jacob and his future, Albert."

"I cannot do it." Albert got up from his chair. "Thank your wife."

"Who needs him?" Zweli said to Albert's face, disdain in his large brown eyes. Prudence's brother had grown up and become a real gangster, with his own crew.

Albert looked around the room and shook his head. "I hope to God I am not looking at dead men." He closed the door behind him.

"He is old and scared," Zweli said.

Flippie looked at the young faces in the room. "You all would do well with a bit more fear."

"Bah!" Zweli waved his hands dismissively. "The whites are rigid and stupid. They will not expect us to stand up to them."

"Don't underestimate them. They have a lot to lose."

"And we have nothing to lose." Zweli raised his fist in the air. "That gives us the advantage." A few of the younger men voiced a chorus of agreement.

"We have just as much to lose, my friend," Flippie said. "But we have more to gain."

"We'll fight them. To the end. An attack on apartheid, on all the whites. *Amandla!*" Zweli shook his fist in the air. *"Umkhonto we Siswe."* The others copied him, their voices unified. *"Amandla."*

The men left one by one under the cover of dark. Flippie found Prudence in the bedroom, rocking the baby in her arms, her back to him. He nuzzled his head in the crook of her neck.

Prudence turned around, the baby between them. "I do not like this, Phillip."

"A noose is tightening around our necks, my love. We have to do something."

"Perhaps you can leave it for the young ones?"

"Young bucks act without thought. They need guidance." Flippie touched the head of his son. Before Jacob's birth, he had wanted to leave. The idea still crossed his mind in times of weakness. But this was his country. His son's country.

The bang on the front door startled them both. "Open up. Police. *Maak oop!*"

The men were inside the house before Flippie and Prudence had time to react, white faces and blue uniforms everywhere, guns pointed at them and their infant son. Jacob wailed, startled by the noise. Flippie tried to block them with his body, but the barrel of a pistol came to rest between his shoulder blades.

"I shoot you dead," a young milk-beard said, his voice breaking in a comic falsetto.

Flippie wanted to burst out laughing, imagining a five-year-old with a gun, but then he saw the raw fear in Prudence's eyes, their baby clutched to her breast. He froze, slowly lifting his hands in the air.

"You Phillip Morgan?" It was an older man. The one in charge.

"Yes, sir. What is going on?"

"I ask the questions, okay?"

The other policemen snickered. Flippie turned his head to see the man and was greeted with a blow to his temple.

"Stand still!" The young policeman hit him again in the small of his back. Pain pulsated through his spine. Flippie's legs gave way and he fell to his knees.

Two men lifted Flippie to his feet. They dragged him outside. He tried to tell Prudence to go to Zweli, but he had trouble speaking, her silhouette in the doorway of their house the last thing he remembered before the police threw him into the back of a van.

Rubber. The smell shot straight up into his sinuses with the last molecules of oxygen. He tasted it, trying to chew at the thick membrane that stretched tight over his nose and mouth. Flippie's eyes darted from one corner of the fluorescent-lit room to the other. Asbestos walls, like those of his childhood schoolroom. Linoleum floors. Even a blackboard to complete the picture.

Flippie's eyes watered, the pressure building until he was sure they would explode in a gelatinous mess down his cheeks. A tall man in a blue uniform stepped in front of him. He gave a nod and suddenly the tentacle released its grip. Air gushed into Flippie's raw lungs.

"You ready now, hey?"

Flippie tried to answer, but spasmodic coughs interrupted him. The force of a *tonfa* blow sent his chair toppling to the side. He tried to stop his fall, but his hands were bound to the chair. His head made contact with the floor. Softening up. That's what the men who took him called it. His skin throbbed, pain coursed through his nerves.

"Get him up, Peaches."

A big pair of hands wrapped around Flippie's shoulders and the world was turned right-side-up again. The two white policemen looked down at him.

"Shall we go another round, Boss? Work him a little more?" It was the big one, Peaches. He had reddish-blond hair and skin as smooth as a baby's. He held the piece of inner tube between his hands, a human face worn into the rubber.

"*Nee, Baas.* Please." Flippie struggled to let his voice be heard. He was tired, so tired. "I'll tell you anything. Please, *Baas.*"

Peaches looked at the tall man for confirmation.

The tall man pulled up a chair in front of Flippie. "Stay close, Peaches, we'll see if he means what he says." He crossed his arms and leaned back in his chair, his legs spread wide. "These things, they are distasteful to me, see?"

Flippie had trouble focusing his eyes. Blood ran from a gash in his temple and his eyelids were almost swollen shut.

"I was brought up in a good Christian house, where we were taught right and wrong, see? I attend church, I'm a deacon."

"*Ja, Baas.*"

"What do you know?" The tall man stood up.

"*Niks, Baas.*"

"You're right you know nothing. God-fearing men like me are being forced to choose between right and wrong, good and evil. And you know what side I will always choose, Phillip? I will stand on the side of good. Of God. Just like my father did and his father, since all the way back when He gave us this land. We are being threatened by the Communists, and it is my job to eliminate that threat, see? And I know you know things that will help me do that."

Flippie stared ahead of him. There had to be something he could tell the man. One thing that wouldn't matter so much, that wouldn't compromise the others. His mind felt thick and slow, the pain in his side the only thing that kept him alert.

"You are going to help us do that, Phillip."

"I don't know how, *Baas.*"

The tall man sighed. "You're educated. A lawyer, *ja*? You help all those ANC buddies of yours keep out of jail. We've been watching you for a long time, see? I'm sure Peaches will appreciate the overtime to help you remember. Maybe we'll even get your wife a free stay in our lovely hotel. Will that help your memory?"

"She doesn't know anything, *Baas.* Please."

A smile ghosted on the man's lips. "Then I'm sure we understand each other. Start by telling me who was at that meeting tonight."

Tessa

There was nothing striking about Dean Kritzinger. He was of average build, average height, with average sandy hair and average hazel eyes. His face was soft and pasty white, and he carried a few extra pounds around, but that didn't matter to Tessa as she sat with him at John Vorster Square police station, waiting for Flippie's release. What mattered was that Dean embodied the only hope she had known in a long time. Dean's own people saw him as a traitor for offering up his evenings and weekends to go into the townships and help blacks find their loved ones, disappeared behind the veil of police custody. Before Flippie's arrest, Tessa had only known Dean as a lawyer-friend of Flippie's, and he knew her as Lilly Maartens, the name that was now printed in her ID book, a friend to the cause. But something had changed. Tessa wasn't sure what to call it, but she welcomed it. She admired Dean, felt safe with him. His talk of marriage and family after only a few weeks didn't feel rushed to her. For the first time, it felt right.

The door of the charge office opened. A young uniformed officer stepped aside as Flippie limped out. He had a nasty gash on his forehead, which would probably be the only visible sign of the police's interrogation methods. Many men had told their stories to Dean. Of electrodes attached to their genitals, of being drowned and revived, their burned fingertips a testament to what they had been through. Tessa reached out to Flippie, but Dean held her back, his eyes dashing to the uniformed men scrutinizing them.

"Can we go?" There was an urgency in Flippie's voice, his eyes darting back to the officer at the door. Tessa and Dean flanked Flippie as they walked into the bright summer day. Flippie sat rigid in the backseat of the car, staring out the window, his hands clasped in his lap.

"You're safe now, Flippie." Tessa turned in her seat, touching his knee. Flippie looked blankly at her for a moment before turning his head away again.

"Give Phillip a little time to catch his breath, Lilly," Dean said quietly.

"I'm sorry." Tessa had arrived in Johannesburg with only the clothes on her back, not sure if Flippie would even want to see her. He didn't hesitate when she asked him for help. He sold the Chevy, helped her with new identity documents, a new life. They had become closer than when they were children. But she knew that something irreparable had happened in that police station, driving a wedge between them. Between him and the rest of the world.

Prudence came running as soon as they pulled up to Dean's house, carrying little Jacob in her arms. Flippie looked at the two of them as if they were a mirage that would slip away if he blinked. He stepped forward and wiped the tears off Prudence's face.

"It's good to have you back, my friend," Dean said, putting his hand on Flippie's shoulder.

"They broke me, Dean," Flippie said quietly. He grasped Prudence's hand, his head low. Prudence looked pleadingly at Tessa. Tessa touched her arm.

Flippie looked strangely at her. "You're wearing a ring." It sounded like an accusation.

"We have some good news," Tessa said.

"Yes." Dean looked uncomfortable. "I know this is sudden, but Lilly has done me the honor of consenting to be my wife."

Flippie shot Tessa a recriminating look. "Congratulations," he said to Dean, forcing a smile.

After lunch, Tessa found Flippie alone in the living room, his face silent and vague.

"I made Malva pudding," Tessa said. "Your favorite."

Flippie turned toward her in slow motion. "Does he know about you?"

Tessa tensed up. She shook her head.

"Don't you think you should tell him?"

Tessa looked back at the kitchen where Dean was doing dishes. She sank onto the sofa next to Flippie, talking in hushed tones. "He doesn't even know my real name."

Flippie stared at his hands, slender fingers laced tightly into each other. "He doesn't deserve you lying to him."

Tessa felt something desperate well up in her. "We're happy. Can't that be enough?"

"He'll find out eventually, Tessa. What do you think is going to happen then?"

"He loves me."

Flippie shook his head. "What about children? What if they're like you? Do you even remember what our life was like? Do you want your children to be treated like that too? Life is hard enough without that to deal with."

"They could be like Dean."

"What happens, then? You'll see your children grow old and die." Flippie sank back, the small bit of fight suddenly out of him.

"I want what you have, Flippie." Tessa realized how much she resented Flippie for being normal. She swallowed back her anger. "Everybody has a right to happiness, to family. Why not me?"

Flippie looked at her, his features cracked by bitterness. "I sometimes wish Jacob had never been born."

His words were like a punch in the stomach. "You don't mean that," Tessa said.

"I love Prudence. I love my son, God knows, but if I think of what lies ahead, that he might one day be thrown into a van and be at the mercy of this government . . . it's too much to bear, Tessa." Flippie broke down, his thin body melting, his shoulders shaking, his face wet against her dress. "I soiled myself, Tessa. In front of them. Like a baby. I was so scared. I told them everything. I betrayed everyone, all I stood for."

"I promise you, Flippie, I'll always be there for Jacob. I'll protect him like he's my own, no matter what." Tessa looked up. Dean stood in the doorway, a look of concern on his face. She pushed her doubts aside. They would be all right. They just had to be. Life couldn't be worth living if it only held misery.

8

Wednesday
DECEMBER 15, 2010

The sound of someone knocking sent Alet's heart racing. She lay sprawled on Tilly's couch, an uncomfortable crick in her neck. She opened her eyes as another salvo of knocks hammered the window.

"Tilly?" No answer. Alet tried to untangle herself from the decorative pillows, stumbling off the couch to open the door.

Maria stood on the doorstep, tray in hand. "*Môre.* Breakfast?"

"For *Mies* Tilly?"

"No, for you. *Mies* Tilly, she told me to bring it."

"She's not here?"

"She left early."

Alet took the tray from Maria and set it down on the coffee table. She found her cell on the floor and tried calling Tilly, but almost instantaneously, a phone rang in the bedroom. "Dammit." She sank back onto the couch, checking for voice mails. There was a message from Theo. Alet slurped down coffee as she listened.

Tilly's car was parked on the curb in front of Trudie's house, the front door open. A must-and-mothball smell permeated the house. The disorder on the dining-room table and china on the floor seemed offensive, and the kitchen was even worse off. Drawers sprawled open. The entire contents of the pantry were on the kitchen table, every container open, some of the food spilling out. A massacre of clothes was strewn over the floor in Trudie's bedroom, open shoe and hatboxes piled on the bed, their lids flung haphazardly across the room.

Alet found Tilly in a rocking chair on the closed-in *stoep* between potted houseplants and piles of old magazines. Her legs were pulled to her chest as she rocked the chair with a bobbing of her head. The air on the *stoep* hung stale and dead.

"Tilly? You all right?"

Tilly didn't look up. "He made a mess," she said simply.

"What's that?"

"Your Sergeant Mathebe."

"I don't think he—"

"I have to clean it all up now." Tilly spat the words. "What was he looking for?"

"It's a murder investigation, Till."

Tilly's lips trembled. She cupped her hand over her mouth and bowed her head. Chestnut curls fell forward, obscuring her face. Alet felt helpless. She sat down on the weathered wicker chair opposite Tilly, her hands sandwiched between her thighs. Sunlight inched around the corner of the house and fell through the window, warming her back. Outside, the thermometer was already climbing above the 40°C mark, the heat forcing every living thing into submission.

Alet noticed a framed photograph on the windowsill. Tilly followed her gaze.

"It's me and *Ma*."

Alet picked up the frame, studying Trudie holding toddler Tilly in the house's front yard. Tilly wore a yellow jumper, her wispy hair adorned with a matching yellow bow. Trudie looked young and radiant in the early-morning light, her hair, the same chestnut as Tilly's, tied in a loose knot on her head. Alet had rarely seen Trudie without her dark glasses. She put the frame down. "Do you have any of these with your dad?"

Tilly shook her head. "He died before I was born."

"How?"

"Accident. *Ma* never really talked about it." Tears glossed Tilly's eyes. "I should have been here for her, asked her about all these things. Instead I—"

Alet leaned across and put her hand on Tilly's, not sure what to say.

"Most of the people who will come to the funeral will offer condolences and talk about how good she was, and they'll be relieved that they don't have to deal with her anymore." Tilly's voice faltered. "She was mean and reclusive, but she didn't deserve to die like that."

"Nobody does."

"Please, Alet. Find who did this to her and make them pay." Tilly's small hands clutched Alet's desperately. "You have to promise me."

St. George's Mall in Cape Town teemed with tourists, their bags filled with cheap African curios. The cobblestone walkway was bordered by stores, restaurants and outdoor stands that sold cheap jewelry, beads and batik work in bright colors. Puddles and wet paving stones bore witness to an earlier rainfall, the air fresh, clean.

Alet sat down at a table outside a small coffee shop. A waitress in a green-and-white uniform placed a cup of strong black coffee in front of her. Alet was early. Theo had been cryptic when he called, said he had found something he didn't want to discuss over the phone.

A young woman weaved unsteadily between tables, begging for money. Her hair was matted, a dirty red-and-white shopping bag hanging from her left arm. Alet watched as she made her way down the lane, sometimes successfully, but mostly ignored or shooed away.

"Hi." Theo sat down opposite Alet. His top button was undone, his tie loosened.

"Can I get you a coffee?"

"I can't stay long."

"Okay, espresso, then." Alet signaled the waitress and ordered. "Did you manage to find anything on Trudie Pienaar?" she asked, turning her attention back to Theo.

"I ran her ID. Nothing showed up in the database."

"She's clean?"

"No. She doesn't exist. No registered date of birth, no passport, nothing."

"Shit. How's that possible?"

"Fake identity? Happens all the time. All you need is a few thousand rand and the right contacts."

"Dammit."

"But that's not why I asked to see you, Alet." Theo leaned forward, his elbow on the table.

"Okay. What, then?"

"After I saw you the other day, I got to thinking. About us and what happened."

"If that's what you want to talk about, we better move this to a bar."

"No. Listen. After the other day, I didn't want to help you. I was mad. I started thinking about your dad and how he told me to stay away from you, like I was trash. And you just disappearing on me . . ."

Alet clenched her fist. She had wanted to apologize to Theo for her behavior the other day, make things right, but he was making her feel defensive.

"Maybe I wanted to get back at you," Theo said after a moment. "Or at him, I don't know. I thought, what the hell, and pulled everything I could find on him and Koch."

"And?"

"Well, for one thing, there were huge holes in the information. All files were supposed to become public record when the Truth and Reconciliation Commission held its hearings."

"Amnesty in exchange for confessing your sins. Everybody hugged and made up and now we're one big happy family. So?"

"You know your dad never testified?"

Alet shrugged. "Perhaps he had nothing to confess."

"Anyway, he totally fell off the grid in places. One day he worked at Brixton Murder and Robbery, his name in the papers, and the next . . ." Theo leaned back in his chair. "I spoke to someone I know who was in the force around that time."

"Who?"

"Doesn't matter. I trust him." Theo's easy manner was gone, his features strained. "He used to be part of an investigative team. Cleaning up the mess, as it were. He said they raided an office in a building in Pretoria. Found rows and rows of filing cabinets and computers. They didn't know what they had at first, but they were ordered to back down by your dad. Most of the files had disappeared by the time they got a court order to go back."

"Whose office?"

"The Afrikaner Broederbond."

"What? All that cloak-and-dagger, secret-handshake, old-white-men-needing-an-excuse-for-a-drinking-club *kak*?"

"You're thinking of the Freemasons."

"Same thing. Besides, wasn't the Broederbond outed in the seventies?"

Theo shook his head. "The Broederbond controlled everything that happened in this country. Every president from 1948 to 1994 was a member, every minister, every covert-operations chief. You didn't take a shit without the Bond clearing you to do so."

"What's this got to do with my dad?"

"Adriaan Christoffel Berg. Member number 16791."

"So he used to be an old-boy. Are you really surprised?" Alet was aware of the prickliness in her voice.

"Ever heard of the Civil Cooperation Bureau? The Security Branch?" Theo lowered his voice. "Vlakplaas ring a bell? They all have Bond ties. Your dad was a detective at Brixton. It was rife with CCB recruits."

Alet took a sip of her coffee to break eye contact with Theo. The Security Branch did the dirty work during Apartheid. One unit used a farm outside Pretoria, Vlakplaas, to interrogate so-called ANC terrorists and sympathizers, making sure that the black/white divide remained a chasm, by any means necessary. Assassination was one of the means. And the CCB was a secret government-sanctioned death squad. No wonder files went missing. Everyone was trying to cover their asses when Apartheid came to an end. There are some things that can't be forgiven.

"My dad's retiring next year, Theo. No way he would have been allowed to stay on till now if he was part of all of that."

"Your dad has powerful friends." Theo's mouth extended into a bitter smile.

"Can you prove any of this? Or do you only have your friend's word?"

Theo pursed his lips. "I'll find the evidence."

"Fine." Alet turned to look at the passers-by, trying not to let her face betray the whirlwind of emotion she was experiencing. "How does Koch fit into this?"

"They definitely worked together while your dad was at Brixton. There are many news articles. Koch helped crack a few big cases. That's all I could find."

Stores were closing their doors for the day, the crowds drawn away from St. George's Mall by the growing blare of pop music from a Malay street festival on the next block. Alet felt the damp cold of the approaching evening creep between the buildings. The waitress brought Theo's espresso and the bill. Theo reached for his wallet, but Alet held her hand out. "On me."

Theo lifted the espresso cup, which looked ridiculous in his big hands. "Thanks." He swallowed the coffee and leaned over to kiss Alet on the cheek. "I'll call if I find anything more."

"Wait." Alet reached in her bag and handed Theo the two women's files she'd found in Oudtshoorn. "I figured I can dig around in dusty archives for the rest of my life or ask you for a favor while I still have my youth and sparkling personality."

Theo raised an eyebrow. "What's this?" He opened the top file.

"Trudie's murder wasn't this guy's first, I'm sure of that. He was way too good. I'm trying to find more unsolved cases with the same MO."

"These are ancient."

"I know, it's a long shot. Humor me."

Alet walked three blocks to her hotel at the top end of the Mall. Her room was old but clean, the dead bolt on the door loose from having been ripped out and replaced a few times. She ran a shower, studying her face in the bathroom mirror when she got out. The deep black and purple bruises had blended into greens with yellow edges around her eye. It looked even worse than before, if that was possible.

Alet sat down on the bed with her laptop and googled "Security Branch." Articles on the Truth and Reconciliation Commission filled the screen. The term "atrocities" kept popping up in articles along with "strong-armed," and "disappeared."

Her thoughts wandered. Was Theo right? Had her father been torturing people for the government at the same time as he was taking her to the fair and buying her pearl earrings for her birthday? Had he helped cause all of these deaths? Alet closed her laptop. She suddenly couldn't handle the thought of spending the evening alone in the room. She found the piece of paper with Mike Engelman's number tucked away in her wallet. He answered on the third ring.

"Mike? Hi . . . it's Alet Berg." There was a pause on the other end of the line. "Constable Berg from Unie."

"Hi, Alet." Mike's voice was deep, sonorous, as if he had been expecting her call all along.

"I wanted to see if you have any matches with the DNA yet."

"Nico said he'd give you a call."

"I see. Thanks." Alet held her breath, convinced Mike had already hung up, a part of her hoping that he had. A sound on the other end of the line betrayed his presence. She took the plunge. "Hey, so, I'm in town. I was wondering, does that offer for lunch still stand? I mean, it would be dinner, of course. Thing is, I'm here alone and I don't know the area and, well, I'm hungry, and drinking alone in your hotel room is sort of sad."

Mike laughed and she relaxed. "Where are you staying?"

"Off St. George's Mall."

"I could meet you at seven if traffic is light."

"*Ja*. Great, hey. Thanks."

Alet's hair was still half-wet. She combed it out and twisted it into a bun at the nape of her neck, securing it with a clip. She only had one change of clothes with her, her fallback outfit of jeans and a black T-shirt. Makeup would do nothing to conceal the bruises on her face, but a little lipstick couldn't hurt.

Alet took a seat at the hotel bar and ordered a whiskey. She entertained herself by watching the hotel guests gorge themselves at the buffet in the adjacent restaurant, crowding around roasted beef on a spit, carved in thin slices by a chef in a cylindrical white paper hat. Japanese, she guessed at the crowd of black-haired Asians. The sounds of Indian accents from other guests were much more definitive, all faces that would not have been here together twenty years ago. Especially not as tourists.

She caught Mike's reflection in the mirror above the bar. His unruly hair fell over his forehead, matching his casual dress, jeans and checkered shirt, sleeves rolled up. He smiled, lifting his left hand in an awkward wave.

"So, I have to confess," Mike said as he sat down next to her. "I practically live on campus. I've only had dinner at one place down here. Small plates and Cape wines."

"If you recommend it, it's good enough for me." Alet pushed her chair out.

"No rush. You can finish that."

Alet glanced at her drink. "That's okay. I'm starving."

They made their way down the Mall, which was now eerily deserted save for the homeless hunkering down with their blankets in doorways. On Long Street, sounds of the city weaved all around them—music from open nightclub doors, people yelling in the street, beggars interrupting their progress on every corner.

"Here." Mike opened the door of a narrow building. The restaurant was cozy, with exposed brick walls, tea-light candles, and large blackboards in unfinished wooden frames. Plates were crowded with mussels, crab cakes, cheeses, and cured meats. Glasses of red wine appeared, following one another in luxurious succession. Alet's tension eased into familiar light-headedness after a few sips. Mike was charming, but she had always had a hard time keeping conversation going with social niceties.

"Thank you for your help in the investigation," she said for the third time.

"Pleasure. How is it going?"

"We just identified the victim. From dentals."

"Oh?" Mike emptied his glass. "Who was it?"

"Her name was Trudie Pienaar. Professor Koch found a lot that our guy didn't. I'm hoping he will help us crack this."

"He's developed amazing techniques in DNA forensics. He's the reason I came to Cape Town."

"You know him well?"

Mike smirked. "We don't really socialize outside work."

Their waitress placed fresh glasses of wine in front of them. Her tight T-shirt was cut low, cleavage bulging from a push-up bra. "Your food will be out now-now. Anything else?" She smiled at Mike, a subtle seduction in the way she leaned on the table.

"I think we're okay." Alet turned back to find Mike studying her as if she were a lab specimen. She shrugged off the thought. Perhaps he wasn't used to social interaction either. These science guys were usually a little strange.

"Is there anything you can tell me about the evidence I gave you, Mike?"

"I think we've confirmed she was of European descent. Probably

Dutch, but so are most Caucasians here. Does that match your profile at all?"

"*Ja.* How about the blood and cigarette butt?"

"The samples were somewhat degraded. I could only determine that the DNA from the blood was female. I haven't been able to match it to your victim."

"Nothing else?"

"Sorry."

Alet changed the subject with reluctance. "So what's your story, Mike? Where are you from?"

"Here."

"*Ja?* Where?"

"Let's see." Mike scrunched his eyes up. Alet thought it a pity that he hid them behind thick black frames. Male fashion sense was so misguided sometimes.

"Well, I did a PhD at RAU. I've been involved with research all over the place, helping out with DNA testing on the fossils they found at Sterkfontein and Klaasies River. Turns out Homo sapiens might have originated in those caves."

"Everyone is South African? As if immigration isn't a nightmare already."

Mike laughed, his body relaxing against the chair.

"So what exactly do you research?"

"My field is DNA mutation. Viruses specifically. Environmental changes affect the host organism and that leads to . . ." He stopped himself. "Honestly, it puts my students to sleep. I'm sure what you do is more exciting."

Alet's half-truths flowed as freely as the wine. Mike was charming and she felt herself relax in his company, actually having a good time as she talked about police procedure and funny things that happened on patrol in the valley.

The waitress brought the bill. Alet watched her blatant flirting with fascination as she reached for her third glass, and missed. The glass toppled in slow motion, the wine fanning into the air before the vessel disintegrated, shards spreading over the table and floor. The waitress squealed as a purple stain sprayed onto her white T-shirt.

"I'm so sorry. You should put that under some cold water right away," Alet said, feeling unapologetic. A busboy came over with towels, and Alet took her bank card out of her pocket.

"It's okay," Mike said. He reached over the table, his long fingers folding over her hand. "It's on me."

Heat rose to Alet's skin unexpectedly.

"Care for a nightcap?"

Alet hesitated, thinking of an excuse. "I have to head back to Unie at the asscrack of dawn tomorrow."

Mike smiled without letting go of her hand. "Just one. Your hotel bar?"

The Cape night was cool, an ever-present haziness in the air. Mike tentatively reached for her hand once they left the restaurant. Alet felt a flutter in her stomach. She pretended not to see it and put her hands in her pockets. They sauntered back up Adderley Street, passing the dissipating crowd of the street festival, merchants breaking down their stalls, the smell of curry and grease clinging to their clothes. Outside her hotel, Mike stopped suddenly, pulling her toward him. Alet felt the heat of his body through her shirt, a muskiness on his skin, his face centimeters away from hers.

"I hope that wasn't too forward. I've wanted to kiss you ever since I saw you in Nico's office."

Alet hesitated a moment too long. Mike put his hand behind her head. Alet gasped at the force of his movement. His lips were hard against hers, urgent. He held her fast. A couple walked past them and entered the hotel, the woman staring straight ahead, her lips pursed, the man lifting an eyebrow.

"How about we go to your room?"

Alet pushed away. "No."

Mike gave a few steps back, rubbing the back of his neck. "I'm s-sorry . . . you called me. I thought . . ."

"I know. It's . . . hey, I've had a great evening, really. Thing is . . ." She sighed, feeling awkward. How to explain this? Mike looked expectantly at her. Alet shrugged. "I've made some bad decisions lately. About men, especially."

Mike nodded, his expression unreadable.

"Well . . . good night, then." Alet headed for the hotel's entrance.

"Alet?"

"*Ja?*"

"Listen, you think, maybe I can call you?" Mike looked vulnerable.

Alet suddenly felt irritated with herself. Mike Engelman was stable, smart, *and* available. He was the right kind of man, her mother would have said, a catch. Any other woman would have loved to get attention from him. What the hell was wrong with her?

"Okay," she said. "You have my number, hey." Alet went through the revolving door, looking back at Mike, his image distorted behind the glass as he waved goodbye.

1969

Benjamin

Every tree, every dirt path, looked exactly like the next. The black tracker, Sipho, crouched down, studying a fork in the path. After a moment he lifted a finger in the air, pointing to the right. He looked at Benjamin for confirmation before the unit proceeded, picking up the pace.

"Berg! Stay on them." Benjamin felt irritated with the rookie. He had seemed competent enough at the base, even got recommended by a commander for having smarts, but here in the bush his youthful arrogance led to mistakes, mistakes which could compromise everybody. The other two men in the unit were dewy-faced milk-beards who thought three years in the police was a cushier ride than two years of military service, not expecting the police to become involved in the Second Chimurenga, the Rhodesian bush war. The only men Benjamin seemed to be able to count on were the two black trackers who could find a target in kilometers of unchanging countryside. They moved with stealth and speed, undeterred by the crushing heat, communicating with hand signals only, so as not to alert the enemy. They trusted Benjamin. He spoke their language. But they were only better than him during the day. At night, he took over.

Benjamin smelled the water before the trackers cut through the last tree to reveal the river snaking across their path. Sipho signaled them to stop while Sechaba dove without bothering to undress, his movement marked by a slight plop, cutting through the water with grace, emerging on the other side in less than a minute. Benjamin scanned the river bank for movement, while Sechaba disappeared among the trees. The rest of the unit crouched down, following his lead. Radio communication with one of the SAP units, Delta four, had been lost five days ago and Benjamin's unit had been sent in to find them. Two days ago they had found tracks belonging to the Zimbabwe African National Liberation Army crossing paths with Delta four. From that moment on, their mission became a rescue operation.

Sechaba returned to the riverbank, slowly shaking his head. Delta four had either stayed on this side of the river or they realized they were being followed and moved downstream to lose the terries. Benjamin gave the signal and the unit moved south. Berg radioed their position in to the base, dodging tree branches as he went, but as usual, the radio only emitted static. The commanders expected them to risk their lives, but the equipment was always failing, support lacking. Benjamin's childhood fear of authority figures had turned to loathing here in the bush, and he found himself kicking against them every step of the way, hampering his chances of promotion.

Sechaba signaled from across the river. Benjamin picked up the pace behind Sipho until he came to the bend. Dark stains marked a collection of rocks where Sipho had halted. As he got closer, Benjamin saw a half-naked white man propped up against a boulder, his skull crushed, his face bloodied beyond recognition. A crumpled SAP bush uniform lay next to him.

"The others." Sipho pushed aside the foliage behind them.

Four more bodies were piled up in the underbrush, each with a bullet wound to the back of the head. Benjamin recognized the unit commander of Delta four.

"What did he say, Captain?"

"It's them, Berg. Get that radio to work and notify base."

"Why are they without clothes?" Berg stepped closer, his face suddenly pale.

Benjamin shook his head. "The stupid bastards went swimming. Probably didn't even realize they were being followed."

"They headed south." Sipho walked away from the bodies, examining the footprints in the mud.

"What about the other two policemen?"

Sipho shook his head. "Taken prisoner. One is wounded. They're a day ahead of us. If we move tonight we can catch up."

"What about the bodies, Captain?" Berg's eyes were fixed on the body by the river.

"They're dead."

Berg looked strangely at Benjamin.

"If we stay, that's us in a few hours," Sipho said anxiously.

Benjamin glanced at the three rookies. He didn't know if they could hold their own in a fight, but if they surprised the terries ahead of them, they might just have a chance. "There's guerrillas on our trail, we move."

"How do you know that, Captain?" Berg's attempts at being alpha male were starting to irritate Benjamin.

"Sechaba dropped back this morning. He says six, maybe seven of them."

The other two privates looked as if they might piss themselves.

"It's getting dark." Sipho headed south without waiting for an order. Sechaba swam back across the river and joined him.

"Stay close." Benjamin signaled the unit. They waded through shallow water to hide their trail. As the sun cast long yellow fingers over the countryside, flaming to a deep red before disappearing beneath a violet sky, Benjamin silently took over from Sipho, pausing only to examine the telltale signs of his oblivious enemy in the bushes. He tracked them as far as the border when they started heading east, for Mozambique. Behind him, Berg and the two others were looking worse for wear, feeling their way through the grass, struggling to keep up.

Around 02:00, Benjamin told Sechaba to set up camp with the others, while he and Sipho went on. By 04:30, they found a fresh trail. One of the prisoners seemed to be bleeding badly, slowing them down. The enemy might decide that he wasn't worth their time. Benjamin picked up the pace. Sipho looked exhausted, but he remained half a stride behind Benjamin. They reached the guerrillas by 05:00. The ZANLA terries had taken up in a farmhouse, a stone's throw from the border. Benjamin and Sipho crawled through the long grass to the periphery of the farmhouse, darkness still providing cover.

"We go in."

Sipho lay on his stomach next to Benjamin. "Sechaba and the others will be here in a few hours."

"It will be too late, Sipho. We're losing our advantage."

Sipho nodded, his surly demeanor giving way to fear. After four tours in the bush, Benjamin had trouble remembering how that felt. They crawled through the grass to the periphery of the farmhouse, darting between chicken coops and outhouses. Sipho stopped suddenly, frozen to the spot near an old tractor at the back of the house. Benjamin's irritation with the tracker changed when he saw why. A white woman's body lay on the ground, her bloodied dress pushed over her head. Blood ran down the tractor's wheels and culminated in the smashed head of a toddler at its base. The child had thick bruises around both ankles.

The shot Benjamin fired into the guard's head at point-blank range woke the others up. Men shouted, firing blindly. Benjamin felt one with the darkness, moving between them, dispatching single rounds, bodies hanging suspended in the moment between life and death as he moved on to the next ones. They were not human to him, only a threat to be eliminated, no more, no less. It was over within minutes. Benjamin placed the barrel of his gun against the temple of the last man standing.

"Where are my men?"

The guerrilla lifted his chin and spat. Sipho hit the man with the butt of his own rifle, sending him sprawling. A dark patch of blood on Sipho's shirt betrayed the fact that he'd been hit. Benjamin couldn't help but be annoyed by this. A good tracker was hard to come by. He should have done this alone.

"I'm not asking again," Benjamin said.

"Go fuck a monkey, white boy." The treble in the man's voice betrayed his bravado.

"You're not worth a bullet." Benjamin clamped his hand around the man's throat, pushing him up against the wall. "Where are they? Tell me and I'll make it quick."

The man's nostrils flared. He tried to kick Benjamin. Benjamin banged his head against the wall. He tightened his grip, crushing the man's trachea. The more the man struggled, the more alive Benjamin felt. This was personal, a connection that bound them to each other, predator and prey. Jooste had once offered him power. Money, control—all these things were arbitrary compared to the true power of taking a life. He alone stood as the judge and jury, the Angel of Death, hiding in plain sight. Blood vessels burst in the guerrilla's eyes.

His body gave a last spasm and for the instant before he let the man fall to the floor, Benjamin permitted himself to think of Tessa.

Sechaba, Berg and the others later found the executed white policemen's bodies in the rows of corn. Benjamin noticed a hardening in Berg's expression. The boy was learning quickly. The other two walked around with dazed expressions, going through the pockets of the dead men, trying to find anything useful on the movement of the guerrillas.

As the others dug the holes, Berg approached Benjamin. "Sipho says you killed all those men by yourself, Captain. Says you moved like a ghost."

"You like to listen to superstitious nonsense, Berg?" Benjamin ran his hand over the bushy beard he'd let grow the last three months, trying to decide whether he wanted to go through the trouble of shaving it off before he went back to Pretoria. At the *trek* centennial long ago he had stood in awe of the men who grew facial hair. Did he look like them now, an adult at last?

"How did you do it, Captain?"

Benjamin turned to Berg, paying real attention to him for the first time. Going by appearances, they were about the same age. Back home, if people saw them walking down the street together, they would assume they were friends, young men out on the town, one fair, one dark, two sides of the same coin. "There is no time to wonder whether you should shoot or not, Berg. Out here, you shoot. While you hesitate, your men die, you die."

Berg nodded. "In college they showed us that video. About the black Communists. Killing nuns in the Congo. Slicing open pregnant women and stuff."

"*Ja.*" Benjamin had seen the footage. Fearmongering by some Italian filmmaker intended to shock with its violent scenes. It was standard fare now during the first week of police college, made the new recruits pay attention, made them realize that this is the enemy, that he has no mercy. For most of the sheltered white boys, fresh out of high school, it brought the point home efficiently, so they could begin to understand the language of hate.

"Do you think that will happen back home, Captain?"

"That's what we're preventing, Berg. We stop it here, we show those terries back home what they can expect if they try to mess with us."

"It's just . . . we say God is on our side. But while I was going through their pockets . . . I found a Bible. I mean, the terrie carried it with him. If he believed that God is on his side and we believe that God is on our side, who is right?"

"We know God is with us, because we are winning, Berg. We are fighting for our people, our way of living, our right to be in Africa. Our God-given right. God gave us this land. It is our duty to keep the black menace, the Communists, out."

"I only . . . He had a Bible, Captain. He probably prayed this morning too."

"The Bantu are less civilized," Benjamin recited. "The more primitive a people is, the less they are able to control their emotions. At the slightest provocation they resort to violence. They cannot distinguish between serious and less serious matters. They are less self-controlled and more impulsive." He locked eyes with Berg. "Page thirty-five of your Criminology and Ethnology handbook. Or did you skip over that part in college? Do you want them to do to our women what they did to that white woman over there, bash our children's heads in?"

Berg had a look of defiance, his jaw set tight. "I read everything, Captain. It doesn't explain—"

"Am I going to have a problem with you, Berg?"

"What do you mean, Captain?"

"When I'm in the bush, I don't need a man who wonders which side is right. I need a man who will have my back. Who will follow orders without question. Otherwise, you are worthless. You might as well put a bullet in your own brain. It's us against them. Understand?"

Berg nodded.

"I said, do you understand?"

"*Ja*, Captain. Us against them."

Benjamin watched Berg join the others as they finished digging the pits, with them, but not part of them. He soon took over leadership of the group, directing the men to cover the pit with leaves and petrol after they dumped the six black men into the hole. Berg dropped a match into the pit. Petrol flames leaped up. Benjamin watched for a long time, remembering the feeling of fire dancing on his skin.

Tessa

She dried her hands, put her wedding ring back on her finger, and practiced a nonchalant smile, preparing herself mentally for what was to come. She had the face of a woman in her mid-twenties, thinner than she should be, perhaps, blond hair cut short in an attempt to fit in with the times, but her eyes betrayed the world-weariness she felt in every thought. Outside the bathroom door, Dean, his hair thinning, his middle-aged paunch spreading, would unwittingly wait for her to disappoint him again.

Tessa picked up the black sash she had sewn for herself and draped it over her shoulder. The solidarity she felt with the other women while protesting on the parliament steps gave her courage. She went as often as she could. Women protesting apartheid did not achieve much in a world run by men, but at least she felt like she was not passively watching the country go to hell.

She found Dean outside in the garden, fiddling around in the dirt, taking a break from the mounds of case files on his desk. "I'm off, darling."

"Ah, my conscientious objector. Be careful?" Dean stood up and dusted his hands off.

People sometimes got physical against the women of the Black Sash. Tessa had had a narrow escape the week before, when someone flung a rock that missed her by centimeters.

"I will." Tessa looked at his dirty hands. "How are the tomatoes?"

"It'll be another week or so. If I can keep Rupert out." At Dean's feet, a golden spaniel wagged its tail. In the year since they got a dog, Rupert had managed to destroy the garden, two leather chairs and so many shoes that Tessa had a hard time finding matching pairs.

"We don't spend enough time with him," Tessa said.

"I know." Dean went on his haunches and rubbed the spaniel behind the ears. "But the kids love it when I bring him along." He often hosted community-outreach events in the townships and Tessa went with him, translating, helping where she could. The people called her *Nobantu*. Mother of humanity. Tessa thought it ironic.

"Makes one wonder if we should even bother having our own," she said casually.

Dean looked at her, a subtle sadness clouding his easygoing demeanor. "Again?"

Tessa nodded. Without warning she started to cry. It surprised her that she still had it in her to be disappointed after all the months of prodding and poking by the doctors amid reassurances that there was nothing wrong with either her or Dean.

Dean had his arms around her. "Perhaps we should give in-vitro a try?"

Tessa shook her head, scared that if the doctors looked too close, they might find the truth.

"Listen, Lilly, don't give up. If they can transplant a heart, they can certainly find a way to give us a baby."

"It won't work."

"It might."

Tessa looked away, unable to meet his eyes. "I can't even do this one thing that's supposed to happen naturally."

"Nonsense." Dean took both her hands in his. "Listen, we'll take a holiday, go away. It would do you good to relax. Let me just finish with the Terrorism Act case . . ."

Tessa pried her hands loose. "You're still working it? We talked about this."

"We have to appeal, Lilly. They're holding people without trial for sixty days now and talking about extending it. Don't you remember what we went through when they took Phillip? What *he* went through? Imagine if they can do that for two months or more without having to justify themselves to anyone."

"Always saving the world."

"That's why you married me."

"Yes." She leaned over and kissed him on the cheek. "But I worry."

"Hey," Dean said, pulling her close. "It doesn't matter to me, you know? The baby, I mean."

"I know," Tessa said, convinced that he was only saying it to make her feel better. She knew the time had come to tell Dean the truth, but the words sounded absurd in her head. He would think she was crazy, leave her. Perhaps Ben had been right. Perhaps they were abominations and this was God's curse. Tessa shuddered.

"Are you okay, Lill?"

"I need to talk to you."

"All right."

Rupert barked. In the house, the doorbell rang.

"You expecting anyone?"

Tessa shook her head. "Maybe Prudence? I invited her to bring Jacob over for a visit sometime this week so I could give him his birthday present. He's getting so big." A lump formed in her throat, but she swallowed it back. Dean squeezed her hand. Tessa couldn't stand his look of pity, so she walked back into the house.

There was nobody at the front door. Tessa was about to close it when she noticed a package on the ground. She started, staring at the block letters on the simply wrapped rectangle. "TESSA." She glanced at the street. Beyond their garden fence lay the white Johannesburg suburb of Sandton, manicured lawns, the smoke from *braaivleis* fires rising up from backyards. But he was there, she could feel his presence. Ben had found her.

Tessa grabbed the package and backed into the house, locking the door behind her. Her hands shook as she tore at the brown wrapping, revealing a plain school notebook. The cracked red binding and curled pages showed signs of wear. She opened it.

A woman's name, Janine Herbst, was written in familiar childish script at the top of the first page. Obsessive pages of intimate details followed, her friends, where she went, even the dates of her menstrual cycle. At the end of the entry was a date and time, December 9, 1948, 0:42. Tessa turned the pages, Sannie van Aswegen, a slew of facts, a date and time concluding the entry. The whole book was filled with names. One entry made her stop. Melanie Steenkamp. Tessa remembered a newsreel in the cinema, black-and-white images of a beautiful blond girl with a bouquet in her arms. Tessa turned to the end of the entry, dated May 2, 1960, 23:10.

Dean was at the back door, wiping his feet, trying to keep Rupert out of the house. Tessa crammed the notebook and packaging inside her handbag on the dining-room table.

"Who was it?" Dean wiped his hands on his trousers.

"No one. Go wash your hands. I just did the laundry."

"Sorry." Dean looked at her sheepishly.

"You need a bath, my piggy."

"You wanted to talk to me about something, Lilly?"

"Tonight, when I get back." Tessa hesitated outside the bathroom door, her thoughts racing. They could empty their bank accounts, pack what was necessary and leave. As soon as she thought it, she realized it was foolish. She couldn't ask Dean to give up his work and hide for the rest of his life. But she also couldn't bear to leave him. She needed to gather her thoughts, figure out what Ben was up to. She grabbed her hand-bag and car keys. "I'm off, darling. There's a plate for you in the fridge."

Dean stuck his head out of the bathroom. "Love you."

Flippie

"I didn't say it back, Flippie. I didn't tell him I loved him too. I was only gone a couple of hours. I didn't even go to the protest. I just needed to think, clear my head. I came back home and . . . There is so much blood. So much."

"Tessa, slow down. What happened?" Flippie gripped the phone receiver between his shoulder and ear, trying to clear a space on his desk for his coffee mug. Prudence looked up at him from her knitting, concern in her eyes. On the floor of the living room, Jacob played with plastic farm animals, herding small sheep out to pasture with the help of a border collie.

"Dean was taking a bath. He is still in the tub, he's . . ." Tessa broke off in undecipherable sobs. "He's dead, Flippie."

Flippie felt stunned, not sure if he had heard her right. He sat down. "How?"

"Ben found me. He shot Dean. I know it was him. I thought he only wanted me, but—"

Flippie felt alarm at the name. "Tessa, listen to me. Go to the office. I'll come as fast as I can."

"I can't leave Dean."

"Tessa! Get out of there. Now." Flippie couldn't hear anything on the other end of the line. For a moment, he panicked. "Tessa?"

"Ja?"

"Please, Sis. I need you to listen to me. It's not safe to stay there. Get in your car and go. Right now, okay?"

"Ja."

There was a soft click. The thought of Dean's body in the house sent a new wave of anguish through Flippie. He tried to get his emotions under control and then called Pote Howard, a private investigator who sometimes consulted on cases. He explained the situation as concisely as he could, hoping that Tessa had made a mistake, that Pote would call back and tell him that Dean was fine, that he had simply slipped in the bath and hit his head.

"The police are swarming the place, Phillip." Pote delivered the news an hour later. "Security Branch. Wasn't much I could do. One of the younger *laaities* let it slip that it was a single gunshot to the back of the head. They are selling it to the reporters as an internal ANC dispute."

Flippie sighed. This was the mantra of the police whenever they "took care" of bothersome members of the ANC. The blacks were so barbaric, they killed their own people. How can we possibly let them control the country? Since the ANC and PAC were banned, no real investigation was ever launched into the disappearance or death of black men. But this would be different. There would be an outcry in the media, whites cowering in their houses, their hatred of the black menace reinforced.

"What about Dean's wife? Anyone mention her yet?" Flippie braced himself for the worst.

"They're not too interested in her," Pote said. "They're making this political. Look, did she . . . ?"

"No. But I need to ensure her safety, so it's better they forget about her for now."

"Understood. I'll see what I can do."

As he drove past the mine heaps, Flippie felt his age, the burden of the fight. His colleague, his dearest friend, had become another victim of a seemingly hopeless struggle. Even in police detention, when he was beaten, stripped of his dignity, when only the thought of Prudence and his son made him fight for life, he hadn't been this hopeless. If the government was willing to kill white people now to maintain power, they would stop at nothing.

Downtown Johannesburg was deserted. Tessa's car was parked outside the high-rise of Dean's office. Flippie found her cowering inside, her dress covered in blood. She rushed over to him as soon as he walked through the door, crying hysterically.

"What happened?" Flippie asked once he managed to calm her down enough to speak.

"His head was all . . . I was only gone for a few hours, Flippie." Tessa sank into Dean's chair, her arms wrapped around her waist. "It was Ben."

"You don't know that, Tessa."

"He sent me this." She showed him the notebook. Flippie had never met Ben, only heard Tessa speak about him. He often wondered if she was exaggerating the relationship, a jilted lover becoming a monster in her mind.

"What does this mean?"

"I think it's . . ." She held her mouth to her hand. "I think he killed them."

Flippie sat down next to her. "Look Tessa, Dean did a lot of work that the government didn't like. This case he was working on—"

"You're not listening to me, Flippie!"

"I am, Tessa. I'm just saying that Dean ruffled powerful people's feathers. It's not the first time the Security Police would have done this sort of thing."

Tessa's face contorted, tears flowing freely. "I was going to tell him, you know."

Flippie put his arm around her. "I know, little one."

"It should have been me."

Flippie felt his own grief rip at his chest. The only way he knew how to cope was to focus on what needed to be done. "We have to get you to safety. If it is this Ben—"

Tessa gave him a sharp look. When Flippie looked into those pale eyes, he often wondered if the old stories and scary movies were true, if she was one of those creatures that lived forever because she had no soul. He pushed the thought aside, ashamed of himself. Tessa had changed with Dean, the selfish little girl had disappeared. She was essential to their work now, facilitating communication, understanding. If she had been a man, her gift would have been invaluable.

"I believe you, Tessa." Flippie touched Tessa's arm. "But we can't rule out the alternative. The government might simply have wanted him out of the way. There's an ANC safe house on a farm about fifty kilometers outside town. You can stay there for a while. I'll organize a new ID book and birth certificate, but it'll take a few days."

"What, then?" Tessa looked lost.

"You need to get out of the city."

"I can't."

Flippie took her face in his hands. "Like *Pa* taught us, remember?"

There was a flicker in Tessa's eyes, a memory they both shared. Andrew packing their bags when they were children, deciding what they could take with them. "Moving is like shedding your cocoon," he'd say. "Nobody will remember the ugly worm you were, they'll only see the new butterfly." Flippie wondered if it had become easier over the years for Tessa to shed her old self. From the pain in her eyes, he doubted it.

Flippie moved a cabinet behind Dean's desk away and unlocked the safe behind it. He took cash from inside and placed it on the desk. "Take this. I'll try to get you more."

Tessa stared blankly at the money. "I forgot Rupert."

"Tess?"

"I left him there, alone. Dean would never have left him."

"Tessa, don't do this."

Tessa grabbed his wrist. "You don't believe me about Ben, but you have to listen, Flippie. He's dangerous."

Flippie gently took her hands. "I'll make sure he can't find you."

Tessa looked up at him, a wry smile distorting her lips. "He said he'd always find me."

Benjamin

Distracted men and the smell of cheap perfume filled the smoky bar. Benjamin glanced at his watch. Van Vuuren was late. He'd reassigned Benjamin to the new Bureau of State Security—BOSS—the moment he set foot back in the country. It seemed that news of his . . . efficiency had reached the higher echelons of the force, and they always needed a man who could get things done.

Benjamin finished his brandy, his limbs softening at last. He took the newly bought notebook out of his briefcase and placed it on the table. Only one entry. A short one. It wasn't hard to find out what he needed to know this time. He started writing the date at the bottom of the page in a careful, almost childish script. A drink appeared on the table, and Van Vuuren sat down.

Benjamin tucked the notebook into his briefcase. "You didn't get me one?" Benjamin touched his hand to his chest. "I'm hurt, Boss."

"Who authorized the hit?" The corners of Van Vuuren's mouth were set in a hyperbole of disgust.

"Sir?"

"Don't play dumb with me, De Beer. The lawyer today, Kritzinger."

Benjamin leaned back. "You did, of course. Congratulations, sir. You took care of a Communist collaborator. Maybe we'll have another secret medal ceremony in the defense minister's office. What do you think?"

"Don't play games with me, boy."

Benjamin smiled at being called "boy." He got up and walked away from the table, chatting with the bartender as he languidly ordered another drink.

The old man's face had taken on a livid hue by the time he got back to the table. "You explain yourself, right now."

"You should go home, Boss. You might miss an important call."

"Look here, I will not let a snot like you dictate what happens in my unit, understand?"

Benjamin watched a stumbling drunk man at the bar. The man clung to a woman young enough to be his daughter. Benjamin found it curious that he felt nothing, no moral judgment, no disgust. He didn't get hard at the sight of the man running his hands over the woman's breasts, his thumbs lingering over her nipples.

The numbness hadn't happened all at once. It was like a spiral winding tighter and tighter as the days went on, crushing everything in his soul. War had changed the value of life for him. All the people around him became inconsequential puppets, obstacles to achieving his salvation. He went through the motions of being among them, following the rigid, ritualized code of behavior that made it so easy to blend in, but he knew that he could put a bullet in any of their brains and feel nothing. God had shown him his true place, a lion among the sheep.

"Are you listening?"

"The decision was not yours to make." Benjamin turned a contemptuous gaze back to Van Vuuren. He once feared this legend, the man who made problems go away. Now he was that man, the ghost they whispered about in government hallways.

"Dammit." Van Vuuren slammed his hand on the table. "I am in charge, which means you work for me, not the other way around. Kritzinger had close ties with certain leftist journalists. His death is going to put them on the defensive. And that is your *fokop*."

"We control the media. Why is this a problem?"

Van Vuuren looked around the room before sliding a thick wad of paper across the table. "There's a leak. One of the *Broeders* talked."

Benjamin unfolded the sheets. A list of names in alphabetical order, hometowns and occupations appeared on the pages. There must have been more than a thousand names.

"It was found during a raid on a newspaper office. All Bond members." Van Vuuren glanced across the room. "There's rumors of a book in an English publisher's safe. If they had any doubts about going ahead with it, your little stunt just gave them incentive."

Benjamin paged through the names until he got to his own. De Beer, B. – Pretoria. University lecturer. His other life, the cover for his real work. Or was it the other way around? He slid the sheets back to Van Vuuren. "I'll take care of it."

"Didn't you hear me? Those journalists disappear and that book hits newsstands all over the world."

"It will happen anyway. You were careless." Benjamin looked at his watch again. He sidled out of the booth.

"We're not done here."

"This is pointless. I have work to do." Benjamin put his hat on and left.

Purple jacaranda blossoms, trampled and bruised, littered the streets of Pretoria after the early rainstorm. Benjamin breathed the damp air while he waited. A cream-colored Mercedes pulled up to the corner across the street a few minutes later. Right on time. A portly older man got out of the car and waved. A petite blond woman in a short skirt and high heels stepped out of a doorway, a coquettish smile on her full lips. The man opened the passenger-side door for her.

Benjamin crossed the street, slipping gracefully between two cars, stopping the girl from getting into the Mercedes. "I need some company," he said.

"Beat it," the man said indignantly. "The lady's spoken for."

Benjamin focused on the girl. Eyes lighter than clouds looked up at him. She gave him the same smile she had lavished on her companion moments earlier. "Maybe later, okay, handsome?" Her eyes darted to the man. "Meet me back here in an hour," she whispered.

Benjamin crouched down. "I've been waiting long enough for you, Carien," he said. The girl looked at him in surprise.

"Get away." The man grabbed Benjamin's arm.

Benjamin pushed him back with little effort. He surveyed the man's disappearing neck, the burst veins on his nose, the thick bags under his eyes. Poor bastard couldn't get a girl like this any other way than paying.

"I need someone for the whole evening." Benjamin smiled at the girl, offering his arm.

She hesitated. "He's a regular."

"I'll give you twice the going rate and a little extra if things go well."

Carien looked at the other man. When he didn't counter the offer she shrugged. "Sorry, Koos. Maybe tomorrow, hey?"

Koos waved her away. "Plenty where you come from, girlie. You're nothing special. Just remember, you're losing a good customer here." He plopped into the driver's seat, and tires screeched as he sped off.

"He's wrong, you know, Carien." Benjamin put his hand behind her neck, caressing it gently. "You're quite special."

"You're not going to cheat me, hey, mister?" She looked at him with sudden vulnerability and his pulse quickened, a promising pinprick under his skin, heat rising from his core. Dealing with Tessa's man, he had walked away from the house as hollow as when he entered it. But this, now, the girl's life pulsing beneath his fingertips . . . Every time he closed his hands around the neck of one of the others, he felt a connection to Tessa, a raw need, a spark igniting the quietly remembered feeling of purpose. Soon, nothing would keep them apart.

9

Thursday
DECEMBER 16, 2010

Knocking. A thin strip of light cracked the heavy hotel curtains. Alet rolled over on her back, her head thick. Details of the previous night slowly came into focus. Dinner. The waitress, and the wineglass. Mike kissing her. And then the hotel bar, where Mpho, the chatty bartender, had poured her a couple of stiff whiskeys while telling her about what he would do if he won the Lotto. Alet made a move to sit up and sank right back into the pillows.

"Housekeeping!"

Alet stumbled out of bed and felt around for her clothes. Another knock, more insistent this time. Leaving the security chain on, she cracked the door open. *"Ja?"*

A housekeeper in a stiff pink uniform stood outside the door. "Sorry, Madam. Checkout was at eleven. Are you staying another night?"

Alet looked back at the alarm clock on the nightstand. 11:40. Dammit. "No. Sorry, hey. I'll be out in a minute, okay?" She turned her T-shirt right-side-out and smelled the pits, a faint odor of sweat and deodorant on the cloth. It'd have to do. She made a halfhearted attempt to tidy herself up, tying her hair in a ponytail and splashing water on her face. Her cell rang.

"'Lo?" Alet pinched the phone between her ear and shoulder while kicking her shoes out from under the bed.

"Constable Berg?"

"Professor Koch?" Alet felt around in her bag for her toothbrush. "Can I call you back now-now? I'm in the middle of something here."

"We have to talk." It wasn't a request.

"You have something for me?"

"When can you be in Cape Town?"

Alet checked the clock again. "Ten minutes, okay?"

Alet's mind was still reeling from what Koch had told her as she pulled up to Mathebe's house later that evening. It was on the other side of Unie, a solid brick building half-hidden from the street by a fence and a couple of oak trees. A gravel path snaked through the small garden to the front door. She shifted the six-pack of Black Labels to her left hand and rang the doorbell. A light went on above her head, the ornate glass-and-metal lampshade casting spotted golden shadows over the stone inlay of the *stoep*.

A woman with short, stylish hair answered the door. "Good evening?"

Alet wondered if she had the right house. The fact that Mathebe didn't live alone had never crossed her mind. "Hallo. I'm looking for Sergeant Mathebe? I work with him."

The woman smiled, the corners of her big brown eyes crinkling. "Johannes is in." Alet was fascinated by the liquid brown sheen of her skin. Her face was open and welcoming, her cheeks round, almost plump, a theme repeated by the rest of her body, the bold floral print of her dress accentuating every curve. "I am Miriam Mathebe." She looked at Alet with expectation.

"Oh, I'm sorry." Alet realized that she was staring. "I'm Alet Berg. Constable Berg." She lifted the six-pack. "I brought this."

A brief crinkle crossed Miriam's brow. She took the beer from Alet. "Thank you. Please, come in."

Alet followed Miriam through a small kitchen, the remnants of a recent dinner still lingering in chakalaka and samp pots. Miriam left the beer on the kitchen counter. The hallway was lined with family portraits, a wedding picture of a slender Miriam and a boyish-looking Mathebe, and a picture of Mathebe in uniform at his graduation cere-mony, pride obvious in his smile. Alet had one that was almost identical.

In the living room, a young boy and a prepubescent girl were watching television.

"This is *Baba*'s friend from work," Miriam said. "Constable Berg, this is Celiwe and Little Johannes."

The children greeted her politely. Little Johannes's eyes wandered back to the cartoons on the screen. He tugged at the bottom of his T-shirt revealing a bulging little-boy belly.

"Time to get ready for bed now." Miriam patted Little Johannes on the back and turned the television off. "Celiwe, I'll be along to ask you about your history lesson in a moment."

The girl sighed. Her eyes had the same droop as Mathebe's, her hair braided into neat cornrows. Miriam raised a warning eyebrow and Celiwe nodded, following Little Johannes out of the room.

Miriam pulled the heavy living-room curtains aside to reveal an open glass door. "Johannes is in the back, Constable Berg."

Mathebe sat on a patio chair, coffee cup in hand. He looked up, a deep frown embedding itself when he saw Alet. She suddenly felt nervous.

"Constable Berg. This is not expected."

"*Ja*. Sorry." Alet had thought about calling, but there was the chance that he wouldn't give her the time of day. Better to beg for forgiveness than ask for permission, she thought.

"Can I get you a refreshment before I put the children to bed, Constable Berg?"

"A beer would be great, Miriam," Alet said. "And call me Alet."

Mathebe gave his wife a questioning look.

"Alet was kind enough to bring refreshments."

Alet smiled. "A peace offering."

"Please sit," Mathebe said. He handed Miriam his empty coffee cup. "I am not sure why you are here, Constable," he said as soon as Miriam disappeared into the house.

"Well, I thought we could share a drink, maybe talk about the case."

"I do not believe it concerns you anymore."

"Look, Johannes, I know we don't see eye to eye, but I need you to hear me out. Have one beer with me."

He opened his mouth to speak, but Alet held her hand up. "One. That's all I ask."

Mathebe studied her face for a moment before he nodded. "I will give you that."

Miriam appeared in the doorway with Alet's beer and a fresh cup of coffee. "Please excuse me while I tend to the children."

"Of course. Thank you."

Alet twisted the cap off the beer bottle and took a sip. Mathebe stirred his coffee as methodically as he did everything else. He took a languid sip.

"You don't like beer?" Alet knew Mathebe was a stiff, but she thought she could get him to loosen up before she dropped this bomb on him. "Must be the only policeman in the history of the force."

"I prefer coffee."

"Oh." Alet took two large sips from the bottle. "It's been a week, you know. I mean, since we found her."

"Yes."

"I know I'm supposed to stay out of it. That I fucked up."

Mathebe pursed his lips and leaned back in his chair.

"*Fok*, messed up. Sorry. I don't mean to . . . What I wanted to say, is that I am sorry. About going behind your back and not respecting your investigation."

A light went on in one of the rooms of the house. Alet heard the muffled voice of Miriam quizzing Celiwe on her homework. She thought about the history exams she'd had to take in school, how the textbooks changed when the ANC came into power. A new history for the New South Africa. She wished that her own history could be changed that easily, her bad decisions erased with something as simple as a revised textbook.

Mathebe studied her, his expression unchanged. "I received a call from Oudtshoorn. Sergeant Maree. He wanted to let you know that he found a case that matched your criteria. The coroner had concluded that the victim was strangled before she was set on fire."

"I'm sorry, Johannes, I—"

"You have continued investigating the case, Constable Berg. You come to my house, apologizing for going behind my back, and yet you are still going behind my back."

"Please, just hear me out."

Mathebe sighed. "Your beer is almost finished."

"There is something very wrong, Johannes. I saw Professor Koch today. He ran DNA on the body. Trudie Pienaar wasn't white."

There was a crack in Mathebe's expression.

"Not in the sense that I'm white or you're black, or April is coloured."

"I don't understand what you are trying to say, Constable. Was she Asian?"

"No." Alet sighed. "So, Trudie looked normal, right? But there's something different about her genes or something."

Alet tried to remember exactly what Koch had told her that afternoon. They had met at the gardens near parliament. Koch led her to a secluded area, away from the tourists. His lisp was so bad that she could barely keep up with what he was saying. She had to ask him to repeat most of it, not understanding any of the scientific gibberish. Once he dumbed it down for her, her mind simply refused to believe that it was true. Koch explained that humans share 99 percent of their genetic makeup with chimpanzees, but that it was that 1 percent that made all the difference. Trudie's 1 percent looked different from other people's.

"What exactly does that mean, Constable?" Mathebe was losing patience.

"It means that she wasn't just a different race. Apparently this gene thing meant that she was . . . a different species." Alet paused, watching a look of incredulity form on Mathebe's face. "I know," she said. "I'm having trouble with it too."

"The victim was not human?" Mathebe's coffee cup balanced at a precarious angle on his lap.

"Koch said it would have been like the difference between us and Neanderthals. They looked like ugly-ass humans, but they weren't human at all. Because some part of their genes was different."

Mathebe raised both eyebrows so high that they almost touched his hairline. "We do not have a case to solve, then. The SAPS does not investigate the death of random animals. Only livestock. Was Mrs. Pienaar part cow or sheep, Constable?"

Alet was taken aback. She wasn't used to Mathebe being sarcastic. "Look, Johannes. I know this is hard to believe, but Koch is sure of the results."

"How did she get here? A spaceship, perhaps? Or did she one day decide to crawl out of a mud puddle?" Mathebe had a sneer on his lips.

"Listen to me, please? I don't know what this means yet, but I think that we are dealing with something bigger than just one murder. It's not just that murder in Oudtshoorn that was similar to the Pienaar murder. I've managed to find thirteen other murders across the country. All of them with the same MO. And there might be more."

"Sergeant Maree said the murder in Oudtshoorn took place in 1958. Even if the killer was a teenager, he would be an old man by now."

Alet sank back in her chair. "There are murders earlier than that. As far back as the forties." Mathebe gave her a questioning look. "I have a friend at the university in Cape Town who has been helping me find them," she said.

Mathebe's nostrils flared. "Are you absolutely sure they are connected, Constable?"

Alet nodded. "I wouldn't waste your time."

"I have to speak to Captain Mynhardt."

"No, please, Johannes. He can't know about any of this. Not yet."

"He will know as soon as he receives Professor Koch's findings."

The faint call of a hyena sounded in the distance. Alet took a deep breath, considering the possibility of walking away. She got up from her chair. "Koch has agreed to keep that part out of it. His lab guy doesn't even know. I think he wants to write some article or something on the discovery."

"So why would he tell you?"

"I don't know. He said something about needing access to the body so he could run more tests."

"This still does not explain why the captain has to be kept in the dark."

"Mynhardt knows my father."

"I am aware of this."

Of course he was. Alet shifted her gaze to the glowing white cross on the hill that overlooked Unie. "Eight of the thirteen murders I found were investigated by my father. They called them the Angel killings." Alet was afraid of making eye contact with Mathebe, of seeing the judgment there. The hyena cried out again, closer this time. She crossed her arms. "There were no suspects. It was the only case in my dad's career he didn't solve."

"Your father is not infallible."

"There's more." Alet bit her lip. She had received a call from Theo that morning after her meeting with Koch, linking the two case files she'd given him with news reports and media coverage of other similar murders. Theo had to search for death certificates to confirm cause of death. "The case files went missing when my father transferred to Security Branch."

Mathebe shook his head slowly. "A lot of files went missing in those years."

"Those files were destroyed on purpose."

"Files were destroyed so that government-sanctioned assassins could get away with murder, Constable. Were your victims activists?"

"They were all Afrikaner women, housewives, secretaries, prostitutes."

Mathebe narrowed his eyes. "Why are you really here, Constable Berg?"

Alet steeled herself. "I have to know the truth."

"And if you find that your father has something to do with these murders, that he protected a killer in exchange for a promotion? What will you do?"

"I don't know."

Mathebe took a moment before he spoke again. "Do you know what the date is, Constable?"

"What?"

"It is the sixteenth of December. *Geloftedag*—the day of the pledge. When the *Voortrekkers* made a pledge to God that they would always commemorate the day if He helped them beat the Zulu at the battle of Bloedrivier, because the blood of the savages stained the river red. A pact made in blood. The Afrikaner and God against the savages of this land."

Alet frowned, uneasy with where this was heading. "Why the history lesson?"

"When I was a boy, we would watch the *baas* and his neighbors walk to church on this day, to celebrate their victory, to thank God and honor their ancestors. After, they would go home and feast and throw their leftovers to the dogs. It was that same *baas* who paid in cheap brandy to keep the workers drunk and under his thumb while he grew even fatter than his father before him. And the lower he pushed those savages, the more they drank to escape despair. I do not drink alcohol, Constable Berg. I do not allow it in my house. When I left my mother's house, I swore I would never be controlled by the *baas* or the bottle like my father and his father. That I would never come home in a drunken stupor and beat my wife and my children because that was the only power I had. I worked hard to become a policeman. Because I wanted the power to change things. Because I wanted to give power to the people who were not chosen by God."

Mathebe's hands balled in his lap. "You are asking me to help you investigate a very powerful man." He looked at the light in Celiwe's room. "If this goes wrong, you will dust yourself off and say sorry, Father. All will be forgiven for you, but I will not have that luxury. My family will not have that luxury. In this land it is still us against them."

Alet picked up her empty beer bottle. "I'm sorry. I should have realized." She headed for the garden gate, not wanting to disturb Miriam and the children. Mathebe was the straightest arrow she knew. If even he was scared, there was little hope of her finding anyone who would help her. "It's not called that anymore, you know." Alet's hand rested on the garden gate. She turned to face Mathebe. "It's called the Day of Reconciliation now."

Mathebe didn't answer. Alet marched back, going on her haunches next to his chair. "I will make a promise to you, Sergeant Mathebe. I will share everything I find from now on. If I don't, you can hand me over to Mynhardt on a silver platter. And if it turns out that my father is guilty, I will respect your decision on what to do with that information." Alet waited, her heart catching in her throat. She felt nauseated, her understanding of the world thrown out of balance in a few short days. There was an uncertain future ahead of her, and she hoped that she had been right to trust Mathebe.

"I am in charge of this case." Mathebe's words came slow as molasses. "It is my duty to see it through. Give the victim justice, no matter who she was."

"You will help, then?"

"I will talk to the captain to get you reinstated."

"Thank you, Sergeant."

"I am giving you until Boxing Day. After that, I will hand everything we have over to the captain."

Alet made her way across the front of the house to where she had parked Tilly's pickup. The porch light went out behind her. Something stirred in the shadows behind one of the oak trees.

"Johannes?" Alet kept her eye on the trees. "Who's there?" She felt for the pickup keys in her pocket. As she turned around to unlock the door, a twig snapped behind her.

"Boet Terblanche, I swear if that is you . . ."

A hyena cried, much closer this time.

"Answer me!"

A soft ping reverberated, dust flying up against her leg. Alet hunkered down before her mind had a chance to process the fact that the shooter was using a silencer. She reached up for the pickup's door handle. The light in the cab went on. *Shit.* Another shot, this one lodging in the side of the truck, barely missing her hand. She jumped in as fast as she could and slammed the door behind her. She turned the key in the ignition, shifting into gear and slamming her foot on the petrol, driving blind. The truck skidded on the gravel, swaying dangerously as the front wheel hit the curb. Glass shattered next to her head.

"*Fok!*" Alet jerked the wheel back to where she thought the road was. She lifted her head just enough to see over the dash. The truck bounded over a bump in the road and she hit her chin on the steering wheel. Blood rushed into her mouth, the horn blaring. The lights went on in Mathebe's house.

"Stay down, there's a shooter," Alet yelled out the window as Mathebe opened the front door. He crouched down and backed into the house.

In the rearview mirror, a silhouette ran across the road. Alet turned the truck around. The figure disappeared between rows of houses before she had a chance to train her high beams on it. She drove back up the block, searching for movement, not sure what she would do if the person started shooting again. Headlights. Alet saw a car starting up a few blocks away. She floored the gas. The truck jerked forward and stalled.

"Dammit!"

The distant headlights disappeared between the houses. Mathebe ran up to the pickup, gun held out in front of him. He got in on the passenger side. "Are you all right, Constable?"

"No! That *fokker* is getting away." Alet turned the keys in the ignition, the engine groaned, then sputtered to silence. "Ugh!" She slammed her hands against the steering wheel.

"Constable?"

Alet looked over at Mathebe, realizing for the first time that he was only wearing boxers. She suddenly couldn't contain herself.

Mathebe frowned. "Why are you laughing?"

"You're buff."

"You have to be fit for the job," he said self-consciously.

Alet's laughter renewed itself. She crumpled over the steering wheel, her eyes tearing up.

Mathebe looked at her stoically. "I do not understand what is funny."

"Sorry, it's just . . . you. In your underwear. And the pickup stalling." Alet wiped her eyes. "It's just too much."

Mathebe put his hand on her shoulder. "Are you all right?"

"I don't know."

"I will get dressed and we can go to the station."

"No." The laughter died abruptly in Alet's throat.

"We have to report—"

"Listen, Johannes. I'm not supposed to be anywhere near this case. If Mynhardt finds out about this, he won't reinstate me. Please. I'm okay, really."

"You are in danger."

"It means we're on the right track. We just need to figure out whose track it is."

"If you are sure." Mathebe opened the door and hesitated. He looked back at Alet, mulling something over before deciding to speak. "We have a comfortable couch."

It took Alet a moment to realize that he was extending an invitation. Her first reaction was to decline, but she thought about going home and the possibility that she might disintegrate into a puddle if she was alone. "Thank you," she said. "I think I will."

Mathebe nodded. "Tonight we rest. Tomorrow we find this criminal."

1976

Jacob

A gunshot rang out. A girl screamed as the limp body of her thirteen-year-old brother fell. Schoolchildren froze, the stones that they had picked up to fling at the police still in their hands. The ones who had adhered to the directive of a "peaceful" march stood dazed, confusion marring their youthful faces. Pop. The second gunshot ignited a fervor that defied reason, ignored fear. The children surged forward. The white men in their police fatigues let the dogs loose.

The placards proclaiming "DOWN WITH AFRIKAANS" and "IF WE MUST DO AFRIKAANS, VORSTER MUST DO ZULU" fell to the ground. The bearers reached for bricks and trash cans, anything they could use to defend themselves against the beasts. An Alsatian's growl turned to a yelp as the first stone hit its side, its body failing under the assault. The children's frenetic rage converged on the dumb animal, bashing it to a bloody pulp. A boy of no more than ten lifted an empty Coke bottle above his head. Pop. The bottle fell from his hands, blood spreading where the bullet had ripped his chest. He looked disbelievingly at the dog, quietly falling next to it. His companions dispersed, their eyes wide with fear. This was not supposed to happen. This was not how this day was meant to end.

The law had been passed two years before. Instruction in black schools was to be given in Afrikaans and English only. Teachers showed up to class with Afrikaans dictionaries, trying to teach their subjects in a language they themselves could barely speak. Jacob had felt the mood change as the screws were tightened one more turn, his own resentment burning.

They had rallied early that morning. As unsuspecting students showed up for school, they were told by the Students' Representative

Council Action Committee that today would be the day of protest, kept secret to catch the police unawares. They would march to other schools in the township, gain strength in numbers, make their voices heard. Their parents didn't know, but the older generation had become complacent, beaten down by so many years of oppression that they would not fight anymore.

Once the march started, they had found their way blocked by the police. But peace held. The procession rerouted, a sense of elation as the students sang "Nkosi Sikelel' iAfrika" over and over, a mantra of hope. Their number grew, joined by township gangsters and brave adults. "God bless Africa, let its horn be raised, listen to our prayers, Lord bless us, we are its family."

But then the line was crossed. Automatic rifle shots hailed down. Government buildings and school buses burned, charred symbols of the oppressor that took their land, their dignity, their power. The violence only receded with nightfall as women searched the streets for their children, the day's events punctuated by raw, inconsolable wails.

Jacob felt nauseated as he looked at the rows of bodies covered by newspapers because there weren't enough sheets. He had not allowed himself to think or feel, only react, running for shelter from the tanks that roamed Soweto. Leaning against the wreckage of a car, he noticed the body of a white man. Around his neck hung a hastily drawn board reading BEWARE AFRIKANERS. Jacob stepped closer. He recognized the man, a social worker in the township, always good for a laugh or to bum a smoke. He stared into the man's glassy blue eyes. It felt unreal to him, this thing that had happened. He never thought that they would be able to strike back. All his life he had believed that the white man was untouchable, yet here one of them lay. He reached out to touch the man's cold cheek, to make sure he wasn't dreaming.

Pop. A hot pain seared through Jacob's left side and he fell on top of the social worker. Pop. Dust rose up a few feet ahead of him. Pop. Jacob rolled off the body and slid under the car, his instinct for survival trumping the pain. Pop. His leg felt warm and wet, but he waited, too frightened to move. Pop. Pop. Shots fired, not at him this time, but in the distance. The nearest building was a sink-plate outhouse. As soon as he was sure they had moved on, he crawled over to it, thankful too for the cover of rapidly descending darkness. Let it end, please, God, he thought as he closed the flimsy door behind him and sank to the floor, the dank stench enveloping him. Just for tonight, let the slaughter stop.

Jacob didn't know how long he'd lain on the outhouse floor before the two women had found him. They had hoisted him between them and carried him to the hospital. A blood trail led to the emergency-room entrance. Jacob felt dizzy. The confusion of bodies and doctors distorted in his fever dream, mashing into one being, a red, undulating monster. "I am Jacob Morgan," he managed to tell the creature as it put its arms around him. The red thing's lips moved, but he couldn't hear what it was saying.

When Jacob opened his eyes again, he was on a gurney, his left side throbbing with a warm pain that extended all the way to his stomach. His mother's careworn face floated in front of him. She wore a black beret and her good Sunday dress. He thought it funny that she had dressed up. The ward was filled with beds, identical to his, their occupants bandaged and beaten down, adults hovering at their sides, their expressions mirroring his mother's.

"Jacob?" She was crying.

"He's all right, Prudence." His father put his hands on her shoulders.

"We scared those Dutchmen *lekker.*" Jacob forced the words through parched lips, ignoring the look in his father's eyes. He had watched his dad deal with the apartheid government for years, defending activists, trying to remain civil, and for what? They, the youth of Soweto, did more to put a dent in the armor of the white man in one day than his dad had done in a lifetime. They had shown them that they would fight back.

"What you did was stupid. You don't think." His dad pointed a finger up at the sky. "You hear that?" Jacob became aware of a constant drone. "The police are coming down on Soweto. The only thing you've accomplished was to give them an excuse to fire on us without asking questions." His dad's anger spilled into white-hot fury, and he turned his head, clinging to Jacob's mother as if she were the only thing keeping him standing.

"No more, Jacob. Please." His mother touched her palm to his father's chest, an intimate gesture that made Jacob uncomfortable.

"We have to get you out of here." His father wiped his eyes. "The police are taking names of everyone who was treated for bullet wounds."

Jacob let his mother help him up and dress him, as if he was a little boy.

"I bought a train ticket." His father stood by the door, hands restless in his pockets, eyeing everyone that walked into the ward. "Tessa will take you for a while."

"I'm not going, *Pa*. People have to stand together. Not *chaile* like rabbits. We've had enough."

"I'm not going to allow you to *toyi-toyi* and be target practice for those animals."

"Please, Jacob." His mom clutched his hands. "Don't break your mamma's heart."

"If I'm in danger, so are you."

"We'll be all right." His dad had the look of finality about him, a steel door lowering between them. Jacob knew arguing would be useless.

A nurse rushed into the ward and handed his dad paperwork. "We documented it as an abscess," she said.

"*Ke a leboha*." His dad had a look of earnest gratitude on his face.

Jacob leaned on his mother, while his father led the way. Outside, the air was hazy and thick with smoke. Riot police manned the perimeter, rifles gripped in front of them, scowling at a crowd of retreating stone-throwers, the smell of tear gas lingering. Jacob's packed suitcase perched on the backseat of the Volkswagen Beetle and he sidled up next to it. His father navigated past the crowds, taking narrow back alleys between shacks and government housing. People spilled in and out of liquor stores and shops, running off with their loot before a bullet had the chance to stop them.

His father jerked the wheel as a stone bounced off the windshield. Jacob crouched behind the front seat. His mother reached for him across the divide and he clung to her hand, fear breaking through the fuzzy reality of the past day, his breath coming in shallow rasps, his pain forgotten. The stones became a horse's hooves pounding in rhythm with his heart. His father screamed. The car skidded to a halt. His mother's grip grew limp. Her body slouched forward.

A police officer flung the door open. "What you doing?" he shouted. "Get out of the car."

His dad raised his hands, his face pale with terror. He addressed the young policeman in Afrikaans. "My wife, sir. She's hurt. We have to get her to a hospital."

"You stand over there. Move."

His father got out and moved away from the car, his hands behind his head. The policeman leaned over the seat.

Jacob felt something explode in him as the man touched his mother. "No!" He reached over the seat to stop the man.

The policeman punched him in the face, a sharp blow that threw him back onto his suitcase. "Want to die today, *kaffir?*"

"Please, Officer. Please. He's my son. Only a boy," his father pleaded from the curb. Jacob had never seen him like that, scared, begging, raw fear forcing him to his knees. His father addressed Jacob in Sotho, pleading with him to remain calm, to do what the police said. Jacob slowly opened the car door, hatred raging in his veins, his hands shaking behind his head, the stitches in his side straining painfully as the policeman trained the gun at his head.

"Please, Officer." His father cupped his hands to the white man like a beggar. "My wife, she needs a doctor."

The policeman sneered. "What she needs is a morgue. If your son's not careful, he'll join her."

"Please, *Baas*. Please. We do not want trouble. We want to get away. Please, *Baas*."

Jacob looked at his father with his knees in the dirt, his pride gone, his dignity shattered. It was too much. Even as he told himself not to cry in front of these men, sobs of anger and grief and shame convulsed his body.

The policeman focused his attention on a column of smoke in the distance. Through his tears, Jacob noticed the look of embarrassment on his face. So they had a conscience, these men. Perhaps they were even human.

"The coloured hospital in Eldorado Park is open," the policeman said, his gun still trained on Jacob. "You go there."

Soweto writhed in fire as they drove away. Jacob reached for his mother's hand in the front seat. It was still warm, the faint line of death barely crossed. But from this, he knew, there would be no return.

Benjamin

The government had fought to keep it out, and yet the brand-new devil's box stood in the faculty lounge. Television. It was the harbinger of civil disobedience, the symbol of deteriorating family values, the mass dissemination of ideas like communism and equality. Benjamin turned the dial and a signal sprang to life. He sat down and stared at the static, the constant *shhhh* mesmerizing.

In the middle of the floor, the girl lay facedown. The back of her head was a tangled mess of bloody blond hair, her shirt torn in the back, one shoe flung to the other end of the room during their struggle. Pity. She'd had promise, for a woman—smarter than everyone else in her class, the previous three years' classes, in fact. Benjamin wondered if Tessa would have made it that far, given the chance. Of the two of them, she was the smart one, but things were different back then. Benjamin glanced back at the girl. She wasn't one of them, that much he knew. Her eyes were brown, her hair bleached. But she had paid enough attention to realize that there was something strange about him. He shouldn't have let her get that close. She had found the tissue samples he had taken of himself: Subject 302091. PRIMATE. UNIDENTIFIED SPECIES.

Light and truth were coming soon, Benjamin could feel it. The work had started to excite him again. Advances were happening so fast that he could hardly keep up with the research. The work that Jooste's man had done back then was oafish, clumsy, the necessary technology still years away. Benjamin had realized it early on, but Jooste had paid him, kept his position in the Broederbond secure, so he had participated in the farce until the old man died and the government shut the project down. Benjamin had often found himself staring at Jooste, trying to catch a glimmer, a flash of Tessa in the old man. He convinced himself that it was there, the way Jooste sometimes stared off into the distance as if he was gazing into another world, the way he tilted his head when something excited him, or curled his mouth when he was thinking. Benjamin often wondered about Dr. Leath and the experiments that had created all of them. With the primitive tools Leath had had at his disposal, did he really know what the result of his experiment would be? Or were they all a great cosmic accident, flung into existence by something nobody could control?

Rage burst through the static of Benjamin's mind. The girl had made the mistake of confronting him, threatening to expose what he was doing if he didn't let her in on the discovery. She was ambitious, he had to give her that. He told her the truth, everything he knew, the confession briefly setting him free. Throughout it all she had studied him closely as if he were an animal that should be put in a cage. He wasn't human. But then what was he? Somehow less than human? Is that what people saw in him, did they somehow know? Or was he perhaps more than human? Could that be what they instinctively feared? The girl would never have kept it to herself. He was too great a discovery.

"Captain De Beer?"

Benjamin recognized the voice. He tried to understand why Adriaan Berg was at the door. The softness of his youth was gone, his face hardened. His nasolabial folds had become harsh, exaggerated, his skin leathery, his dark hair finely specked with silver. Benjamin noticed a wedding band. How quickly life marched on for them.

Berg stepped into the room, staring past Benjamin at the body, his dark eyes betraying shock. "What's her name?" He hovered at the door, as if coming closer would make him part of the deed.

"Does it matter?"

"You called us for help. I can't fix this if—"

"She was an ANC activist." Benjamin recited the standard excuse. "Tried to pass as white, see? Spread propaganda on campus. She had to be taken care of." He was supposed to act like it mattered, he was supposed to know her name. Grethel . . . Something. Hansel and . . . No. Gretha. Gretha . . . Le Grange. *Ja.* "Gretha Le Grange."

"Anyone see you?"

"Nobody here on Sundays."

"Security logs?"

Benjamin snorted. "Dump her down a mine shaft and get it over with. Do your job."

A muscle jumped on Berg's jaw. "You have to come in with me."

Benjamin locked eyes with Berg. "Why?"

"This isn't your first *fokop* . . . Captain." Berg spat the word out as if it was poison. He didn't need to say more, it was written on his face. They were going to make him leave, disappear. Benjamin thought about calling in a favor, but the Bond was in a mess, everybody scrambling to cover their own asses. The book had been published earlier that year, and though it had been banned, the list of Broederbond members had become the most photocopied document in the country as people searched for the names of neighbors and friends to see who had been part of the secret organization that ruled the land.

The TV was still on. Berg reached to turn it off.

"Leave it," Benjamin said, a warning in his voice.

Berg folded his arms. "General's orders, you have to come with me."

Benjamin turned his attention to the box. Gray flecks on the screen. The *shhhh* of static. A face surfaced from a faded memory.

"Captain De Beer!"

Benjamin copied the sound, his front teeth grinding together, his lips an exaggerated trumpet. "*Shhhhhhh.*" He saw Tessa's face. Tessa who became Lilly Maartens, Lilly Kritzinger. As if a new name would have made her something other than what she was. At Security Branch they had different names too—Goose, Shortie, Doppies. The fools believed that a different name would keep the things they did at work separate from the Bibles they carried to church and the wives and children they kissed. They called Benjamin "Angel" because of his complexion. If only they knew how close they were. Benjamin De Beer had been a vulnerable little boy, human. But he was something different now: the angel of war, the angel of death, the angel of God's vengeance. Not human at all. He looked back at the static and jerked at what he saw. *Matrone* Jansen, in the storeroom, the strap in her outstretched hand.

"Did you hear me?" Berg touched his shoulder. "The unit is waiting outside to take you to the station."

"*Shhhhhh.*" Benjamin closed his eyes, trying to block Berg out.

"What the hell's wrong with you?" Berg went to the door, signaling two uniformed men to come in. "I think he's gone apeshit."

The first policeman grabbed Benjamin's arm. "Time to go, *bra.*"

Benjamin looked up at him, his hand buried beneath his shirt. There was a moment of clarity where he tried to reason with himself, but it receded. He slid the Tokarev from his waistband and shot the policeman in the throat. He hit the second man in the shoulder, then knocked him unconscious with the butt of his gun before pointing it at Berg. "Too slow, Berg. Shoot first, ask questions later. Have you learned nothing?"

"There's no walking away from this, De Beer." Behind Berg's bravado, Benjamin saw the fear of death in his eyes, the fear of him.

"You can stand there talking, Berg, or you can save your friends. Number two should be fine, but number one is having a little trouble breathing." He grabbed the chair next to him with his free hand, holding it in front of him.

Berg looked at the men on the ground and back at Benjamin, his face set in a grimace of frustration. Benjamin backed out of the room and closed the door behind him, setting the chair under the door handle.

"I'll find you," Berg yelled as he slammed his body against the door. "I'll destroy you."

The chair wobbled but held. Benjamin took the stairs to the ground floor, walked out of the building, past his car, and into the street. He slowly lifted his left thumb above his head.

"Where you headed?" The driver who pulled to the side of the road wore a dirty blue work shirt. The inside of his pickup reeked of sweat and grease.

"South."

"I can get you as far as Colesberg, okay?"

Benjamin opened the door. "That works."

Tessa

"It's just a nightmare, *Ngwana*. It's all right." Tessa sat on the edge of the narrow bed holding Jacob in her arms, his skin clammy against her, his pajamas soaked with sweat. He was too thin, she thought, as she pressed him to her, feeling his ribs. It had been almost a month since he had come to live with her in Kimberley, and still he screamed in his sleep. It broke her heart to see him cry. She rocked him, stroking his head. On the cusp of manhood, he was reduced to a child again, wetting his bed some nights, mostly staring into the flat landscape.

"I want my *ma* back, *Rakgadi*."

Tessa tried to comfort him in Sotho. "Try to go back to sleep?" Jacob pulled away. "I can't." He looked up at her, pleading.

"Then let's get a head start on the day, huh?" Tessa smiled. "I baked bread last night and we have fresh eggs."

Jacob nodded, a smile trickling through his anguish. Tessa took his hand and they made breakfast in the little kitchen. In an hour the room would be bathed in yellow-curtained sunlight. It always brightened her mood. Tessa fried up baked beans and eggs on the gas stove, putting Jacob in charge of coffee. She had tried her best to establish a normal routine. In the mornings Jacob helped her with chores before he went to the *location* school and she to the private Catholic school where she taught history. After school they sat at the table together, he with homework, she with exam papers. It reminded her of her childhood, sitting at the kitchen table helping a very young Flippie with his assignments. It was a quiet life, not very exciting, but Tessa had had enough of the kind of excitement that usually sprung up around her. All she wanted now was to blend in, stay hidden, the kind of life Andrew had always insisted on.

"No, wait," she said as Jacob sat down. She went out into the garden, her little yard blooming in full color. She had started a vegetable garden, a tribute to Dean. She picked a bunch of white daisies from one of the flower beds and arranged them in a small porcelain vase.

"There, much better." Tessa pushed the vase to the center of the table.

Jacob pushed food around on his plate, his head resting in his other hand. "I don't think I'm hungry." He dropped his fork and pushed his chair out.

"Please eat, Jacob. I promised your *pa* I'd look after you."

"So I can die later?" Jacob stood up. "I shouldn't be here."

"Your death in the streets of Soweto won't do any good."

"You're white, Auntie. You don't know what it's like."

Looking at the determination on his face, Tessa was suddenly afraid. "Stay here with me," she begged. "You can finish school. Make something good of your life, find peace. *Kgotso*."

"Peace doesn't work! Look where it got us." He looked away, his shoulders shaking.

Tessa got up and held Jacob close to her. He endured her embrace rigidly. After breakfast, he helped her clean up. She packed his sandwich for lunch and walked to the garden gate with him. "*Ke an o rata.*" Tessa touched his shoulder.

"I love you too, Auntie."

Tessa watched him get on the bus. Every cell in her body wanted to help him, make life better for him, try to heal the damage life had wreaked. She wondered if Flippie had told Jacob the truth about her.

Tessa gathered her things in a square basket—the student notebooks she had brought home to grade, the whistle she used when she coached the girls' netball team. She heard the front gate open, and she parted the curtains to see Markus Wexler, a middle-aged local farmer, coming down the garden path, wearing his Sunday suit, his short sandy hair neatly combed, his beard trimmed. Ever since Tessa had started teaching at the school, several of the female teaching staff had tried to set her up with young men in the district. The idea that a young widow was sitting alone at home obviously didn't sit well with them. Tessa had found all the men from the area myopic and boring, until she met Markus. They had a standing dinner appointment every Friday night, and their get-togethers had the district's ladies speculating on a wedding date. Markus was divorced, and he, like Tessa, had no real interest in romantic love, but they enjoyed each other's company and had quite a bit of fun feeding the rumor mill.

Tessa surprised Markus at the door, a wicked smile on her lips. "My, you got dressed up just to see me, Markus? Could it be that today is the day you ask for my hand?"

Markus looked taken aback for a moment. "Oh, no. I mean, I would, but I . . ." He smiled when he caught on. Tessa laughed, charmed by how easily he got flustered. "I wanted to come by and let you know that I can't make dinner."

"Oh?" Tessa was surprised at her disappointment.

"I have to pick my son up from the airport. He is coming to stay with me for a while."

"Jeffrey, right?" Tessa smiled reassuringly. "I can't wait to meet him."

Markus, for his part, looked nervous at the prospect. After their divorce, his ex-wife had moved back to Britain with her family and taken their son with her. Markus hadn't had much contact with Jeffrey after that.

"He . . ." Markus searched for the words. "He got into a bit of trouble over there. His mother thought it might help if he was away from his friends for a while."

"You'll get to spend some time with him."

Markus smiled back at her. "*Ja*. It will be good." He dug his hands into his pockets. "In any case, could you ask Jacob to come to the farm this weekend? I could use a hand. Unless you need him here?"

"I'll drop him off tomorrow morning," Tessa said quickly. Jacob had shown little interest in anything except when Markus sometimes asked him to help out on the farm. Tessa had seen something come alive in his eyes when he tended to the animals. It's what he needs right now, she thought, excited to tell him about it later.

"I'll be off, then," Markus said, and he pecked her on the cheek. Tessa felt grateful once again to have met him. Markus had become like family to her and Jacob. He'd never asked her why there was a black boy living with her, and he'd done his best to help smooth things out whenever questions were raised in town.

Tessa drove to school in her white Anglia. Flippie had laughed when she'd told him she was a teacher now, the thing that she once kicked against becoming. But she found it satisfying, especially when she could sneak in history lessons that weren't in the syllabus, something other than the victor's revisionist myths.

It was almost five o'clock by the time Tessa finished coaching the netball team and returned home. She pulled up to the house, surprised to see that there were no lights on.

"Jacob!" Tessa called when she opened the front door. She was met with silence. She walked through the house, finding it empty. Jacob's room in the servant quarters out back was clean and neat. He usually slept in the house, but they had to keep up appearances for the townspeople, just in case there were whispers. A single sheet of notebook paper lay on his bed. Tessa reached for it. His uneven script seemed to move in front of her eyes. She had to read over it several times, the ground suddenly malleable under her, as if she might sink into it.

Rakgadi,

I thank you for giving me your home, but I have to go where I am needed. Umkhonto will train me to be a strong man for my people, so do not worry. I borrowed crown for the train from your tea tin. I promise to pay you back when I can.

—Jacob

10

Friday
DECEMBER 17, 2010

"Unie Police." Alet answered the phone, unable to keep the boredom out of her voice. Mathebe had retracted his complaint and Mynhardt, desperate for an extra man, had reinstated her that same morning. She was stuck on desk duty for the time being, but at least she was back in uniform.

"*Ja*, hallo?"

"Unie Police. Can I help, sir?"

"*Ja*. Right. Those *fokken* kids from the *location* is hanging around outside again. You better come do something, 'cause today is the day that I *bliksem* them all."

"Calm down, Mr. Brink."

"Oh, Alet, I . . ."

Captain Mynhardt and April walked past the service desk. April waved at Alet, a smile on his face. Mynhardt motioned to him to go ahead.

"Can I place you on hold?" Alet pushed the mute button before Petrus could answer. "Captain?"

"We got called out to the squatter camp. Trouble with one of the farmers because of missing cattle. Can you hold the fort by yourself?"

"Of course."

Mynhardt pointed his index finger at her. "Remember, my girl. Thin ice. Anything happens, you put a call out to Strijdom or Mathebe."

Alet nodded with a smile, resisting the strong urge to throw him the bird under the desk. She picked up the call again. "Okay, Petrus. What's the problem?"

An elderly couple hovered right outside the station door while she listened to Petrus's rant. The man held on to the woman as if he needed her assistance to stay upright. They were well-dressed, a bit too glossy to be from the area. Alet covered the mouthpiece when they approached the service desk. "Be with you in a moment. Take a seat." The couple didn't move, the woman's gaze remaining fixed on Alet.

"What did you say?" Petrus was working himself into a frenzy.

"Just tell me what you want me to do, Petrus."

"Those *skollies* only come into town weekends to cause trouble."

"They're kids, Petrus."

"Kids my *gat*. There was that broken window last week. And I swear it's them that let the air out of my tires. A bloody nuisance, let me tell you."

"You sure it's them? Maybe you got a puncture when you visited your girlfriend. Those farm roads are rocky, hey."

Petrus responded with a nasty swearword and hung up. Alet suppressed a smile and turned her attention to the couple. "Can I help you?"

The woman stepped forward. "We're looking for Constable Berg." Her accent was sharp, American, her tongue lingering on Buhrrrg.

"That's me."

The woman smoothed her hand over her white bob and glanced back at the man. He nodded, refusing to look at Alet.

"I am Monica Saunders and this is my husband, Bill. We're Mabel's parents."

"I'm not sure . . ."

"Oh, I'm sorry. Mabel Braverman." The woman on the side of the road.

"*Ja.* Of course." Alet walked out from behind the desk. "I am so sorry about what happened."

Bill Saunders's eyes became glassy, his lip quivering. "We were told you found her. That you tried to help."

"Would you like to sit?" Alet motioned to the charge office's wooden bench.

"We don't want to take up much of your time. We just . . . hoped that you could tell us what happened. Nobody will to talk to us." Monica Saunders balled her fists. "We have a right to know. We're her parents."

Alet touched the woman's shoulder. "I understand. Please."

Monica nodded and sat down, Bill followed her. Alet knew she was supposed to refer them back to the investigating officer, but if anything like this had happened to someone she loved, she would have wanted to know too. She tried to relay only the facts, keeping her feelings out of it. She didn't mention names or that she was under investigation. Bill sobbed openly as she spoke. Monica looked dazed.

"I'm very sorry," Alet said again.

"There's nothing else you can tell us?" There was hunger in Monica's eyes.

"That is all I can say."

"We can't . . ." She reached for Bill's hand. "You're sure there's nothing else?"

"I have told you more than I should. May I ask why Mr. and Mrs. Braverman were in South Africa?"

Bill lifted his eyes. "Mabel, she—"

"Bill." There was a warning in Monica's voice.

"Maybe it will help them," he pleaded.

"Mr. and Mrs. Saunders, we want to bring this perpetrator to justice. If there is anything you know . . ."

Monica nodded. "You have to understand. They tried everything else." She looked at her lap as she spoke. "My daughter was desperate and John, he loved her."

"I don't understand." Alet searched the two old people's faces.

"They came here for a baby." Monica said the words reluctantly, tension tightening her mouth.

"I'm sorry?"

"They couldn't have a child and they couldn't adopt. John had a record. It's all so stupid."

"Do you have the name of the adoption agency?" It was unusual for Americans to adopt black babies from South Africa. AIDS was rampant and the paperwork a nightmare.

Monica looked at Bill. He crossed his arms and stared out the window while he spoke. "Mabel said there was a man who could help them."

"They were buying a baby on the black market?" Alet leaned forward. "Did she tell you how?"

Monica shook her head. "She only told me that they had to come here and stay for the night. The contact said he'd find them. I was afraid that it might be a scam, but she wouldn't listen. Please, Constable. You have to understand. They weren't bad people."

Alet escorted them out, promising to call if anything else came up. Monica asked again if there was anything else she could tell them. Bill didn't say a word, melting away silently as Alet shook his hand.

"There has to be a connection." Alet got into the police van and handed Mathebe one of the bottles of Coke she had bought at the co-op. "I've never trusted Wexler."

The van's windows were cranked open all the way, the air inside the vehicle still stagnant. Alet pressed the Coke bottle against her cheek.

"There is no evidence of his involvement." Mathebe put his straw down on the dashboard and drank directly out of the bottle.

"Mabel Braverman's mother said that they had instructions to stay overnight in Unie. The only place they could have stayed is Zebra House. So what if that's the way Wexler contacts them? He plays host to the tourists, whatever, nothing looks suspicious from the outside." Alet tried to remember the previous Thursday night at Zebra House. They probably planned everything right there in front of her and she was too busy worrying about Boet Terblanche to notice anything. "I mean, seriously, have you ever wondered why anyone from overseas would want to visit Unie?"

Mathebe considered it. "There is a problem with this."

"There are many problems with this." Alet ran the Coke bottle down her neck, the condensation on her cheek evaporating rapidly. "Which one were you referring to?"

"Where do they get babies?"

"Are you kidding? When I worked in Jo'burg we had to haul women off the street who offered their kids for sale on the highway. Some of the Zimbabweans rent kids out to beggars for twenty rand a day. Problem is, the beggars get more money if the kids look sick, so they drug them. Finding an unwanted child is not hard. The tough part is getting them out of the country. I think that's where Wexler comes in. He might have more people involved in this."

"But where is the baby now?"

"Here's what I think. The Bravermans meet Wexler on Thursday night and set up a meeting place for the exchange. But there is a murder in town and the police are on the lookout for anything suspicious, so they decide to hold off for a few days, do some sightseeing, whatever, until things cool down. But then the Bravermans get hijacked, so the baby gets sold to someone else."

"This is all speculation."

"It's a theory. I haven't heard any from you."

Mathebe was quiet for a moment. "The Braverman couple was here to buy a baby."

"*Ja.*"

"To buy a baby and forge adoption papers costs money." He turned to Alet. "Where is the money?"

"Well, I don't think Wexler is stupid enough to process baby payments through Zebra House's books."

"The initial contact would have to be overseas. They would use foreign bank accounts." Mathebe shrugged. "We might not be able to trace it at all."

"Ugh. There must be a way."

Mathebe looked intently at the co-op entrance. "It seems that Mr. Terblanche has bought a new irrigation system."

"What? How do you know that?"

"I have been investigating this case too, Constable. Mr. Terblanche put the order in three days before we found Mrs. Pienaar. He promised Mr. Brink that he would pay in full by the end of the month."

"So?"

"I had a look at Mr. Terblanche's finances." Mathebe reached over and opened the glove compartment. He handed Alet an envelope.

Alet withdrew the bank statements inside. Boet's name and address appeared at the top, and string of negative numbers and interest charges ran down the page. "The drought's been bad. There isn't a farmer here who isn't struggling."

"Mr. Terblanche has two mortgages."

Alet pretended to study the bank statements. "It might be from something else," she mumbled. "His wife's parents might have promised them money."

"Perhaps." Mathebe finished his Coke.

"Okay. So let's say he has something to do with this baby-buying business. We still don't know how it's connected with Trudie's murder, if at all. Besides, Boet has an alibi."

Mathebe shook his head. "He was asleep at home with his wife."

"And how does Trudie fit into all of this? I mean, I don't think she was even friendly with the Terblanches."

"Perhaps not. But I found something else. Mr. Terblanche only owns half of the land he is farming. He leases the property where the body was found."

"Who does it belong to?"

"Mrs. Pienaar."

Alet looked at Mathebe in shocked silence. Could Boet be capable of murder? She didn't want to believe it.

"I do not know what it means yet," Mathebe said, "but Mrs. Pienaar was murdered on her own land. It is possible she found out that Mr. Terblanche is involved with the baby trade. Mr. Terblanche could have killed her to keep her silent." Mathebe shifted his weight. "There is also the matter of Dr. Koch's findings." He had that tone of incredulity again, a look of distaste. "Mrs. Pienaar being . . . a different species."

"Look, we don't know if it has anything to do with her death, hey. It might just be this weird thing nobody knew about." Alet put Boet's bank statements back in the glove compartment, happy to be rid of them. "What we need is a connection between Trudie and the other Angel-killing victims."

"If the two cases are related, there might be a link between Colonel Berg and Mr. Wexler."

"Well, we don't know that they're related," Alet said, aware that she sounded defensive. "Wexler is fit enough to get a body up that mountain, but he must have been in nappies when the first girl died. What bothers me is that someone felt threatened enough to shoot at me last night. Who knows that we found out about all of this? I mean, we barely know what's going on ourselves."

"I have retrieved a bullet for evidence."

"How are you going to explain that to Mynhardt?"

"I am holding it somewhere safe until we need it. How you are going to explain the condition of the truck to Miss Pienaar?"

"I'll think of something." Alet leaned her chin in her palm and stared out the passenger-side window at a row of white pickups parked next to the co-op. What did these people have against colour? A group of young black boys hung around the entrance, their bare legs dusty, some of them wearing baseball caps back to front, trying to look like gangsters, showing off for girls walking by. Too young, Alet thought, too eager to grow up.

"You have to talk to Mr. Terblanche."

Alet looked back at Mathebe. "Why? You interviewed him already."

"We did not have this knowledge yet."

"He's not the talkative type, you know?"

"That is the job, Constable. You keep asking questions until you find the right answers."

Alet sighed inwardly. "*Ja*. Of course." The bent figure of Jakob caught her eye as he went into the liquor store down the street. "Okay, Sergeant. I'll get right on that." She opened the van door.

"Be careful, Constable Berg."

"*Ja* . . . okay." Alet got out of the van, suddenly feeling awkward. "You too." As she walked down the street to the liquor store, a car horn honked behind her. Joey Joubert pulled up beside her.

"Alet! On the job again?"

"*Haai*, Joey. *Ja*. As of this morning."

"I knew all that other stuff was nonsense. The old *tannies* are all yapping, but I told them no, you shut up. If Alet shot someone, they deserved it."

"Thanks, man." Alet glanced at the liquor store.

"Are you coming tomorrow?"

"Uh . . ."

"André is performing. For the fund-raiser."

Right. It was the church bazaar weekend. "I don't know, Joey. I'm dealing with some things at the moment."

"Oh come on, doll. It's a chance to dress up and have fun. You could use some. There's a special menu. Lemon meringue for dessert. Your favorite. And there will be booze."

Alet raised an eyebrow.

"Only wine." A sarcastic smile splayed across Joey's pouty lips. "If it's good enough for Jesus, it's good enough for *Dominee* Joubert." He touched her arm. "I'll save you a place at my table, okay? You can catch me up on who offed old Trudie. I know of a few *tannies* in town who prefer her six feet under."

Out of the corner of her eye, Alet saw Jakob walk out of the liquor store, a brown paper bag clutched in one hand.

"Fine. Okay."

Jakob turned the corner at the end of the block.

"Starts at eight."

Alet waved at Joey as he drove on. She hurried to the corner. A few farmworkers stood outside the store, still in their blue overalls.

"Do you know where Jakob went? He was here, just now," Alet asked them.

One of the men shook his head and looked away. Nobody else responded. Jakob couldn't have gone far. Alet moved down the street at a walk-run. It was late afternoon and Unie was buzzing with workers coming in from the farms and people spending their All-pay government money. Later, drunken fights would break out. A few would end up in jail. But for now, all that existed was the anticipation of a good time.

Alet stopped short as she got to the big stone church. In the distance, on the rise that snaked up the mountain overlooking Unie, she noticed Jakob's skinny body swaying up the path. "Jakob!" Jakob turned around, smiled, waved at her with the hand that wasn't clutched around a bottle neck, and continued up the mountain. "*Ag, Jissis.*" Alet ran after him. The incline was steeper than she thought, the day's heat rising off the barren ground. She really had to do something about getting back into shape. Sweat was pouring down her face by the time she reached him. "Jakob. *Fok.* Stop, okay?"

"What now, *Mies?*" Jakob grinned, the picture of innocence.

Alet walked closer, trying to catch her breath. The bottle in Jakob's hand had not been opened yet, but the smell of alcohol seeped out of his pores. "How much have you had to drink? It's not even five o'clock yet."

"*Nee, Mies.* Is just a little happiness. Is all okay."

"I had a *moerse* time catching you, man."

"These legs are old but they're fast, *Mies.* Just see." Jakob started speed walking up the mountain.

"Jakob! You come back here or I will *bliksem* you myself."

Jakob stopped. "Ai, *Mies*. What now? Why you so *bedonnerd*?"

"I have to talk to you."

"Not now, *Mies*. Let a man have his *dop* in peace." He did a little jig. "Hey, hey, it's Friday!"

"We can do it here or I can take you to the station for the night."

"*Ai, nee. Ai, nee.*" Jakob sank down haunches in the middle of the road, shaking his head. "You're always ugly to me, *Mies*. I already tell you everything."

"I need to ask about *Baas* Boet."

"I don't know anything, *Mies*. I told you. True's bob. The *baas* is a good man. I told you, but you people never listen."

"He hit you, Jakob."

"Was nothing." Jakob waved his hand in front of him. "Long forgot. Finish and *klaar*. No problems between us."

"Okay." Alet walked closer to him. "Tell me, Jakob. Does *Baas* Boet know *Baas* Jeffrey Wexler?"

"*Baas* Boet likes to *dop* at Zebra House, *Mies*. You know. I sometimes catch a ride when he goes to town."

"Did *Baas* Jeff ever come to the farm?"

"I don't know, *Mies*."

"How about *Mies* Trudie Pienaar?"

Jakob dropped his bottle. He covered his head with his arms.

Alet waited, but Jakob didn't move, didn't make a sound. "Jakob?" She bent down and touched his shoulder.

Jakob jerked and he fell back, his arms swinging, trying to stop his fall. His face was wet.

"Jakob, what's going on?"

"She's dead, *Mies*. That's all I know. Burned black. Black dead. Dead, dead, dead." Jakob's wrinkled face contorted. "She never coming back again. Never ever."

"You knew *Mies* Trudie?"

"She was good. A good lady. Better than all of them." Jakob gestured to the town below them. "Whole stinking lot."

"How did you know *Mies* Trudie, Jakob?"

Jakob pushed himself off the ground. He swayed unsteady for a moment before retrieving his bottle.

"Jakob, answer me."

Jakob turned away and staggered up the mountain.

"Jakob!"

"Just leave it, *Mies*," he yelled without looking back. "Maybe another day, hey?"

Alet let him continue his trek, determined to try again once he'd slept it off.

She was busy changing out of her uniform when her cell rang. She sank down on her bed in only a pair of shorts, her tank top dangling over one arm, listening to Mathebe's update. "That must be wrong, Johannes," she said after he finished. "I thought you identified Trudie from dentals."

"The record was from a dentist in Oudtshoorn. I ran the fingerprints we found at her house for confirmation. The query came back this afternoon."

"Well, she looked bloody good for an octogenarian, is all I can say. Look, she must have used a fake ID, or there was a major cock-up when they digitized the records. Wouldn't surprise me."

"I do not know how to explain it, Constable Berg, but the captain is asking questions."

"Shit." Alet pretended not to notice the silence on the other end of the line. "So who did Trudie's fingerprints match up to?"

"Lilly Maartens. Birth date, March 1931."

"Hold on. What day?"

Alet heard a rustle of papers on the other end of the line.

"The second."

"The date on Trudie Pienaar's ID is the second of March '58?"

"Yes."

Alet forced a breath out pursed lips. Why would Trudie have taken the identity of someone so much older than she was? "What else do you have on Lilly Maartens?"

"One moment."

There was a click as Alet was put on hold. She tried to get her top over her head, but Mathebe picked up again.

"Place of birth, Winburg. There is a record of marriage. Nothing else."

"No DOD?"

"No."

"And the husband?"

Papers rustled. "Dean Kritzinger. Lawyer. Some mention of activity in the ANC. He died during a home invasion."

"Okay." Alet's phone beeped. Call-waiting. "Look, I have to go, but I wanted to ask you something. Have you found anything that links Boet Terblanche's foreman to Trudie Pienaar?"

"I have not. Why do you ask?"

"Probably nothing, but he was very upset this afternoon when I tried to talk to him. I think he knew her better than he's let on."

The second call disconnected before she had time to pick it up. Mike Engelman's number came up. Alet listened to the voice mail. Mike's voice rambled through static.

"Alet. I just saw the papers. I . . . well, I know you are working with Professor Koch, but I'd like to offer my help with the case. Please call if you need anything. Anytime. Okay? You have my number. Please call."

Alet had read the article online that morning, complete with a fuzzy photograph of Trudie, sensationalized with doom-and-gloom statistics about the increasing murder rate, which was the highest in a country not at war, it claimed. The reporter identified Mynhardt as the officer in charge of the case, no mention of her or Mathebe. She wondered if Mike really wanted to help or if this was his way of feeling out the waters after the other night. Either way, she didn't want to deal with it, not right now. She turned her phone off and finished dressing. Grabbing a six-pack out of the fridge, she headed over to the main house. Tilly answered the door after a couple of minutes. A fragility hung about her, her pale skin punctuated by dark shadows.

"I've got refreshments."

"Come in." Tilly led the way through the house. Most of the earlier chaos had been replaced by stacks of boxes in the hallway.

"You want something to eat? Only toast and Marmite, I'm afraid." Tilly picked up an empty plate from the kitchen table and dumped its contents into the sink.

"No. I'm good." Alet took two beers out of the pack. "You've been busy."

"I'm putting the house up for sale." Tilly took a beer from Alet and twisted the top off.

"How are you holding up?"

Tilly shook her head. "I thought I could make up for things if I stayed here." She sighed, leaning back against the kitchen counter. "But that's stupid, isn't it?" Her voice wavered. "Anyway. Perhaps it's time to start fresh."

"What will you do?"

"I don't know. Maybe go overseas. Jeff said he'd help me out."

"Really?"

"Anywhere is better than here, hey."

"Cheers to that." Alet clinked her beer bottle against Tilly's. "Jeff and your mom knew each other, right?"

"Let's go sit on the *stoep*. It's cooler there." Tilly grabbed two more beers.

Alet followed her to the back of the house. Tilly opened the glass door and all the windows of the enclosed *stoep*. She tucked her feet under her on the old couch. Alet took a seat at the other end.

"You didn't answer me before."

"Mmm?" Tilly stared out at the backyard, where the trees were becoming monochromatic in the twilight.

"Your mom and Jeff."

"Oh. Um . . . she worked for him for a little while when he first bought Zebra." Tilly changed her empty bottle for a fresh one. Alet had only taken a couple of sips of her first. "You know, the last time I spoke to her, we argued," Tilly said. "I think Wednesday, maybe. It might have been Tuesday. You'd think I'd remember."

"She was in the garden every morning. I should have noticed that she was missing. There was just so much *kak* going on."

"It's okay." Tilly sounded removed. "I don't blame you. She was difficult."

Alet studied Tilly's profile, trying to figure out how she was going to broach the subject. "Do you think, perhaps, I could take a look at her things?"

Tilly dipped her thumb into the mouth of her beer bottle, making a popping sound as she pulled it out.

Alet wasn't sure if Tilly had heard her, or if she was just ignoring the request. She tried again. "I'll be honest, we don't understand any of this. Maybe there's some clue in her past that can help."

"Your colleague already ransacked this house. He came in here and . . . Do you know what it was like? Finding out what happened to her and then walking in here? Her whole life violated, thrown on the floor like it was garbage."

Alet wondered why Mathebe had gone to such lengths, had been so uncharacteristically messy. She supposed he was trying to be thorough.

"You people." Tilly's voice was shrill, a subdued hysteria suddenly bursting to the surface. "You have prodded and invaded, worse than whoever did that to her."

"Tilly—"

"She always kept to herself. Now the whole world has made it their business to lay her bare."

Tilly hid her face in her hands, a low moan escaping from the pit of her stomach. Alet moved closer and put her arms around Tilly. Tilly shook her off.

"I'm sorry." The words seemed meager. Alet sat quietly, waiting for Tilly's guttural moans to quiet down.

Tilly slumped into a fetal position on the couch, her head leaning on the armrest, her knees pulled up to her chest, her arms disappearing under her body. "Do you know how it happened?" she said at last. "Did she . . . suffer?"

"She was strangled before the fire. I honestly don't know if she suffered."

Tilly pushed herself up. "I can't do this. I have to go to work. Please lock the door behind you." She walked into the house, leaving Alet alone on the *stoep*. Moments later, Alet heard the front door close.

"Do you have any idea what time it is? I have a family."

Alet switched the cell to her other ear and glanced at her watch. "I'm sorry, Professor Koch, but something came up."

"Let me take this in the study."

There was a click on the line. Alet imagined Koch assuring his wife that a call at midnight was nothing serious. She looked at the items spread out on her bed. She had taken a box of Trudie's personal things from the house, hoping Tilly wouldn't miss them till morning. In the box she found an old biscuit tin with peeling green paint, filled to the brim with faded photographs. Alet had tried to arrange them in some sort of chronological order. As she trailed her eye from the beginning of the line to the end, a whole lifetime passed, pink-cheeked youth slowly disappearing, giving way to a gaunt adult face, the bloom of beauty progressively worn down by time. The early photographs were sepia, a blond little girl growing into adolescence. In the later ones Trudie always looked away from the camera, her hair color and style changing constantly. There was only one picture that had her facing the camera, taken in the seventies, judging by the bell-bottoms and long hair of the man in the picture with her. She must have been about the same age as Tilly was now. There was an expression of surprise on Trudie's face, as if she'd been caught off-guard. The flash made her pale eyes look like they were shining, as if she was something ethereal, staring out at Alet through time.

"This couldn't wait till morning?" Koch's mood had soured considerably between his bedroom and his study.

"I have something here, Professor. I need you to tell me if it is possible."

"*Ja?*"

Where to begin? "I've found personal photographs of the victim." Alet picked up the most recent one. "She was in her forties or so when she died, right?"

"It's hard to determine a precise age forensically after a person reaches adulthood, but I concur that it is possible."

Alet thought of the last time she saw Trudie in the garden. Trudie always dressed dowdy, her clothes that of an old woman, her hair the same color as Tilly's, tied in an old-fashioned knot, always covered by some sort of hat, her eyes hidden behind dark glasses. "What if she was older?"

"Well, there's a range of about fifteen years."

"No. I mean, what if she was a lot older?"

"I thought you identified the victim. Don't you have a birth certificate?"

"Professor, you said she was a different species. Have you found out anything more about how she might have been different from us?"

"The genotype wasn't compatible with that of modern humans, although the phenotype might have mimicked Homo sapiens closely. To determine the exact expression of the gene from the DNA is virtually impossible. I can only give you an approximation. I thought I explained that."

"Listen, Professor, I almost flunked biology in high school, so just answer my question in plain English."

Koch sighed. "I can't. Not with any degree of certainty."

"Okay. Let me put it this way. I have a photograph here of what looks to be a three-year-old girl before the First World War. This same girl is a teenager in the next photo, but it was taken in the late thirties. I have one of her in her early twenties, but her hair is in a beehive and she is wearing a miniskirt. In what looks to be her late twenties her bangs are teased so high she might have blown away if the wind caught her at the right angle. Now my fashion sense is dubious at best, but I don't think anyone has gotten a perm on purpose since the early nineties. Shall I go on?"

"You're sure it's the same person? Not a family resemblance?"

"I'm not sure of anything anymore, but it looks like her. I need you to tell me if it's possible."

Koch was silent for a moment. Alet heard his breathing, the sound of pages being turned. "According to a recent study, older males have longer telomeres and this causes them to produce offspring who live longer. If there was a mutation of the sperm, the effect might be greater. I don't know. This is speculation."

Alet scribbled "telomere" in messy script on her notepad. "Can you confirm this from the victim's DNA?"

"Doubtful. Another possibility is jumping genes. The signal to age might have been blocked. There are very rare cases of this happening, but it is usually accompanied by severe retardation."

"Just tell me, is what I'm proposing possible?"

"Anything is possible. We haven't even started glimpsing the possibilities of gene manipulation."

"Okay. Thanks. Please let me know if you find anything else. Oh, and I'm sending you all the crime-scene evidence I could find on the older victims. Perhaps you can pull DNA, see if they have the same . . . jumping thing going on?"

Alet hung up. If Trudie had aged more slowly than normal humans, it meant that she really was Lilly Maartens. Alet was wired. She needed to clear her head. She thought for a moment about the shooter from the previous night, put her holster on, and went for a run.

1980

Jacob

He woke up shivering on checkered linoleum. A generator droned outside the building. Above him a single fluorescent bulb flickered and buzzed. He tasted blood. Why was he naked? He struggled to remember. The ghost of electrodes on his penis, under his arms. The pain as the circuit was completed, electricity coursing through his body. He had bit his tongue. The man in shorts and *vel* shoes flipped the switch. There were three of them, maybe four, coming in and out, dust and burrs clinging to their socks. He had struggled to understand them.

"You don't speak Afrikaans, my boy? You going to learn fast, hey."

A buzz. Muscles contracting, threatening to snap, the sting rippling thick under his skin.

"For starters, why don't we give you a nice Afrikaans name? What is with this English Jacob *kak*." He sneered. "You look more like a Jakob to me. Plain old proper Boer name. YAH-kohp, *ja*?" Another buzz. His heart pounded, his veins on the edge of bursting.

The other man hunched down, looked him in the eye. "He looks like a *moegoe* to me, Goose. How's about we up the juice. You'd like that, hey Jakob?"

"*Nee, Baas.*"

Buzz.

He had cut the wire fence, limpet mines in a sack flung over his shoulder. Letso crawled through first, then held the wire back for Jacob and the others. They planted the mines on gas tanks and watched from afar as the whole plant went up in flames, patting each other on the back for hurting the enemy where it mattered. Jacob had never seen fireworks, but in his mind that was what they looked like, a fireball lighting up the sky for freedom.

Letso was with him when the police found them. The other MK members had left for Mozambique already, but Letso wanted to see his girlfriend. At first the policemen seemed confused, as if they were expecting someone else at the Soweto house.

"What did you say your name was?" The clutch plate squinted, asked him to repeat. He called over to the other Dutchman. "His passbook says he's Jacob Morgan." Then, suddenly, they got excited, speaking goat among themselves. Jacob Morgan, known MK terrorist. They arrested him and Letso, took them with bags over their heads to this place. When was that? Days? Weeks? When the electrodes didn't break him, they brought in a cattle prod.

"You going to help us, Jakob." The man had caressed the shaft with fat fingers. His face was sunburned and he reeked of beer and *braaivleis* smoke. Two other men lifted Jacob out of his chair, holding him down prostrate over the table. "You see, my boy, I don't really care if you live or die. But perhaps you can be useful." One of them pulled his underwear down, he could not tell which. Hands gripped his flesh, holding his buttocks apart. He felt the steel prongs resting on his skin, as if the man was deciding what to do. Then it penetrated him. He felt flesh tear deep inside.

"*Sis*, man. It smells."

"He's full of *kak*," one of them giggled.

It hit him, ripping through his spinal cord, crushing his brain, his body simultaneously shrinking and bursting into the room. His eyes couldn't see, his ears couldn't hear. All that existed was the pain's thick grip on him, its limbs entwined with his, pulsating, wringing, stealing his breath, his light. When darkness came, he gratefully gave over to it. But then he didn't die. He was still where they had left him, discarded flesh, used up, on the floor like dirty laundry.

A stranger sat on the chair, looking down on him. A rigidity prevailed in the way he dressed, the precise cut of his short hair and mustache, the calculating look. A man carrying death with him, Jacob thought.

"I know what you've done, Mr. Morgan," the man said. "Your friend Letso told us all about it, see?"

Jacob lifted his head off the ground to look at the man, every tiny muscle protesting.

"But don't worry. I understand what the ANC has done to you and your people."

The man didn't make sense. Jacob had trouble focusing on what he was saying.

"The people you think are liberating you, they are actually destroying you. You see, they are really the bad people here." He smiled sympathetically. "They killed your mother, didn't they?"

"No."

"They had people there in Soweto. Gangsters. They started the violence, so kids would get killed, so their cause would seem justified. Isn't that so?"

Not true, not true.

"They had snipers there that day. Shooting everyone who wanted to leave, making it look like the police. That's what happened, isn't it Jacob? Your mom was shot when you tried to run away. The police didn't do that. It's the ANC that likes lots of black bodies for the overseas cameras. They lied to you, see?" The man got down on his haunches next to Jacob. "They don't care about you."

The man put his arm around Jacob's waist and helped him to a standing position. He walked Jacob over to the chair and lowered him into it. Sitting up was painful.

"I bet you think I'm full of it, don't you? But Communists take the lives of innocent women and children. All I'm trying to do is stop them. Deep down you know that, don't you Jacob?"

Jacob trained his eyes to the ground, afraid to speak.

"What happened in the MK training camps, huh? When you were there. How did they treat their own people?"

Jacob had slept in a tent full of teenagers like himself when he first arrived at Quatro in Angola. Young people arrived daily, eager to join the fight. During the day they were drilled hard, taught how to build bombs, how to shoot, but at night he lay awake, listening to the women cry while the guards raped them. Lephutsi had been fifteen when they'd shot him. He was stupid as a pumpkin, one of the commanders had said, and the name stuck. Someone had accused Lephutsi of being a spy. Jacob never believed it, but they had dragged the boy away, his eyes pleading with Jacob to say something, to save him. "Comrades, no! Is not true. I am with you. I fight for Umkhonto. *Amandla. Aman-*

dla. Amandla." Lephutsi's desperate yells continued until a single shot rang out in the distance.

"You can work for us, Jacob," the man smiled. "Be an *askari*. Otherwise the government will hang you for terrorism, you know. That job you pulled at SASOL? Bad news." The man leaned against the table, staring Jacob down. "But maybe you think it's noble to die for the cause."

Jacob wasn't sure what the cause was anymore. He swallowed the blood in his mouth. "What do you want from me?"

"We need someone in the ANC. You see what they're up to and report back to me."

Jacob lifted his head, afraid to ask.

"My name is Berg. Don't talk to anyone else, hear? You help me, I'll treat you well. You have my word."

Jacob nodded.

A doctor was sent in. He had confusing thoughts, unraveling as soon as they shimmered in his mind. Perhaps his interrogators used this same doctor for all their prisoners. Perhaps he even knew what they did to Steve Biko. Jacob asked, but the doctor told him to be quiet.

Jacob was helped to a room with a bed and a Bible. The door was left unlocked, but he had no desire to escape. He was in bed with his enemy now. There was nowhere to run.

A month later, he and Letso crossed the border into Botswana, armed with a true story of torture and a flimsy story of escape. They were welcomed as heroes in the camp, adoration in the younger boys' eyes, respect from the elders. Letso played the game well, lapping up the attention, but Jacob couldn't look his people in the eye.

"It's because of what they did to him." Letso proclaimed when one of the commanders, Bongile, asked. "They do very bad things to comrade Jacob and me. But we never talked. He is a brave man, I promise you."

Jacob could feel Bongile's distrust, vivid as a hand running down the back of his neck, eyes following his every move. Jacob knew that even when he was sleeping, Bongile kept watch in the dark. He thought about telling Bongile everything, taking his chances. But the Security Branch men had threatened him. The *askaris* called it "burning bridges." Rumors would be spread in the community that they were traitors so they could never go back. Jacob didn't think his dad would survive the shame of having a government spy as a son.

Within a week the order came that they were going back across the border, running a shipment of AK-47s to Johannesburg. Two other men, Rocky and Jonas, would go with them. Letso protested, but Bongile claimed he needed experienced men. They left at dawn. Letso sat in the front seat of the combi, Rocky drove. Jacob was in the back with Jonas, a surly older man. It was barely light out, heat squeezing the air dry.

"So you the guys who escaped from the Security Police?" Rocky rolled his window down, leaning his arm out the window, his hand resting lightly on the steering wheel. The drone of air rushing by swallowed his words.

"*Yebo*. That's us." Letso had a glint in his eyes. Jacob had seen it often since their return. He sank deeper in his seat, cringing at the thought of what would follow.

"Those *ropes* let you walk out of there?"

"*Haw wena!*" Letso looked mortally wounded. "We were prisoners. Valuable! No way they let us go."

A smile played on Rocky's lips. "Then how did you get away?"

Letso frowned, the cloak of drama and intrigue hanging over his suddenly erect shoulders. "We were cunning. Fast like the Thokoloshe."

Jonas turned to Jacob, looking him up and down. Jacob broke eye contact first, focusing on the wind tugging at the edge of Rocky's shirt collar in front of him.

"But what did you do?" Rocky's tone shifted. "Exactly how did you escape?"

"I waited for night." Letso seemed unaware of the menace Jacob felt from the other two men. "The whites were *braai-ing*. We could smell the food, hear them talk. They were drunk, very drunk, on spirits and beer. I knew it was our chance to *chaile*."

That much of the story was true, but it wasn't just one night. The white policemen had a *braai* almost every night, thick steaks roasting on the open fire, empty bottles of brandy lining the walls of the compound. They let Jacob and Letso join them. There were other *askaris* too, men who had once fought for the ANC but now worked for the police, sitting in a group to one side, part of the unit, but always separate. Berg sometimes made an appearance. He never got drunk. He only sat in the corner nursing a whiskey, watching the whites all act like idiots. The others talked about him in hushed tones. Jacob had wondered why Berg inspired such loyalty from men he had once tortured. One of the *askaris*, Kalo, was a former Angolan soldier who had served with Berg in Namibia. He told stories about how they kept scores of their kills on chalkboards at base camp, had some sort of competition going, Berg always in the lead. He never talked down at the black soldiers like the other policemen, but treated them with courtesy, Kalo said, made sure they had the same rations as the whites. The man was ruthless, but fair.

Rocky turned off the main highway.

"This isn't the road," Letso said.

"Back way. We can't be stopped by the police," Rocky said. "Go on with your story."

Letso looked back at Jacob. "This man here, he is a brave man. When one of the crunchies walks past the window, he asks for a beer. The Dutchman he thinks it's funny, because he comes inside with two beers. When he opens the door, this man jumps him, knocks him out. No problem."

"So you just walked out of there?"

"We ran, *chana*. They shoot, but they're all too drunk to hit us."

"That's it?" Rocky stopped the combi. Jacob looked out the window. As far as he could see there was nothing around them, just flat dry dirt. He turned back and looked down the barrel of Jonas's Tokarev. In the front seat, Rocky had pulled his own pistol, pointing it at Letso.

"*Haw wena!*" Letso's expression changed to one of shock.

"You know what, my *bra*." Rocky pushed the barrel of the pistol into Letso's forehead. "I don't like your story. I think I have a better one. See, I think you didn't escape at all. That you spy on us for those crunchies."

"Never." Letso's voice was shaking. "*Amandla*." He held his balled fist up in the air. "We are with the people."

"Your words do not deceive us, traitor scum."

"It's not true," Jacob shouted. "I hate them."

"Get out," Jonas said.

They led Jacob and Letso away at gunpoint. Letso protested his innocence, but Jacob knew the decision had been made.

"Stop here," Rocky ordered a few paces farther. "On your knees."

Pop. The sound of the gunshot next to Jacob's head hurt his ears. He felt a fine hot spray on his face. Letso's body slumped forward, his big eyes frozen forever in an expression of surprise. Without thinking, Jacob grabbed the barrel of Rocky's gun. Rocky was tough, strong, but MK had taught Jacob how to handle himself. He wrestled Rocky to the ground, warding off blows from elbows and knees, keeping his focus on the weapon. Out of the corner of his eye he saw Jonas training his Tokarev on them, trying to get a clear shot at Jacob. Jacob knew he had to keep moving, had to keep Rocky between himself and Jonas. Pop. Pop. Jacob wasn't sure which gun had fired. Rocky was on top of him, wrestling the gun away. Pop. Rocky's body suddenly went limp. Pop. Jacob freed the gun from his grip. He fired in the direction of the shots. Pop. Pop. Pop.

Jonas lay on his back, blood gushing from his thigh. He lifted his gun, training it at Jacob. Pop. Click. Jonas's arm dropped to the ground, his body jerking before it went still. Jacob held his breath. A perfect silence rested over the barren plains, the way it must have been before any of them, white or black had laid claim to it, before there was even a creature such as man. For a moment he wondered how he would get the gun shipment back to Botswana by himself, before he remembered. The ANC had labeled him as a traitor. He was no longer welcome. They had killed his friend. He was supposed to be dead too.

Jacob took the combi. He followed the dirt road on until he reached a small farming town two hours later. The gas-station attendant filled the tank, his eyes returning to Jacob's shirt collar. Jacob inspected himself in the rearview mirror as soon as the man walked away to get change. Dry blood clung to his ears and neck, Letso's blood. Jacob went into the shop to look for a place to wash his face.

"Where you think you going, boy?" The old white man stepped out of the restroom in the back of the shop. He pulled the door shut behind him. "This is the white toilets."

Jacob stared at the man, hatred surging. He felt Rocky's Tokarev next to his skin. His hand slipped under his shirt.

"Didn't you hear me? What are you standing there for?" The old man banged his walking stick on the floor for emphasis, his head trembling with righteous indignation.

Jacob's fingers brushed over the butt of the gun. It would be nothing to kill the old bastard, to kill every person in that shop. It really didn't matter which side he was on, they all wanted him dead and he despised them equally. He let go of the gun and clutched both hands together in front of him, bowing his head. "Sorry, *Baas*. Is okay, I say."

"Stupid *kaffir*," the old man muttered.

Jacob let him pass, comforted in the knowledge that he had let the man live, that he had that power. He hurried to the call box outside, hesitated for a moment, and lifted the handset. He tried to remember his father's number. After his mother's death, their relationship, already fragile, had broken down. Would the old man ever forgive him for what he had done? Jacob dropped the coins into the slot.

"Berg."

"It's me, *Baas*. Jakob." Jacob pasted the subservient darkie act on. His life depended on it. "Letso, he's dead. The Commies knew. You gotta help me, *Baas*, or I'm next. No joke, I swear."

There was a short silence. "Come in." Berg gave him an address. "And Jakob?"

"*Ja, Baas?*"

"Don't worry. I'll take care of you."

Flippie

Thick sheets of rain obscured the road, glaring red taillights the only sign of a car coming to a halt in front of Flippie. It had been slow going since he'd left his practice almost an hour ago. He needed new glasses. His old pair kept sliding down his nose, the cheap frames not up to the challenge of his thick bifocals anymore. Getting old was harder than he ever would have guessed. Flippie had a pinched nerve in his back and the pain kept him awake at night. The doctors said there was nothing they could do. He'd have to live with the pain or leave the country to get help.

The car in front of him disappeared behind veils of water. Alongside the road, drivers with more respect for the elements had pulled over to wait the storm out, but Flippie wanted to get home. He didn't have the stamina for waiting anymore. All he wanted at the end of the day was a nice cup of tea and to watch the news in his favorite chair. Sometimes the neighbor women sent their daughters over with a plate of food and a dustcloth, but most nights he was content to turn in early. Sleeping was better than remembering in the dark hours.

A man appeared suddenly in the middle of the road, waving his arms. Flippie slammed on the brakes. His car skidded on the wet road. He missed the stranger by less than a meter. By the time his heart stopped racing, the man had disappeared into the grayness again. Flippie rolled down his window, yelling into the void where steam rose from the asphalt. "Anyone there?" Rain pelted him in the face, his glasses fogging up. The pounding of the water on his car drowned out any answer to his question. He was just about to pull away when a brown hand slapped the windshield.

A young man appeared at his window. "Sorry, *Ntate*. My *bakkie* stalled. Can you give a jump?" He had an earnest look about him, his clothes poor, his manner subservient.

Flippie strained to see in the direction the man was gesturing, barely making out the outlines of a pickup on the side of the road. "Of course, son. Get in."

"I'm too wet, *Ntate*. Don't want to ruin your nice seats. Can you pull over there?"

Flippie followed behind the man at a snail's pace. He took care to stop as close to the old pickup as he could. "The cables are in the boot. I have to unlock it."

The first blow landed on his jaw as soon as he stepped out of the car, hard and unforgiving, not from anything made of bone and flesh. The man looked like two. No. There really were two of them, more. Blows barraged his skull. He held up his hands to stop them, but they knocked him on the ground, hit him in the chest. An excruciating pain radiated from his legs. So many men to kill an old man. Didn't they know he had nothing?

The man who had waved in the road knelt next to Flippie. "Time to *chaile*, old man," he said. The knife plunged deep inside Flippie. His lungs felt heavy, breath a battle, life ebbing as burdened seconds ticked by, the rain patting him, warm and gentle. It washes away my blood, Flippie thought. My blood joins the blood of those who have gone before me. I am one with the land now, one with them. Nobody can separate us from our home now.

Tessa

Tessa cleared up after the mourners, the mess people made when it wasn't their own home. Someone had dropped a piece of milk tart on the floor and trodden it into the carpet. Tessa got down on all fours to scoop up as much of it as she could. When she looked up, a face flashed on the TV screen. Pale skin, pale eyes, fine curls the color of newly plucked cotton, a look of pure joy. The girl was posing for the camera, arm in arm with a plump girl about the same age. Tessa paused, mesmerized by the image.

Jeff followed her gaze. "Looks a bit like you, luv," he said before switching the channel to cricket.

"No. Go back, please."

Jeff sighed and turned the knob. The girl's photograph appeared in a small screen next to the news reader's head again.

"I can't hear anything." Tessa rushed to the TV set and turned the volume up.

". . . believe it may be connected to the so-called Angel killings that have been committed in the Johannesburg area the past three years. Anybody with information regarding Johanna Jacoba Dreyer, or any of the previous victims, is urged to call the following number."

A toll-free number appeared at the bottom of the screen.

"In sports today—"

Jeff switched the channel back to the rebroadcast of the day's Transvaal cricket match. "Leave those, luv," he said. "I'll do it later on. Come sit by me."

Tessa thought about protesting. She liked to get things done, but then she saw the look on his face, his tough-youth exterior replaced by a melancholy maturity. She set a stack of cake plates down and nestled in the crook of Jeff's arm, her ear resting next to his heart so she could hear the quiet steady thump.

"What are you going to do now?"

"Not quite sure." Jeff held her a little tighter. He had found his father slumped over his desk earlier that week. The doctor said it was a heart attack.

Tessa felt a pang thinking of Markus dying alone like that. "Will you stay?"

"I'm not much of a farmer. But I might be persuaded . . ." He ran his big hands over her hair, entangling his fingers in the ends. "If you made an honest man out of me."

"No." Tessa pushed away from him.

Jeff looked surprised by the violence of her reaction. "Tru, I thought . . ."

"Jeff, this isn't the time to talk about this." Tessa got up and rushed toward the dishes to give her hands something to do.

"I think it's a fine time." Jeff stood up, moving closer to her. "I know we said this ain't serious, but I've changed my mind, luv. I thought you might've—"

Tessa jumped as the phone rang next to her. She didn't bother hiding her annoyance when she picked up the receiver. "Hallo?" The line crackled, the person at the other end silent. "Hallo? Who is this please?"

"*Rakgadi.*"

Tessa wasn't sure if she could trust what she heard. "Jacob?" More static.

"*Ja.* It's me."

"You're alive." Tessa's heart beat faster. "Where are you?"

"I want you to—" Droning in the background overpowered his words, the blast of a horn, voices and music.

"Jacob, please, I have to see you."

"No can do, *orraait*? There's no going back no more. Not for me."

"It doesn't matter. Nothing matters. Just come home."

"Can't." Jacob's voice carried an air of defeat. "Too late, Auntie. *Pa*, he's . . ."

"What about Phillip? Jacob? Can you hear me? What happened?"

"Sorry, Auntie. Sorry, sorry."

"Tell me where you are, then."

Somebody yelled, "Hey, *bra*," in the background. Jacob responded, forced joviality in his voice. Tessa tried to make out the muffled conversation, banter about girls, something about heading back in the morning.

"*Rakgadi*, I can't talk longer. If they find out I'm talking to you—"

"Who, Jacob?"

"I'm in bad stuff, Auntie."

"Jacob, I can help. Don't worry about your dad. He loves you."

Jacob's laugh was without irony, a scoff at her ignorance. "Is *klaar*. Finished. You hear?"

"What are you talking about? You're scaring me."

"*Pa*'s dead, Auntie." Jacob's voice broke. "They got him last night."

Tessa felt herself go cold, her mouth suddenly dry.

"I'm sorry, Auntie."

"Jacob, please tell me where you are. Please." Tessa's body shook.

"I have to go. You promise you don't look for me, okay? Is better like that. You look for me, now-now they gonna find you. Then it's tickets for both of us, see?"

"Jacob, wait." He didn't answer. Tessa forged ahead. "There is land in Unie. It belonged to your grandpa. If you ever need a safe place, go there. I'll—"

There was a click, a dial tone instead of static. Tessa's fingers cramped around the receiver. She slowly put the phone back in its cradle.

"Trudie?" Jeff reached for her. Tessa succumbed to his embrace, her mind reeling. Jacob had to be mistaken. Flippie couldn't be dead. She knew she should call, find out, but as long as she stood there in Jeff's arms the possibility still existed that it was just a misunderstanding.

Jeff combed his fingers through her hair. "Everything all right, luv?"

There was something so innocent in this big man with his strong arms and broad chest, something so eager to please her, that Tessa's instinct was to lie to him. She pushed away. "I can't marry you, Jeff," she said before she could change her mind. "There are things about me you wouldn't understand."

"I don't care about the past, luv."

"You know nothing about me." Tessa crossed her arms. "You don't even know my real name." She watched his certainty waver. "You want a family. Well, I can't have children."

Tessa noticed his disappointment before he had time to hide it from her. "That doesn't matter," he said. "I love you."

"It matters. More than you realize right now." Tessa bowed her head. "And it matters to me." The knot in her stomach tightened as she thought of Dean, the child they could never have. Flippie. The pointless despair of it all was suddenly overwhelming and she couldn't stop the tears.

"It's okay, luv." Jeff touched her cheek.

"No." Tessa pushed his hand away. "There is a man," she said. "If he finds me, he'll—"

"I won't let anybody hurt you."

"Ben will kill you. He's done it before. I'm not going to let . . ." She closed her eyes, struggling to let go. She hadn't told Dean who she was. It had strained their marriage, a barrier that she never could get past. She was reminded of the disconnect every time he called her Lilly. But in the end her lies had done nothing to protect him. She was sick of secrets, the guilt she felt about his death. Jeff and Markus had been like family, yet she kept secrets from them too.

Jeff gripped her shoulders. "What's going on? Please tell me. Let me help you."

Tessa wondered if she even had it in her to completely trust another human being again. She struggled against the thing that separated them, the words stones in her mouth. "My name is Tessa." She held her hand to her mouth, tears flowing freely now. "I am Theresa Morgan." Her name felt new and ancient all at once, a thing that had remained hers, the bedrock under the changing seasons. She looked up at Jeff, studying his reaction. "I was born in 1901."

11

Saturday
DECEMBER 18, 2010

Joyboys was packed. Mismatched lounge chairs and couches strained under the weight of rotund posteriors eager to take refuge from the sweltering heat. The converted vestry had no air-conditioning, but the walls were thick brick, and huge ceiling fans teased the multicolored drapes on the windows. Almost everybody had heard about the death of the suddenly sainted Trudie Pienaar, but an occasional intake of breath with a shocked hand in front of the mouth signaled the uninformed.

Joey moved about the coffee shop in a wifebeater and denim shorts, his hair gelled into a faux Mohawk. He stopped at each table, the belle of the ball, taking orders for sandwiches, chocolate cake and iced coffees in exchange for gossip and flirtation with the ladies of the district. In the kitchen, Gertie, Maria's counterpart, stacked orders on trays, mumbling in Xhosa every time Joey placed a new order ticket on the serving hatch.

Alet observed the scene from the doorway. In front of her, three elderly ladies waited for a table to open up. She walked around them, trying to get Joey's attention.

"Wait your turn, girlie," said one of the women, her hair rinsed a cotton-candy blue.

"I'm not here for cake, Mrs. Dippenaar." Alet bristled. "I'm in uniform."

"So is he." Mrs. Dippenaar pointed a gnarly finger across the room, where Strijdom sat with his wife, two huge pieces of quiche in front of them. Captain Mynhardt and his wife completed the party.

Alet rolled her eyes. She turned back to Mrs. Dippenaar. "*Ja, Tannie*, but I'm actually working, see?"

Mrs. Dippenaar raised an eyebrow to her two friends, the meaning clear. Word about Alet's misadventures had gotten around. She shrugged it off. Let them play judge and jury. If life in a small town had taught her anything so far, it was that people were only interested in the truth when it fit their way of seeing things.

"What will it be, doll?" Joey's overpowering aftershave partly masked the smell of sweat.

"Can we talk, Joey?"

"Darling, look at this place." Joey tilted his head, his expression mocking her request.

"Won't take long, man. And I'll take an ice coffee to go."

Mrs. Dippenaar pursed her lips. One of her companions whispered something in her ear and she nodded vigorously, giving Alet the evil eye.

"Come into the kitchen with me. Gertie's struggling to keep up." Joey weaved through the beaded curtain to the kitchen.

Gertie looked shell-shocked, sweat forming dark patches on her brown uniform. "No more, *Baas* Joe, no more." She had kicked her shoes to the corner, navigating the linoleum floor barefoot.

"Relax, Gertie, darling." Joey stood behind Gertie and gave her shoulders a playful pat. "Deep breaths. It's only till lunch. Then they'll all go over to the *braai* and we won't have to worry till tonight."

Gertie gave him a dubious look. Joey took a huge tub of ice cream out of the freezer and started scooping the contents into an industrial-size blender. "You'll love André, Alet," he said while cleaning the scoop. "He was on TV, you know."

"*Isit?*"

Joey dumped milk into the blender. "*Ja.* Two episodes on Egoli. He's got talent." He reached for the instant coffee, a glint in his eyes. "And by talent I also mean his enormous schlong."

"You didn't!" Alet stole a glance to see if Gertie had heard Joey above the hum of the blender.

"Uh-huh." Joey looked like a cat that had stolen cream. "Might even become a thing." He sighed wistfully. "Joey du Plessis . . . No, Joey Joubert-du Plessis."

The beginning was always exciting. Alet thought of Mike, the fact that she hadn't returned his call. That addictive thrill usually preceded a *fokop* by a hair's breadth for her, and she didn't know if she could face another one this soon.

"*Baas*, Joey, take those trays," Gertie yelled over the din.

"Just a sec, Gert." Joey poured a third of the blender's contents into a Styrofoam cup. "I'm dying to hear what you think of him, Alet." He handed her the coffee shake. "On the house."

"Thanks. Look, Joey, I need to ask you something."

"Mmm?" Joey lifted a tray from the counter. "Hey, Gertie, is this table eight? I need another slice of carrot cake, my girl."

Gertie clicked her tongue. "You didn't write it on the slip."

"Joey?"

"*Ja*, doll. What is it?"

"You know Boet's foreman, Jakob? Did he know Trudie?"

Joey raised his eyebrow. "Is he a suspect?"

"I'm only trying to figure something out."

"There was talk when I was a kid. I don't know."

"What talk?"

"People said he often spent the night there. And I'm not talking the maid's room, if you know what I mean." Joey winked. "Big scandal."

"Are you saying Trudie had an affair with Jakob?" Alet found the idea preposterous even as she uttered the words. She tried to picture staunch Trudie with the wacky farmhand.

"Ooh. Jilted lover kills the object of his affection!"

"No." Alet raised her index finger to Joey. "Don't you dare tell that to anyone, hear? All I need is more misinformation."

"You're so boring."

"Do you know anything else about Trudie and Jakob?"

Joey shrugged. "Ask Tilly. She lived with her, didn't she?" He leaned over the tray. "See you tonight. Mwah."

"Letta, there was a call. Hit-and-run," April shouted over the heads of the people at the service desk. Saturday mornings brought the inevitable slew of minor crimes on the farms that had gone unreported during the week.

"Okay," Alet said. "I'll take over here."

"No, hey. Sarge asked for you to go out, see?" April looked put out.

"Mathebe took it?"

April nodded. "Guy's dead."

"Shit." Alet handed April her untouched coffee shake. "For you."

"Sheesh. Thanks, hey." April smiled, forgiving easily.

The body had been discovered just outside town, on the road to the golf course. While cattle starved and crops failed in one part of the district, here, just over the hill, sprinkler systems kept the course a luminous green that looked almost radioactive amidst the barren brown hills.

Mathebe and Dr. Oosthuizen stood at the side of the road, their discussion muted, Mathebe nodding and asking an occasional question to which Oosthuizen responded with expressive hand gestures. He stopped his explanation midsentence, pushing his glasses higher on the bridge of his nose as Alet came within earshot. A covered body lay perpendicular to the side of the road, skid marks thick on the road's tar.

"Sergeant?" Alet shaded her eyes from the sun, realizing that she'd left her cap at Joyboys.

Mathebe gave a nod of acknowledgment and walked over to the body.

"We need you to help with an ID," Oosthuizen said. He gestured for her to step closer.

Alet had a sinking feeling. The two men looked at each other before Oosthuizen lifted the sheet. The body of a black man was on its side, one leg at an unnatural angle. The right arm was splayed overhead.

Oosthuizen lifted the arm up carefully to expose the face. "It's the Terblanche foreman?"

Alet put her hand to her mouth. She managed to nod in confirmation.

"I should have a report for you by this evening." Oosthuizen covered Jakob again.

"When did you find him?" Alet tried to get her emotions under control.

"An hour ago," Mathebe said calmly. He shook hands with Oosthuizen.

Alet followed him to the squad car. "This was an accident?"

"You said you saw him yesterday, Constable. That he was drunk."

"*Ja*, but—"

"It is conceivable that he ended up on this road. There are no streetlights. A speeding car might not have noticed him until it was too late."

"Jakob knew our murder victim. He works on the farm where her body was discovered. Don't you think it's somewhat suspicious that he suddenly turns up dead?"

The crease between Mathebe's thick brows deepened. "Yes. I do."

"So it's homicide."

"We have to wait for the autopsy report, but Dr. Oosthuizen feels the injuries to the body are not explained by the impact alone."

"He was killed before?"

"Severely beaten, but some of the injuries had started to heal. Where are you going, Constable?"

Alet headed for the van. "I'm sick of people lying to me." She slammed the door shut and sped off before Mathebe could stop her. *Fokken* Boet Terblanche. No matter which way she looked at it, he seemed to be there. She felt stupid for denying the possibility that he could be anything but the man she'd once thought him to be. Jakob was loyal to Boet. Could that loyalty have made him protect Boet from a murder conviction? She honked at a slow-moving car in front of her. When it didn't move any faster, she sped around it.

Alet stopped in front of Zebra House, her mood flammable, double-parking next to the red pickup. It was only when she got out that she noticed the smashed left headlight and the dent on the driver's side. She had explained the smashed passenger window with an attempted break-in when she returned the vehicle to Tilly, but she was sure that that had been the only damage.

"Where's *Mies* Tilly?" Alet asked a bewildered Maria as she stormed into the restaurant. A few heads looked up from their rum-and-Cokes.

"*Mies?*"

Alet didn't wait for Maria to answer. She stormed through to the empty kitchen and opened the office door. Jeffrey Wexler looked up from his laptop. In the corner, Tilly lay curled up on a small sofa, her face pale, her expression blank, her chestnut hair limp and greasy in a low ponytail. She barely acknowledged Alet's presence.

"Constable Berg. I do believe it's customary to knock, even in the boondocks."

"Tilly, I need to speak to you."

Tilly turned her head away. "Not now, Alet."

"We can do it here or at the station."

"What?" Tilly narrowed her eyes, her irises disappearing.

"Jakob is dead." Alet watched a semblance of emotion creep into Tilly's expression. "How did he know your *ma*?" Tilly bit a hangnail on her ring finger. Alet turned her attention to Wexler. "What's wrong with her?"

Wexler got up from his chair. "Can I offer you a cup of tea?" He gestured toward the kitchen. Tilly didn't move. Alet nodded and followed him.

Once the office door was closed behind them, Alet got in Wexler's face, her voice seething. "What is going on here, Mr. Wexler?"

"Calm down, luv."

"Look, you pissant, it's Constable Berg. And I've had just about enough of all the *kak* you people have been dishing me, see?"

"Mathilda is having a rough time."

"No shit. Doesn't explain the state she's in right now. Or the way the red pickup looks."

Wexler showed no reaction, calmly filling the kettle with water.

Alet crossed her arms. Her dislike for the man was intensifying exponentially. "Well? I'm waiting."

"I believe Dr. Oosthuizen gave her a sedative prescription."

"She's high?"

"She's been through a lot."

"And the pickup?"

"Probably a little run-in with a lamppost. Nothing serious. Lucky, really, considering the state she's in."

"I'll need the keys."

Wexler gave her a questioning look.

"The vehicle has to be ruled out in our homicide investigation, Mr. Wexler."

"Homicide?" Wexler paled.

"Ja. Jakob was the victim of a hit-and-run. And Mr. Wexler? I'll need you to stay in town until all of this is sorted out."

Alet went back to the office. Tilly had not moved from the sofa. "Come, Tilly, you can't stay here." She knelt next to Tilly when she didn't get a response. "I need you to sober up. Okay? I need you to come with me and explain what happened last night."

Tilly blinked hard, trying to focus through hazed confusion. She nodded slowly. Alet helped her up. Heads arched together as they walked through the restaurant, their progress carried on a flutter of whispers.

Dominee Joubert stepped up to the microphone, his voice hollow and metallic over the speaker system. "We need three more to fill the tug-of-war, Brothers and Sisters. The winning team gets free tickets to tonight's cabaret at Joyboys featuring André du Plessis."

Alet wondered if *Dominee* Joubert had gone to the trouble of finding out who André really was yet. She waited until the feedback from the speaker died down.

"We need to talk to Boet, Jana." Alet and Mathebe had been looking for Boet at the church bazaar and found Jana working the concessions stand, selling tickets for the *braai.*

"He was helping out with the sheep auction. Two farmers donated this year."

Alet had heard about this charity sheep auction. There was an unspoken rule that whoever put in the highest bid was supposed to donate the sheep back to the church. The same sheep ended up being auctioned multiple times through the day.

"It's about your foreman—" Alet was interrupted by the man in the fake-fur Santa suit and white polyester beard. It took her a moment to realize that it was Boet. He made brief eye contact with her before laying his hand on Jana's shoulder.

"Haai, Koeks." Jana turned her head, her kiss lingering uncomfortably long. "Are you ready for the little ones?" She patted his padded stomach. "Boet plays Santa every year. The kids love it."

"So what's this about, Jakob? Does he need to be bailed out again?" Boet had a forced joviality about him. Probably a few too many bazaar beers. Alet noticed sweat beading on his forehead. In this heat that suit had to be torture.

Mathebe stepped in. "Could we talk privately, Mr. Terblanche?"

"Why?" Jana snapped.

Alet caught Mathebe's eye. The way he looked at her made her uncomfortable. She turned her attention back to Boet. "Jakob's body was discovered this morning."

Jana put a swollen hand on her chest. The other was stuck to her swollen stomach, as if it might fall off if she let go.

"What?" Boet frowned. "That can't be right."

Mathebe clasped his hands in front of him, nodding confirmation. "Mr. Mens was struck by a vehicle late last night."

"I just saw him yesterday." Shock sobered Boet. "He asked for half day. Said he had business in town and took the smuggler's truck in." He addressed Alet. "Do you know who it was?"

"Nobody has come forward. We're waiting for the autopsy."

"I see." Boet had the same look in his eye that he'd had the day of the murder, a surprised fear, as if he was barely keeping it together.

"One more thing. Do you either of you know anything about the Thokoloshe?"

Mathebe's neck stiffened.

"The what?" Jana's upper lip lifted in an incredulous sneer. She reached for Boet's hand, interlacing her fingers with his. "That's just kid nonsense and superstition."

"It's the nickname for a man named Skosana."

"Never heard of him," Boet said mechanically.

"Skosana has been known to frequent Magda Kok's."

"That woman," Jana said with disgust. "Nothing but trouble. Beautiful little girl she has. Shame she has to grow up like that. The police really should do something."

"Thanks for your help." Alet walked away, leaving Mathebe a few paces behind. He caught up to her at the school gates.

"Constable, what are you doing?"

"Boet's lying. Did you see his reaction when I asked him about Skosana? He almost pissed himself. Boet Terblanche is eyeball-deep in this. I say we go after him and see what shakes out."

"Are you sure you are the best person to judge Mr. Terblanche's involvement?"

"What?"

"I'm asking if what you see is not influenced by something else."

"I don't know what you—"

"You had promised you would not lie to me again, Constable."

Alet sighed. "That's personal."

Mathebe held up his hand. "Mr. Terblanche is a suspect."

"Look, it happened way back, hey. I was . . ." She struggled for the words, finding it difficult to explain. "I had lost a lot. Everything. It's not an excuse, but . . . When I came here, I was lonely, see? It was a mistake. But it is over. Long gone. Forgotten."

"You are sure?"

"I can do my job."

A group of teenage girls walked past the gate, chatting noisily. Mathebe motioned to the van and got in.

"Let me work Boet, find a crack," Alet said as she closed the door. "He's ready to break, I can tell."

"You have to stay away from Mr. Terblanche."

"But—"

"This has to happen the right way, Constable."

A call came in over the radio. Pileup on the N12. Mathebe responded to the dispatcher.

"We need to wait this out. Find evidence first." Mathebe turned the siren on. "We cannot proceed with what we have at the moment." He looked over at her. "Patience, Grasshopper."

Alet did a double-take. Did Mathebe just make a joke?

Alet booked off shift at six and walked home. Between two accidents on the N12 and keeping the bazaar-goers from blocking the streets, she didn't really feel like going to a show to chitchat with a has-been TV celebrity amid a sea of sunburned drunks. Jakob's death bothered her. He had been a good *oke*, no matter his love for the bottle. She should have taken him in last night, let him sleep it off in a cell. Perhaps he'd still be alive.

Alet closed the groaning gate behind her. She thought about the night she climbed over the fence and ruined her blouse. The same night that Boet followed her home. His clumsy goodbye as he left her flat. The light that went on in Trudie's living room as Alet slammed the door behind him.

"*Fokker.*" Alet took her cell out of her backpack and dialed Mathebe with shaky hands.

"Constable?"

"When you went through Trudie's house, what did it look like?"

"I do not understand."

"Did you mess it up?"

"I always try to be respectful."

"So it was in chaos when you got there?"

"There are photographs of the scene."

"You took prints, right? You ran them against Trudie and Tilly. Anyone else's pop up?"

"Only a partial index finger print in the living room that did not match Mrs. Pienaar or her daughter. But we do not know how old it is."

"Johannes, I think he was in the house."

"It is possible. Most victims know their killers."

"No. You don't understand. There was a light that went on in the house that Thursday night. Trudie was already dead. Boet saw it too."

"Mr. Terblanche was at your house?"

"He wanted to talk about what happened on the mountain." Alet sighed. "Look, I told you the truth. It's over."

Mathebe was quiet for a moment.

"That print might be the killer's, Johannes. Can we run it?"

"There is not enough of it. We need a print to compare it to."

Tilly sat on the *stoep* of Alet's flat, a mug of coffee at her feet. She had changed into clean clothes and her hair was wet.

"Johannes, I'll call you back." Alet hung up the phone. She walked up to Tilly. "How do you feel?"

"Like someone left an ax in my skull."

"That's why I stick to beer."

Tilly cracked a smile.

"What happened last night?"

Tilly shook her head slowly. "I don't know."

Alet sat down next to her. "Can we cut the bull? Or do I have to play bad cop and make stupid threats and lose a friend? Jeff is selling babies to foreigners, isn't he?"

Tilly hesitated for a moment, then nodded.

"How long?"

"Since he bought Zebra House." Tilly looked pleadingly at Alet. "You have to understand, these kids, they aren't wanted. They're born with long-gone fathers and mothers with little education and low-paying jobs, if they have one at all. They have no chance."

"You get to decide this?"

Tilly clutched her hands in her lap. "When you see those kids begging at the shops, when you know that most of them go hungry at night or eat grass just to have something in their stomachs, you think, I have the power to change this, to make a difference. They'll have access to schools, parents who love them, a future."

"You don't know that."

"The people who come here are willing to do anything for a child."

"They are desperate for a reason, Tilly. Maybe they can't go through legal methods because they have red flags next to their names. Who even knows what happens to those babies once they're out of the country? What kind of person pays for a stolen baby?"

"They are wanted."

"I'm sure it keeps Jeff in good Scotch too, and you . . ." Alet stopped herself. "Okay. So Jeff organizes the sale. He has a contact, presumably. Where do they get the babies?"

"There is someone the women know to go to if they are in trouble."

"Or do they get pregnant on purpose to get money?"

"It's not like that."

"What about the American couple from the other night? What happened to the baby?"

"There was an exchange."

"Wait. They had a child with them when they left here?"

"*Ja.*"

"*Fok.*" Alet flipped her cell phone open and dialed the station. "April? Listen. Get hold of the captain. I don't care how, just get him. Let him know that the Americans had an infant with them. I'll explain later. Tell him to authorize an alert, right away."

Alet hung up. "Why didn't you tell me this earlier?"

"Jeff said he'd take care of it."

"And you believe anything that man says?"

"It was too late already. And then *Ma* . . ." Tilly's face contracted. "I know this looks bad, but I swear, I just wanted to help."

"How does Boet figure into all of this?" Alet spoke through a clenched jaw.

Tilly frowned. "Boet?"

"*Ja.* Is he your contact? Do women on the farm come to him if they want to sell their children?"

Tilly shook her head. "No. They go to Jana."

"Absolutely not." Mynhardt was wearing a checkered shirt and dress pants. He'd probably been on his way to Joyboys when he received the call.

Alet stared at Mynhardt in disbelief. "Captain?" She and Mathebe stood in front of Mynhardt's desk like chastised children.

"Nobody's dragging a pregnant woman out of the main social event of the year in handcuffs."

"Tilly is willing to testify."

"It's her word against Jana Terblanche's. Tomorrow we'll calmly ask Mrs. Terblanche to answer a few questions. And you, my girl, will stay as far away from her as possible."

"It's my case."

Mynhardt pointed a finger at her. "Sleeping with Boet Terblanche lost you that."

"Captain, I—"

"Alet. I've been patient with you." Mynhardt looked at Mathebe. "Both of you. This isn't the Wild West, my girl. There's a chain of command and I am at the top of it as far as you're concerned. You're going to tell me everything or I'll make sure neither of you ever works in the force again."

Alet looked over at Mathebe. His stern mask had slipped and she saw a vulnerable man there, his impeccable posture melting at the shoulders, his tie askew. "It was my fault, Captain. I asked Sergeant Mathebe to hold off on reporting certain facts. You understand why."

Mynhardt glared at her, his thick red eyebrows knitted together. "And there were things we weren't sure of yet."

"I'm listening."

Mathebe cleared his throat. "I can take it from here, Constable Berg." He didn't wait for Alet to object. "We believe that Mrs. Terblanche used her position as teacher at the farm school to find women in trouble. She promised them money for their infants and received a commission from Mr. Wexler."

Mynhardt sat down in his chair, his arms crossed. "How does this tie in with Trudie Pienaar and the Terblanche foreman?"

"Mrs. Pienaar had known Mr. Jakob Mens. She is the one who got him the job on the Terblanche farm."

Mynhardt had a look of incredulity, but he motioned for Mathebe to continue.

"We think that Mr. Mens found out about the trafficking and told Mrs. Pienaar. That she perhaps threatened to expose the operation. That one of the parties involved might have killed her to keep her quiet."

"It doesn't make sense," Alet broke in. "Tilly would have known about it if Trudie found out."

"We cannot rule her involvement out," Mynhardt said. "She could be trying to set the others up so she can get away with murder. You said yourself that there was someone in the house. Mathilda has keys, I presume?"

Alet had never doubted her instincts about people this much. Tilly had been devastated by Trudie's death. Was she just a gifted actress?

"It would also explain Mathilda's motive for killing the Terblanche foreman," Mynhardt said. "To shut him up."

"What?" Alet's head was spinning.

"Paint flecks on his body match Ms. Pienaar's vehicle, Constable."

"That vehicle belongs to Zebra House. Anyone could have taken it."

"What else is she going to say, Alet?" The corners of Mynhardt's mouth tightened in a sarcastic grimace. He turned to Mathebe. "Go on."

Mathebe nodded. "Miss Pienaar has been cooperative. She has given us the names of couples that have come here for children in the past two years."

"For all we know, these adoptions were perfectly legal." Mynhardt leaned back in his chair. "If the mothers consented and the paperwork was in order, there isn't much we can do."

"Come on, Captain." Alet balled her fists. "I don't think buying children can be considered legal, no matter how you look at it."

"It might have been an adoption fee. Reimbursement for the mother's expenses."

"And Wexler? Last time I checked, he wasn't running an adoption agency."

"You can stop your hysterics, Constable." Mynhardt stood up. "I'll examine the evidence, but I don't see how we can charge anybody. Even so, it seems like a victimless crime. Besides a very flimsy connection to this baby business, do you have anything on Trudie Pienaar's murder?"

"We are waiting on forensic evidence, Captain," Mathebe said. "We know she changed her name from Lilly Maartens to Trudie Pienaar. She might have used other pseudonyms, which is why we cannot find anything on her."

Alet clenched her jaw, waiting for Mathebe to reveal the anomaly in Trudie's DNA, but he didn't continue. She looked over at him. He had his lips pressed together, his gaze fixed on Mynhardt, his expression inscrutable.

"I want daily updates." Mynhardt grabbed his jacket from the chair. He patted the pockets, feeling for something before putting it on. "Strijdom will take charge of the Braverman case."

"What about the baby?" Alet barely kept her sudden anger in check.

"I informed Captain Groenewald. He will take it from here." Mynhardt motioned to his office door. "Good night."

Alet followed Mathebe through the canteen to the backyard. All the vehicles were checked in, the station running on a skeleton crew. Mathebe sat down on one of the plastic chairs.

"Thank you for that," Alet said. "Not telling him about my dad, I mean."

"We agreed."

"*Ja*, but thanks anyway." She pulled up a chair next to him. "What are we going to do about this?"

"Exactly what the captain told us to do, Constable."

"Let those bloody bastards get away with it?"

"It is as the captain said. It is Miss Pienaar's word against everybody else's." Mathebe glanced at the station's back door. "The captain's too."

"You picked up on that, huh?"

"I have suspected it."

"Would explain the 'perfectly legal' paperwork in any case."

"The captain and Sergeant Strijdom are members of the golf club. Their families went on vacation together last year. I believe the captain bought a beachfront property in Umhlanga Rocks."

"On a policeman's salary? That's a lot of unwanted babies."

Mathebe nodded. "It might be more than children. Selling dockets. Not logging drug evidence."

"What do we do? Go to the Hawks?"

"There is nothing we can do at the moment. They have started cleaning house. Evidence is disappearing. Activity will cease until they believe there is no threat. We must tread carefully, Constable. Everything we do will now be watched."

Alet got up from her chair. "Well, since they know we know, let's make them sweat a little, hey? See if it makes them do something stupid."

"What do you mean, Constable?"

"Want to go to a show, Sergeant? I'll *stick* you for a ticket."

The performance had already begun by the time Alet walked into Joyboys. Onstage, André du Plessis, a middle-aged man in a multicolored waistcoat with shoulder-length hair and a goatee, stood in front of the microphone, strumming on his guitar, crooning an old Afrikaans folk song. Alet scooted through the tables in the dim room, keeping a firm hold on Mathebe's shirtsleeve behind her.

"Alet?" Joey looked questioningly at Mathebe.

"Johannes is joining us. Can you make room?"

Joey made eye contact with a few of the patrons who were looking in their direction. "Show was sold out, you know."

"I will wait outside," Mathebe said.

"No." Alet smiled and pulled him forward, patting him on the shoulders. "You have my spot. I'll stand." She pulled the open chair next to Joey out for him. "I insist."

Joey shot Alet a look of dismay while Mathebe sat down. "Wine for you, Sergeant?"

Mathebe held his hand up. "No. Thank you. Water is all right."

"We've already served appetizers, but I'll see if Gertie has anything left."

"Please," Alet said. "I'm starving."

André finished the song and the room erupted in applause. He lifted his porkpie hat and made an elaborate bow. "Thank you, Unie!" He took the microphone off the stand. "I want to thank you good people for having me out here. *Lekker* times with friends, hey?" A chorus of drunken approval went around the room.

"We're going to take a little break to enjoy the lovely dinner our host, Joey, has prepared for the evening, but before that, *Dominee* Joubert is going to lead us in prayer."

Alet looked around the room while *Dominee* Joubert droned on. Mynhardt, Strijdom and their wives sat a few tables away. Mathebe gave Alet a panicked look as she left their table. She bumped into a chair on purpose to make sure that everyone saw her walk over to Boet and Jana's table at the opposite side of the room. Jana had her left hand folded over Boet's on top of the table, the other still glued to her stomach.

"Amen."

She gasped when she looked up into Alet's face. Like most of the women there, she was dressed to the nines and plastered in makeup that was at least two shades lighter than her skin tone. She quickly regained her composure, an insincere smile masking her discomfort. "I didn't expect you here, Alet."

"I wanted to come say hallo." Out of the corner of her eye, Alet could see Mynhardt getting up from his table. His jacket was slung over the back of his chair. "Can I have a seat? I think it's time we talked, got a few things straight, you know?"

Boet looked at Jana, waiting for her cue. Jana's smile didn't slip. She spoke in low tones, her teeth clenched. "I think it's best that you leave."

Alet pulled an empty chair out next to Boet. His eyes pleaded silently with her. "We're all friends here." Alet patted him on his forearm, watching Jana's neck stiffen.

"Slut." Jana hissed the word.

"Jana," Alet pouted her lips. "That's not nice, hey."

"Leave." Jana crouched over the table. "You have no rights here. I'm his wife. I'm carrying his son."

"You're planning on keeping him? I'm disappointed. I wanted to put in an offer. What do babies go for these days?"

Jana lunged at Alet, her mouth open, teeth bared, her face swollen and red. Shocked faces turned to them from the buffet line, the room suddenly silent.

Boet stepped between the two women, holding on to Jana. "Alet, please," he hissed.

Alet looked him in the eye. "So you knew. *Jissis*. How do you sleep at night, Boet?"

"Whore. You stay away from us." Jana pushed away from Boet.

"I know what you've done, Jana, and I know who you're in bed with. I'm coming after you and your whole operation."

"You see all these people here?" Jana pointed at the room. "They stand with their own. Life is going to get very hard for you here in Unie, trust me."

"I'm sure it will, Jana." Alet leaned in, her voice low. "Problem is, I don't care anymore. Captain!" Alet turned just as Mynhardt and Strijdom reached the table. "Hein." She smiled. "Hope you're enjoying your evening. Have you met André? I'm just about to make his acquaintance and I'm so excited." She walked away, stopping at Joey's table, forcing herself not to run for the door. As Joey made introductions, fawning over André, Alet watched Mynhardt and Strijdom out of the corner of her eye. They exchanged words with Jana. Boet stood to one side, his arms crossed, tension in his face. As soon as André took the stage again, Alet slipped out. She found Mathebe up the block, pacing nervously.

"Did you find anything?"

Mathebe hesitated for a moment before reaching into his pocket. He handed Alet a pay-as-you-go cell phone. "It was the only thing in his jacket."

"Great." She attempted a high five, but Mathebe looked at her with exasperation. "Don't worry, Johannes. Nobody saw you, right? Mynhardt has already had a few, and the evening's just started. He won't notice it until later, and he'll think it fell out and got lost."

"I have broken the law. We cannot use this as evidence now. It was the wrong thing to do." Mathebe reached for the phone. "I have to take it back."

Alet put her hand on his arm to stop him. "Johannes, we need to nail these bastards or this will never end. You know that. Besides, this would probably have ended up in the trash when they started covering their tracks anyway." She lowered her voice. "You did the right thing." Mathebe let his arms drop. Alet tucked the cell into her purse before he could change his mind. "Can you cover the first half of my shift tomorrow? I need to get this to Cape Town."

Mathebe nodded reluctantly, still looking like a guilty schoolboy.

"Alet?" Theo answered the door in a pair of shorts and a baggy T-shirt, his face swollen with sleep.

"I tried calling."

"I turn my cell off after nine. Students panic about deadlines at strange hours. What can I do for you?"

"I need you to trace the numbers on here for me." She handed him the cell Mathebe had taken from Mynhardt's jacket. "And also . . . can I crash on your couch?"

"Um . . . That's not the best idea."

"I'll try to restrain myself, but you can lock your bedroom door if you're scared I'll seduce you."

"It's not that. I have company, see?"

"Oh . . . even better. She can protect you."

"Alet—"

"Please, Theo, you know what the service pays. My hotel budget is blown for the year."

Theo leaned against the door frame. He looked like he was in physical pain.

"I'm willing to beg."

Theo ran his hand over his face. "Okay. Fine. Come in."

Theo's town house was small but stylish, the interior all clean lines and muted earth tones, not a coaster or magazine out of place.

"I could never live with you."

"What?"

"I mean, you'd have a nervous breakdown in a week."

Theo smiled. "*Ja*. Well . . . I'll get you a blanket."

"Theo?" A petite young woman came out of the bedroom wearing a robe. She had high cheekbones and skin the color of desert dunes.

"Lana. Sorry, did we wake you up?"

Lana looked questioningly at Alet.

"I'm Alet. Hi. Nice to meet you. Sorry about the late-night intrusion."

Lana turned back to Theo. "Your ex?" There was a note of panic in her voice.

Alet was surprised that the girl knew about her. "Lana, right? *Haai*. Theo is helping me out, because he's a nice guy. That's all that's going on here. Promise."

"I should go." Lana's voice wavered.

"Please stay," Alet said. "I'll find somewhere else to crash, I didn't realize . . ."

"It's okay. I have work in the morning." Lana didn't make eye contact. She turned and scrambled back into the bedroom.

"I'm sorry," Alet mouthed. Theo shook his head and followed Lana. Alet tried not to listen to the exchange coming from behind the closed door. She took Trudie's file from her backpack and drew a timeline on the cover, starting with Trudie's death, going back to her birth certificate date of 1958. She extended the line to Lilly Maartens's birth date in the thirties, ending in a question mark. If Trudie claimed to be in her fifties when she died, and Lilly/Trudie looked to be in her late twenties in the fifties, that meant that she aged at a rate of roughly 1:3. Alet did the math in her head. That would put her real birth date somewhere around the beginning of the century. So who was Trudie before she was Lilly Maartens? And how did Jakob fit into this whole thing? Alet filled in the dates of the known victims' murders on the timeline. She hated the feeling that she was missing something. She paged through the file with the case reports Theo had forwarded her, laying them out chronologically, young blond women with pale eyes staring back at her.

"I'll be damned," Alet said out loud. At the time of their deaths, the women were the age that Trudie would have appeared to be then.

The bedroom door opened. Lana was dressed in a cute knee-length cocktail dress and high heels, her black hair pinned up with a pearl clip. She looked like a woman who had her life together. A good match for Theo. Alet felt a dull pang at the thought.

"Lana," she said. "Please stay."

"It's all right, Ms. Berg."

"I hope you guys are okay?" Alet said when Theo came back from walking Lana to her car.

"I don't know. Things are kind of new. We'll see." Theo opened the hallway closet, took out bedding, and dumped it on the couch next to Alet. "Here. It's not going to be the most comfortable night's sleep you'll ever have." Theo glanced at the files and timeline Alet had spread over the coffee table. "This your victim?"

"*Ja*. I think I've found the connection between her and the other Angel Killer victims."

Theo moved the bedding aside and sat down next to her. "We probably need to talk."

"Hey, I'm sorry about Lana, Theo. I feel bad."

"No. I mean, about Adriaan. And Nico Koch."

Alet's stomach knotted. "You found something?" The sound of her voice was harsh, a little too loud.

"Okay. Vlakplaas wasn't the only Security Branch unit that was a death squad. The Citizen's Cooperation Bureau was so bloody hush-hush that the one hand didn't know what the other was doing. There were units all over the country. Remember the Lubowski murder?"

"The civil rights lawyer? The one who was gunned down in Namibia?"

"*Ja*. There's no proof, but word is that he was killed by a CCB guy because they didn't know that Lubowski was really a Security Branch informant."

"What's that got to do with my dad?"

"My source tells me that Adriaan was one of the CCB commanders." Theo frowned. "You sure you want me to go on?"

Alet nodded.

"Adriaan had a number of assassins in his unit, some *askaris* who were turned, some Security Branch men. All of them highly skilled. They had access to guns, bombs . . . they sometimes resorted to chemicals, switching a target's medication out, putting thallium in beer, even poison in clothes and on toilet seats. There were several bio-engineering shell companies that developed this stuff. Nico Koch worked for one of them."

"And he knew my dad through working with him on murder cases."

"*Ja.* They go back a long way. Anyway, Koch was hired by one of these shell companies when your dad was transferred out of Brixton. High-level stuff."

"So Koch is the Mengele to my dad's Himmler?"

"You need a drink?"

"Make it whiskey. Don't bother with ice."

Alet's hand was unsteady as she took the drink from Theo. "I assume all of this was government-sanctioned?"

"And funded. They even tried to develop some sort of chemical agent that would only kill blacks."

"That doesn't even make sense."

"Not now. But back then their ideologies were more important than facts. They couldn't see past it. Blacks were less human than whites to them. Probably thought they could zero in on some animal gene or something." Theo shook his head. "Nothing came of it, as far as I know. There were rumors of tests across the border—"

"So why is my dad not in jail?"

"The people close to him were loyal, kept their mouths shut. Sometimes the killing was contracted out to township gangsters who didn't even know they were doing work for the government. They just got the name of a target and a bunch of money once the job was done."

"What else?"

"That's all I have now. I'll keep digging."

"Thanks, hey." Alet touched Theo's thigh, letting her hand linger a moment too long.

Theo looked up at her, before pulling away awkwardly. "You're the one who left, Alet. Remember?"

"I'll go. The backseat of the car will do for a few hours."

"No. Stay. I'll go to Lana's place. Make yourself at home." Theo got up to leave, but turned around in the doorway. "Look, I have a good feeling about Lana. I don't want to mess it up if . . ."

"She seems great."

Theo smiled. "You think so?"

Alet nodded. "I'm sorry about tonight. I really am."

"We're okay. Don't worry." Theo pulled his sweatshirt over his head. "There's bread in the fridge, coffee by the kettle. I'll call you in the morning, okay?"

Alet tossed around on the couch for a while, trying to get comfortable, her long legs dangling over the armrest. She gave up after a while and started poring through Theo's research files, reading every incident report, every name, every abuse. After a while the crimes lost their borders, meshing into a dark litany of human atrocities. Why didn't she know? She was only a child around the time of the Truth and Reconciliation Commission's hearings, and the adults always changed the TV channel whenever the broadcasts came on. Nobody talked about it in church or in school except as a nuisance, the inference always that the blacks were lying. By the time she'd reached college, a weariness prevailed across the land. Nobody wanted to talk about it anymore. It was better to pretend that they were all just one big politically correct family, even as the hatred curdled underneath it all.

Alet went down the list of TRC witnesses, not recognizing any of the names. There was one reference to her father by a witness named Jim, but Jim never showed up to testify.

Alet cross-referenced the name Jim with the available witness information. Jim's birth name was given as Jacob Morgan, born in 1961. Morgan. The name sounded familiar. Alet made a note to look it up.

Morning light steadily penetrated the blinds in Theo's kitchen. Alet put the last piece of paper down and got up to make coffee, her limbs stiff from the awkward reclining position that she'd been sitting in all night. She was exhausted, struggling with a confusion of emotions, with the fact that it was shame, not pride, that now seemed to define her heritage. So many deaths, lies going back for almost a century, and she'd had no idea. She had accepted the notion that it had been better before, and yet she'd never given it real thought. It was easier to cling to a comfortable illusion than to look for the truth. But the truth was steadily encroaching on her world, and she had no idea which of her illusions would be shattered next.

1985

Benjamin

The toddler waddled to the elephant enclosure, her large eyes sparkling with excitement. "Fant," she shouted, her small outstretched
hand reaching toward the enormous animal. Her father yelled at her,
ordering her back. A thin, bedraggled woman with stiff hair followed
a few steps behind him, pushing the child's empty stroller. It wasn't the
same woman Benjamin remembered Adriaan Berg being married to.
Wife number two seemed much more . . . compliant.

Sudden tears glinted in the toddler's eyes at the reprimand, followed by wailing. Mrs. Berg number two picked her up. "Stop that,
please, Alet. *Pa* will never bring you to the zoo again if you don't behave." A look passed between her and Berg, difficult to place, but certainly devoid of warmth.

Benjamin sauntered behind them, blending in with the crowd,
while observing the family. He was surprised at Berg for bringing
his family to such a public place. There had been a bombing at an
Amanzimtoti mall just the previous week, five civilians killed and
forty injured. It was the latest in a string of ANC bombings aimed at
soft targets. Whites lived in fear, the police on edge. The shops were
practically deserted for the Christmas season.

The girl, Alet, calmed down a bit as the woman put her in the
stroller. They headed to the next section of cages. Primates. Benjamin followed, the smell of animal feces rank as they got closer. Berg
seemed to issue some instructions to his wife, leaving her and the child
alone to stare at the baboons while he disappeared in the direction of
the public toilets.

"You can see the familial resemblance," Benjamin said as he sauntered up behind Mrs. Berg number two.

"Sorry?" The woman had a vapid expression. Benjamin wondered how Berg tolerated her presence day in and day out. He supposed Berg liked them like that, easy to control, fewer questions about his late-night activities.

"I mean, your ancestors didn't look too different from these guys, you know."

"You saying I'm a monkey?"

"I believe you mean ape."

"I'm not an ape. That's only the blacks. That's where they come from, you know."

Benjamin took a deep breath. Stupid and ignorant, like most of them, content to let the government and the church dictate their thoughts. This was the mythical Afrikaner nation, the chosen race. He had so desperately wanted to be accepted by them once. What for? He hunched down next to the stroller. "And what's your name?"

Suspicious eyes met his. The little girl clutched a yellow baby blanket, sucking at its edges.

"This is Alet. She's eighteen months today." The pride in the woman's voice sounded funny to Benjamin, as if she was expressing pride over breathing or emptying her bowels.

"She looks a bit like a baby chimp to me. Don't you think?"

Mrs. Berg number two opened her mouth, shock on her face. Benjamin stood up and turned in time to stop Berg from sending him crashing into the fence post.

"You're loud and slow, Adriaan."

Berg grabbed the collar of Benjamin's jacket. "Get away from them." Benjamin's knee caught Berg in the stomach. Berg let go. "I'll kill you," he gasped. He reached for his hip, coming up empty.

"Forgot something, Adriaan?"

Berg didn't take his eyes of Benjamin. "Take Alet to the car, Gerda." Mrs. Berg number two hesitated. "Now," Berg barked. The woman scurried away, looking over her shoulder every few steps as she made her way up the lane to the zoo's entrance. Berg never took his eyes off Benjamin.

"Let's walk," Benjamin said, noticing the onlookers, stopped midstride to observe the spectacle. He started down the lane, wondering for a moment if Berg had it in him to walk away, but then he heard the crunch on the gravel behind him. He leaned on a banister as soon as they were far enough away to have some privacy. Inside the cage, a hawk sat in the crook of a tree, blinking slowly as it surveyed the newcomers.

"What do you want, De Beer?" Berg's body was poised to react.

"Be civil, Adriaan."

Berg crossed his arms. "You're wasting my time."

"I have tolerated your interest in my work for some years now, Adriaan. I was flattered by your persistence, frankly. But your clumsy excuse for an investigation is becoming annoying."

The frown on Berg's face eased. "So it was you."

"The Angel Killer," Benjamin laughed. "Was that your idea?"

"One of the constables. The girls all looked the same, he said, like angels."

"And you didn't stop the media from latching on to that."

"I thought it was poetic, your old squad name finding you again. The old boys still talk about you, you know? None of them realizes what a monster you really are."

Benjamin sighed. "You're a hypocrite, Adriaan. You hide behind policy and crude ideals, thinking it absolves you. Believe it, if it helps you sleep, but at the end of the day there is no real difference between you and me."

"I take care of threats to our nation. I don't go around killing my own. Us against them, remember?" Adriaan's face swelled red with indignation. "What you do is . . . barbaric, killing innocents, just like the *kaffirs* do." Berg had regained his composure. He locked eyes with Benjamin. "That last girl? Her name was Liezl Brits."

"Oh?" Benjamin feigned interest.

"*Ja*. She was a nurse. A sweet girl who taught Sunday school and liked to visit her *ouma*."

"A real-life Red Riding Hood."

"What you did to her . . . it destroyed her family. Good people."

"And the powerful Adriaan Berg promised them he'd catch her killer. Is that right? They must be so disappointed."

"She was a real person, not just some—"

"I'm offended that you've resorted to cheap tricks, Adriaan. Did you think I'd feel remorse? Do you really think I randomly pick women out of a crowd? That I'm not absolutely sure of what I'm doing every single time? There is nothing you can tell me about darling Liezl, or any of them, that I didn't already know. Nothing. As a matter of fact, I think I can teach *you* a thing or two about poor little Liezl."

Adriaan narrowed his eyes. "I showed her family and friends your photo, to see if they recognized you."

"They have no part in this."

"*Ja*, I realized it soon enough, but as I passed your photo around, I realized something. You see, the photo was the one on record, from when you joined the force. What was that? Almost thirty years ago?"

"Feels like yesterday."

"Records give your birth as 1938. You're supposed to be pushing fifty and you don't look like you've grown chest hair yet. I looked into stolen identities, but then I remembered you from the days in the bush. Took a few phone calls, but I found a picture of the unit."

Benjamin kept his emotions in check, even though he wanted to pummel the knowing smirk off Berg's face.

"You had a beard back then, De Beer, always wore those dark glasses, but I'll be damned if you look a day older now than you did then, than you did in that ID picture."

"What can I say? It's good genes." Benjamin chuckled at his own joke, then at the confusion on Berg's face.

Berg frowned. "How do you do it?" His eyes narrowed. "Are you taking some kind of drug? Or are you just a freak of nature?"

Benjamin waved Berg off, his mood souring. "What I want to talk about is your lovely family." He felt something akin to pleasure again as he noticed tension tightening its grip on Berg's body, his vulnerability clear. Van Vuuren had been right all those years ago not to allow married men into the unit.

Berg stepped up to Benjamin, their faces inches apart. "I will hunt you down if you touch a hair—"

"Get off me, Adriaan." Benjamin's voice was void of emotion. "You need to hear what I have to say." Berg stepped away. Benjamin straightened out his jacket. "Your newly found conscience is interesting, but irrelevant. Because you're going to walk away from this case, forget I exist."

"Others are involved in the investigation. I can't just—"

"I'm sure you can lead things in a different direction." Benjamin winked. "Wouldn't be the first time, now would it."

"Captain," Berg pleaded, a hint of distress in his voice. "Those girls didn't deserve it. To burn them like that . . . They are your people."

"My people . . ." The words felt strange to Benjamin. He wondered at how different the meaning of that concept was to Berg, triggering feelings of protection rather than annihilation. The hawk swooped down suddenly, then soared as high as the cage would allow. "I'm doing what needs to be done, Adriaan. Like you."

"Look, I get it." Berg's tone softened. "I was there too, remember? We were children who signed up to be policemen and ended up in a war zone, ordered to kill. You can't switch that kind of thing off when you get back home."

An image of the bush flashed before Benjamin, the body of a freedom fighter dragged behind a patrol vehicle for miles until his skin was sloughed off and you couldn't tell whether he was black or white anymore. The Casspirs would roll over the ones still alive to finish them off. Benjamin still woke up at night, the sound of bones crushing under tank wheels echoing in his mind. He had seen hundreds of bodies dumped into mass graves. He knew these men like Berg, what they were capable of. What he himself was capable of. His chest suddenly felt constricted. "So what do you do?"

"The blokes in my covert unit, they channel it, use it to help our cause, protect our people. They hunt these MK bastards down and eliminate them."

Benjamin turned to Berg. "Is that a job offer?"

"If that's what you want," Berg said. He gripped the railing with white knuckles. "No one can know, of course. But you are one of us."

The hawk swooped again. This time, when it ascended, something small wriggled in its claws. A hunter fulfilling his purpose. There was no purpose in what Berg and his oafs did. Not for Benjamin, anyway. It was a distraction, nothing more, men desperate to hold on to power in a land where they were outnumbered. He didn't believe in that cause. Not since God revealed to him how He made Benjamin superior to them. Oxygen filled his lungs again. "You're desperate. Adriaan Berg has never not caught his man. That's got you panicked." Benjamin backed away from the railing. "Keep your deal. We're done here."

"I'm warning you, stop with the girls. I won't let you—"

"You haven't been able to track me down in fifteen years, Adriaan. I know you've been looking. You think you can do it now?"

"I'm close or you wouldn't be here."

"Perhaps. But it was so easy to get Gerda and Alet alone today. Do you really think you can get to me before I get to them?"

The punch took Benjamin by surprise. He staggered a few steps, but regained his balance fast enough to stop the next blow. He was on top of Berg before the man had a chance to react. Benjamin's body went through the motions with practiced grace, striking a blow to Berg's solar plexus. Berg gasped, his arms still reaching for Benjamin.

"Too slow, Adriaan." Benjamin spun Berg around like a rag doll, grasping the man's throat. He felt Berg's struggle become faint disappointingly soon.

Shouting. Two bruisers were running toward them. One of the men grabbed the back of Benjamin's jacket. Benjamin released his grip. Berg's body flopped to the ground. Benjamin swung around, punching the man hard enough that he let go and fell down.

"You want in on this?" Benjamin took a step toward the second man.

"No, friend." The man held both hands up in front of his face. "You just go, see?"

Benjamin looked back at Berg trying to push himself off the ground. Adriaan Berg was a vengeful man. Benjamin knew he'd have to make sure Berg realized that he didn't make idle threats.

On his way through the parking lot, Benjamin saw Gerda's bewildered face in the passenger side of a gold Mercedes. The lock clicked as he approached the car. "I'd like to talk to you, Gerda." He bent down, his hand resting on the glass. "How about you open up?"

Gerda shook her head. "My husband said . . ." She tried to contain a squirming Alet.

"Gerda!" Benjamin put his hands on the roof of the car, rocking it. "You're not listening. I said, open up!" He slammed his body against the car for effect. Gerda screamed. Alet sat dumbfounded for a moment before emitting her own wails. There was a commotion at the zoo gate. Berg and the bruisers had been joined by more men. Benjamin brought his fist down. The glass in front of Gerda cracked, fracturing the image of her face, her features diminished to small pieces that didn't add up to a whole. Benjamin looked down at his bleeding hand, the image of flames springing forth from his body flashing before his eyes. Purified by fire, chosen to do God's work. More yelling, a mob of voices building to an unbearable cacophony. Berg and the others weaved their way through the lot, their united bravado building to a frenzied pitch.

"Pay attention, Gerda." Benjamin said. "You make sure your husband backs off or you won't see me coming next time. Not till it's too late for Alet." He turned and ran until the footsteps behind him faded away and Johannesburg enveloped him in its darkening fold.

Jacob

A small white coffin drifted on the sea of bodies, anchored on both sides by two men. Women sang a plaintive hymn, underscored by the harmonies of deep male voices, their feet kicking up dust as they walked past small round houses with thatched roofs, cattle and goats grazing on the sides of the road.

"Only a baby," a woman said next to Jakob. She dabbed her eyes with a handkerchief. "What could a baby do?"

A tall boy put his arms around her shoulders. "They are dogs, *Ma*," he said. "One day they will pay."

Policemen watched the procession, rifles in hand, staying close to their yellow vans. Jakob averted his eyes when he recognized one of the policemen, hoping he'd blend in, just another black face in the mass, praying that today wouldn't be a repetition of past events. Funerals were the only legal way of gathering afforded to black people now, the only way for the ANC and PAC to rally their followers. Things got out of hand on more than one occasion, escalating into riots, lives lost in the process. In Langa, seventeen people were killed at a funeral that Jakob attended. The police said the funeral-goers had petrol bombs and bricks. The media echoed their story, but he saw the truth.

The procession bottlenecked into a small graveyard outside the township. A young man in a white shirt smiled knowingly at Jakob from the other side of the open grave. Jakob turned his attention to the minister, Hadebe, an ANC man known to the police, an instigator in the community. Jakob had met with him earlier, claiming to be from the training camps, looking for young recruits, throwing around a few names he remembered from his own training days to boost his credibility. Reverend Hadebe eagerly took the bait. Since Archbishop Desmond Tutu had received the Nobel Peace Prize, religious men across the country were getting involved in the struggle, pushing others to sacrifice themselves as they kept the pulpits warm with rhetoric.

A restlessness welled in the funeral-goers after Hadebe's graveside speech about the struggle, the need to fight for freedom from white oppression. Hadebe raised his fist above his head. Sporadic fists followed his example, their number growing until *"Amandla"* sounded in united voices. Jakob held his arm in the air, feeling hollow as he uttered the word, forcing enthusiasm for the sake of the unfolding play.

"No more speeches or singing. You are done here!" One of the white policemen had planted himself on the edge of the graveyard, megaphone in one hand, rifle in the other. The ones behind him mirrored his stance. "Disperse immediately and go to your homes."

Jakob hoped that Hadebe had it in him to keep the people under control. The gathering dispersed amid whispered sentiments that Jakob had heard in every desperate little town. Poor, oppressed all their lives, they clung to the leaders who promised them freedom through blood. Jakob had been there, in Jabulani, Soweto, when Zinzi Mandela read her father's response to P. W. Botha's offer of freedom, if Mandela renounced violence.

"Let Botha renounce violence." Zinzi's hand shook as she read from the paper, fueled by rage. "Let him say that he will dismantle apartheid. Your freedom and mine cannot be separated. I will return."

The message raged through churches and beer halls across the country. Jakob had seen a renewed hope, but he didn't share their optimism. Violence would bring more violence, and the government had bigger guns.

"Jim! You will eat with us." Hadebe put his hand on Jakob's back, steering him through the river of people.

"Thank you, Reverend."

A group of youths glared at the policemen as they walked by, talking rapidly among themselves. Their leader, a tall boy, bent down to pick up a rock. Jakob loosened himself from Hadebe's grip and clamped his hand over the tall boy's.

"Let go of me." Dark eyes filled with hatred looked up at him. "They killed my sister. Now they stand there and laugh at us."

"A rock against a rifle?" Jakob shook his head. "You not so clever, my friend."

"I'm not your friend." The youth tugged to get loose from Jakob's grip.

Jakob looked at the other young men. "Is right." He let go of the youth and motioned toward the police. "Go ahead. Maybe we sing tomorrow at your funeral."

The boy looked at him, close to tears. "What do you know, huh? You're not even from here."

"I know there's better ways to hit those crunchies." He tapped his index finger to his forehead for emphasis. "But you gotta use the stuff up here, *bra*. You check?"

The boy didn't answer, a mistrustful look on his face. Out of the corner of his eye, Jakob saw a raised rifle.

"Disperse. Go to your own homes." The tinny megaphone voice commanded. "I give you five minutes."

Jakob lowered his voice, talking fast, his eyes locked on the boy as he recited what Kalo had told him to say. "I come from Botswana. MK. You think I crash funerals for fun?" Jakob put his hand on the boy's shoulder, aware that it was trembling. "The people need men like you to fight for them, make a real difference. You come to the Reverend's house later. You'll see, we'll make this right. You dying today will do nothing." The boy hesitated for a moment. Then his fingers slackened and the rock dropped to the ground. Jakob smiled. "Now go home and be with your mother."

Hadebe had his arm around Jakob again as soon as he turned around. "You're a good man, Jim. A man of the people." He lifted his palm in a solemn greeting to the group of young men, a look of understanding passing between them.

They left that same night. The tall youth was one of the six that signed up to go to the training camps. A hum of energy filled the combi as they piled inside, each with their meager belongings in a plastic grocery bag.

Hadebe shook Jakob's hand with an exaggerated motion. "You look after them, good man. Make them warriors."

Jakob nodded, bile rising in his stomach as he pulled away from the curb. He could stop, tell them there was a mistake, someone else would come for them later. But that was the problem. Someone else would come. Kalo usually ran things, but Jakob was trusted now, enough to operate by himself. If he showed up empty-handed, that trust would disappear and he'd be as good as dead. Behind him, nervous chatter filled the gaps between upbeat songs on the local radio station. Ten kilometers outside town, a car began to flash its headlights furiously behind them.

"Why are we stopping?" One of the youths leaned over the seat. Bewildered faces reflected in the rearview mirror.

"It's a comrade. Don't worry." Jakob pulled over. He knew the signal, but he was still surprised when it was Kalo that knocked on the window next to him.

"All good, Jim?"

Jakob nodded.

Kalo looked over his shoulder at the passengers. "So many fine young men. Comrades, welcome." The youths seemed to relax as Kalo opened the combi door and reached over to shake each of their hands, asking their names and thanking them for joining the cause with a sincerity that sent a chill through Jakob. Only he seemed to pick up on the subtle mocking in Kalo's voice.

"Botswana is far still. I have refreshments. You," Kalo motioned to the tall youth. "Help me get it from my car."

Two of the other young men got out as well. They returned with a case of beer, some cigarettes and a bottle of cane. A burst of excitement followed. Jakob doubted that they had ever had this much free liquor at their disposal. He watched as they tore into the case, opening cans, lighting cigarettes, no doubt feeling like they were adults.

"We treat our men right." Kalo's broad grin spread to the faces in front of him. He caught Jakob's eye. "Be there in an hour," he said under his breath. He walked away, the car's headlights flashing again before he drove off.

Jakob watched the young men behind him pouring beer into

their mouths, with the gluttony of those who grew up with little and weren't sure if their luck would last. It was over already. There was nothing he could do. Before, he could blame Kalo or Berg, claim that he didn't know what they were up to, but this was his doing. He felt an overwhelming panic take hold of him, the white line wavering in front of his eyes. A horn blared, the sound elongating as Jakob jerked the wheel to get the combi back to the left side of the road, adrenaline flooding his system as he narrowly missed the oncoming truck. Nobody moved in the seats behind him.

"I was wrong about you, Jim." Kalo crushed a cigarette under his shoe as Jakob stepped out of the combi. Darkness shrouded the open veld around them. "You're no sissy girl." He walked over and slid the back door open, the smell of spilled liquor and cigarette smoke pungent. The six young men lay motionless in the back.

Jakob looked away. "What now?"

"We're going to necklace them. Like they did in KwaNobuhle."

Jakob looked back at Kalo, disconcerted at the man's gleeful demeanor. He let his eyes trail over the bodies in front of him. "They aren't dead?"

"Sedated." Kalo held his hands up. "It would be good if people thought MK killed them, no? Who but the Commies necklace their own people?" He grabbed the ankles of one of the bodies. "There's tires and petrol in the boot."

Kalo lined the boys up, each with an old tire forced around his shoulders. He emptied the petrol over their heads. As he struck a match, Jakob emptied the contents of his stomach on the ground.

"A small price for the good life, I say." Kalo laughed, his body a totem of mockery. "Reward money will keep us in drink and fine women for a long time." He wiped his mouth and reached for a beer from the case in the back of the combi. "This will settle your stomach." Kalo opened the can and held it out to Jakob, his eyes steely.

Fear gripped Jakob. If he tried to run, would he get far enough that Kalo couldn't gun him down? He had done all they asked for, sold himself to them, tried to forget that he was ever anyone else. Why was he now being punished? In that insane moment he believed that Kalo had made a pact with the Devil to read souls, that he could see the weakness when Jakob allowed himself to think.

Kalo's body suddenly jerked with laughter. "For a brown man, you look very white, *bra*." He patted Jakob on the back. "Relax, Jim. I joke." He emptied the can on the ground. "We'll go into town. I know a nice place."

Jakob nodded, forcing a laugh in step with Kalo's, the image of his mother flashing before him, her hand warm on his skin.

Tessa

"Don't push us too far." President P. W. Botha had said, addressing the National Party's Congress in Durban. "We have never given in to outside demands and we are not going to do so now." After the coverage of the speech, the global condemnation, Thatcher was still on their side, but it looked like even Reagan would have to yield to an American anti-apartheid act. The rand plummeted, the stock exchange shut down for a week, and sanctions loomed. In the Cape, police had openly beaten black men and women with *sjamboks* as the people peacefully marched for Mandela's release.

Tessa sighed, her eyes skimming the article. The bus stopped to pick up passengers. Tessa briefly made eye contact as a woman sat down next to her. She tried to focus on the newspaper article, but her attention wandered to the translucent skin of the woman's hands, clutching the seat in front of her. Blue-green veins formed lumps amid dark liver spots, the yellow nails thick and uncared for, a slight tremor visible each time she let go of the seat to touch a tissue to her nose. Tessa forced herself to look up at the woman's face. Folds of paper-thin skin zigzagged over hollow cheekbones and sunken eyes.

A sense of dread suddenly took hold of Tessa. In a few months' time it would be her eighty-fifth birthday. It was happening to her too now, the thing that she had watched everyone else succumb to. The mirror held a strange fascination for her these days, the possibility of her mortality becoming a certainty. She counted fine lines, the rose-like roundness of her face fading. It was harder to keep her figure slender. Her joints had a faint ache in the mornings when she got out of bed. Sometimes she even welcomed it, the promise that her life would eventually end.

The walls of the bus suddenly seemed to close in on Tessa, and she got off at the next stop. She walked the last two kilometers to Triomf, her heels chafing, the raw sting of a blister growing stronger with every step she took. The government housing took on a look of uniform neglect in the distance, rusted cars in the yard and kitsch adornments on the porches. A male voice barged from a house as she turned onto Toby Street, a woman's voice joining in a shrill retort. Triomf was where poor whites had settled into government housing, masters now where Sophiatown once stood. Tessa unlocked the front door of her house and slid inside, her breath coming easier once she'd bolted the lock and put the safety chain on. The house remained silent, Jeff still not home. He came home late more often now, smelling of booze, turning into a middle-aged man in front of her eyes. He had found work at some sort of export business, he said. Tessa asked about it in the beginning, but dropped the subject after too many vague answers and ill-conceived lies.

The day Tessa had heard of Flippie's death, she had left everything in Kimberley and moved back to Johannesburg. She was frantic to find Jacob. Jeff had followed her, like a lost dog. Tessa's obsession with Jacob wedged itself between them by degrees. She cared for nothing else. She had met some of Flippie's acquaintances at the funeral, asked around after Jacob as best she could, attending secret ANC meetings, pledging her support. But whites weren't trusted, no matter what the bylaws stated. A darkness began to seep into Tessa's soul as the months dragged on, devouring the hope she clung to by degrees as every lead turned into a dead end. Some mornings she couldn't see her way through the day, so she stayed in bed, staring at the stucco ceiling for hours. Those days were becoming more frequent. She could no longer keep the thought away that Jacob had also permanently disappeared, the last of her family gone.

The argument between the man and woman next door grew louder. A young child's cries joined in the cacophony. Tessa lay down on the bed and wrapped her pillow around her head. When she opened her eyes, blue lights bounced off the walls. Tessa got up and slowly parted the curtains, careful not to be seen. There were two police cars parked in the street. A man with greasy blond hair and wearing a dirty T-shirt sat on the *stoep*. Two policemen pulled him to his feet. He rammed into one of them, sending him down the steps. The other one grabbed him and punched him in the face. The first policeman ran back up the steps, grabbed the man's head, and bashed it into the wall of the house until blood streamed out of his nose.

"Pig! You leave him alone." It was the woman, her long permed hair teased into a bushy mess, her bra visible under the falling straps of her tank top. The policeman shielded his face to ward off the blows as she attacked him. Two more men struggled to get handcuffs on her as she screamed and cursed. The pair was escorted to the police van. The woman tried to bite one of her captors, who slapped her in the face.

The van took off, followed by the patrol cars, and the residents of Triomf closed their curtains again. Tessa became aware of a whimpering noise near her window. She tried to block it out, but it persisted. She tried to convince herself that it was only her imagination, but as she unlocked the door and took a tentative step outside, the whimpers intensified.

"Hallo?" Tessa scanned the dark yard at the spot where there was a break in the fence between the two houses. Tessa advanced toward the fence. The noise seemed to come from a clump of bushes just on the other side. "Who's there?" Getting onto her knees, she parted the foliage to find a toddler, a girl, judging by the dirty dress she was wearing. The child's hair was jaggedly cut, close to her head, crusted with food. Tessa reached out. The child tried to get away but stumbled, unsteady on her legs.

"It's okay."

The child made another attempt at standing up. Tessa reached out again and grabbed her before she could fall again. The girl reeked of urine and feces. Tessa turned her head away as she carried the toddler to her house. She put the girl down on the kitchen table. The child let out a wail as Tessa switched the light on.

"I'm not going to hurt you, okay?" Tessa carefully unhooked the diaper pins and peeled the rough fabric off, trying not to retch. A nasty rash and half-moon-shaped bruises lined the tender skin of the toddler's back. Something ripped inside Tessa. She grabbed a pair of scissors and cut the dress off the girl, too disgusted to try to undo the buttons. The toddler screamed hysterically as Tessa lowered her into the bathtub, her cheeks glowing red under a layer of filth, her eyes and nostrils caked with gunk.

"It's all right now, little one." Tessa spoke soothingly, gently lapping lukewarm water over her body, revealing large hazel eyes and curly chestnut hair by degrees. Brown water seeped down the drain. She stood there until the tub had completely drained, dirt forming lines on the white porcelain. The girl had calmed down, her body limp in the towel as Tessa held her. Suddenly, she glimpsed her salvation.

"Whose child is that?" Jeff stood in the doorway, a soft slur tainting his words.

"I'm taking her, Jeff." Tessa's words were without apology. "Her parents are gone."

"What?" Jeff stared at the girl.

"Next door. They were arrested."

He sighed, seemingly relieved. "We can call someone to take her."

"They didn't even tell anyone there was a child." Tessa broke into tears, her body shaking as she clung to the toddler. "She's just a baby."

Jeff stepped closer to her, reaching uncomfortably, the girl between them. "The police will sort this, luv."

"No." Tessa broke free from his grip, keeping her hand protectively on the child's head.

"Be reasonable."

"She's not going back." Tessa's pale eyes challenged.

Jeff tugged at his tie as if it was choking him. "She's someone's child, Tessa."

"Look at her, Jeff." Tessa tore the towel away.

Jeff's face mirrored her initial horror, his brow contracting. "Maybe Child Services—"

"I'm taking her away." Tessa picked the girl up. "Tonight. She'll be safe. Nobody will find us."

"Does this plan include me?"

Tessa hesitated for a moment before answering. "Nothing's changed."

"No. Apparently it hasn't." Jeff sat down on the edge of the bath-tub, wiping his eyes with his palms. "I don't think I can do this, Tess."

Tessa felt a willfulness spring up. "Then I'll manage without you."

Jeff looked as if she had slapped him. "So that's it?"

"I need to get her away from here before those people sober up and remember they have a child. That is all that matters now, keeping her safe. We can talk about the rest later if you want."

"I don't know that there's anything more to talk about." Jeff's body deflated. "I'm going back to London. Maybe for good." He held his breath, watching her for a reaction.

Tessa could only muster a curt nod. The life in her arms was the only important thing now. She could do it, save this one person. To-gether, they would start over. One more time.

Adriaan

Adriaan hid behind the low fence of a house on Toby Street. Triomf spread all around, an eyesore of welfare and depravity, where the em-barrassing dregs of white culture sank to the bottom. "You're sure it's the right man?" he asked the constable next to him.

"He matched the description, sir. I was staking the place out. The occupants are wanted for questioning about that missing child, see? Then your man rocked up. Went in almost an hour ago."

Adriaan looked at the neighborhood around him, old cars and junk on the neglected lawns. Could this be where De Beer had been all along? Hiding in plain sight? His dramatics at the zoo had only convinced Adriaan that he was on the right track, too close for the monster's comfort. If anything, De Beer's threats to his family served to intensify Adriaan's investigation. He kept the media in the dark, even gave them a few misdirections, but he had made sure that every milk-beard on the force memorized De Beer's description. Contacts were roused from their hiding places, bribes distributed, threats made. Then, today, it had all paid off.

The front door of the house across the street opened. Adriaan sig-naled the unit to stand by as he recognized the tall frame of the man who walked out wearing a motorcycle helmet. De Beer went through the front gate, headed toward a dirt bike parked up the block.

"Police! Stay where you are." The constable next to Adriaan jumped up without waiting for the signal, his gun trained on De Beer. "I said, don't move!" He stormed at De Beer, grabbing him by the scruff of his jacket. De Beer slipped out of the jacket in one graceful move and punched the constable, then grabbed his gun from him.

Adriaan fell back when he heard the pop, pulling his own weapon as the constable's body thumped to the ground. There was another barrage of pops as the other policemen opened fire. Adriaan carefully looked over the fence, meeting De Beer's eyes, the gun pointed directly at Adriaan. Adriaan hugged the ground as a bullet grazed the fence. "We have a man down," he yelled into the radio. "Suspect on the move, riding a Honda dirt bike." He touched the fallen constable's neck. There was almost no pulse.

Two squad cars approached, sirens blaring. Adriaan raced down the street, watching the motorcycle disappear down the block. It was too far away, but he fired a shot anyway. Chaos descended. Sirens could be heard kilometers away as the squad cars gave chase. Adriaan sat down on the curb where the constable had fallen, his head between his hands, frustration gnawing at him. De Beer had to be stopped. This was the closest Adriaan had ever gotten, and the man had still managed to slip away.

"Hey, you." A teenage girl, around sixteen, slouched onto the *stoep* of the house where he had hidden moments before, a cigarette hanging from her lips. "What you people doing?"

Adriaan waved her away. "Go back inside."

"You find the people who took that baby?" She crossed her arms when Adriaan didn't reply. "I told my *pa* the moment they moved in. I said they'll be trouble. She acting all high and mighty as if her *kak* wasn't brown, not talking to anybody. Now look. And what are you people doing?"

"We're working on it, miss. Now go back—"

"Time you people stop arresting people for nothing and start doing your job, Mister Police." She flicked her cigarette onto the grass.

Adriaan turned away from her. De Beer's jacket lay where it had fallen in the street, stained with the constable's blood. He crouched down, picked it up, and went through its pockets. Nothing. His fingers brushed a piece of paper in an inside pocket and he pulled it out, hoping for a note or a receipt, anything that might give a clue as to De Beer's whereabouts. It was a small photograph with yellow scalloped edges, its subjects, a boy and girl, faded in sepia tones. The boy was young, maybe eleven or twelve, but there was no doubt in Adriaan's mind who it was. The girl in the photograph bore a resemblance to De Beer—eyes the same shape, fair hair, pale skin—but there was something different about her, a kindness in her expression that De Beer's empty stare lacked.

Adriaan crossed back to the teenager. "Can you look at this?"

She eyed him warily, not moving from her spot in the doorway.

"Please? You want to find the little girl, don't you?" Adriaan walked up to her, pushing back his revulsion at her cheap perfume. He noticed that she wasn't wearing shoes, her toenails painted a bright red. He held the photograph out to her.

She looked at it for a moment, then nodded. "I guess it could be her."

"Who?"

"The one from across the street."

"And the boy?"

She shook her head. "Never seen him."

"When was the last time you saw her?"

"I don't know. Maybe a week ago? When little Tina went missing, I suppose. Ursula hasn't been the same, never comes out now. It's bad, losing a child, hey."

"Thanks for your help."

"You come ask me anytime, hear?" she said, smiling.

Adriaan smiled back, an understanding passing between them. He'd known her kind before. She wouldn't be the first white trash who tried to get out of here by spreading her legs for a policeman. It was always good for amusement. God knows, with Gerda taking Alet and threatening divorce, he needed it. Adriaan tucked the photograph into his pocket as he walked away. De Beer wasn't living with the woman, so what was he doing there?

Two more squad cars pulled up to the house. "Turn over the house," Adriaan yelled at the men who got out. "Get prints. Statements from the neighbors." As a constable drove him back to the station, he studied the two faces in the photograph again.

"Was she one of the victims, sir?"

"Keep your eyes on the road, Constable."

"Sorry, sir. She just looks—"

"Yes, like an angel." Adriaan smiled.

12

The Dutch Reformed church on Adderley Street seemed anachronistic, standing between two modern buildings. People in shorts and T-shirts crowded the sidewalk in front of it. Behind the iron fencing, its imposing gray walls were interrupted by barred windows and a heavy wooden door. From where Alet stood, it was easy to imagine it as a fancy prison, designed to keep the congregation in a purgatory of psalm-singing until everyone had handed over their tithes.

Patchy sunlight invaded the city's shadows. Alet pushed up her sweatshirt's sleeves, glancing at her watch. As if on cue, a man in a gray suit opened both church doors, then kicked at the stops. The *dominee* appeared behind him in black robes, taking up his post next to the door. Families in suits and knee-length dresses sauntered out, men stopping to shake hands and exchange a few words.

Alet searched the faces, locking eyes with Koch as he walked down the church stairs. A short frumpy woman in mauve walked arm in arm with him, her graying brown hair teased into an eighties-style helmet of hairspray. Alet yawned, waiting for Koch to cross the street, while Mrs. Koch talked to a woman who Alet presumed was the *dominee*'s wife.

"You could have called."

Alet was unfazed by Koch's irritation, her own taking precedence. "I did," she said. "Your *ousie* told me where you were."

Koch crossed his arms. "Well?"

Alet mirrored his defiant stance. "Tell your wife you're going to be late for lunch. You and I have a few things to discuss."

"This can wait."

"Actually, it can't. You're going to tell me the truth about you and my dad. Right now."

"I don't know what you're talking about."

"No? I know about your employment history, Professor. What you did back then for the government."

Koch stiffened. "I am a scientist."

"Doesn't give you the right to kill people."

"I didn't kill anybody." Koch waved a finger in her face, his mouth pulled taut.

"Look, you're going to tell me, or I'll go to the university board and tell them who they have in their employ. Maybe the papers would find it interesting too. You influencing the young minds of the country and all."

"You wouldn't."

"Try me."

Koch met Alet on the corner after briefly talking to his wife. Alet followed him to Greenmarket Square, the streets bustling and breathing with tourists. She waved off a very dark-skinned man holding a wooden hippo statue as Koch marched straight ahead into an old hotel bar that overlooked the square.

"So, what do you know?" Koch placed two Black Labels on the table, taking the seat opposite Alet.

"You did research for a government front company that supplied death squads with chemical weapons. And my dad was in charge of one of those squads."

Koch looked at her in surprise, eyebrows raised in an unspoken question.

"I only just found out."

"What do you want from me?"

"The truth. I need to know how it all fits in with this murder investigation."

"I don't understand," Koch said, the fight out of him.

"Did they experiment on people?"

"Tests were done on animals—primates, pigs, dogs."

Alet raised an eyebrow. "You're sure about that? What use would they have for a man like you?"

"I did what I was told to do. Everything was highly compartmentalized. They recruited researchers from around the country, and everyone worked on their little part, with no idea of how it fit into the bigger picture."

"But you knew, didn't you?"

"People were too afraid to talk. They had us sign secrecy agreements, even bugged our houses. The tests mainly dealt with organophosphates like paraoxon, paraquat, agents that could only have been used for one purpose."

"Which was?"

"They claimed the work was to protect our troops from chemical attacks in Namibia, but most of the agents were designed for offensive purposes, all small-scale production."

"Assassinations."

"I think so. They had rooms full of food and liquor that were being picked up by Security Branch men. Cigarettes. Clothes, even. All laced with the stuff." He took a gulp from his beer before continuing. "It had been in the news around that time. Opposition leaders hospitalized because of thallium or unknown agents. It's not hard to connect the dots."

"What about breeding super wolf-dogs?"

The corner of Koch's mouth lifted in a sneer. "You read the tabloids."

"The official documents are still classified, so I take what I can get."

"Genetic research like that takes time, money. The company was sold and privatized before we made any real progress."

"And people?"

"What?"

"Did you use people in these experiments? If the government was willing to experiment on humans, they may have been doing it for a long time. Longer than you know."

"Nonsense. Look, I was just as surprised as you when I saw those results." Koch sighed. "We didn't know anything back then. Those experiments were failures. The technology for that kind of thing simply didn't exist. It's impossible that they'd have known more in 1900."

Alet leaned on the table, cradling her chin in her hand. "Then help me out, Professor. I don't understand how this is possible."

"Evolution, perhaps? A different species could have evolved along-side Homo sapiens for thousands of years, living and passing as human."

"And we didn't find out about it until now?" Alet thought about Koch's theory for a moment. "Okay, suppose that happened. There had to have been more of them, right? A single being can't evolve on its own. They had to breed."

Koch's eyes narrowed behind his thick glasses. "I think we can presume that."

"Where are they, then? Could they be the other victims? Someone found out about these non-humans, saw them as a threat, and tried to eradicate them?"

"No." Koch swept his hand through the air emphatically. "The DNA evidence you sent me from those old cases was all human. No match to your victim whatsoever."

"Dammit." Alet rubbed her temples. It would have been a neat solution, a motive at least. Somewhere out there was a faceless killer she just couldn't get a grip on, and it was frustrating the hell out of her. "And my dad? How does he fit in to all of this?"

"I really don't know anything, Alet." Koch fiddled with the label on his beer bottle, pulling at the edges and sticking them back down again.

"That's *kak*, Professor," Alet said. "Why did you agree to keep this quiet?"

"I thought that's what you wanted." A thin layer of perspiration had formed on Koch's pasty face.

"I expected you to write a paper about it. Get published. Have your name in the scientific spotlight. Unless of course you suspected that it had something to do with the work you were doing for the government, the larger thing they were working on?"

Koch pressed his lips together, the corners drooping. He looked like all the authority figures she'd ever encountered, the *dominees*, the teachers, the principals, the drill sergeants, the station chiefs, all of them asserting their authority without opposition because they were white and male.

Alet shook her head. "You can't go public about what you did back then, because you're scared you'd be found out, prosecuted. But you're desperate to get back at my father. You wanted me to find out about what he did. Expose him to his only daughter. I just can't figure out why."

"I really don't see what—"

Alet held her hand up to stop him. "I don't think you understand, Professor. The time for amnesty is over, the TRC went home. So help me understand why I shouldn't take everything I have to the government."

"It's personal. Nothing to do with this case."

Alet crossed her arms, her gaze unwavering. "You should talk to me, Professor."

Koch held his hands up in a sign of surrender, letting them flop back down on the table. "I suppose it doesn't matter anymore." He stared at the TV screen above the bar as he talked, suddenly unwilling to look her in the eye. "Your dad . . . We were friends of sorts, you could say. Worked a few cases together in Pretoria, sometimes shared a *dop* while trying to reason things out. Catching the bad guy, watching the pieces come together, it was a huge rush to be part of all that. Adriaan was obsessive, relentless. I admired that, wanted to be part of it, see?" An expression of self-ridicule lodged on Koch's face.

"My daughter got into trouble because of some hippie she was seeing at the time, arrested for aiding the ANC. Known ANC sympathizers had been disappearing regularly at that point. The police would detain them indefinitely. Their families didn't know if they were in jail or dead. You have no idea what it was like back then." Koch looked pleadingly at Alet. "I was frantic when I got the call. I went to Adriaan, begged him to help. He took care of it, brought her home, kept her name off the government lists. He even fixed it so the boyfriend wouldn't be a problem anymore." Koch bowed his head. "The relationship changed after that. If he said anything, changed his mind, my girl would have been in a whole lot of trouble. So when Adriaan Berg pulled at my leash, I came running."

A sourness ate away at Alet's insides. Her dad was a bully, a man who manipulated his friends and colleagues to get what he wanted. Adriaan enjoyed watching the people around him dance. It was one hell of a gene pool she'd inherited.

Koch finished his beer. "It's all well and good to say now that what we did was wrong, Alet, but I would've done it a million times over to keep my girl safe." He looked at her, a sarcastic chuckle escaping his lips. "After all he did, your father walked out of two trials and a national inquiry without a scratch on him. He's untouchable."

"Things have changed, Professor." Alet emptied her beer. "This is the New South Africa, after all."

Mike Engelman's number flashed on Alet's cell. She hesitated for only a moment before she silenced the call, slipping the phone back into her sweatshirt pocket. She felt as if she were wading through water, her mind thick, her limbs slow to react. She finished the piss coffee from the vending machine outside Theo's cramped office and crushed the cup in her hand.

Theo hunched over his keyboard, entering variables into a database. "Jeffrey Wexler has been arrested a few times," he said. "Petty crimes when he was younger, one charge of assault, never married, no children. Mathilda Pienaar is clean. I'll print these out for you."

"What about Jacob Morgan's dad? Phillip?"

Theo typed, his eyes squinting at the screen. "Human-rights lawyer. Assaulted and killed on the way home one day. There were suspicions that it was an assassination, but no evidence supported the claim."

"Of course." Alet leaned her head back, then jerked upright when she felt herself drifting off. "What about the rest of his family?" She yawned, running her fingers through her ponytail. She had taken a shower that morning at Theo's place but she still felt greasy and awful. She got up and leaned on the back of Theo's chair, a sliding green bar tracking the progress of the report on his computer screen.

"Got it." Theo turned in his seat. Alet moved too slowly and they butted heads. "Shit, sorry." He touched his palm to her face, let go immediately.

Alet covered her tearing right eye with one hand, light flickering in the darkness before her. She wondered if she'd have a new bruise just as the old one was fading. "No worries." She tried to focus her other eye. "What does it say?"

Theo turned back to the screen. "His grandfather was a Corporal Andrew Morgan. British forces during the Boer War. Seems he stayed and married a black woman, but the marriage was declared illegal after the Immorality Act passed." Theo scrolled down the page. "The name Theresa Morgan pops up in a few places. No idea what the relation is, though—there's no birth certificate. Could be his mother or his sister."

Theo typed the name into the database. "No. There's a record here of her graduating from high school in Bloemfontein in forty . . . seven. So probably a daughter."

Alet leaned in. "Nothing else? School or hospital records?"

"She disappears from the paper trail. Why are you so interested in Jacob Morgan, anyway?"

"Don't know. He was the only witness willing to testify against my dad. He's important somehow." Alet noticed the time on the computer screen. If she didn't get on the road soon, she'd be late for her shift. "Call if you find anything?"

"*Ja*. Sure."

Alet grabbed the pile of paper from the printer. She turned to find Theo's brown eyes fixed on her, a strange expression on his face. She suddenly felt self-conscious about her greasy hair and baggy clothes. "Thanks, hey. I'd still be at square one if it wasn't for this."

Theo nodded, his lips pinched together.

"How were things with Lana?" Alet wasn't sure she wanted to know the answer.

Theo clasped his hands together in his lap and leaned back. Alet knew the gesture. It was the same one he had made when he first told her about the brass finding out about their relationship. That had been one of the hardest nights of her life, knowing what she'd have to face in the morning, judgment on the faces of the officers, and later, inevitably, her peers. She had fought tooth and nail to get into STF, worked twice as hard as the blokes, had to prove every second of every day that she wasn't a liability, and it had all been for nothing. Theo had informed her of what would happen, plain and simple, as if he was reciting a grocery list, his manner detached, void of emotion. She had felt utterly alone and she had hated him for it.

"I don't think we should see each other anymore," Theo said.

"For a new *stukkie*, that Lana is kind of bossy, hey. Better watch out." Alet kept her tone light, hoping to sidestep whatever was coming.

"It's not her." Theo looked up, meeting her gaze. "You barge into my life after how long, show up in the middle of the night . . ." He sighed, running his hand over his face. "It's no good, Alet."

"You said we were okay."

"All I've done since you've turned up is think maybe we could try again."

"Can't we?" Alet felt vulnerable, the seconds ticking by in slow motion as she waited for his reply. The expression on Theo's face changed, his eyes accusing as he shook his head. Alet felt a tugging at her insides. She faked a smile, failing at being nonchalant. "I know our track record isn't great, but . . ."

"Look at you. Did you even eat today?"

Alet's vulnerability morphed into rash defensiveness, burning hot in her throat. "What's that got to do with anything? Sorry I don't prance around in cocktail dresses and makeup all the time but—"

Theo held his hand up. "It's not that. I just don't want to be part of the carnage again when things fall apart."

"Fine." Alet dug her keys out of her pocket, avoiding his gaze. She wanted to shake him, wipe the self-righteous expression off his face. She bit back her anger. "I don't see how trying to find a killer makes me the bad guy here."

"It doesn't."

"What, then?"

"I can't do this. The way things are going . . . I don't believe you've changed at all."

"*Fok jou*, Theo." Alet walked out before he had a chance to reply.

On the mountain pass, just before the descent into Unie, Alet pulled over to the side of the road. She stared down at the town, a spit stain in the dirt, the sun leaving only a thin orange strip along the ridge of the mountain. Street lamps sputtered to life. Trudie had left her home in the dark and ended up on a mountaintop many kilometers away, stars looking down as her killer doused her body in petrol and set it on fire.

"What the fuck happened?" Alet said to no one. The anger in her voice was amplified in the stillness of the evening. She hadn't realized how much all of this was wearing on her, on the people around her. Emotion welled out of her exhaustion. "Never let a man see you cry," her mother used to say. "He'll know you're weak and punish you for it."

Alet understood that her mother could only have been talking about her father. Alet's grandmother hadn't seemed surprised when she and her mother showed up on her doorstep. She poured them Rooibos tea from the pot she always kept brewing on the stove and made up the spare bedroom. Adriaan showed up the next morning. He had just come off shift and was in a fervid rage. Gerda refused to let him in. When he threatened to break the door down, she called the police. Nothing came of that, of course, but at least the other policemen had calmed him down. He disappeared from their lives for a long time after that. Alet had thought he had abandoned her forever. A part of her now wished he had.

When Alet walked into the station an hour later for her shift, she knew that something was up. April greeted her without enthusiasm, his shoulders tense, his answers to her questions short. Mynhardt wanted her in his office right away, April said. No, he didn't know what it was about. Strijdom glared at her as she passed his desk. He had the air of a man prepared for battle, waiting for the signal to storm into the fray. Alet's pulse sped up as she knocked on Mynhardt's door, waiting for the irritated, *"Ja?"* on the other side. As she stepped into the office, a cold rush numbed her limbs. Mynhardt stood in the middle of the room, wearing the look of a beaten dog. There was panic in his eyes, fear rank enough to smell.

"Alet."

Alet focused on the figure behind the desk. *"Pa?"*

Adriaan's skin was a sun-kissed caramel, a faint white tan line on his temple from his glasses. Tension tightened his full mouth, belying the fact that he had just spent a week honeymooning on an island.

"I'll leave you." Mynhardt backed out of the room, flustered, closing the door behind him.

"How was Mauritius? I thought you're only back on Tues—"

Adriaan waved the question away. "What do you think you're doing?"

Alet felt like she was four again, lining up for inspection. "I don't understand."

"Don't lie to me. I won't tolerate it. Tokkie told me what's been going on here. So now you answer my question. What the hell do you think you're doing?"

"What did Mynhardt tell you?"

"Captain Mynhardt."

"*Ja.*"

"I told you to keep your nose clean. Now your superior calls me to tell me that you're withholding evidence, accusing people left and right."

"Did he also tell you that he is up to his *fokken* eyebrows in the muck?"

"Alet." Adriaan's voice cautioned, but she didn't care.

"It's true. He's selling children to the highest bidder."

Adriaan narrowed his eyes. "Do you have proof?" He crossed his arms, his eyebrows raised.

"He took care of it."

"Really?"

"Check his bank accounts."

"Captain Mynhardt did me a favor, letting you come here. The only reason you still have a job is because of him."

"I wouldn't make something like that up, *Pa.*"

"And what's this about you being under investigation?"

"I did my job. Read the file."

"Captain Mynhardt told me about you and that married man." Adriaan studied her for a moment, eyes boring into her. "I really thought you could turn things around. You've been a disappointment." He turned his head away. "It won't be easy getting a transfer once this gets around, but maybe I can—"

"I'm not leaving Unie until this case is solved." Alet clenched her fists, bracing against the blow.

"I don't think you heard me, Alet. You are out of options. You'll do as I say."

Alet's heart beat in her throat. "I'll go to the Hawks if you try to force me."

"Have you learned nothing? On the job you shit with one hole. You go fling stories around about other officers, run to ICD, and you're done."

"I don't care, *Pa*. I'm not running away from this. You wouldn't have either."

Conflicting emotions seemed to take hold of her dad's expression at that moment. There was a pride she hadn't seen in his eyes in a long time, but also an almost imperceptible hint of hate. It knocked the wind out of her, and for a moment she wanted to acquiesce, just to make it go away.

Adriaan got up from the chair. He stood close, his voice low. "Don't assume that I'll always be there to protect you, Alet," he said. "There are rules. And there are consequences when they're broken."

Alet looked straight ahead, not trusting herself to reply. She waited until her dad left the office before she moved again. Outside the door, the station fell silent. April quickly busied himself with a docket when he saw her.

Strijdom leaned against the service desk, a wry smile on his face. "You've got a nerve," he said. "*Chot* whores like you don't belong in uniform." Alet bit her lip, determined not to give him the satisfaction of a response. Strijdom sniggered. He took his cap off the desk and sauntered out of the station, a self-satisfied grin on his cracked lips.

"What a *doos*," Alet said once he was out of earshot. She took a deep breath to get her emotions under control. "April, I . . ."

April briefly looked up before getting back to the book in front of him. "Don't. Okay, Letta?"

"Why are you being like this, man?"

April dropped his pen. "I'm getting married next month, you know that. My girl wants a family. A house. Nothing *kiev*, just the basics, but I can't . . ."

Alet nodded. "I'm not doing what they're saying, okay? There's something very wrong going on here, April. I only want to do the right thing."

"*Ja?* Then don't rock the boat, see?"

"I can't promise that."

"Maybe if you had something to lose, like the rest of us."

"I'm sorry, okay?"

"Right. Well, I'm knocking off." April slid the docket book across the desk. "You're on your own."

• • •

It was close to midnight, the station eerily quiet, all the desks empty, computers turned off. A cool breeze snaked its way through the open doorway. Alet rang Theo and wasn't surprised when her call went straight to voice mail. She went to the canteen to make coffee. There was a long night ahead and she could hardly keep her eyes open. She decided to go through the stack of paper that Theo had printed out for her. The information on Theresa Morgan seemed random— vaccination records, piano-exam certificates, a single hospitalization for a ruptured appendix. If it was the same Theresa Morgan, she would have been in her late forties by the time she matriculated. Alet considered this for a moment. School records weren't digitized back then. It would have been simple for her to claim she was in a certain grade if she looked the part, no one would have thought to look further than a falsified report card. Was it possible that Theresa had the same gene mutation as Trudie? Or that she could possibly be—

Alet felt her pulse quicken as she wrote Theresa Morgan's name at the top of her timeline. She added Lilly Maartens's name and birth date. If Theresa Morgan became Lilly Maartens, it would mean that Theresa could be Trudie, that there was a link between her and the man who was going to testify against Alet's dad. She thought about calling Mathebe, but it was late already. Tomorrow, she thought, when she'd had some sleep and could organize her thoughts.

Alet looked at the picture of Trudie again. The woman had moved around, changed her identity, hid from the world because she wasn't aging, because she was different. Perhaps she'd found solace in the fact that she could start over. Alet understood it intrinsically, the hope that going where nobody knew you would somehow change who you were, give you a do-over. But it was a sweet delusion. You could never truly get away from the past. Or what it had done to you.

1992

Jacob

"I can no longer explain to our people why we continue to talk to a government, to a regime, that is murdering our people."

On the small TV screen in the rec room, Nelson Mandela addressed thousands of ANC supporters. It had been two years since a new prime minister, F. W. de Klerk, had taken over the National Party government. He started his term strong, legalizing the ANC and other opposing parties and securing Mandela's unconditional release. Racial distinctions were stricken from the laws. A whites-only referendum followed, indicating that they too were ready for reform, but then the government stalled.

"What's that *kaffir kak?*" Tokkie Mynhardt planted himself at the bar, a deep scowl between his thick red eyebrows.

"*Ag*, nothing, *Baas*. Just news." Jakob switched the TV off. "Coming right up. Klippies and Coke. *Lekker*, man." He poured the brandy and slid it over to Berg's right-hand man.

"You still have that bottle of Chivas here?" Mynhardt's question had a hint of desperation, as if a lot more than the right kind of alcohol was at stake.

Jakob checked under the bar. "*Ja, Baas*, he's here. Is only half." If Mynhardt was asking about the Chivas, it meant that Berg was coming. Mynhardt mostly ran things, giving them orders for whom to target and eliminate, but Jakob knew he wasn't smart enough to plan the missions they were given. Mynhardt was a yes-man, quick to anger, disciplining with a fist, blindly rushing to action, but he was slow when it came to anything more than boozing and following orders.

"Okay, get. You make sure you're here when he comes."

"Is right, *Baas*." Jakob grabbed a six-pack of beer from the fridge.

"Tell the others to stay put."

Jakob raised his hand in acknowledgment, closing the door behind him. When the bigwigs came, they usually ended up in an orgy of boozing and wild antics. The *askaris* made themselves scarce on those weekends, lying low and going into town until the hangovers subsided and nobody thought it would be good sport to chase a black through the sand dunes with a *sjambok* anymore.

"You sharing?" Trivedi stood in the dark outside the house, the embers of his cigarette glowing. He stepped into the light cast through the window of one of the bedrooms, an attractive Indian with streamlined features and large dark eyes. He was shorter than Jakob, but a lot more muscular, with a funny bowlegged walk, as if his nuts might chafe if he brought his legs any closer together. They weren't friends, exactly. None of the *askaris* really were. Everybody was too busy watching their own backs, a constant wariness making it difficult to think of anything more than survival.

Jakob held out one of the Black Labels. "Boss says everybody has to stay out tonight."

"Up to no fucking good." Trivedi took the beer from Jakob. He flopped down on one of the benches next to the *braai* pit, leaning back against the wall. The pitch black around them was relieved only by stars, their glow unnaturally bright away from the city. Jakob sat down as well, though he was not sure that he wanted to stay. Trivedi was the most vocal of the *askaris*. It wasn't a good idea to be associated with him.

"So what do you make of it?"

"What's that?" Jakob feigned ignorance.

"The crunchies getting together all hush-hush in the middle of the night?"

"Don't know." Jakob tipped the beer can up to his mouth. "Maybe he wants us to nail more monkey fetuses to someone's door." He giggled, remembering all the "missions" Mynhardt had sent them on for so-called "intimidation tactics." The man was a buffoon, full of dumb buffoon ideas. Unfortunately, he was greedy too, making them run dangerous errands to buy diamonds across the border or fence stolen cars. Mynhardt claimed it was government business, but everybody knew in whose bank account the money ended up.

"You think that's all?" Trivedi fidgeted with the ring of the beer can.

Jakob shrugged. It was hard to believe that anything would ever really change. If anything, Mynhardt and Berg and all the others seemed even more manic in dealing with "the threat" these days.

"It's all well for them, *bra*, but either way the shit strikes in the end, we're the ones who are fucked."

"How so?"

"You never thought of it? If they win an election, they keep their thumbs on us. If they lose, what do we tell the new black government when they ask why we fight against them, kill our own people?"

"You think the ANC will win?" The idea seemed strange to Jakob, exhilarating and terrifying all at once.

"Numbers, *bra*! There's a shitload of us, not so many of them. And the referendum—"

"Bah!" Jakob crushed his beer can and reached for the next one. "Blacks are killing blacks now. It's worse than before. Look at Boipatong." Nearly forty black men, women, and children had been killed there, and many others maimed, when members of the Inkatha Freedom Party attacked ANC supporters.

"You're not stupid, Jim-boy. You know what's been going on. Those right-wing AWB Afrikaners have been training Inkatha, giving them weapons, promising the sun and moon, and we all live happily ever after if they fight the ANC. Their own Zulu territory? Inkatha didn't just think of that by themselves. Divide and conquer, see? No way a Zulu wants to be ruled by a Xhosa, and those white bastards are working it."

"So the whites will win," Jakob said. A part of him secretly hoped for change, a new tomorrow. But hope was dangerous. It made you second-guess what the bosses told you, made you wonder if you could stand up to them. That's the kind of thinking that got you killed.

Trivedi leaned in. "Eventually," he said quietly, "they will run out of bullets." He stood up, his head tilted to one side. "Gold Mercedes by the sounds of it."

Jakob had also become aware of the engine noise in the distance. That was one thing about being out here in the middle of nowhere: you could hear trouble coming. Trivedi's lips curled into a snarl. He tread unsteadily to the *askari* quarters at the back of the house without another word. Jakob finished the rest of his beer, heading back when he could put it off no longer.

Agitated voices came from inside the rec room. Jakob hesitated at the door. Tokkie Mynhardt gave him a sideways glance. Berg didn't acknowledge his presence at all, a stream of profanity continuing from his mouth, his face growing redder by degrees. Jakob had rarely seen Berg like this. He usually had an exterior of detached calm, the Devil slithering under the surface, but tonight he raged out of control.

"What are you standing there for, *kaffir*?" Berg suddenly focused on Jakob, as if he was seeing him for the first time. Jakob's limbs felt numb. "I don't keep you around so you can stare at me like a bloody baboon." Berg slapped his hand down on the bar. "I said!"

Jakob snapped out of it, his sense of self-preservation kicking in. "Is right, *Baas*." He smiled, his lips straining against his teeth. Something had changed. He prayed that his usual clown act would get him through the night. "You tell me. You the boss man, I say. What can Jakob do?" He slipped behind the bar, grateful to have something between him and Berg. "A Chivas for the pain? *Lekker*." Jakob slid the glass of whiskey and Coke over to Berg, trying to contain the trembling in his hands. Berg inhaled the dark liquid, emptying the glass in one go. Jakob refilled it, making the drink stiffer than before.

"When are they back?" Berg picked up the conversation he was having with Tokkie as if they hadn't been interrupted.

"Tomorrow." Mynhardt's speech was thick, his eyes dull. He put his right hand on Berg's shoulder. "The delivery was made. Don't worry, *Broer*. A minor *fokop*. We'll make it right."

Berg stood up suddenly, his bar stool teetering for a moment. He kicked at it and it toppled, hit the floor and bounced once. His eyes flashed black as he took a step toward Mynhardt, his voice seething. "We are hanging on by our fingernails. Let me tell you that if it was up to a *fokop* like you, we would have lost this war already."

"Take it easy, Adriaan."

"Your unit got snagged by MK, because they were trying to sell a target's car. Did you know about that? They are on TV telling the world what we're up to."

"Nobody will listen—"

"You shut your mouth, you flat-faced *kak*." Berg spat the words in poison salvos. "The general is riding me because of you. We're losing our country to those Communist bastards. Do you know what they will do to us? They will murder your children in their beds and *naai* you up the ass before they slit your throat." Mynhardt shook his head. It fueled Berg's rage, his tanned skin flushing dark, the veins on his temples bulging as if they might burst at any moment. Berg grabbed Mynhardt behind his neck and drove the man's head against the bar with a dull thump. "We can't afford your minor *fokops*." Mynhardt slumped to the ground.

"Is okay, *Baas*." Jakob jumped out from behind the bar, sure that Mynhardt would die that night if he didn't do something. "He heard you. Sorry for sure, *ja*. Hey? We'll fix it, we'll fix it." He squatted next to the disoriented Mynhardt. "No worries. Is going to be sharp-sharp, *Baas*." He stood up, his lips quivering. "I'll get you another *dop*, I say. No pain." As Jakob tried to go around Berg, they locked eyes, the cold hate sending a shock through Jakob's core.

The first blow came fast and hard, catching him under his right eye. He had trouble seeing. The next one caught him in the stomach. Berg grabbed him behind his head with both hands, repeatedly driving Jakob's face into his raised knee. Jakob thought he had lost consciousness, because the next moment, he was up in the air, the rec room spinning below. He felt his stomach dip as Berg flung him to the ground. The breaking of bones echoed in his ears, too many shards of glass tearing through his body for him to pinpoint what was hurting.

Berg wasn't done. "Think you're going to be my *baas*, huh? Take away everything that I've worked for? That's what you scheme, all of you, fucking up on purpose so we fail. Think when this is all over you're going to sleep in my bed and fuck my wife? Is that what you think? You and all your little *kaffir* brothers?"

"Not me, *Baas*. Please." Jakob's voice drowned in a gurgle.

"I will kill you first, hear? I will kill the fucking lot of you."

Jakob tried to lift his arm to fend off the next blow, but he couldn't move it. Berg's boot was in his face, kicking at his mouth, pressing down on his face. The smell of cow dung on Berg's sole was the last thing Jakob remembered.

Benjamin

At night the past haunted him. It drove him into the damp streets, and he walked for hours, trying to think of anything but Tessa. How long had his soul been in this abyss? He had been so close to her that time in Johannesburg, so close to making himself known, but all he could do was watch her at a distance, too scared that it was the wrong time, that God wasn't finished with him yet. The longing had gnawed at him, the memory of her body ghosting his nerve endings until he thought he would lose his mind. When he gave in at last she was gone, and Berg was waiting. Did she know that he was watching? Did Tessa betray him? In the end it didn't matter. If it wasn't for the cruel hope that he'd find her again, he'd have walked into the freezing ocean at the base of Table Mountain, one of the many who disappear, mistaken for a seal in the shark-infested waters. But that was not God's way. Benjamin was being tested.

The fog hung thick over Table Mountain, its tendrils trailing into the city. Benjamin buttoned his jacket and turned onto Adderley Street, weaving his way past the holidaymakers, some of them shouting lewd one-liners at one another. Tomorrow they'd be in church, condemning lesser men. A voyeuristic fascination pricked Benjamin as he watched them. There was a man among the rowdy group, large, fair, barely able to stand. He separated from them, slinking into an alley. Benjamin made eye contact as he walked past, the man leaning precariously as he urinated against a wall. Benjamin's initial disgust gave way as recognition sparked. He stopped, turned back.

"What you looking at, mate? Never seen a man piss before?"

It was him. The man Tessa had been with the last time Benjamin saw her. Could it be? Had God sent him a reprieve? Benjamin nodded at the man and walked on, blending with the shadows ahead. He watched Wexler stumble out of the alley and cross the street, oblivious to the screeching tires and elongated horn blasts accompanying his progress. His friends had deserted him.

Benjamin followed as Wexler bumbled down the lane. Moonlight filtered through the fog, bathing the parliament gardens in diffused half-light that gleamed off garish Christmas decorations. Wexler lost his footing on the cobblestones and fell down. He lay still long enough for Benjamin to wonder if he had passed out. As he stood over the man, trying to decide between reviving him or dragging him away, Wexler suddenly flipped over, his eyes focusing slowly. "I know! You're Ben." Wexler stared at Benjamin with fascination. "I always thought she was taking the piss."

Benjamin watched dispassionately as Wexler made several ungraceful attempts to get on his feet, his big frame awkward. Tessa had chosen this man above him, given herself to him, told him her truths. This laughable cliché of a low-class gangster.

Wexler's skin flushed pink once he got to his feet. "Fancy a drink, mate?"

"How do you know me?"

"No mistaking you." Wexler patted his pockets. "Could you spot me a few quid, though?" He grinned. "I seem to have misplaced my wallet."

"Where is she?" Benjamin frowned. "I can't find her." The simple sentiment brought a familiar lump of panic to the surface.

Wexler's face pinched to a point. "You know, I don't think she wants you to, mate."

Benjamin felt blood rushing to his face. He barreled toward Wexler, all his pent-up frustration and rage focused on this one man, the gatekeeper between him and what was his. He warded off Wexler's defensive blows without much effort, knocking the man back to the ground. "If Tessa told you about me, Jeffrey," he said, "she must also have told you what I can do to you."

"Sod off." Wexler's drunken bravado did little to conceal his fear.

Benjamin straddled Wexler, his hands closing around the man's throat. Wexler kicked up and Benjamin fell back, misjudging Wexler's strength. Benjamin slammed his body down on Wexler with force, pinning him down, his face close to Wexler's, his thumbs applying pressure to Wexler's larynx.

"Tell me where she is."

A grunt came from Wexler. Benjamin eased his grip.

Wexler coughed. "She's scared of you."

"No. She just doesn't understand yet." Benjamin could smell the sweat and beer seeping from Wexler's pores, the odor of smoke masking that of a woman. Benjamin looked Wexler in the eye. "I see you've moved on."

"She didn't want me." Wexler crumpled. "I don't know where she is. I swear."

Benjamin felt a strange empathy with the man, their proximity suddenly unbearably intimate. He let go of him. The man was willing to die to keep Tessa's secret. Or perhaps he really didn't know. Benjamin felt disappointed, confused by God's message. The city suddenly bore down on him, unforgiving of his failure.

"Wait."

Benjamin turned around. Wexler was still on the ground where he had left him.

"Why not let her go, mate? There's plenty of girls, eh? Man like you can have his pick."

"She is all I ever asked for." It slipped out, this truth that Benjamin had held close. It felt as if his skin was chafing, his nerve endings raw. He wanted to take the words back, rip them out of Wexler's consciousness. The fearful child hiding inside of him was tethered to life by the smallest grace, a grace named Tessa, and the knowledge that she was out there in the world somewhere.

Wexler scrambled to get away as Benjamin advanced. "I'm sorry, mate." His voice melted into Cape Town's noise, as if he was already being erased. "She left me too, you know."

Benjamin stopped, the words resounding, landing in a part of him that wasn't numb, a knife twisting at the thought of what was. Of Tessa stealing off in the night. He nodded slowly, his rage deflating. Desolation weighed his steps as he left Wexler behind, faded into the city's streets, became one with its shadows.

Tessa

"There. That wasn't so bad." Tessa reached out for Tilly's hand as she walked out of the dentist's office. The girl grimaced, exposing one of her front teeth that had just started coming in.

"*Ja,*" Tilly said dramatically. "It was."

"But you missed a school day."

Tilly's expression mimicked a cartoon character thinking, her index finger held to her mouth, her head tilted to one side.

"And . . ." Tessa dragged it out, loving the eager anticipation in the child's eyes.

"We get waffles and ice cream!" Tilly gave a little leap, her short chestnut hair flopping in the air. Tilly looked nothing like Tessa. Her olive skin was noticeably darker, her features were rounder and far less delicate. Tessa knew that a deceased father would explain only so much as far as the dramatic difference in their appearances was concerned, but people were usually satisfied with something as simple as matching hair color, and Tessa matched Tilly's as close as she could, covering her white roots on a weekly basis with a home-coloring kit.

"Mathilda did well today," the dentist said, lingering in his consultation room's doorway.

"Tilly." The girl rolled her eyes.

"*Ja.*" Tessa smiled, rolling her eyes too. She was surprised when the dentist let his gaze linger for just a little too long. She was used to it in Unie, where eligible women were few and every young farmer had only one purpose when they came to town on weekends, but she didn't expect it here in the city, from a married man to boot.

"When is your next appointment?"

"We won't get back to Oudtshoorn until February, I think." Tessa removed her purse, moving to the receptionist's desk.

"It is 152 rand."

Tessa felt anxious as she handed over the notes. The lease money on Andrew's land was barely enough to get them through the month after the mortgage on the house on Pierneef Street. The pickup had broken down earlier that month, which was all it took to destroy the last of her savings.

"Waffles now." Tilly shifted her weight back and forth from one leg to the other. "I'm hungry."

"How about I make waffles when we get home, huh?"

"No! You promised. Wimpy Bar waffles."

Tessa nodded. "I did." She kissed Tilly on the nose and took her hand as they walked down the block to the shopping mall. They took a window seat at the Wimpy and Tilly eagerly grabbed a laminated menu, then pretended to consider her options.

"Just Rooibos tea for me," Tessa told the waitress after Tilly gave her order.

Tilly prattled on about the trauma of having her teeth cleaned. Tessa listened patiently, her eyes drifting outside. A woman, her figure bent with packages, made her way through the parking lot, shooing a limping beggar away from her car. A security guard stepped closer and the beggar hobbled off to the shade of a nearby tree.

"*Ma*, you're not listening to me." Tilly glared at Tessa.

"I am, darling. But I need you to talk a little less and finish your food. I'd like to get home before dark."

"I'm full." Tilly pushed the half-eaten waffle away.

Dry heat rose up from the asphalt as they walked back up the street, Tilly's leftovers wrapped up for Tessa's dinner. She anticipated the hot air that would assault them as soon as she opened the pickup's door.

"Can I have that, *Miesies?*"

Tessa was startled by the voice, a faint memory flickering in the back of her mind. She swung around, grateful that Tilly was inside the car when she saw the beggar standing a few feet away from her.

"I'm hungry, *Miesies*."

"I don't have money."

"I just ask leftovers, is all." He gestured to the plastic bag in Tessa's hand. "Please, *Miesies*. Please."

"Here." Tessa held it out to him.

The man reached for it, his hand shaking. "*Dankie, Miesies. Dankie, dankie.*" He hobbled away. "*Kgotso.*"

"Jacob?" The man looked nothing like the boy who had once lived in her house. He was frail beyond his years, his flesh seeming to cling to his bones by mercy alone, his skin weather-beaten. He turned around to face her, brown eyes full of sorrow.

"Hey, *kaffir*." It was the security guard. "I told you to *fokof*. I will *bliksem* the *kak* out of you." He lumbered forward, his face red from the heat, a police-issue *tonfa* in his hand.

"*Nee, Baas, nee!*" Jakob crouched down, his body curled into a ball, arms outstretched to stop the anticipated blows, the leftover container falling in the dirt. "Jakob didn't do anything. Honest! Please, *Baas*."

"No!" Tessa stepped in front of the security guard. "You can't do that. Not anymore."

The guard looked confused for a moment. He pushed Tessa out of the way, landing a blow on Jacob's arms. Jacob covered his head, a strange high-pitched yelping escaping his lips. The security guard lifted the *tonfa* to strike another blow. Tessa grabbed at the stick, trying to ward him off. He pushed her off easily.

"Help!" Tessa started screaming. A few passers-by watched the commotion from across the street. "Help us!" She yelled at them.

The dentist came running out of the building, the receptionist on his heels.

"He attacked us." Tessa pointed a finger at the security guard.

"Chris?" The dentist gave the security guard a questioning look.

"This piece of rubbish has been bothering people at the mall. I saw him following these people."

"He works for me." Tessa faced the dentist. "He was waiting for us to finish."

The dentist studied Jakob where he lay on the ground, a look of disgust on his face. "He looks like a *skollie*."

"No." Tessa balled her fists. "He is with me."

"Are you sure?"

"Of course." Tessa crouched next to Jacob, touching him gently on his shoulder. "Jacob, it's time to go now." He only emitted the strange yelping sound in response.

Tessa switched to Sotho. "It's all right, son. I'll take care of you." She saw recognition in his eyes.

"I tried to come to the place you told me, *Rakgadi*. It was so far away." Jacob wiped his eyes. "It was too far."

"Please come, son. Get into the car. It will be all right now."

"*Sis*. Holding on to a black like that." The security guard sneered.

The dentist eyed Tessa, unsure of what to make of the scene. She opened the back of the cab. Jacob slowly climbed inside, every movement strangely graceful. Ignoring the stares, she got into the pickup and pulled into the street.

"Why are we taking that *kaffir* with us, *Ma*?"

Tessa smacked Tilly on her leg, harder than she intended, her emotions threatening to take control. "Don't you ever let me hear you use that word, hear?"

Tilly's mouth scrunched up, tears welling in her eyes. "Everybody else does."

"Not you. That man back there . . ." Tessa's voice broke. "I knew him long ago. He is a good man, you hear? A person."

Tilly nodded, tears flowing freely. Tessa felt a pang of remorse as she saw a welt forming on her daughter's leg. She turned her attention to the road, not trusting herself to speak for the two-hour journey back to Unie.

13

Monday
DECEMBER 20, 2010

Alet picked Mathebe up at his house. Miriam waved from the *stoep* as she ushered Celiwe and Little Johannes back indoors.

"Miriam is taking the children to her mother in Grahamstown today," Mathebe volunteered.

"So you're home alone? Are you going to do push-ups all day and leave your socks on the floor?"

Mathebe's back stiffened, and Alet smiled. She put the van in gear, telling Mathebe of her hunch about Trudie being Theresa. "I called Bloemfontein this morning. They're checking with the area schools to see if there is any record of Theresa Morgan. I think we should grill Wexler about Trudie, see what he knows."

Mathebe nodded. "What about your father?"

Alet shrugged. "He's in PE with his wife and her family until Christmas, probably getting daily updates from Mynhardt on whether I'm being a good girl, so no worries." Mathebe gave her a look that she decided meant either that he was worried about her or that he thought she was full of it. She pulled up to the curb in front of Zebra House. The smell of breakfast wafted through the air.

"Coffee?" Maria greeted them at the door.

"Thanks, Maria. And we need to talk to *Baas* Jeffrey."

Maria's eyes darted to the office. "*Baas* Jeffrey . . ."

"Is he here?"

Maria shook her head. "He left last night."

"Where?"

"I didn't ask, *Mies*."

"Fok."

Mathebe reached for his radio.

"Get in touch with the airports," Alet said. "He's going to try leave the country." Alet turned to Maria. "Do you have the keys for the office, Maria?"

"Nee, Mies. Only the *baas* and *Mies* Tilly."

"Has *Mies* Tilly been here?"

"I don't know, *Mies.*" Maria was close to tears. "I just do my work. I don't know what's going on here."

"What do you mean? What's going on here?"

"Mies, last night during dinner *skollies* showed up here. They yell. They knock things over, scare the customers and *Baas* Jeffrey he does nothing."

"What *skollies*? Have you seen them before, Maria?"

"Nee, Mies. They are rubbish, not from here. They had *pangas,* guns." Maria gestured to her side, her voice getting higher. "I could see, here under their clothes." She pulled a tissue out of her bra and dabbed at her eyes as she spoke. "The short one he hit Lukas when he tried to stop them, said they'd kill him. The other two broke plates and glasses, threw the chairs."

"What did they want?"

"I don't know, *Mies.* Lukas and I hid in the kitchen. When we came out again the place was all broken. A big mess. Lukas says they took bottles from the bar. We had to work all night to clean up."

"Why didn't you call the police?"

"Baas Jeffrey said no, *Mies.* Wouldn't do no good. He says Lukas and me have to stay here. Then he just goes and leaves."

Mathebe walked over to the bar. "Maybe there are fingerprints."

"Aikona. I do a good job," Maria sobbed. "Don't go saying I don't."

"It's okay, Maria." Alet said. "We only want to catch them."

"You talk like *Baas* Jeffrey is a criminal, *Mies.* If he goes, the job goes. Then what will become of us?"

"We don't know that yet, Maria. Don't worry. We just want to find out what happened." Alet took Maria upstairs to one of the empty guest rooms, trying to calm her down.

Mathebe met her at the bottom of the stairs as she came down again, his face ashy. "The captain has arrested Miss Pienaar."

"What?"

"For Mr. Jakob Mens's death."

"But the evidence is circumstantial, if that. There's no way he's going to make that stick."

Mathebe cupped his hand around his mouth for a moment. "They need to discredit Miss Pienaar. With Mr. Wexler gone, the only other person tied to the case is Mrs. Terblanche."

"And Mynhardt made sure everybody knows about me and Boet Terblanche."

Mathebe nodded. "It does not look good."

"Dammit." Every way Alet looked at it they had their backs against the wall.

"I think you need to listen to your father, Constable Berg. You need to remove yourself from this case as soon as possible."

Alet turned to Mathebe, unsure that she had heard him right. "You want me to what?"

Mathebe held his hand up. "If you stay, they will get desperate. They will try to hang you." He looked over his shoulder. Outside the guesthouse, a police van pulled up.

"What about you?"

Mathebe smiled. "I am not a threat. You are the troublemaker."

"So what do I do?"

"You have to ask for leave. Say you are thinking of quitting."

"Mynhardt's not going to fall for that."

"Then you have to make your father believe, Constable."

Alet imagined the exchange between herself and Adriaan. "That's going to take more acting skills than I've got, hey."

"You will do all right. Parents want to believe. And you are your father's daughter."

Alet didn't quite know how to take that, but she didn't have time to worry about it just then. While Mathebe ran the investigation, Alet took Maria and Lukas back to the station to show them mug shots. Both of them identified Skosana without hesitation and pointed out one other man, a known associate.

Alet tried to piece things together. Wexler ran the operation, that much was obvious. Somehow Skosana and his henchman, Ngwenya, were involved. But something had gone wrong. Perhaps Trudie discovered what was going on, and Wexler had Skosana kill her? Tilly said the Bravermans paid the money and left with the baby. This happened after Boet and Jakob found Trudie's body. It didn't make sense. Why would Skosana go after the Bravermans? And why would he leave Ngwenya behind at the crime scene? More important, why would the Thokoloshe risk coming in to Unie and causing havoc at the guesthouse? She had to find a way to get to Skosana.

Joey's car was parked outside, but Joyboys' doors were locked. Across the street, a young coloured man sat outside a newly erected stand, tinkered together from an old caravan and some zinc plates. A hand-written cardboard sign next to him advertised twenty-four-hour coffee for R10. Alet walked over, fishing loose change out of her pockets.

"Howzit!" The man jumped out of his flimsy folding chair. "Some tea, some coffee? I got some *lekker* Coke, nice and cold. What can Giel do for the law today?"

"Just coffee, Giel. Black." Alet handed him her two R5 coins. "How long have you been here?"

"Since the weekend." Giel smiled. "There was a need."

"For twenty-four-hour coffee in Unie?"

"Is right, *ja*. Sometimes people drive past on the highway and it's late. Sometimes a thirsty man need a little something after bar-time before going home to the missus, I say." Giel winked. "You check, Constable?"

"I check, Giel. *Baas* Joey from Joyboys is going to think you're giving him competition."

Giel's broad face beamed with pride. "Is free enterprise, I say. You got to be sharp-sharp. Joyboys don't like it, they can stay open twenty-four hours too. Is like my *pa*, Poena Junior Junior used to say. If you don't grab opportunity by the balls, it'll kick you in the behind. Sorry, sorry, Constable," Giel held his hands up. "That's no talk in front of a lady." He placed a paper cup under a push-button coffee machine. "You sure you don't want cappuccino? Vanilla latte? We do all sorts here. Five-star service."

"Just black." Alet's eyes trailed the electric cable snaking out from underneath the stand, through the bushes, and along several extension cords. She wondered who Giel convinced to subsidize his twenty-four-hour electricity needs.

Giel pressed a button on the machine and, after a short delay, thick black liquid spewed into the cup, the process terminating in death-rattle sputtering. "Is nice, is nice." Giel handed Alet the cup.

"*Jissis* that's strong!"

"Quality. No watered-down coffee here. People need to stay awake, see? It's serious business this."

Alet perched her lips on the rim of the cup, careful to let only a little bit of the liquid into her mouth. The bitterness traced an acid trail through her mouth and down her throat. "Have you seen *Baas* Joey today, Giel?"

"I have."

Alet sighed. "Okay. Where?"

Giel stretched out his arm, the tip of his index finger pointing at the converted vestry.

"Why doesn't he answer the door, then?"

"He's in there. True's bob. I've been here the whole night."

Alet wondered if Giel worked the stand twenty-four hours, or if he had help. She crossed back to Joyboys, leaving her coffee cup on the doorstep before she knocked again. "Joey! I know you're there. Open up, man. I need a decent cup of coffee. Joey?"

Alet was met with silence. She walked around the building, testing the handle of a narrow back door she'd never seen anyone use. The ancient metal resisted her efforts, then gave way noisily. She found herself in Joyboys' dressing room. Hangers were strewn across the floor, and an old wooden school bench, used as a dressing table, was turned over. Alet pushed the black curtain in the doorway aside and walked onto the small stage, the scene still set for André's performance. Trickles of light penetrated Joyboys' high windows, bouncing around the myriad of mismatched crystal chandeliers hanging from the ceiling. A support beam creaked from the heat of the day. Alet squinted into the half-light. It felt like the shadows in the restaurant were moving, alive, taking form in the negative spaces between refracted light shards. Alet jumped down from the stage and reached for a light switch against the wall.

"Don't."

The sound of Joey's voice spun her around. Alet searched the dark room for a human form. A pale face appeared from underneath a blanket on one of the mismatched sofas. Alet flipped the light switch. As she walked closer to Joey, she gasped.

Dark bruises stained the skin around Joey's eyes, the lids almost swollen shut. Dried blood caked his nose, tracing a path that joined up with a rivulet from a large cut on his lips.

"Are you okay?"

A sarcastic laugh emanated from Joey's throat. He pulled the blanket up under his chin. Alet knelt down next to him, touching his shoulder. Joey jerked, pulling away from her.

"You need a doctor." Alet reached for her radio.

"*Nee.*"

"Joey, I don't know if you've had a look at yourself, but you're going to need stitches for that cut. It's going to leave a scar."

"The mark of Cain." Joey's voice was dull, matter-of-fact.

"What happened?"

"Does it matter?"

"Of course it bloody well matters. You've been assaulted. Did they take anything? They might be out there going after someone else."

"He won't. It's only me."

"Is it André? You guys fight or something? I'll have him *kak* himself in a cell tonight, hear?"

"Alet, no." Joey raised his voice. "André had nothing to do with this."

"Where is he, then?"

"It's not him!" Joey sat up, throwing the blanket off. His shirt was ripped, some buttons missing. Alet noticed bruising on his clavicle.

"*Fok*, he got you good."

"Wouldn't be the first time. Turns out I'm not too old for a good old-fashioned hiding."

"*Jissis.* Your *pa?*"

Joey coughed, his arms wrapping around his waist, his face scrunching up. "*Eina.*"

"You have broken ribs. I'm calling an ambulance to come get you."

"No. It will get out. People will . . . Don't. Please?"

Alet nodded reluctantly. "But I'm calling Oosthuizen, okay? He needs to take a look at you." Joey stared listlessly at the floor while she called the clinic.

"How long has this been going on?" Alet sat down next to Joey as they waited.

"I was seven, maybe eight, I don't know. *Pa* caught me skinny-dipping with a coloured boy in the farm dam."

"You were too young for him to think—"

"He knew. He always knew. Said he needed to put me on the narrow path."

"By beating you?"

"Spare the rod . . ." Joey coughed again.

"Don't defend what he did."

"I behaved, made sure I went to Oudtshoorn or George to . . . you know." Joey smiled wryly. "I thought that maybe he'd come to accept it. The laws are different now, you know? Men marry each other in church. I thought that if he saw me serious with someone, that I wasn't just fooling around . . ."

"André."

"I really liked him, Alet." Joey dropped his gaze, subservient shame settling over him like a dense fog. "It's my fault. I embarrassed *Pa* in front of the whole town."

"Is that what he said?" Alet's anger flared. "He's the one who should feel ashamed. He can be lucky I don't—"

"If you do anything, I'll deny it."

"Joey, I don't understand."

"He's my father. He has a place in the community. I won't ruin his life anymore."

"Any more than he ruined yours?" Alet sighed when Joey looked away. "What are you going to do?"

"I have friends in George. I can try to get a job at a hotel there or something."

Alet heard a car pulling up outside. She opened the door for Oosthuizen. Joey placidly let Oosthuizen examine him, their exchange conducted in semi-whispered confidences. Oosthuizen managed to convince Joey to go with him for X-rays. Joey had trouble standing, so Alet helped him to Oosthuizen's car.

"Thank you, Doctor." Alet closed the car door once she got Joey inside.

Oosthuizen nodded, walking over to the driver side. Alet suddenly realized that Oosthuizen had never asked what happened. He already knew. He'd probably been the one who helped *Dominee* Joubert keep the abuse of his son under wraps all these years.

"Bastard," Alet muttered through clenched teeth as she watched Oosthuizen's car turn the corner at the end of the block. This town . . . these people. It was getting to her, all these so-called God-fearing souls who couldn't care less about the cesspool at their feet.

Alet plunked down on a plush chair inside Joyboys, her cell resting in her hand. She thought about her future, surprised at the sudden clarity she felt. Since coming to Unie, she'd had an overwhelming feeling of powerlessness as she went through the motions of each day, just trying to get to the other side. She had tried to become invisible, hoping to please her father. The realization stung, but it was time to wake up from that daze, to rip open the wounds and face the truth. Not only for the sake of the victims, but for her own sake as well.

Alet flipped the phone open and dialed Adriaan's number.

"It's gotten to me, *Pa*, I'm sorry," she told Adriaan after stilted greetings were exchanged. "I don't think I can be here anymore."

"Alet, I told you, I'll make a few calls."

"I mean, I don't know if I'm cut out for the police." There was a long silence on the line.

"Are you telling me you want to quit?" The disdain in Adriaan's voice was unmistakable.

"I don't know. It's just, everything is going wrong. I need time to figure out what to do."

"Perhaps a break is a good idea," Adriaan said tersely.

"I don't have any leave." Alet knew she was pushing it, but she forged ahead. "I just don't think I can hold it together right now."

"I'll talk to Tokkie," Adriaan sighed. "Tell him to give you unpaid time. Frieda and I will pick you up tonight."

It took careful treading, but Alet managed to convince Adriaan that she needed to spend some time alone, maybe have a real vacation so she could gather her thoughts. He reluctantly agreed, ordering her to be in Port Elizabeth by Christmas. As she hung up the phone, Alet thought about how good she had become at manipulating people. Family trait? Thinking of herself as Adriaan's daughter, a chip off the old block, didn't make her proud anymore.

• • •

"It's my word against theirs." Tilly slumped over on the concrete bench in the court's holding cell. White paint chipped off the gate where countless detainees' hands had gripped the bars over the years, while they stared out at the courtyard, waiting. Alet had escorted many a drunk and disorderly local there after they had slept it off in the police station's cells next door. Cases weren't heard over weekends, so by Mondays, the miasma of stale alcohol and vomit hung thick in the air.

"Tilly, I'm desperate. Please, man. There must be something that proves Jeff paid Mynhardt off."

"I'm the only one who spoke with the buyers. The only one they can identify." Tilly hugged her knees against her chest. She looked childlike, her chestnut curls sagging over her narrow shoulders. "I didn't think about protecting myself. I trusted him." She shook her head. "Stupid."

Alet leaned against the bars. "Boet only owns half the farm. Seems old Mr. Terblanche leased the rest." Alet dug her middle finger into her palm. "Records indicate that the farm belongs to your *ma*. The part where she was found."

Tilly looked up, a startled expression on her face. Alet wondered if she knew the truth about what her mother was, if she should tell Tilly about what she'd found in the town's archives, the fact that the farm was transferred into Trudie's name by Tessa Morgan, and that they might be the same person.

Tilly shook her head. "We always lived on Pierneef Street. *Ma* never went out to the farms."

Alet decided not to say anything more until she figured things out for herself. "Okay. You think I can have a look through her things? Just to make sure we didn't miss anything?"

"You're asking permission now?" Tilly's gaze challenged Alet.

"I was trying to—"

Tilly clicked her tongue, waving Alet away with a dismissive hand.

"Tilly, I think the killer was in the house the night she died, that he might have been looking for something of hers."

"Maybe he found it. There's nothing of value there now."

"At least let me have a look."

Tilly shrugged. "Do whatever you want, Alet. It's not like I can do anything about it now."

"Captain Mynhardt and Sergeant Strijdom have gone through the house." Mathebe looked apologetic. "I do not believe we will find much."

"Maybe they missed something."

"Miss Pienaar is a suspect in a crime. The captain has taken the case on himself. It might not be wise to go."

"I'm not backing out now, Johannes."

Mathebe sighed. "I did not find anything the first time, Constable."

"Maybe you just didn't realize it was important." Alet bit her lip, certain that Mathebe would take offense.

A frown lodged between Mathebe's eyes. "Yes," he said. "That is possible." He pulled the van out of the police-station lot and took the road to Trudie's. As they turned onto Pierneef Street, Alet noticed a car with a Cape Town registration parked in front of Trudie's house.

"Koch, maybe?" Alet replied to Mathebe's unspoken question. He got out of the van and followed her through the gate and up to the house.

"Alet! Hallo." Mike Engelman emerged from the peach trees that lined the path to the back of the house. "I was just going to slip this under your door when I heard the car." He held up a manila envelope.

The surprise of seeing him in these surroundings took Alet aback. In the daylight his features seemed more prominent, the intensity of his blue eyes contrasting with pale skin. His thick-rimmed glasses were gone, and she noticed the gelatin edge of contact lenses around his iris. "Beautiful" was the first word that popped into her head. It surprised her, but she had to concede that it was correct. Mike Engelman wasn't handsome in the traditional sense, but there was something fragile about him she couldn't put her finger on. It imbued him with an essence of elegance, even grace. I should probably try to stay sober on dates, Alet thought.

"Hi." Mike extended his hand to Mathebe. "Mike Engelman. I work with Professor Koch."

"*Ja*, um . . . Mike, this is my partner, Sergeant Mathebe."

Mathebe shook Mike's hand. "Good to meet you, Mr. Engelman."

"Doctor Engelman," Alet said.

"Call me Mike." A dimple appeared in Mike's cheek as he smiled at her. "I'm on my way to Humansdorp. They're reopening the Klasies River project."

"First humans," Alet said.

"Right." Mike's smile grew broader. "You remembered."

"*Ja*. I . . . Hey, sorry for not calling. It's just that we've been working on the case. There's a lot going on."

"You have a suspect?"

"We're getting there."

"Anyway, Professor Koch asked if I could drop this off." Mike handed her the envelope he had tucked under his arm. "The DNA results you wanted."

"Oh." Alet took the envelope from him. "Thanks."

"Well, I should go." Mike extended a hand to Mathebe. "Nice to meet you, Sergeant. Alet."

"Mike, wait." Alet glanced at Mathebe.

"I will start," Mathebe said.

Alet waited until he disappeared into the house before she turned back to Mike. "I really am sorry for not calling you back."

The dimple disappeared from Mike's cheek. "That's all right," he said. "Best for you to focus on the case. I hope you get him." He leaned over and gave her a kiss on the cheek. "Let me know if there's anything I can do."

Mike got into his car and drove away. Alet opened the envelope. As she finished reading the report, she reached for her cell.

Inside the house, Mathebe had already dragged a box marked PERSONAL to the dining room and was busy unpacking it, inspecting every item and laying them out on the table. Alet glanced over the table. "Is that a diary?" She took a small black notebook out of the box and started flipping through the pages. "Planner. To-do lists." She scanned the pages, finding no entries for the day Trudie died. She carelessly dropped it back onto the table.

"What did Dr. Engelman give you, Constable?"

Alet handed the envelope to Mathebe. "Seems Tilly is not Trudie's biological child. They're not even related. I just called the provincial records office. They had no record of an adoption. I'm waiting for Jo'burg to get back to me."

"I see." Mathebe paused in his work, his eyes narrowing.

"This could be the link between Trudie and the baby ring. Maybe Tilly was the first."

Mathebe considered this for a moment. "Miss Pienaar is twenty-six. The baby-smuggling only started about ten years ago. I think it is too soon to assume that Mrs. Pienaar was part of it."

"But—"

Mathebe held his hand up. "We should find evidence, Constable. It is better that way."

Alet had the sudden urge to go have a drink at Zebra House, but Zebra House was shut down for the investigation. And who knew if Joyboys would even open up again? It was bad enough before, but Unie was really turning into a shithole now.

Mathebe emptied the box and took a picture of the contents. Alet went through everything again, inspecting antique pillboxes and costume jewelry, flipping through books as she repacked it. Mathebe dragged the next box over. It was filled with clothes, mostly modern pieces interspersed with unusually beautiful coats or embroidered blouses, anachronistic mementos, Alet thought. She felt the pockets and seams of each garment, finding an old pound note in the pocket of a jacket with an unusually tiny waist and a small studded earring stuck into the folds of a hoopskirt.

Mathebe's cell rang. "Sergeant Mathebe speaking. Yes. I am."

Alet packed the clothes back into the box while Mathebe gave monosyllabic answers to the caller. She thought of the picture of Trudie holding a very young Tilly. They looked like so many pictures of mothers holding their infant children. Nobody could guess at the deception. Every box they had unpacked held subtle remembrances of a distant past: a turn-of-the-century coin collection, a silver brush with ivory inlay—small affirmations of Alet's theory, but not enough to prove it.

Mathebe hung up. Something that could have been misconstrued as a smile pulled at the corners of his lips. "Mr. Wexler has been arrested in George. He was chartering a plane to fly him to Namibia."

"Yes!" Alet couldn't contain her excitement. "Got the bastard. Can't wait to get my hands on him."

"Constable, you are on leave."

"Right." Alet had almost forgotten about it.

"I will go right away." Mathebe stacked the last of the boxes.

Alet dusted her hands off. "Call me when you're done with Wexler."

Mathebe hesitated, something obviously on his mind.

"*Ja?*"

"You and Dr. Engelman . . ."

Alet knew where this was going. "We had dinner."

"He is involved in the investigation."

"I know. Nothing happened."

Mathebe gave a curt nod. He turned and left, closing the front door behind him. Alet could hear the front gate moan outside as he opened and closed it. She had climbed over the fence that night to avoid making that noise. Alet walked into the living room and looked out from between the net curtains. If the killer had stood right there, he would have seen her go into the flat with Boet. The light had only gone on as Boet left. Did he do it to make it look like Trudie was still alive? If that was his plan, why wait? Why would he have cared about watching Alet and Boet?

Alet called Mathebe's cell. "Hey, was Jana Terblanche ever fingerprinted?"

"She has no arrest record."

"She must have been fingerprinted for an ID book or passport or something. We need to run her prints against the partial you found in the house."

"Mrs. Terblanche was in Oudtshoorn the night after the murder."

"That's what Boet said."

"You do not believe him?"

Alet thought about it for a moment. "I don't know. Either way, they were both on the farm the night of Trudie's murder."

Alet began a systematic search of the house, starting on the doorstep and working her way back. She checked for loose floor and ceiling tiles, drawers and hiding places that they might have missed. By the time she reached the enclosed *stoep* in the back, she was ready to throw in the towel. If Trudie's killer had been looking for something in the house, he must have found it.

Alet's eyes itched from the dust. She rubbed them, but that only made it worse. She walked out toward her flat to take a bath and wash all the filth off her. Walking around the back of the house, she noticed how dry Trudie's flower beds were. A strange guilt crept over her. She dragged the sprinklers out into the beds and turned them on. Drawing the hose out from its coil, she watered the large flower beds. The smell of wet soil wafted through the air. Alet imagined the distressed plants giving a sigh as the water seeped to their roots. In the twilight, a pleasant coolness descended on the garden, and Alet gave her own sigh. She regretted the fact that she had never offered Trudie help. Maybe if she had spent more time with her, she would have noticed that something bad was about to happen; maybe she could even have prevented it. She shook off the thought. "If only" was never productive, she knew that. It created the illusion that she had control.

The front gate moaned. Alet craned her neck to see around the peach trees as Tilly walked down the path, her step tentative as if she didn't inhabit her own body. She looked startled when she noticed Alet.

"Are you okay, Till?" Alet felt hesitant about approaching Tilly, unsure of where they stood.

"I've been released on bail." Tilly looked haggard, her blouse wrinkled. "Boet Terblanche came to see me. He made an offer on the land. It was low." She crossed her arms. "He thought I'd probably want to let it go."

"Meaning what?"

A sarcastic laugh escaped Tilly's lips. "He thinks I'll be sent to prison. He didn't say it, of course, but he didn't have to." Hazel eyes looked pleadingly at Alet. "What's going on?"

"I don't know that I should—"

"Who else?" Tilly said hotly. "Who is going to tell me? My lawyer? Your buddy, Mathebe? I have nobody left, Alet. Just tell me what you know."

"Let me get you a drink?" Alet guided Tilly to her flat. Tilly stared at the beer Alet handed her as if it were a crystal ball.

Alet sat down next to her on the *stoep*. "Trudie's DNA does not match yours."

Tilly's face betrayed no emotion. "Go on."

"We're still searching for adoption records, but so far there are none. We just caught Jeff Wexler. I suspect that he might know something about this."

"You think Jeff knows who my real parents were?" Tilly's voice was flat.

"I don't know," Alet said, wondering why Tilly wasn't responding to the news. "It's a possibility."

"I don't want to know." Fine lines formed around Tilly's lips as she formed the words. She tilted the beer bottle back.

"Tilly—"

"I've had dreams, Alet. Since I can remember. The same ones. I used to wake up at night crying, terrified. My *ma* . . . Trudie said she would never let things like those dreams happen to me. She denied it was real, but she couldn't erase what was left behind," she tapped her index finger against her forehead, "the stuff in here. Once it's done, it never goes away, see?"

They sat in silence, watching the bright colors of the garden become muted and the sky turn from bright blue to pale pink. Alet felt a melancholy settle over her as she thought of children like Tilly, locked behind doors, their lives dependent on the whims of others, most of them only discovered when it was too late. She understood Tilly's need to save, misguided as it may have been. She was saved too.

"I need to know about your *ma* and Jakob Mens," Alet broke the silence. "What happened?"

Tilly sighed. "*Ma* found him in Oudtshoorn. A filthy hobo, crazy, off his rocker, living off scraps and handouts, but *Ma* treated him like he was Jesus himself, returned from the dead. Jakob could do no wrong. She got him the job with old Mr. Terblanche. I guess they struck some kind of deal. Jakob would come to the house sometimes. I'd hear them late in the night, talking, when they thought I was asleep. Once I walked in on her holding him like he was a baby. It was just weird. The kids at school treated me like a leper when word got around that a black slept in the house. I hated him back then, I won't lie. But I didn't kill him, Alet."

"Do you remember anything from the night of the accident?"

Tilly shook her head. "When I woke up the next day, I felt wrong. I could barely see straight and my head . . . It was almost like I had the flu really bad. I tried to go to work. Jeff told me to stay put in the office."

"Wait. He said you took a sedative."

"No. I threw that stuff out. It made me feel weird."

"So you don't remember taking anything?"

Tilly shook her head.

"What exactly happened before you went to bed?"

"I closed the restaurant. Maria, Lukas and Jeff were gone already. I was exhausted. I couldn't focus on the paperwork so I just put everything in the safe and locked up."

"What about before you closed?"

Tilly frowned. "Only Dr. Oosthuizen was there, finishing his drink. Sometimes just hangs around for conversation. He's kind of lonely. I think Petrus was there too. Or maybe he left already, I can't remember."

"You said your mom and Jakob talked. Do you remember about what?"

"No, but when I went through her stuff I found the last name 'Morgan' on some of the old papers. I remember that they sometimes mentioned it. I thought it might be distant family or something."

Alet leaned in. "Papers?"

"Birth certificates, marriage licenses, report cards. That sort of thing."

"I didn't find anything."

"I took them." Tilly looked away. "It was just a lot of old papers. I didn't see what they had to do with any of this."

"Could I see them? They could help us."

Tilly nodded reluctantly.

"There's something else I need to ask you. What did you and Trudie really argue about before she was killed?"

"I told you."

"Come on, Tilly. I need the truth."

"It has nothing to do with her death."

"Perhaps not. Why don't you let me decide?"

Tilly folded her body up in the chair. "*Ma* found out."

Alet frowned. "About Wexler's operation?"

"That I was involved. She told me she was ashamed of me. Of what I had become." Tilly's voice broke. "Rich coming from her, don't you think?"

• • •

Later that day, Tilly brought Alet a concertina file filled with years and years of documents, birth certificates, old ID books, marriage licenses, school report cards. Alet dumped the contents out on her counter. A plain hardcover school notebook thumped out. Her pulse quickened as she opened it and ran her eyes down the page.

"What's that?" Tilly asked, helping herself to a beer.

Women's names, details about their lives, dates. Every page revealed increasingly obsessive observations, intimate invasions of lives, with no clue to the identity of the author. She recognized at least four names that had been in the Angel Killer files.

"I'm not sure, hey. Can I hold on to these?" Alet motioned to the pile of paper. "Promise I'll get them back to you."

Tilly nodded. She muttered something about a decent bath and disappeared out the door. Alet dialed Mathebe. His phone went straight to voice mail. This couldn't wait. She had to get down to Cape Town, have Theo confirm that the other girls were also murder victims. If he would even talk to her. Alet grabbed a backpack, black T-shirts, underwear and a toothbrush. On the way out of town, she stopped at the twenty-four-hour coffee stand and handed Giel two R5 coins.

"Going somewhere, Constable?"

"Cape Town, Giel. Get me one of those industrial-strength coffees of yours, hey?"

"Now you use the service I provide, see?"

Alet smiled. "*Ja*, Giel. I see."

"Maybe you should wait till morning, Constable? The roads, they not nice so late. Just now I lose a customer. That's never good."

Alet suppressed a smile. "Sometimes you just have to do something right now, Giel. Not now-now, but now. You check?"

Giel looked at her thoughtfully for a moment. "*Ja*, Constable. I check."

1994

Benjamin

The flight descended into Johannesburg. The jowls of the man next to Benjamin vibrated in the turbulence. Outside the window, yellow landscape and flat buildings rushed toward them. Every time Benjamin climbed aboard an airplane, his awe was renewed. God would not give man the ability to fly, so man invented the means himself, traversing the country in a matter of hours, not months. What else could man not achieve? He felt a wave of shame roll over him at the thought. He could never let go of the feeling that God was watching him, controlling him, withholding what he desired most until he did as he was commanded. Though it had turned from a sharp pain to a dull ache, the longing for Tessa was still with him every waking moment. With the country on the verge of change, on the very precipice of a new beginning, something as irrational as hope had sprung up in him too. There was talk that the name of the Johannesburg airport was going to be changed from Jan Smuts to Oliver Tambo International. New names everywhere, new beginnings. Perhaps he too could begin again.

The airplane's wheels made bumpy contact with the runway. Benjamin waited, watching the sagging looks of exhaustion on the faces of the men and women walking down the aisle, their clothes as wrinkled as the pillow-lines on their faces. He closed his eyes. An article on DNA manipulation had excited him, shown him the way forward. The time had come for him to return to his work. He'd reached out to old Bond members on the boards of universities across the country, received offers from prominent departments. The interviews were a mere formality.

"You are chosen." *Matrone* Jansen's voice was so real that Benjamin suddenly broke out in a cold sweat, buried memories wrapping tentacles around him. He frantically looked for her in the empty seats behind him, and realized that he was the last passenger left on the plane.

"Sir? Are you all right?" The flight attendant had a pale round face and high cheekbones, her platinum-blond hair pulled into a French braid. Her manicured hand rested on the back of his seat as she leaned into the row to talk to him. She smiled, red lipstick staining her teeth.

Benjamin looked up into the palest blue eyes. "It's you."

"Sir?" A frown crept over her face, marring her static smile.

She knows what I am, Benjamin thought. That I have found her. He smiled. "I'm all right." He reached over and gently touched her hand. Her name tag registered in his peripheral vision. "You don't have to worry, Fransien. Everything will be fine."

Tessa

"It's ugly." Tilly spread the newspaper on the kitchen table. The Y-shaped color blocks of the New South African flag filled the front page.

"Why do you say that?" Tessa leaned over the table, examining the design.

"Joey said, his *pa* said, that green, red, and yellow are the colors of the ANC and it runs through the red and blue because they're taking our land."

"Did he, now?" Tessa wasn't fond of little Joey Joubert, the *dominee*'s son. He was far too big for his shoes, planting unsavory ideas in Tilly's head. If Joey's stories were anything to go by, the *dominee* had difficulty practicing the tolerance he preached.

"You know what I think the colors mean?" Tessa traced the outlines with her index finger. "Green is for our land and farms, yellow for our gold, black and white for all the different people and blue for the two oceans that surround us."

"And red?"

"Red for the blood that was spilled to bring them all together."

"Joey says that the blacks are going to get houses for free now and we have to pay for it. Is it true?" Tilly let out a suppressed giggle. "He says we should take cover the day after the election because refrigerators and TVs are going to fall from the sky for all of them."

Tessa tried not to get angry. "If people all had houses, wouldn't that be a good thing?"

Tilly looked at her for a moment, her confusion clear. Tessa hated how much Tilly was being indoctrinated into the narrow-mindedness of this town, her teachers and friends rigid with conservative ideas, unwilling to think for themselves for even a moment.

Tilly's mouth drew to a point, trying to hide a trembling lower lip. "They will kill us when they win."

"What are you talking about?"

"Everybody says so, *Ma*. The blacks are going to wipe us out. Why do they want to do that?" Tilly's voice was shrill, her eyes watery.

Tessa didn't know what to say. How could you explain a history of hate? Tilly was only a child, but Tessa knew just how much there was to answer for, and the day of reckoning was upon them. "We will have to hope that people are willing to forgive one another, Tilly," she said at last.

Tilly frowned. "We didn't do anything. Miss Nieman says we gave them everything and they burned it to the ground. That they just destroy everything and it's in their nature."

"Mathilda!" Tessa felt her own eyes filling with tears, the task of schooling her daughter in the true history of the country, a guilty burden, the suffering she had seen firsthand too much to relate. She should have told Tilly everything from the beginning, but she foolishly hoped that teaching her respect for all people would be enough. Where would she even begin? Censorship had kept the truth off the bookshelves and out of the news for so long that nobody was willing to believe it anymore, the mythology of the long-suffering Afrikaner who conquered this land with God's blessing too tempting, too easy. Believing in your own suffering gave you license to ignore that of others. Tessa bit back the anger. "Set the table," she said, turning her back to Tilly. "Use the good plates."

"Why do I have to dress up for this guy?" Tilly crouched next to the sideboard, balancing plates on her right arm. The plates' pattern was one that Andrew had chosen for Sarah, so long ago now. "Who is he, anyway?"

"No!" Tessa lurched forward trying to catch the pile as they slipped out of Tilly's arms. The fragile porcelain smashed to pieces on the stone floor. *"Jissis,* Mathilda. What's wrong with you?"

Tilly looked at Tessa with wide eyes. "I'm sorry, *Ma.*"

Tessa knelt on the floor a wash of emotions running through her as she picked up the white shards. Sarah, Andrew, Flippie. She remembered how Sarah refused to let anyone else wash the plates, how carefully she wrapped them in blankets every time they'd had to leave town.

"Ma? I'm sorry."

Tessa looked down at the shards in her hands, blood trickling over the white porcelain from a cut on her finger. They were just things, she knew that, but they were a tenuous link to her memories, proof that she didn't just dream them up. It felt more and more as if her past was slipping through her fingers, as if the world was trying to wipe history away every time someone on TV or in the papers twisted the truth of what they'd done.

The doorbell rang. Tilly gave Tessa a look of consternation.

"Go answer." Tessa cleared the broken porcelain and carried it to the kitchen. She thought momentarily of trying to glue them back together, but realized it was hopeless when she pulled a splinter out of her palm. They were good for nothing but trash now.

"Ma, it's—"

"What?"

"Dominee Joubert is in the sitting room."

"What does he want?"

Tilly shrugged. Tessa rinsed the blood off her hand. Wrapping a kitchen towel around it, she made her way to the front room. Joubert sat in the leather recliner, the best chair in the house, her chair, where she always sat reading or listened to the news. He was in his forties, his blond hair thinning rapidly, his sharp nose and small eyes giving him a vague resemblance to a vulture. Or maybe that was only what she thought of him.

"Mrs. Pienaar." He looked briefly at her towel-wrapped hand.

"What can I do for you?" Tessa sat down opposite him on the old upholstered couch, her insides clenching. She couldn't stand the man. She went to church on Sundays for Tilly's sake, made an effort to fit in with the community, but like so many others, Joubert used the pulpit to further his bigoted agendas, and Tessa had a hard time biting her tongue in his presence.

"As you know, the election is in a few weeks."

"*Ja?*"

Joubert gave her a tight smile. "We trust in God's plan, but we are outnumbered."

"By us, you mean?" Out of the corner of her eye Tessa saw Tilly lingering in the doorway.

"The *volk*. We need to stand together. I trust you understand that?"

Tessa didn't answer. Joubert sniffed, his mouth thinning to a slit. "There has been growing concern in the community about you, Mrs. Pienaar."

"Me?" The mock surprise in Tessa's voice did not escape Joubert, his hands crossed prudishly in his lap.

"More precisely about what happens in this house."

"If you have something to say, *Dominee* . . ."

"As you wish. You have a child in the house, Mrs. Pienaar. As a leader in the community, I look out for all of God's flock. Even the ones who stray."

Tessa felt her ire build, her civility hanging on by the loosest of threads. "Go on."

Joubert looked at his hands while he talked, as if looking her in the eye was tantamount to communing with Lucifer. "It seems that one of the Terblanche farmhands has been spending a lot of time in this house. Congregation members have told me that they believe he spends the night. I presume in the servant quarters, of course, but some believe otherwise."

Outrage blushed Tessa's cheeks. "Guests in this house sleep in the spare bedroom."

A look of satisfaction glimmered in Joubert's eyes. "You think that wise? There is talk."

Tessa gritted her teeth. "Of course there is."

"If not for your reputation, certainly for that of your daughter, I simply wish to—"

"I know what you wish to do, *Dominee*."

"Then you understand."

"Too well. But let me assure you that since this is my house, I will conduct it any way I see fit. If I wish to have a black man in my house, let him eat at my table and let him spend the night, it has nothing to do with the members of the congregation."

"Mrs. Pienaar, there is such a thing as decency. Be an example for your child, at least."

"I know what decency is, *Dominee*. Do you? Perhaps you should worry about the example you're setting for your own child."

Joubert's neck stiffened. "I'm sure I don't know what you mean."

Tessa stood up. "Things are changing, *Dominee*, even in Unie. You should all be on your knees instead of worrying about decency. Please, do not look for me or Tilly in your pews again, and know that you are not welcome in this house." Tessa slammed the door behind Joubert as soon as he stepped outside.

Tessa turned to find Tilly skulking behind her. She sighed. "Is the table set?"

"Did you have to do that, *Ma*?"

"Don't worry about it."

"But all my friends . . . Joey . . . they say I'm . . . Why does Jakob have to come here?" Tilly wasn't a beauty, especially as she stood there with her upper lip curled in accusation. The girl had her mother's arrogant eyes and her father's puffy features. She was too easily influenced by others, dissuaded by present pleasures. Could it be that taking her away from her parents hadn't saved her after all? Were ignorance and hate ingrained in her the day she was born? Tessa immediately felt guilty for these thoughts. If it were true, after all, what could be said about her? About her real parents? Andrew and Sarah had taught her humanity. She would have to try harder, for Tilly's sake.

Tessa was startled when the doorbell rang behind her. Jeff stood on her doorstep, tall, barrel-chested. At fifty-something he was certainly not the boy she had met many years ago, but age had given him an air of distinguished calm. In her anger she had forgotten that he was coming. He had called her out of the blue the day before, asking if he could come to Unie to see her. As he stood there in front of her, the expectations of long ago on his face, Tessa regretted saying yes.

"Hallo, luv." Jeff's joviality ebbed when she didn't respond. "What? Have I changed into such an old fart?"

Tessa leaned in to give him a cautious hug. Jeff wrapped her easily in his arms, lingering too long.

Tessa gently pushed him away. "This is my daughter, Mathilda. Tilly, this is Jeff Wexler. An old friend of mine."

"*Isit?*" Tilly raised a sassy eyebrow.

Jeff let his gaze trail from Tilly back to Tessa, the unspoken memory of the night when Tessa brought Tilly home between them. Tessa hoped she could trust him to keep their secret.

Adriaan

It was just before ten on Sunday morning, two days before the election, the streets of downtown Johannesburg unusually quiet except for optimistic faces heading toward ANC headquarters for a voter registration program. A policeman stopped a beige Audi at the barricade near Shell House. The white man behind the wheel looked over at his passenger, his hand edging closer to the bulge on his calf. They waited while the policeman searched the car.

"Go." The policeman slammed the trunk and waved them through.

The men parked the Audi on the corner of Bree and Von Wielligh streets, got out, and walked away. Five minutes later, the ninety-kilogram bomb exploded. Concrete disintegrated in the wake of the force. Glass rained down from the sky. Bodies arced weightless through the air, flesh torn from bone. The blast was heard all the way to Pretoria, an hour's drive away. Then silence. As if all who heard it held their breath.

A solitary wail broke the spell, ringing in chaos. A woman ran through the debris, her hands in the air, blue domestic overalls sprayed with blood.

"A witness states that the police let the bombers through." The reporter, a man with a receding hairline and a stiff British accent, held an enormous black microphone to Adriaan's face.

Adriaan fought the impulse to knock it out of the man's hand. "We cannot confirm that at this time."

"Is it possible the police were complicit in order to jeopardize the election?"

"There is absolutely no proof to support that claim."

More foreign journalists yelled through the throng of cameras. Adriaan knew that the world was gaping at the war zone behind him, the bent steel rods protruding from leaning walls that stopped halfway up the building, the nine black bodies on the sidewalk, the people whose wounds were being treated by paramedics. He bit back his rage. The people responsible for this were idiots. The whole world was watching, sympathies increasing a hundredfold for the Commies.

"Surely, you have to admit that the police are guilty of negligence."

Adriaan checked himself before answering. "A thorough investigation into today's events will be conducted, and all guilty parties will be prosecuted to the full extent of the law. The South African Police Force will not allow anyone who terrorizes the citizens of this country to get away with it."

"But, Colonel, how did such a large explosive device go undetected by your men?"

They weren't listening to him. All they saw was a uniform to hang the blame on, a symbol of a past that refused to let go. Whites were the bad guys now and blacks were the heroes, on the verge of taking Troy. How quickly they forgot about the ANC bombs that had killed pregnant women, children, limpet mines destroying families on vacation. Nobody wanted to hear that now. He had to smile and shake hands with those bastards, pretend that he was pleased by the direction the country had taken, or they'd have his neck. But Adriaan knew how to play the game. He had already covered his tracks. His men were loyal. They knew that implicating him in anything would mean their own downfall. And they also knew what he was capable of if they had a change of heart.

"Colonel, is it true that—"

"That is all I can give you for now." Adriaan walked away from the microphones. "Keep them out," he barked at a constable in riot gear as he crossed the cordoned-off area.

"Call came in for you." Kalo, dressed in his constable uniform, waited behind the wheel of a squad car at the edge of the scene.

Adriaan closed the door. "Media?"

Kalo shook his head. "A warrant officer from Murder and Robbery. Stofberg. He gave an address. Said you should come immediately."

"Jissis. Has he been in a coma for the past five hours? We have to deal with this *kak."*

Kalo started the car. He made a deft U-turn, barely avoiding a news van coming down the street. "He said you'll definitely want to see this."

Only one yellow van stood parked in the driveway of the address Stofberg had given. It was a house in Linden, one of the Jo'burg suburbs. The house looked old, mildly neglected. Even from the street, the distinct odor of something burning assaulted the senses, thick and noxious. Adriaan walked in without announcing his presence, the smell intensifying by degrees. Little natural light penetrated the thick curtains in front of the windows inside. He and Kalo found one of the new black hires in the kitchen taking photographs. The constable had a relaxed arrogance in his attitude that no white policeman would have dared around Adriaan.

"Where is Warrant Officer Stofberg?"

The constable pointed down the hall. He turned his back and sauntered out into the backyard of the house.

"Keep an eye on him, Kalo. Teach him his place if he gives you any trouble."

Kalo smiled. His teeth seemed unnaturally white against his dark skin. Kalo had made a small fortune working for Adriaan, every kill rewarded, every mission carried out with relish. He owned a huge house in Soweto, a brand-new BMW, two wives and family who had grown accustomed to luxury. But the more precarious the whites' position became in the country, the more his demands grew. Adriaan wondered if Kalo could still be trusted once the well of money dried up.

Stofberg, a short man in his forties with an intelligent face, came out of one of the rooms at the end of the hallway. "Colonel Berg. I appreciate you coming." He extended his hand.

"I'm not at Brixton anymore, Stofberg. And you know we're in the middle of a shitstorm. So what do you want?"

"I thought that . . ." Stofberg retracted his hand. "Perhaps you should see for yourself." He turned around and led the way into one of the bedrooms.

The door frame was scorched black, the inside of the room almost totally destroyed, the floor covered in water. On the bed was a human form, female, the outer layer of skin burned black, exposing raw flesh underneath.

"Neighbors called when they saw smoke. The whole house almost went up in flames."

"Where's forensics?"

"Everybody's been called to Shell House. Only me and Lucky left to process it."

Adriaan studied the scene with a practiced eye. "The fire started on the bed." He held out his hand. Stofberg handed him a pair of latex gloves.

"*Ja*. The firemen had the same conclusion. The house is being rented by three flight attendants. The other two are out of town, so it's possible that this is the third girl, Fransien van der Merwe."

"Why am I here, Stofberg? The girl probably fell asleep with a lit cigarette."

"After she threw petrol all over herself? The firemen confirmed an accelerant was used." Adriaan carefully lifted the skull, finding traces of scorched blond hair beneath it. "Do you have a photograph of her?"

Stofberg left the room briefly and came back with a small square frame. A smiling young couple, their arms around each other, looked back at him, the man making bunny ears behind a girl with white hair and high cheekbones. Adriaan knew without a doubt that Benjamin De Beer was back in Johannesburg.

"You were the lead on the Angel Killer, Colonel. I read all the files. I thought you could perhaps—"

"The Angel Killer hasn't been active in years."

"But he has also never been caught."

Adriaan looked at the Fransien van der Merwe in the picture. She was only a few years older than Alet. "We followed all the leads. We got nowhere. The murders stopped. He's probably dead."

"But, sir . . ."

"Listen to me, Stofberg, I'm not going to tell you this is the Angel Killer just because a blond girl was burned in her bed." Adriaan barely contained his agitation.

"You were close. I studied the file." The accusation was clear in Stofberg's voice. "If it's him there will be more girls, you know," he said when Adriaan didn't answer.

380

Adriaan peeled the gloves off. He recognized the flimsy concern that veiled Stofberg's true ambition, the potential for besting the legend of Adriaan Berg by solving the one case he couldn't. He gave Stofberg a smile. "You think you can do better? Be my guest."

"Wait. I pulled the case files. While you were working on the Angel Killer case, you requested DNA tests on some old unsolved murder case of a student in Pretoria."

"*Ja*, so?"

"You also had samples processed. But there's no record of the results in the file."

"After all these years and the state of that evidence locker, I'd be astonished if you found anything. Look, I'm a busy man, Stofberg. Can you get to the point before our new government takes over?"

"What was in that report, Colonel?"

"It was a dead end."

"I think you found him, Colonel. That you matched him up with that early case. That you know who he is."

"If we could convict criminals with theories, you'd be a champion, Stofberg. As it is, you have nothing. Why would I let a killer go free?"

Stofberg stared at him without answering. Adriaan snorted and walked away. Stofberg was digging, getting too close. Adriaan would have to make sure his line of inquiry was quashed.

After De Beer left his blood on the car door at the zoo, Adriaan had had it tested. The results came back negative for human DNA. It had puzzled the hell out of the techs. It sounded like nonsense, the stuff of myth and nightmare, a monster preying on humans. Nobody would have believed it. But Adriaan had known Benjamin De Beer, had seen what he was capable of. There was no doubt in his mind that the man wasn't human. Not a day had gone by since the incident at the zoo that Adriaan hadn't thought about taking that animal down. He kept his investigation off the books, though, leading the official line of inquiry away from De Beer. The trail had been cold for so long, Adriaan had almost given up.

Kalo pulled into Berg's parking spot at John Vorster Square. In front of them loomed the granite monolith. Adriaan had always been proud to walk into that front entrance. This was all he ever wanted to do. Find the criminal, destroy the enemy. But the thought of going in there now, dealing with the bureaucratic fallout of the bombing instead of hunting De Beer, felt oppressive.

"You right, Boss?"

Adriaan came out of his reverie, contemplating the meaning of De Beer's return. "I need you to do something for me, Kalo. On the quiet, see?"

Kalo nodded.

"I need to find someone. Double pay if you do."

Kalo's smile seemed to extend beyond the confines of his face. "You give me a name, Boss. It's done."

"I don't have a name. Couldn't find anything on her either." Adriaan took the faded photograph out of his wallet, pointing at the girl.

"Nice. You want me to take care of her?"

Adriaan considered it for a moment. "No. Not yet."

14

Tuesday
DECEMBER 21, 2010

"Homicides, all of them. According to the coroner reports they were killed before their bodies were burned." Theo yawned. He dropped the notebook on his desk. "Only the last two in here were part of the Angel Killer investigation, though."

"He started a new notebook."

"If it's the same guy, he only played with the idea of fire in the beginning. Or he was a huge bungler." Theo pointed to the list of names on his computer screen. "These first girls, in the late fifties, only had partial burns. The strangulation marks were still visible. After the mid-seventies, the bodies were all beyond recognition. That's a really slow learning curve."

"Or he changed his MO. But why?" Alet looked at the printouts of case-file pictures spread out chronologically on the floor in front of her, all of them blond females, all of them vaguely resembling one another. She took out the picture she'd found of Trudie from the seventies, when her hair was long and blond like the others, a startled expression on her face as if she didn't expect the camera. Her eyes were pale and ethereal. Alet dropped it into the final spot. Something bothered her about the picture, but she couldn't put her finger on it; an unsettling memory, buried just beyond her reach.

Theo got up and walked to the kitchen. "Coffee?"

"It's too late, I'll never sleep."

Theo glanced at his watch. "Wine?"

Alet nodded.

"I thought you said that the DNA matches were negative." Theo

383

took a bottle of red wine from the rack and dug around in the drawer for a bottle opener.

"*Ja.*" Alet sat down on the floor, crossing her legs. "Koch said Trudie was the only one with the gene mutation."

"So was she killed because she looked like the others?"

"I don't know. I think she might have been the reason he killed them."

"What do you mean?" Theo poured the wine and handed Alet a glass.

"The victims got progressively older. Look here—they all died around the time their biological age matched up to hers. That can't be a coincidence."

Theo looked over her shoulder at the photographs. "A very old guy, then."

"Who likes blondes." Alet put a fist to her mouth, trying to stifle a yawn.

"We're talking about a huge chunk of the male population." Theo sat down next to Alet. "Why didn't he just kill Trudie Pienaar if she was his target? What do these other woman have to do with it?"

Alet's cell vibrated on the table. "Johannes? What took so long? It's after midnight already."

"Mr. Wexler admitted to selling the children."

"And Mynhardt?" There was a short silence on the other end of the line. "Please don't tell me—"

"He refused to say anything more."

"He can't explain how he pulled the whole thing off without implicating Mynhardt and Jana Terblanche." Alet shifted in her seat, watching Theo at the computer. Theirs was an uneasy truce. She had apologized to him for her outburst, he in turn for his unflattering remarks, but the air wasn't quite clear. Alet didn't know how to broach the subject, didn't know that she wanted to. But she needed him to help her solve the case. She'd deal with the rest later.

"Theo managed to pull the numbers off Mynhardt's cell, Johannes." Alet caught Theo's eye and smiled at him. Theo gave her a small nod and turned back to the computer screen. "Mynhardt and Wexler definitely talked, especially around the date when the Bravermans were in town."

"It does not prove anything by itself."

"What about the Skosana incident the other night at Zebra House?"

"Mr. Wexler said Skosana was angry that he had not arranged another buyer. He wanted to get paid a second time for the same child, a six-month-old girl."

Alet felt alarmed that the baby was still in Skosana's possession. "Where are they keeping her?"

"Mr. Skosana has a girlfriend on the Terblanche farm."

"Magda Kok." Alet could kick herself. She remembered the cradle. It had been right there in front of her. Magda looked after the children while they were waiting to be sold off. "Did you send someone out there?"

"Child Services has taken custody of the baby and the older child. There is a warrant out for the arrest of Gareth Skosana and his associates."

"Ngwenya?"

"I will interview him when you do your pointing-out."

"Oh. *Ja*. That." Alet had forgotten about the witness statement she was scheduled to give at the scene. The charges against her would not be dropped until her hearing. She had to convince a review board of the events of that night. If Ngwenya could be implicated in the Braverman killings, her shooting him might be viewed as justified.

"I need to talk to Wexler."

"Constable—"

"Please, Johannes. He knows the truth about Trudie. I know I can get him to talk."

A brief silence. "Perhaps you are right."

Alet hung up the phone, a heaviness settling over her as she emptied her glass. Theo motioned to refill it, his hands poised on the wine bottle. Alet waved him away. "No. I . . . I need to go to sleep." She sank into the couch, her head too heavy to hold up any longer.

"I'll get you a pillow and a—"

Theo's silhouette fractured in her vision. She fought the depths pulling at her, trying to keep up conversation, but sleep enticed her to its molten core, and she gave up.

•   •   •

A persistent buzzing clawed at Alet's inertia. She tried to find the cause, her senses muffled. Her fingers found her phone on the ground next to the couch, its vibration sending an unpleasant tickle up her arm. Its journey between the floor and her ear was glacial.

"Hallo?" Alet was met with silence, the call disconnected. She tried to pry her eyes open. Theo's name came up as a missed call; in fact, there were several missed calls, two from Koch. Alet noticed the time on her phone. "*Fok*." It was ten-thirty already. She was supposed to have met with Koch at nine. She sat up, realizing she was only wearing her T-shirt. Her jeans lay neatly folded on the coffee table.

Alet pressed the redial button on her phone.

"Alet?" Theo aspirated her name, relief in his voice. "I've been calling all morning."

"I just woke up." Alet tried to clear the fog from her mind as she dressed. "Last night . . . I must have been exhausted."

"You were pretty out of it."

"What's going on?"

"Turn on SABC 1."

Alet reached for the remote on the coffee table. The screen sprung to life after a few seconds, the image of a black female reporter in a beige suit jacket jerking onto the screen.

". . . death toll on the roads now nearing eight hundred for December. I'm here, on the outskirts of Khayelitsha Township, where a car veered off the road hours ago and crashed into a convenience store."

Behind the reporter, men were working on the crumpled wreck of a blue sedan, its nose smashed into the wall of a small square building covered in bright advertisements. Groceries lay scattered on the sidewalk. The frame cut to a prerecorded clip. A man, dressed in a hotel porter uniform, gestured toward the wreck, other brown faces looking over his shoulder at the camera. "I had to jump to get out of the way. Others too!"

The reporter's face appeared on the screen again. "The cause of the accident has not been confirmed yet, but it is believed that the driver, identified as a professor at the University of Cape Town, lost control of the vehicle."

Alet felt cold.

"It's Koch," Theo confirmed. "They've been running the story for the past couple of hours. I spoke to the police. He's in critical condition . . . Alet?"

Alet took her hand away from her mouth. "We were supposed to meet today, Theo." Alet grabbed her jeans from the pile on the coffee table and finished dressing. She lost her balance, one leg in her pants, and banged her knee against the table. "*Eina. Fok!*"

"Are you all right?"

"*Ja* . . . I don't know." Alet sat down on the couch and took a deep breath. "You think this might be the killer? That he found out Koch was onto him?"

"It was a car crash, Alet. The policeman I spoke to said it looks like he swerved to miss a baboon in the road. They're all over the place that side of town."

"This stinks, Theo."

"I know." Theo sighed. "Listen, I ran prints against that partial. It's not Jana Terblanche."

"What about Mynhardt?"

"Corruption is one thing, Alet, but murder—"

"You read the TRC testimony. Just because Mynhardt was never prosecuted doesn't mean a thing. If he was involved with a death squad, he's capable of this. He's been making a lot of money with this baby thing. If Trudie threatened to expose him . . . Don't tell me he wouldn't have done whatever it took to keep her quiet."

"I thought you were looking for this weird serial-killer guy."

"This is all connected somehow, Theo. Please. Rule Mynhardt out, then, if nothing else."

"Okay, okay."

"I'm going to the hospital. I'll see you after."

Alet had learned a long time ago that if you looked confident in what you were doing, people rarely questioned you. The same was true when she walked into intensive care and announced at the desk that she was Koch's daughter. The receptionist directed her to a waiting room where the other family members had gathered. Alet slipped down the hall to Koch's room. She could pick out the familiar smell of blood masked by disinfectant. Koch's wispy gray hair was pasted to his scalp, and his frozen face had a sallow color. A gash ran from his forehead down the side of his nose and right cheek, and a plastic brace enfolded his neck and back. Wires attached to hidden places on his body, springing forth from his hospital gown in a tangled web. A huge plastic tube snaked from his mouth, the respirator beeping with reassuring regularity. It was hard to reconcile this damaged body with the peculiar little man who had given her such grief.

Alet opened the locker next to Koch's bed. His glasses were sealed in a plastic bag, the right lens cracked, the frame bent, resting on a shelf next to a pair of shoes, a watch and a wedding ring. It was a miracle they weren't looted off his body at the scene. A tan briefcase had been slid into the top shelf of the locker. Alet reached for it.

"Miss Koch? You shouldn't be in here." The nurse smiled sympathetically. "I know it's hard. I promise we'll let you know if there is any change."

Alet quickly closed the locker door, the briefcase tucked under her arm. "I wanted to take his things home before they . . ."

The nurse nodded. "That's probably a good idea." She touched Alet's arm. "There's always hope," she said. "Remember, your father is in God's hands."

"They ran a toxicology report, didn't they? What did they find?"

The nurse's hand froze, a confused frown nestling into her homely features. "I don't know if the results are back yet."

"Do you know how it happened?"

The nurse shook her head. "I'm sorry."

"Thank you." Alet walked past the waiting-room door and out of the hospital, her heart racing. Only once she was on the road did it feel like she could breathe again. She couldn't accept that it had been an accident. Koch had found something and he was going to tell her, she was sure of it. Someone wanted to make sure that it didn't happen.

Alet turned into the university's empty parking lot and reached for Koch's briefcase. It contained a wallet, keys, a half-eaten ham sandwich carefully rewrapped in cellophane, folders with grade sheets for the semester and three rolls of cherry-flavored sweets. Alet went through everything, desperate to find a clue as to why Koch wanted to meet, but nothing seemed out of the ordinary. She cut through the campus, Koch's keys in her pocket. The grounds were eerily quiet, the quad empty in the lazy afternoon sun, the academic staff on vacation.

Only the truly dedicated would be here now, instead of spending vacation time with their families.

Alet had found Koch's key card in his wallet. She went up the nearest stairwell to the third floor, but she realized she'd made a wrong turn somewhere when she hit a dead end. She traced her path back to the stairwell, the sound of her footsteps exaggerated on the tiled floors. Koch's name was on a door at the end of the next passage. She reached for his keys in her pocket and tested a couple before finding the right one. Koch's office had no windows, so she flipped the light switch, dreading the fact that the fluorescent lights might be seen by a zealous security guard.

The room was pristine, the way she remembered it, the faint smell of body odor lingering in the stagnant air. She sat down behind his desk, bumping her foot against the backboard. It was cheap, probably not designed for tall people. Koch's computer wasn't password-protected. Not a good sign. Digging around on his hard drive, it was obvious that he didn't keep anything of value there. Koch was old-school, from an era of paper and filling forms out by hand. Alet sighed as she eyed the mammoth row of locked filing cabinets against the wall.

She unlocked the cabinets with a small key on Koch's key ring and started searching for the obvious first. UNIE, POLICE . . . she even looked to see if there was a file under her own name or that of her father, but came up empty. She realized that she would have to go through each and every one of them, A through Z. The files were mostly administrative, student papers, exams, grade sheets. Koch, for all his neatness, was a pack rat. Curious, she flipped through the file marked ENGELMAN. It contained a research proposal, something about radiation and the mutation of virus DNA when present in a host organism. She wasn't sure what it meant, except that dead rats and bunnies were probably involved.

A noise came from somewhere down the hall, an unintentional stumble. Alet dashed to switch the light off. She listened as faint footsteps grew more distinct and stopped just outside Koch's office. The door handle wiggled, resisting the intruder's attempts to open it. There was a pause. At the sound of someone fiddling with the lock, Alet darted to Koch's desk and ducked under it, folding herself double to fit the small space. The fluorescent lights sputtered to life again.

The intruder was a man, judging by his sure, heavy step. He stopped in front of the desk, his brown *vel* shoes inches away from her. Alet heard him page through the calendar on Koch's desk and then drop it without ceremony. He walked over to the filing cabinets and started to pull paper out of the files. He wasn't trying to be neat, that was for sure.

Alet's phone vibrated in her pocket. She fumbled to find it, adrenaline flooding her veins. For a moment the room froze in silence, Alet sure that the sound of her furious heartbeat would betray her presence. The intruder took two steps, then veered toward the bookcase next to the desk. Alet tried to see under the backboard, but the space was too narrow. She could barely make out the hems of a pair of jeans.

The man was dumping books from Koch's shelves. Alet heard a metallic clicking sound. She stuck her head out from under the desk, craning to see what he was doing, and realized with a shock that the man wasn't standing next to the bookshelf any longer. Alet put her arms out just in time to stop her skull from slamming into the side of the desk as the man grabbed her from behind. Alet screamed. He pulled her by her hair, his other hand wrapped around her neck. She fought for breath, struggling against him, managing to push him off. He tried to grab hold of her again, but she stomped on his instep. He cursed and let go. Alet tried to stand up, but he thrust her back to the floor and ran. She grabbed the desk and pulled herself up. Her legs shook so badly that she could barely stand.

"Come back here," she yelled as she reached the door, the hallway empty. She realized the absurdity of her words. What was he going to do? Turn back and duke it out with her? By the time she reached the stairwell there was no sign of the man.

Theo had raced over to Koch's office after she called him, his face ashen when he laid eyes on her. "You should have brought me with," he said, visibly shaken. "We have to get you to the hospital so a doctor can check you out."

"I'm not going to a hospital." Alet got up from Koch's chair. She felt a little dizzy, but the feeling passed. Paper and folders formed a carpet on the office floor, books stacked knee-high.

"Alet."

"Theo, I'm fine." Alet touched her throat. It felt bruised, swollen.

"You could have internal injuries."

Alet held her hand up, motioning for him to stop.

"Quit being so pigheaded," Theo said through clenched teeth.

Alet went over to the gaping hole in the bookshelf. "He obviously knew about the safe." Attached to the wall, no more than fifteen centimeters deep, was a flat rectangular steel box that nestled perfectly behind the books on the shelf. Alet had found the key to it in the bunch from Koch's briefcase. Inside was an envelope thick with R100 notes, a folder, and Koch's passport.

"What was he looking for?"

"Maybe this?" Alet removed the folder from the safe box. A wave of nausea washed over her and she had to hold on to the bookshelf until it passed. Theo gave her an I-told-you-so look. He helped her back to Koch's chair and took the folder from her.

"Research notes." Theo leafed through the pages. "Looks like the outline of a book. Something about the practical implementation of forensics in the field. Lots of notes here on cases he worked with your dad. I'll have to read it, but it doesn't look like anything damning. Bone-dry textbook stuff, if you ask me." He put the folder down. "Alet, do you remember anything about the guy who attacked you?"

Alet suppressed a giggle at the seriousness of his expression. "I was a little preoccupied while he was strangling me, Theo." The hazy image of a pair of brown shoes and jeans danced in front of her, a dark outline walking away. She took a breath and tried to remember with detachment. He had grabbed her from behind. Sense memory brought back the pressure around her throat. She pushed back the panic, fighting her raising heart rate. "He was taller than me."

"A lot?"

Alet shook her head. The smell of leather, something clinging to her skin. "He wore gloves."

"Good. What else?"

"His clothes were . . . It was jeans and a shirt but it didn't look modern. It was too . . . formal . . . I don't know." His skin against hers. "He smelled sweet, but not pleasant."

"What about his hair?"

Alet frowned, willing the memory into being, but stopping short. "He ran away." She could remember nothing higher than his dark back, as if the rest of him didn't exist. "I think he was wearing a hat or a balaclava maybe . . ." Frustration gripped her. "I just can't remember."

"It's okay. Don't worry." Theo suddenly had his arms around her, holding her to him. Alet felt the wetness of her eyes sinking into his shirt. She wanted to push him away, swallow it back, but then something dawned on her. She felt safe. It had been a long time since she'd felt this way. Theo ran his hand over her hair, pressed his lips to her forehead, the gesture so tender it made her well up again. She looked up into his eyes, dark brown melting into hers. Then their lips touched, she didn't know how. They both seemed perfectly still, holding each other steady while the world around them spun into chaos.

Theo broke the kiss first, a frown sneaking across his brow. "Are you okay?"

Alet pushed away, suddenly irritated with herself. "I'm sorry." She couldn't look him in the eyes. She focused on his pursed lips, his jaw tight, unforgiving. "I'm heading to George."

Theo's shoulders folded in on his chest. "You can stay. I—"

"Mathebe is waiting for me. I need to talk to Wexler tonight. Get ahead of this thing."

Theo ran his hand over his face. "That's it, then?" His arms shielded him against her.

"I don't know."

Theo's face grew hard. "Fine. Let me know when you do."

"Please understand—"

"It wasn't an offer of marriage, Alet."

Alet balled her fists. "Don't be a bastard."

Theo snorted. "Don't just expect me to be there every time you need help. I need to look out for myself too."

She tried to find something to say, but she could only think of harsh comebacks. Why were things between them always so complicated? She wasn't even sure what she felt for him. Perhaps the things she felt around him, the flirting, the closeness, were just ghostly reminders of what they'd had before, ruined the day their careers in STF were over.

"I have to go," Alet said to break the uneasy silence. She handed the contents of Koch's safe to Theo. "Please hold on to this. See what you can make of it."

Theo nodded and wordlessly followed her to her car. Their eyes met briefly as she backed out, an intensity in his expression that she couldn't read.

A constable from Bloemfontein called Alet as she was nearing the George city limits. They couldn't find anything on Theresa Morgan; it had been too long. But one of the secretaries gave them the number of a woman who used to teach at the school around the time Theresa would have gone there, a Mrs. Uys. Alet called the number as soon as the constable hung up.

"Hallo?"

"Mrs. Uys?"

"*Ja?*" The voice sounded sprightly for a woman in her nineties.

"I'm sorry," Alet said. "I'm looking for a Mrs. Marie Uys, who taught music at a high school in Bloemfontein around 1940."

"Oh. My mother-in-law."

"My name is Constable Alet Berg. I'm with the SAPS investigating an old case. I was wondering if I could talk to her."

The woman at the other end of the line paused for a moment. "She's in a nursing home, Constable Berg. She gets confused easily, and we couldn't take care of her anymore."

"Could you please give me the number? It's crucial that I talk to her."

George nestled against the coastline in the distance. Alet took the exit, snaking down the hill through the township, toward the city center. She pulled up to a gas station to write down the number.

"Marie Uys speaking." Mrs. Uys measured out each word, as if it was an effort get them out.

"Mrs. Uys, I'm Constable Berg, with the police. I'm trying to locate someone and I was hoping you could help."

"What's that?"

"Mrs. Uys, can you hear me?"

"*Ja.*"

"I'm wondering if you remember a student. Theresa Morgan."

"Who?"

Alet sighed. The old woman was hard of hearing and the poor cell reception didn't make things easier. "Theresa Morgan." There was a long pause. "Hallo? Mrs. Uys?"

"Tessa."

Alet's pulse quickened. "*Ja.* You remember her?"

"Why do you want to know about Tessa? Who are you?"

"I'm looking for her, Mrs. Uys. I was hoping you could help. I know it's been a long time but—"

"She was gifted, but lazy. Never practiced. Her dad died, you know. A nice man. Back in . . ."

"Mrs. Uys? Are you still there?"

"*Ja?*"

"Do you remember what happened to Tessa?"

"She was always with that boy, you know. She was nice, but he never spoke a word to anyone."

"Mrs. Uys, do you remember his name?"

"What's that, dear?"

"The boy Tessa was friends with. What was his name?"

"Oh. Let me think. It was a good Bible name. Reuben? No. I don't . . . *O ja*, Tessa used to call him Ben."

Alet navigated the subdivision's stop streets. The houses were all surrounded by high walls, some with spikes or barbed wire, some with signs warning that they were electrified. She remembered walking down the street to play with neighbor kids when she was a child, riding her bicycle to school and netball practice. The streets in George were devoid of children, and even adults seemed scared to leave the confines of their own fortresses. Alet pulled up to the curb across the street from the George Police office, where Mathebe stood waiting for her. She motioned for him to get into the car.

"I have a name. Ben. Tessa Morgan's teacher, Mrs. Uys, said they were going to get married."

"Is there a last name?"

Alet shook her head, disappointed that Mathebe didn't seem excited by the break.

"Then we have little to go on." Mathebe looked uncharacteristically weary.

"It's a start," Alet said. "Be glad it isn't something more common, like Hendrik or Johan."

"Did Mrs. Uys know what happened after they got married?"

"She lost contact after Theresa's father's death. But listen to this: this Ben would have had to do military service back then when he got out of high school, right? Maybe we can find him that way." Alet tried to remember her timeline. "Andrew Morgan died in 1948 when Theresa was at the university. So around that time? It's worth a try."

Mathebe nodded. "We have to go," he said. "The room is prepared for us."

"Has Wexler changed his tune yet?"

"He refuses to implicate anyone but himself and Miss Pienaar. I do not know that there is more we can do."

Alet stopped Mathebe before he could get out of the car. "One more thing, Sergeant. Do you know anyone in Cape Town? We need to find out if there was anything unusual about Koch's accident that wasn't in the report."

"I will make a call."

Jeffrey Wexler looked up listlessly as Alet and Mathebe entered the interrogation room. He had dark circles under his eyes, his pink complexion almost as pale as his cropped gray hair. He leaned on the table with his elbows, his back rounded, his hands cuffed. Alet sat down opposite him. Mathebe remained standing, his posture rigid as a stick figure's.

"Mr. Wexler."

"Alet, luv. How nice of you to visit."

"Constable Berg," Mathebe said tersely.

"Psh!" Wexler looked away.

"Can I get you anything?" Alet said calmly. She smiled at him. "A Coke, maybe?"

Wexler shook his head, his fingers drumming on the table.

"Look, Jeff, we found evidence tying you to Trudie's death."

"You have nothing." Wexler smiled. "If you did, I wouldn't still be in a holding cell."

Alet put her finger to her mouth, enjoying the feeling of slipping into a different persona, the one she used whenever she had to interrogate a suspect. It was self-assured, even a little arrogant. Most importantly, it made her feel invincible. She sometimes wished she had the guts to take it home with her. She dropped the file in front of Wexler. "We've contacted all of the foreign visitors in your guest book. Their local police were quite obliging to help us out with this. I think the thought of babies being sold and smuggled into their countries didn't sit well with them either.

"Quite a few of the families are willing to testify to escape prosecution. Their stories are all the same. An overseas contact instructed them to go to Zebra House. The money was left, in cash, in their rooms when they checked out. Then they were met on some desolate stretch of highway by someone with a child. We have a statement from Tilly Pienaar and some foreign bank statements in your safe." Alet leaned forward. "You are going away, Jeff. How long is up to you."

Wexler looked unimpressed. "What do you want?"

"I know you and Trudie go way back. That you helped her abduct Tilly."

"I'd like that Coke," Wexler said in a bored tone.

Alet looked over at Mathebe. "Sergeant? Would you mind?"

Mathebe hesitated for a moment, then nodded, leaving the room.

Wexler leaned back, a self-assured grin on his lips. "If you know so much, luv, why do you need me to tell you anything?"

Alet bit her lip. She had hoped that he would cave, but if he wouldn't talk to Mathebe, she was stupid to believe that he would just spill the beans to her. She decided to change tactics. "Why are you protecting him? Mynhardt, I mean."

"Couldn't give two hoots about him, luv. But I'm in here, and as you pointed out, I'll be in here for a while. You obviously have no idea who your boss is."

"Oh, I'm pretty sure I do."

"If you did, you would drop this and go back to where you came from, darling."

"What about Skosana? A big man like you ran away from the Thokoloshe? What is he? A meter and a bit?"

Wexler banged on the table, his mouth locked in a grimace of disgust. "You want to know about Mynhardt? You talk to Skosana. He's been paying Mynhardt off for years to look the other way. Sometimes they exchange favors. It's Christmas, after all."

"What about Trudie? How does she fit into all of this?"

Wexler locked eyes with Alet. "She doesn't." Even as he said the words, Alet knew he was hiding something. She could smell his sweat, see the panic in his eyes. The guilty ones always started sweating.

Alet leaned on the table, dropping her voice to barely a whisper. "I know who she was." She hesitated for a moment, not sure if her gamble would pay off. "I know her real name was Theresa Morgan and I know her secret."

Mathebe walked back into the interrogation room, a can of Coke in his hand. He looked from Alet to Wexler with a confused expression. Wexler put his face in his hands and started sobbing.

1996

Adriaan

"Our aim is to bear witness to what has happened in our country. Investigate human-rights violations, restore the victims' dignity, and in some cases, consider amnesty for those who have applied."

"So criminals will walk free?" The speaker was a brash Australian, his face barely discernible in the sea of journalists and microphones.

Cameras flashed intermittently, pointed at the Truth and Reconciliation Committee panel at the front of the room. The archbishop folded his hands, a look of exasperation passing between him and the other members. They had been at it for almost an hour, trying to explain the spirit of Ubuntu to the press of the world. A difficult concept, perhaps, but in this land, where retribution for the sins of the past would end in bloodshed, the spirit of African forgiveness was the only viable option.

"We all have to live together now," one of the female members on the panel volunteered. "You must remember, no section of the population, white or black, escaped the violence, the abuse of their human rights. We want to avoid a victor's justice. Nobody is exempt from appearing before the commission."

"But certainly those in the apartheid government will have to pay for what they did?"

"We are here to hear the truth. It is the only way to heal our land, to reconcile our people. It is a crucial step in our peaceful transition to democracy. It is up to the accused to prove that his actions were politically motivated, or that he was forced to commit these atrocities by those higher up on the command chain. If it is found that he has fully disclosed his crime, and that it was proportionate, amnesty will be considered."

"But, Archbishop—"

"Ladies and gentlemen, we have a long road ahead of us. Perhaps you will gain a better understanding once you have spent some time here with us."

Adriaan turned the television off. He sat down next to the bed, where the shriveled figure of Van Vuuren lay, an oxygen mask over his face. "How do you like that, Brigadier? Seven thousand have applied for amnesty. Everybody pointing fingers, crying to mamma that they were only following orders."

Van Vuuren looked at him with dull eyes, a man counting his last hours. Around him the room seemed to echo the sentiment. This was what Van Vuuren was left with after devoting his life to his country, to his ideals. Adriaan felt depressed by the sparse surroundings, the furniture old and dilapidated, the curtains threadbare and dusty.

"The generals have denied that they knew. Imagine that, hey. Back then they gave out medals, now they're hanging their men out to dry. And you . . ." He smirked. "Well, your timing has been impeccable, hasn't it? You always knew when it was time to quit the party."

Van Vuuren started coughing, his body convulsing from the effort, his chest heaving for air. The doctor had said it was a matter of days now. With him died Adriaan's only hope of proving that he was acting under orders. Not that he had any intention of appearing before the commission. He refused to justify himself to a bunch of dimwits hugging it out. What he did was necessary for the survival of his people, for their place in this country. They all wanted apartheid, but it was men like him who had to get their hands dirty to make it possible.

Adriaan reached for his hat. "Well, so long, you old bastard," he said. "You're getting what you deserve." Van Vuuren turned his head away.

Adriaan made a call on the pay phone outside. Kalo picked up.

"Is it done?"

"Jim won't be a problem."

"Good." Adriaan couldn't help but smile. The *askari*'s name had been on the list of asylum-seekers, and he had dispatched Kalo to deal with it. Nobody else would talk. He had made sure of it. "I have your money," he said. "Meet me at the usual place."

There was a message from the general on Adriaan's desk when he walked into John Forster Square. He looked briefly at the internal memo and then dropped it into the trash. A meeting had been scheduled for the following week. Adriaan had a pretty good idea what it was about. The police were getting rid of the old guard, one by one, sparing themselves the embarrassment if one of their own popped up in front of the news cameras confessing their sins, a golden handshake included in the deal if they went quietly. The police was getting darker and more incompetent every day, promoting new officers who could barely read and write. Affirmative action, they called it. Adriaan had another word for it. He'd be damned if they pushed him out. He had quite enough on all of them to give them an incentive to keep him happy.

He glanced at the clock, a strange nervousness in his stomach. After much pleading and subtly veiled threats, he had arranged with Gerda to meet Alet for the first time in eleven years later that day. He wondered who his daughter had turned out to be. From the occasional surveillance he put on her, he knew she was smart, a bit of a loner. Like her old man. The thought made him smile. Adriaan opened his desk drawer and pulled out an envelope with photographs, retrieving the latest one. It was of Alet at the movies, dressed in a sloppy sweater, her wide-set eyes rimmed with black eyeliner, her dark hair long and unkempt. If she had grown up in his house, he would never have allowed her to walk around like that.

Adriaan glanced at his watch. Once his business with Kalo was done, there would be just enough time to shower and change. In the car, he double-checked the magazine of the Makarov he had stashed under the seat, a souvenir taken from a consignment they had delivered to Inkatha before the elections. It had come in handy on occasion, a gun that was traceable only to the terrorists of the old days, the heroes of the present. His bile rose at the thought.

Adriaan exchanged the Mercedes for an old Toyota *bakkie* he kept at a garage near the airport. He took the highway back into Johannesburg and pulled the *bakkie* into an alley across the street from a Hillbrow bar. The area had been abandoned by whites years ago, and violent crime was now rampant, the derelict apartment buildings filled with prostitutes and illegals. He watched the entrance in his rearview mirror. Kalo appeared in the doorway a few minutes later, clinging to a girl who teetered on a pair of bright pink heels, her skirt so short that Adriaan could take a good guess at the color of her underwear. Kalo slipped the girl money and slapped her on her ass when she turned to go back inside. He swayed across the street.

"Hey, Chief!" Kalo reeked of Klipdrift and day-old sweat. He climbed into the passenger seat.

"What did you say to the whore?"

Kalo smiled. "She should keep my seat warm."

Adriaan reached into his jacket and pulled out the envelope. Kalo opened it, counting the notes inside, his face twisting in mock concern.

"Is a little light, my *bra*."

Adriaan stiffened. He couldn't get used to the familiarity, the disrespect the blacks thought they were entitled to now. "It's what we agreed on."

Kalo shook his head. "A man like me has responsibility, Chief. Things are getting expensive, hey. *Eish* . . ." He pursed his lips together as if considering the situation. "If that Jim went to the commission, who knows? You'd be in big trouble. But I found him. I made sure he doesn't talk ever. I take care of you, *bra*. You're my number-one priority." He touched his chest. "I'm not a greedy man, hey." He smiled, the village idiot.

"How much?"

Kalo bounced the envelope in his palm as if he was weighing it. "One more like this, I think."

Adriaan kept his expression blank, his hate in check. "I don't have it on me."

"No worries, *bra*." Kalo patted him on the shoulder. "I check you're good for it."

"Let me give you a ride." Adriaan turned the key in the ignition. "We can stop at the cash machine."

Kalo's grin broadened until it threatened to engulf his face. "You look out for me, Chief. Like I look out for you. 'Cause we're brothers."

Adriaan drove through the alley, making a right deeper into Hillbrow. Instead of taking the ramp to the highway, he stopped under an old underpass covered with graffiti. Traffic rumbled overhead, the noise amplified by the concrete structure. Kalo's initial confusion gave way to understanding when he saw the Makarov in Adriaan's hand.

Kalo's nostrils flared. His lips pulled away from his teeth in a macabre smile. "Is just a joke, Chief. A joke. You know Kalo will never talk."

"You've become greedy, Kalo."

"No, Boss. Honest."

Adriaan pressed the gun to Kalo's forehead. "Get out."

"I found the girl."

"What are you talking about?"

"That girl from the picture."

Adriaan lowered the gun.

"I was going to tell you, Boss. Bonus for the money. No lies. But I give it to you free now, okay?"

"You told me years ago you couldn't find her."

"I saw her. Same as the picture. I swear."

"You've been lying to me, Kalo."

Kalo raised his hands, the whites of his eyes large. "No. Honest, Chief."

"Where is she?"

"I tell you, Boss. Sure I tell you. But Kalo needs to go home first, okay?"

Adriaan lifted the gun. "You tell me now."

"*Eish*, no. I don't—"

Adriaan pulled the trigger. Kalo's eyes looked right at him, his mouth still open in denial as blood and brain matter spattered the interior of the car. Adriaan clenched his jaw at the mess, a high-pitched ringing in his ears. He'd have to clean it up now. He'd be late. He wondered if Kalo had been telling the truth about the girl. She could be the way to get to De Beer, and Adriaan might have wasted his only chance to find her. He brushed the thought aside. Kalo was loyal to nothing except money. If he really knew the girl's whereabouts, he'd have put a price on the information a long time ago. Adriaan leaned across Kalo and opened the passenger-side door. He kicked at the body until it fell out of the car and landed with a dull thud on the ground. Adriaan made a U-turn and drove back to the airport.

Tessa

"My son, he went to work that morning. When evening came, I was worried. I stood by the gate to look for him. But he did not come. Then my neighbor ran to me. She said to come to her house. To come look on the TV. I did not understand. It was the news, on the TV. They said the police shot terrorists. White police, they stood there with AKs. The one smiled at us. They showed the bodies of men on the ground. They were all young men from our village. Then I saw him. My son. He was dead. My son he was not a terrorist. My son was a good man. He worked to bring money, because my legs are bad, there is no job for me. Nobody came to tell me my son was dead. I had to see it on the TV."

"Trudie, luv." Jeff reached across the bar to switch the radio off, a warning in his voice.

Tessa slowly came back to the present, her thoughts still with the grieving mother from Craddock. Across Zebra House's bar, ruddy-faced men in khaki shirts averted their eyes to the bottom of their brandy-and-Cokes. Tessa wiped her cheeks, realizing they were wet, sorrow crushing her chest in empathy with the woman, like all the women she'd listened to over the last few months. Clips of the TRC hearings were broadcast every day, every story more horrific, more heart-wrenching than the next.

"*Ja.* Put the game on instead of that rubbish."

Tessa locked eyes with the young Terblanche, home for the holidays from Agriculture College. He had become muscular, built like a rugby player, his hair longer than his father would have allowed when he was still living at home. A petite young blond thing in a tie-dyed top clung to him, all giggles and blandness. She wasn't from around there. Old man Terblanche was sick. Lung cancer, his wife had told Tessa the last time she saw her in town. By the look of him, Boet Terblanche was already throwing his weight around, trying out the role of master.

"Nobody here wants to listen to them whine, *Tannie* Trudie." Boet's defiance gave way to insecurity under her glare. If he was being shown the ropes at the farm, he probably knew that they needed Tessa's land.

"This woman did nothing. Her son was killed for nothing. Aren't you interested in the truth? In the history of what happened in this country?"

"That's what she says, but you know they were all in on it. Murdering people, even their own, calling themselves freedom fighters. 'Cause that's the African mentality. They're a bunch of savages." A few of the men at the bar nodded in agreement, egging Boet on.

"You don't think what those policemen did was savage?"

"They did their jobs. These blacks claim they were so oppressed? Let me remind you, nobody in this country has been more oppressed than the Afrikaner in the Boer War, or has everybody forgotten that? Our people suffered more for this land than the blacks ever did. But we didn't go out killing everybody. We rebuilt the nation. We didn't need to become terrorists or thieves or murderers to do it."

Tessa's neck muscles stiffened. She felt so angry that tears burned behind her eyes again. "Do you know anything about your own history, Boet? Do you know about the Broederbond? The Citizen's Co-operation Bureau? Let me tell you, there is blood on all our hands. Nobody in this country is innocent."

Boet lifted his chin, a young man's arrogance glaring down at her. "I know my history, *Tannie* Trudie. Those people can change it now to make themselves look like little angels because they're in charge, but we all know what they did."

"They had no choice. Things would only have gotten worse if—"

"They all just want free handouts, or they take it." A chorus of "*Ja*," and "Hear, hear," went up around him. Boet had a light in his eyes, his confidence growing. "Those people don't want to work for anything. Nobody in here has had a good night's sleep in a long time because of the cattle thefts. Even if they get caught, nothing happens to them. Murderers don't spend more than a few years in jail now, so why should they care? They are trying to wipe us out. That, *Tannie* Trudie, is the truth of what's going on in this country."

"Don't you dare talk to me about truth, all of you. All these years you've had it *lekker* while the people working on your farms lived like animals. The consequences of what you did are only coming back to haunt you now, that's all."

"I've worked for what I have," said De Hart, one of the farmers. The others chorused agreement.

"You had opportunities, education, support, you had—" Tessa struggled to get the words out, outrage tripping her tongue. From across the restaurant, Tilly glared at her, her arms full of empty glasses and dirty plates as she cleared tables. She's embarrassed by me, Tessa thought.

Jeff put his hands on Tessa's shoulders. "Tru, why don't you take a break?"

Around the room, hostility radiated back at Tessa. She felt acid panic rising from her stomach. Everybody's eyes were on her. She frantically scrambled out from behind the bar, breaking into a run once she got outside.

"Trudie!" Jeff caught up to her on Kerk Street. "Wait, luv."

"You didn't say anything. You just stood there while that bastard . . ." Tessa heaved for air through her sobs, unwilling to look at him.

"Look, Tru, you have to understand where they're coming from. Young Terblanche has a chip on his shoulder, sure, but a rumor's been going around that the ANC might start a land reclamation, that they will lose their farms. They're all from here. Most of them have never gone farther than Oudtshoorn since the day they were born."

"Ignorant, stupid! Just like their fathers and grandfathers."

"They are just people, and they're scared." Jeff pulled Tessa to him, but she pushed away.

"They still think they're owed something." Tessa's words were almost incoherent, her hysteria growing. "They cling to this myth, this lie of their so-called noble ancestors."

"Nobody wants to be told that they're bad, Tru. My mum always used to say that everybody loves to remind you of their suffering, because suffering makes them right. Let them have their Boer War and their indignation. It's all they know. All they have left."

"I was there, Jeff. I've seen what people can do to each other. White, black, it doesn't matter. All I feel when I listen to those hearings is shame, regret that I didn't do more. My own daughter thinks I'm a loon, but how can I remain quiet? And if I speak up, nobody will believe me."

"Let me take you home. Tomorrow when you come back—"

"I can't go back. I can't pretend that the world works the way they believe it does."

"Running away is not the answer."

"I'm done with running." Tessa looked up at him, defeat bowing her body. "Where could I even go?"

"At the end of the day, we all have to get along, Tru." Jeff reached for her, but she brushed him off.

"I own myself, Jeff. I'd rather spend the next hundred years alone than saying yes to those people."

Jeff nodded. Tessa watched him walk back to Zebra House, something hollow settling inside her.

Benjamin

The organ sounded the last bars of the hymn. As one, the congregation sat down in the polished pews. The young *dominee*, pink-cheeked and energetic, bounded up the steps to the grandiose pulpit, black robes flowing behind him. "Good morning, brothers and sisters," he said, his hands outstretched. "I welcome you in the name of Jesus Christ our Lord. Our reading today will come from Nehemiah Nine." Bible pages fluttered throughout the cavernous church like butterfly wings.

". . . they reveled in your great goodness. But they were disobedient and rebelled against you; they turned their backs on your law."

It was one of *Matrone*'s favorites. Benjamin looked up at the *dominee*, whose face gradually changed to a deeper hue as he finished the reading, ready to feverishly dissuade his congregation. God chose Israel, like God chose Benjamin. But Israel worshipped other gods, turning away from the one true God.

"What is your false god, brothers and sisters?" The *dominee* pointed a finger down the middle of the congregation. "What is keeping you from following Him?"

Benjamin dropped his gaze, blood pulsing in his ears. Had he strayed without knowing? He had always done what God demanded. The notebooks would prove it, come the Day of Judgment. Each and every one of the girls was anointed for sacrifice. God had shown him the path, pointed them out to him. But there was still one of them left. Benjamin rebelled against the thought as soon as it surfaced. Tessa was promised to him, he would not kill her. But she is also one of them, the thought pushed back. So are you. The last two abominations of man to walk the earth. No. God had promised him salvation. The Bible shook in Benjamin's trembling hands.

"Renew your vows with God, then, brothers and sisters. Go on your knees and beg him to show you the way. Let us pray so that you may tell Him how you will dedicate your life to Him. It is only in blind faith in His plan for us that we can be saved. In Jesus's name, amen."

Around Benjamin, all bowed their heads. The *dominee* gave the congregation a moment to pray silently, to vow to rid their lives of the false gods of their choosing. Sweat beaded on Benjamin's forehead, the air suddenly stifling. Please, he begged silently. Please, not Tessa. You promised. But God spoke to him. Wipe the earth of abominations, Benjamin, and you shall inherit the power of the kingdom of Heaven. Benjamin grasped the edge of the pew. He had trouble breathing. "Please," he begged. "Save her. I'll give you anything else." A woman with white-blond hair looked over at him, her lips pursed in disapproval. Benjamin put his hand over his mouth. He got up and almost ran down the aisle. The *dominee*'s raised voice drowned out his hollow footsteps on the polished floor. A young girl looked up at him with pale gray eyes as he struggled to open the heavy door. No. No. No. Benjamin's heart pounded.

He broke into the sunlit street and leaned against one of the huge white pillars of the church, crisp spring air filling his lungs, the voice of God silenced by the bustling of the Cape Town morning. Black faces filled the streets outside now, walking with a confidence, even daring, in their step. Sometimes they even ventured inside, to show that they could.

"He's not really my cup of tea either." The bald man closed the door behind him.

"E-excuse me?" Benjamin tried to regulate his breathing.

"The *dominee*. Too much doom and gloom, too many grand gestures. But my wife likes him, thinks he spices things up." The bald man walked over to him, his hand outstretched. "Nico Koch. You're the new man, aren't you? Forgive me. I recognized you from that lecture last year on quadruplex structures and the possible retardation of cell damage."

Benjamin took Koch's hand. "You know my work?"

"Son, everyone in this field knows your work. Which is a rather small sampling, I'm sorry to say. The university is lucky to have you."

"It's not official yet."

"Well, I hear the committee was impressed by your research. Or rather, I told them they should be. Those idiots wouldn't know the difference between genes and genomes."

The pressure in Benjamin's chest eased. "I've been following your work too, Professor Koch. I was hoping that perhaps I could pick your brain about a project I've been working on." He made a dismissive wave with his left hand. "But there will be plenty of time for that," he said.

"Well, in any case, it will be nice to have a fellow church man in our midst." Koch motioned to the imposing building behind them. "Few can reconcile religion with science these days, Dr. Engelman. They do not recognize that God's hand is in everything. Pity to be so close-minded."

Benjamin smiled. "Please, Nico, call me Mike."

15

Wednesday
DECEMBER 22, 2010

Alet's cell rang as she exited the gas-station shop. She balanced the coffee and fast-food bags in one arm and answered, watching Mathebe paying the attendant at the petrol pump, his brow knotted with concentration as he signed the slip and double-checked the numbers.

"Alet? Mike Engelman."

"Mike. Thanks for calling me back. Are you still in Humansdorp?"

"*Ja*, but I'll probably head to Cape Town soon. You must have heard."

"I'm sorry about the professor." Alet didn't know how to ask Mike without sounding crude, but she had run out of options. "Listen, I know this is a bad time, but I was hoping I could take you up on your offer for help. We found something the professor was researching and I'd like you to take a look at it, see if it has any bearing on the case. You understand what these things mean."

"Can you fax it to the university?"

"I'd rather not. There are some . . . anomalies the professor found in the DNA evidence, and I'd rather explain it all to you in person."

There was a brief silence. "I can drop by this morning on my way back."

"Um . . . thing is, I have to be in Joubertina for a pointing-out."

"Pardon?"

"I have to walk the local police through the crime scene of that hijacking. You know, my face . . ."

"Oh. Right. I suppose I can postpone going back for a day."

"Thanks, Mike."

Alet got into the passenger side of the van. She and Mathebe ate their breakfast in silence, watching the world around them slowly wake up as the sun peeked out over the mountains, the flow of traffic growing denser on the highway with each passing minute. Alet's pickle fell out of her bun, sauce staining her black T-shirt and jeans. As she tried to clean it up with a napkin, Mathebe reached over and handed her a wet-wipe from the glove compartment.

"I wanted to let you know that you did good work last night, Constable."

Alet looked up in surprise. "Thank you, Sergeant."

It had taken almost twenty minutes for Wexler to calm down enough to tell them about his history with Trudie. An "associate" of his in London had a nice business going, dealing with unwanted children from Eastern Europe, and he had wanted to expand. When he'd found out that Wexler had contacts in South Africa, he suggested a partnership.

"Why Unie?" Alet had pressed.

"Because it's isolated. Because . . . she was there," Wexler answered simply. "We tried again for a little while, but . . . it wasn't the same. People change, I suppose."

It seemed that it wasn't just the killer who had carried a torch for Trudie. Once Alet got Wexler talking, he offered information with little resistance. How he'd met Trudie when he was still in his teens and fallen in love. How he'd followed her to Johannesburg when she went searching for her nephew.

"What was his name?" Mathebe's pen was poised over his notepad.

"Jacob."

"Jacob Morgan," Alet said. Wexler nodded. "Also known as Jakob Mens?"

"Yes."

Alet felt a warm glow at the small victory. She had suspected it, but there had been no concrete evidence. "And Tilly?"

"Took her from the neighbors' yard in Triomf. Should have seen the state of her." Wexler shook his head. "All Trudie had wanted was a child. When she couldn't save Jacob . . ."

"Did she know what you were doing? That you got Tilly involved in your . . . business?"

"Mathilda figured things out pretty quickly once she started working at Zebra House. She wanted in. Said she needed money. All she ever talked about was getting the hell out of town one day. Never had the guts to actually do it. Shame, really. If she'd known the truth she might have."

Mathebe stepped closer to the table. "Did Mrs. Pienaar ever tell you why she decided to come to Unie?"

"Well, there was the farm. She went on about roots, and belonging. I never saw any of that, though. Poisoned roots, if you ask me. Trudie didn't have it in her to take what those people were dishing. But she was tired of running."

"Running from what, Mr. Wexler?"

Wexler's brow knotted. "His name was Ben."

Alet caught Mathebe's eye. His expression betrayed nothing. She turned back to Wexler. "Do you have a last name for Ben?"

"The only thing she told me was that I'd be dead if he ever got to us. I thought she was off her rocker till the day he found me."

"Wait. What?"

"In Cape Town, few years back. I was on a bender with some of my old mates. Showing them a good time and all. Buggers took off with some slags. Then this bloke corners mc out of nowhere."

Alet grabbed a chair and sat down, scared that she didn't hear right. "Are you telling me that you had contact with this Ben?"

"Scared the piss out of me. Got me by the neck. Couldn't swallow right a month after."

"What did he want?"

"Her, Trudie. Wanted to know where she was."

"And?"

Wexler sat a little more erect. "I said I didn't know. He sodded off."

"Just like that?"

Wexler gave her a sardonic smile. "I wasn't his type, I suppose."

"What did he look like?"

Wexler's gaze traveled to the ceiling as he remembered. "Tall. Thin. Wanker was right strong. Held me down, sure. Didn't look like he was trying."

"What about his face, his eyes, his hair? Give me something to go on."

Wexler crossed his arms, looking at Alet and Mathebe in turn. "Well, honestly, he looked a good lot like Tru."

"We have to get a sketch artist in with Wexler. If we release an iden-tikit . . ." Alet reached for one of the coffee cups perched on the dash-board. She peeled the lid back and sipped carefully, trying not to burn herself. "A man named Ben, no last name, approximately a hundred years old, looks like the murder victim, but taller. The press is going to have a field day."

Mathebe returned his take-out container to the bag. "Mrs. Pienaar changed her appearance."

Alet nodded. "She looked different in just about every picture. Glasses, wigs, hair dye, makeup, self-tanner, you name it."

"The suspect might have changed his appearance too." Mathebe turned to Alet. "It was your father's case. He would know what was in the missing Angel Killer case files, the list of suspects. He could—"

"No." Alet crossed her arms. "We have Koch's notes on the Angel case now. Maybe Mike will find something in there."

"We could be wrong about your father, Constable." Mathebe spoke softly, as if calming an upset child. "This case might have nothing to do with his death-squad involvement."

"Doesn't change what he did. What he is."

"Mrs. Pienaar deserves justice."

"And she'll get it." Alet reached for the door handle. "I'll see you in Joubertina."

Mathebe stopped her before she could get out of the car. "Perhaps, Constable, you should ask yourself why it is that you do not want to ask for your father's help."

"I don't know what you mean." Alet closed the door. She walked over to her Toyota a few parking spaces away. She felt irritated as she got onto the highway behind Mathebe, loath to be alone with her thoughts. Was Mathebe right? Was she really so angry with her father that she needed him to be in cahoots with a killer just to prove that she was justified? Maybe he simply couldn't solve this one case, the most prolific serial killer of his career. He couldn't have known about the earlier victims. It had taken a modern database and multiple computer searches to connect the dots.

Mathebe broke away at the exit. Alet eased up on the petrol when she saw Mathebe tapping his brake lights, realizing that she was almost bumper-to-bumper with him at 120 kilometers per hour. Green hills morphed into dry savannah the farther inland they went. The traffic was ungodly on the two-lane highway, and it took them nearly three hours to get to the Joubertina city limits. Captain Groenewald met them at the station. A Sergeant Mazingane was to escort Alet to the crime scene and walk her through the pointing-out. Mathebe stayed behind to interview Ngwenya.

"I can't go with, you understand?" Groenewald's tone was apologetic. "There can be no question of me leading a witness, or being anything but impartial in this case." Alet nodded. It was standard procedure. The investigating officer could be nowhere near the pointing-out, in case he was accused of intimidation. The whole case could fall apart in court.

Mazingane pulled over at the rest stop where the Bravermans had been killed. Alet stopped behind the police van. Two other officers were present—to observe, they said.

"Will you please show us where you stopped your car, Constable Berg?" Mazingane was draped in an air of new authority. At first glance, he looked a little like a young Mathebe, but he wasn't nearly as careful with his words and actions, his manner verging on insolence every time he addressed her.

"Over here." Alet walked about thirty meters past the rest stop's concrete benches and planted herself in the spot. She looked back at the crime scene: Mazingane writing on his pad, the frowns on the faces of the other two. Everything looked mundane, even innocent, the terror of that evening scrubbed away by the clear day. Around them lay miles of flat dry farmland, the highway trilling with car horns as traffic slowed down as soon as they saw the parked police cars.

"What did you do once you exited your vehicle?"

Alet closed her eyes briefly, remembering the sequence of events. "I called to the woman on the ground."

"It was dark. How could you see her?"

"Before. In my headlights." Alet pointed to Mazingane's feet. "About there."

"What exactly did you say, Constable Berg?"

"I think I asked if she was okay."

"You think?"

"I did."

"Walk us through what happened next." Mazingane motioned her over.

"I knelt next to her. I tried to stop the bleeding."

"She was alive."

"*Ja.* I heard something behind me. Then Ngwenya hit me."

"Show me."

"I was here." Alet crouched down. "He caught me here." She touched the right side of her face. "I turned. He knocked me down." Alet fell back, simulating what happened. Something sparked in her memory. She tried to grab on to it, but Mazingane interrupted.

"Then?"

"I fired a shot. He ran to my car."

Mazingane looked over at the other two officers, a knowing look passing between them. Alet took a deep breath. She hated their judging expressions.

"You fired again, correct?"

"Twice."

"You were aiming at the fugitive."

Alet bit the inside of her cheek. "I couldn't see him."

Pop. Pop. The sound of the gunshots reverberated in her mind. Pop. Ngwenya running, the car starting. Pop. Pop. Two shots, drowning another noise. Alet replayed the memory. Pop. Pop. She looked back at the picnic table, the patch of trees farther down the road where they discovered Mr. Braverman's body. She had been focused on Ngwenya. Her face was throbbing, the taste of blood. Pop. Pop.

"There was somebody else here."

"Mr. Braverman?"

"No. I heard a noise."

"What noise?"

"I think there was a car by those trees there. It drove away when I fired."

Mazingane glared at her. "This was not in your statement."

"I was trying to stop the suspect. I didn't remember it till now."

"Didn't remember it, or made it up?"

Alet locked eyes with Mazingane. "There was another car here, hidden behind the trees. I think it was the Bravermans' car. The baby must have been in the back. Don't you see?" She took a few steps toward the trees. "Ngwenya's buddies killed Mr. Braverman over there by the car. Mrs. Braverman tried to run, but Ngwenya caught up to her and killed her here. When I stopped, Ngwenya hid behind the picnic table. He must have thought he could deal with me too, but he didn't plan on me having a gun. The others abandoned him when they heard the shots." Mazingane showed no reaction. She went on. "Look, Captain Groenewald said there was another set of tracks. Was it by those trees?"

Mazingane didn't look up from his notepad. "Anyone can use this rest stop. We have no evidence except your new testimony that those tracks were left at the same time that the Bravermans were killed."

"There should have been forensic evidence of more than one attacker. If you processed the scene properly." Alet turned her palms up when Mazingane didn't respond. "Well?"

Mazingane's mouth curled up in one corner. "There was," he said.

Unic was languid in the afternoon heat. Alet stopped at the grocery store. There was no food at the flat and she was starving. She scoured the shelves, settling on a loaf of bread, a tin of apricot jam, a six-pack of Black Labels and a hand full of Wilson Toffees. She handed the toffees out to the little ones hanging around outside. When she looked up, Mynhardt was leaning against her car, which was parked halfway down the block.

Alet walked over, dreading what was coming. "Captain?"

"You are supposed to be on holiday."

"*Ja*, I . . . I had the pointing-out this morning, so I thought I'd stop at home."

"Your dad said you are planning on leaving for good." Mynhardt didn't take his eyes off her. "Is that so?"

Alet felt a stubbornness rise in her. "I don't know, Captain. I don't always have to do what my dad says, you know?" Mynhardt nodded to someone behind her. She turned to see Strijdom at the store's entrance. "Is there a problem?"

Mynhardt stepped close enough that she could smell his breath. She turned her head away. He grabbed her arm, his fingers digging into the flesh. Alet thought about hitting him with the six-pack, but it would be a waste of beer.

"I'd listen if I were you," Mynhardt said.

"Is that a threat, Captain?" Alet defiantly met his eyes.

"Make of it what you want, my girl." Mynhardt let go of her arm. He knocked her groceries out of her hand like a spiteful child and walked away.

Strijdom followed, a wry smile on his face. "Watch it," he said as he walked past her. He ran his hand over his brush cut, scanning the street to see if anyone was watching.

"*Fokkers*," Alet muttered under her breath as she picked up her bag, her anger seething at the thought that either of them called himself police. More like uniformed gangsters. If Wexler wouldn't testify, she had to find another way to prove they were dirty.

Mathebe knocked on her flat's door around four o'clock. "There is rain coming," he said when she opened the door for him. Alet sniffed the air, realizing that she had forgotten what rain smelled like. She left the door open and made room for him among the folders and photographs laid out all over her couch. Mathebe's eyes darted over the disarray. Alet put her half-drunk beer back in the fridge.

"Coffee?"

Mathebe held up his hand in reply. "I cannot stay long. The captain asked me to come in for overtime."

"How did it go with Ngwenya?"

"He knows he can be reached in jail if he talks. Captain Groene-wald is trying to make a deal with his lawyer. Protection and a more lenient sentence if he testifies against the men who killed Mr. Braverman."

Alet hated the thought that Ngwenya might get off easy. "Will it work?"

"I do not know. He fears for his life."

"We need to find Skosana. I'll go talk to Magda Kok again. See if she knows anything."

"I will go with," Mathebe said resolutely. "Have you found out anything more about Mrs. Pienaar's movements the day she was killed? How she ended up on the farm?"

"Not much. She was in the garden that morning around seven. Tilly said she phoned Trudie around eleven when she started prepping for lunch at the guesthouse. Trudie had found out what Tilly had done for Wexler." Alet opened her notepad to a sheet of paper with her initial timeline. "We don't know anything about what she did after that, but the neighbor down the street saw her going for her daily walk around six. Sometime after that she must have driven to the Terblanche farm and was murdered between midnight and two a.m."

"Could she perhaps have gone to confront Mrs. Terblanche?"

"If that was the case, why didn't she go to the house? Her car was discovered kilometers away. I've taken that route up the back side of the mountain, Johannes. It's a difficult climb in broad daylight, never mind at night when it's pitch black."

"It was her farm."

"Tilly said she hadn't set foot there in years."

"Miss Pienaar might not be aware of everything her mother did."

Alet nodded. There was a lot that Trudie had kept hidden from Tilly. "There's something else that's bothering me, Johannes. That guy who attacked me in Koch's office?"

"Yes?"

"Well, it always looks so easy to strangle someone on TV, but have you ever tried it? This guy put everything he had into it and I still managed to stop him. I mean, we know this Ben could hold down Wexler, a big guy, without effort. It should have been easy for him to take care of me."

"It was not him?"

Alet shook her head. "Hand me that pile?"

Mathebe picked up a stack of folders next to him on the couch. Alet plopped down on the ground and spread the autopsy reports from each file in front of her.

"*Ja.* See?" Alet handed Mathebe the first report. "Says here there were finger marks on the victim's neck. This one too. And this one."

"These are the earlier victims. The later victims were completely incinerated."

"But all of them had cracked hyoid bones, so we know they were strangled first. Wait." Alet rifled through to the bottom of the pile. "Here. This is one of the later victims, part of the Angel Killer investigation." She scanned the report, then pulled out a copy of the file she'd found in Koch's safe. "*Ja*. Liezl Brits. Koch made a case study for his book. Hyoid bone cracked. He found subcutaneous bruising in the shape of fingers." Alet put the files down. "I'll go through all of these, but I bet you that's how our bloke gets off. Skin on skin. He burns the bodies purely to get rid of evidence. A practicality. Or maybe it's some kind of ritual, I don't know. But the real high is the strangulation. That's his reason for killing. In his mind he was probably strangling Trudie like that, over and over, until he found her. They were practice runs for his sick fantasy."

Mathebe's features distorted in concentration. "Then I believe we have a problem, Constable."

"What's that?"

Mathebe removed Trudie Pienaar's autopsy report from the pile, his eyes narrowing to droopy slits as he studied it. He looked up at Alet. "Dr. Koch's autopsy report states that the hyoid bone was broken, not cracked."

"*Ja*, Koch said . . ." Alet suddenly realized what Mathebe was referring to. It was a clean break. It would have been almost impossible to do that with bare hands. Trudie's killer had used a garrote.

Alet sorted through case evidence long after Mathebe left, a newly opened cold beer within reach. Why did Ben change his MO? Why use a garrote on Trudie if he had killed all the other girls with his bare hands? Perhaps he had been injured somehow, a broken arm or something that made business as usual difficult? Would a super-strong killer who lived three times as long experience the same muscle deterioration as a normal aging human? She reached for her phone.

"You've reached Professor Engelman. Please leave a number and a brief message."

Alet disconnected the call before the beep. She had left a message already. Messages. Mike Engelman hadn't shown up in Unie, which worried her. In light of what had happened to Koch, nobody connected to this investigation was safe.

Alet pored through Trudie's stack of documents. There were report cards, a high school certificate, all in Theresa Morgan's name. There was a marriage certificate in Lilly Maartens's née Kritzinger's name, and ID books and birth certificates in all three of the aliases. There were love letters between Lilly and her husband, most of them written when he was away, helping people when their family members were arrested by the police. He sometimes hinted at giving up, his despair clear, but Tessa always urged him on, begged him to do what she couldn't. Alet's discomfort grew as she read on, feeling as if she was violating Trudie's life, but she had to make sure that there wasn't anything here that could lead her to the killer. The names on all of the documents matched up to the aliases she already knew Trudie had used, except one, the deed to a *plot* in Bloemfontein. It was registered to Theresa De Beer. Alet stared at the name. It hadn't shown up anywhere else.

The gas needle hovered on the right side of half after Alet turned the key in the ignition of her Toyota. Enough to get her where she needed to go. She dialed Theo's number as she pulled into the street. "I think I might have a last name, Theo. De Beer. Can you run Ben De Beer through Tempe records and see what you get?"

"Hold on," Theo said. "Let me check the list I have." The sound of typing filled the silence. Alet remembered Theo's fingers gliding over the keyboard, barely touching it, his broad shoulders hunched ever so slightly forward as he squinted at the screen. "Got a Benjamin De Beer here, discharged from Tempe military base in 1948 because of medical reasons. Only did basic service."

"That matches the timeline. See if you can find anything more on him." Alet hesitated. "Also, check police personnel records."

Theo sighed. Alet imagined the tightness around his lips, the slight flaring of his nostrils as he tried to suppress his agitation. She of all people knew that loyalties died hard. A part of Theo always got riled when there was a crime connected to the police, as if he took it personally.

"Look, Theo, his MO change has been bothering me. He went from only partially burning the bodies, you know, only a limb or something, to incinerating them totally. Like with Trudie. The change happened before my dad began investigating the Angel Killer in the eighties. It might be the reason that nobody found a connection with the older murders until now."

"What's this got to do with the police, Alet?"

"The bush wars. South African forces were in Namibia from 1966 till 1989 fighting SWAPO. Also in Zimbabwe fighting ZANLA. They disposed of enemy combatants by burning the bodies in mass graves. Ben was discharged from the army. The only other way he could have been involved in those wars was if he was police. I know it's a long shot, but we should check anyway."

"I don't know if the database is digitized that far back." The sound of Theo massaging the keys filled the silence again. "Fourteen De Beers in the service during that time, eight posted in Zimbabwe. Two named Benjamin, one a constable promoted to sergeant, David Benjamin De Beer. The other, a captain. Benjamin De Beer, no middle name, commanded a squad in the early days of the bush war . . . *O fok.*"

"Theo?" Alet was brought back from the hypnosis of the black road ahead of her by the alarm in Theo's voice.

"Alet, Constable Adriaan Berg is listed here as being under his command."

"My dad? Are you sure?"

"*Ja.* Date of birth matches. He was eighteen at the time."

Alet clenched the steering wheel. Her father was covering for someone after all, but it didn't seem likely that De Beer would have been one of his men. Instead, he must have been protecting De Beer because he was one of the higher-ups, one of the puppet masters of the death squads. Either way, Adriaan Berg had allowed a serial killer to go on killing innocent women. Theo confirmed that De Beer had transferred into Security Branch after his deployment. That was where the trail blacked out. Her father would go on to make a name for himself as a top detective at Brixton Murder and Robbery, until he too would disappear into the vortex. He would come out the other side without a blemish to his name, a respected and valued member of the South African Police Service. Alet wondered if it was his reward. You scratch my back . . . but Ben didn't reappear. What happened to him? Killing blondes didn't exactly pay the bills.

"Thank you, Theo," Alet said as she turned off onto the dirt road that led to the Terblanche farm. "Can you see if there are any other connections between them? I'll call you later."

The wind had picked up since she left Unie, the gentle rolling clouds of the afternoon replaced by a dark canopy. Twirling sand and debris were illuminated in her headlights. Alet stopped the car and called Mathebe. There was a cell blackout for about twenty kilometers once you turned off the road, the signal blocked by the mountains. She'd only get to use her phone again once she was near one of the farmhouses with a signal booster or on higher ground. Mathebe answered, his voice fighting for a place in the crackling static.

"Listen, Johannes, I think we found the guy. His name is Benjamin De Beer. Theo is going to send you everything he can find on him. I'm on my way to talk to Magda Kok." The sky lit up briefly, a bright bolt of light illuminating the landscape, followed a few seconds later by a low rumbling.

"It can wait until the morning, Constable."

"She knows where Skosana is. He can link Mynhardt to this whole mess. And he was on the mountain the night Trudie was murdered. I know he saw something."

"He will not talk. And you are risking—" Static swallowed the rest of Mathebe's words.

"Listen, I'll come to your place as soon as I . . . Hallo?" Alet checked her cell. A single bar flickered, then disappeared. She dialed Mathebe's number again. The call failed. Alet tried sending a text, and an error message appeared almost immediately in reply. Dammit. In the distance another streak of light cracked the sky. Great, Alet thought. Drought for six months, and now the heavens were ready to piss on her. She sure as hell wasn't going to let a little water stop her. That little *kak*, Skosana, had been slipping through their fingers for long enough.

Eight slow kilometers farther, the first raindrop cracked through the dust, colliding violently with the Toyota's windshield. Lightning bounded on the mountaintops and the sky exploded in a sudden downpour. The road was difficult enough to navigate under normal conditions, but with visibility nonexistent beyond the hood of her car, it was impossible. There was no way around it, she had to stop. Standing in the middle of the narrow road was dangerous, she knew that, but she was scared that pulling to the side might send her over the edge—not quite the ending she had in mind.

Alet stared out through the windshield. On nights like these she always opened all the curtains and switched off the lights, marveling at nature's display. It comforted her for some reason, made her feel safe. Perhaps it had something to do with her father snuggling next to her on the *stoep* when she was little, reading her stories, the smell of pipe tobacco on his clothes, his rough hands turning the pages. The same hands that touched death. The time she had with him had been short, a blip in the story of her, of who she became, yet he had always been a force against which she measured her worth. What, then, would all this mean?

Two dull beams of light penetrated the sheets of water in her rearview mirror. Alet immediately honked the horn, unsure if the approaching car could see or even hear her. Who would be stupid enough to drive blind in this? The headlights grew sharper. She pressed down on the horn again, keeping it compressed, the sound a jarring wail. The car stopped behind her. A shadow briefly flickered across the headlights. Someone tried the door handle on the passenger side. When it didn't open, a hand slapped the window. Alet felt for her 9mm in her backpack, found it and unclasped the holster. She leaned across, holding the backpack on her lap, and cautiously rolled down the window a few centimeters. Rain splashed in her face.

Boet Terblanche's eyes appeared in the opening. "Open the door."

Alet closed her hand around the butt of the gun in her backpack.

"Come on, Alet, I'm drowning out here." Boet jumped in as soon as she complied. He was drenched, his hair pasted against his scalp. "What are you doing out here? I almost rear-ended you."

"I should ask you the same bloody thing," Alet said. "How the hell can you drive in this?"

"I have to get home. You're blocking the road."

"So sorry to inconvenience you, Mr. Terblanche, but I think your dinner can wait until this eases up and we can actually see the road."

"Open the door and shift over. I'll drive."

Alet paused at the urgency in Boet's voice. "What's going on?"

"Just do it, for God's sake, Alet." His voice came through clenched teeth. "There was an alarm call from the house. Jana is alone. Move!"

The fear in Boet's eyes was clear. The emergency signal would have been received at the police station in Unie, but nobody could get out to the farm in this weather.

Alet climbed over the gearshift while Boet ran around the front and sidled into the driver's seat. "Slow down. You're going to get us killed," she said as Boet stepped on the petrol. The car skidded across the road.

A bolt of lightning hit the top of the mountain, followed rapidly by another. "The storm is moving," Boet said. He leaned across the steering wheel, wiping condensation on the glass in front of him.

"When did the alarm go off?"

"Right as this started. I was at the remote encampment. They stole twelve head of cattle last night. Cut right through the fence and took them across Thuys De Hart's property. He thinks his foreman might be in on it. Saw him talking to some strangers yesterday. Today the foreman says he's sick, then disappears."

Alet tried to discern the landscape. Nothing looked familiar. "How far away are we?"

Boet squinted. "Another two kilos."

They were moving faster now, the Toyota hugging curves, mud splattering up against the windows as they drove through puddles. Boet slowed for the turnoff. Alet jumped out to get the gate, shielding her eyes from the rain. By the time she got back into the truck, she too was drenched. Instead of following the path up the mountain, Boet turned the other way to get to the house. Water ran from the mountainside in deep grooves, past the property. The river had come up, water rising fast in the normally dry bed. The sedan stalled.

"We have to go by foot." Boet was already out of the car.

Alet grabbed her backpack. The water was almost even with her car's door when she opened it. She held the backpack over her head, fording to the bank, her trainers heavy as she followed Boet up the slippery drive. The house was cloaked in darkness. Boet flipped the switch of the exterior light, but nothing happened. Alet stayed close to him, struggling not to fall on the uneven terrain. Boet pushed against the house's back door. It gave way without effort.

"Jana?"

Alet pulled her gun out of her backpack, flipping the safety off.

The hairs at the back of her neck stood on end. Boet felt around in the scullery for the light. It too was out. Either the storm had knocked the power out, or someone had cut the lines.

"Jana!" Boet's voice betrayed his fear. "Answer me, dammit."

Alet heard him open a drawer in the kitchen, rummaging through it, small objects hitting the floor. A flashlight beam blinded her momentarily.

"Sorry. Here." Boet shone his flashlight on the counter. He turned, the beam briefly illuminating the barrel of a shotgun.

Someone shoved Alet. She fell, her gun sliding across the floor. The attacker climbed over her, his heel making contact between her shoulder blades. The force knocked her flat on her stomach. Two men were yelling at each other in Xhosa right outside the door. "Boet! Are you okay?" She frantically ran her hands along the floor, feeling for her gun.

"*Ja*, I . . . They got into the gun safe."

"*Fok*." Alet's hands made panicked contact with the legs of a chair. "Get the flashlight. I can't see anything."

Boet crawled to the flashlight. He shone the sputtering beam along the floor. "Alet!"

Alet's hands closed on her gun just as a shot exploded from the doorway. She fired in the direction of the sound, emptying the magazine. More yelling, more voices. She scrambled for her backpack. Boet was somewhere in the dark, one of the phantoms moving around in the room, the flashlight abandoned on the floor. She turned her backpack over, contents spilling on the floor, her fingers closing around the spare magazine. With trained efficiency, she expelled the spent magazine and reloaded.

Alet heard floorboards creak as Boet made his way down the passage to the bedroom. She got to her feet, reached for the abandoned flashlight and shone it at the doorway. A man lay crumpled in the scullery, his dark skin wet, an even darker liquid pooling around him. A shotgun lay trapped under his body. Alet switched the flashlight off and moved past him to the back door. She listened for voices, footsteps, anything. When she was sure the coast was clear, she pushed the body on its side, recognizing the man's face from the mug shots of Skosana's associates. She retrieved the shotgun. It was warm, wet, slippery.

Alet found Boet kneeling next to the open closet. Jana sat bound inside, brown tape, the kind used for packages, wound around her head to keep a gag in place. Boet tore at Jana's restraints. Her eyes were wild, blood from a gash on her forehead running down her cheeks. She spat the gag out as soon as Boet got the tape off her head. Clumps of hair stuck to its surface.

"They forced me to open the safe." Jana clung to Boet. "They held a gun to my head."

"It's okay." Boet helped her to the bed. "The baby?"

"They hit me," Jana managed through sobs. "I haven't felt him move since."

"She needs a hospital, Boet."

Boet looked over at Alet, as if he had forgotten she was there. "My pickup is still on the road," he said, his voice pleading, desperate.

"Where's Jana's car?"

"We keep it in the barn. On the other side of the river." Hopelessness deflated his features.

"You have a quad bike." Alet remembered seeing him ride it on her patrol one day.

"She's not strong enough."

"She's bleeding, Boet. There might be internal injuries. If you don't get her to Oosthuizen right now, you might lose them both. Go get the bike."

Boet hesitated, the inability to make a decision paralyzing him. He looked at Jana like a lost dog.

"Boet!" Alet grabbed his shoulder. "Now. I'll stay with Jana."

"Go," Jana said weakly.

"Take this." Alet handed him the shotgun and the flashlight. "They might still be out there."

Alet sat down on the bed next to Jana, the awkwardness of the moment thankfully obscured by the dark. "We're going to get you out of here," she said to fill the silence.

"Why are you here?"

Alet took a deep breath, steeling herself. "It's not what you think. I was on my way to see a witness . . ." The implication hung between them in the dark. Alet braced herself, surprised when a sob from Jana took the place of an expected insult. "Jana? Are you all right?"

"I'm scared, Alet."

"I know. Me too." It felt strange confessing it to this woman.

"It's my fault. If my baby dies—"

"You couldn't have helped this. Do you hear? This is their fault. They did this."

Jana's clenched her hands. "They came here for a reason."

"What do you mean?"

"The Thokoloshe." Jana's voice broke. She turned her head away from Alet.

"He provides the children. I know."

"He said we were cheating him. He wanted more money."

"Is that why he went after that couple?"

"We had agreed on a price."

"He found out you were making a lot more than him and wanted his cut." Alet kept her voice even, her judgment to herself. The Terblanches obviously had no idea that they were dealing with a sociopath.

"We paid him," Jana said weakly.

A dull thud came from the back door. Alet pulled herself away from Jana and went into the passage, gun held out in front of her. The beam of the flashlight appeared, Boet's sturdy outline behind it. "How is she?"

"I think she's going into shock."

Together they helped Jana up, supporting her on either side. Alet grabbed a blanket off the bed and hung it around Jana's shoulders. They shuffled down the passage into the kitchen. Jana barely noticed the body as they sidled past it. Lightning tore the sky outside. Alet noticed fast-disappearing footprints in the mud leading to the mountain. Skosana and his men. She helped Boet to get Jana on the four-wheeler. He climbed up in front.

"Hold on." Alet draped the blanket over Jana's head. It was like a Band-Aid on a slit throat, for all it helped against the rain.

"Get on the back, Alet."

"You need to get through the river, Boet. You won't manage with the extra weight."

"You can't stay here."

"I'm armed. I'll be okay. Call Mathebe as soon as you get a signal. Tell him what's happened."

"Take this, then." Boet handed her the flashlight. He turned the bike around and headed down the road to the river. Alet went back inside, grabbed her holster out of her backpack, and strapped it on. She made her way to Boet's office, on the other side of the living room. The safe gaped open, empty, papers strewn haphazardly across the floor. The phone line was dead. Alet felt along the underside of the desk for the panic button and pressed it again. She went back to the bedroom and took her soggy shoes off. Jana's shoes were too small for her. She rummaged through the dresser drawers for dry socks, then layered several pairs on before slipping into a pair of Boet's work boots. Her mind was made up. If she didn't go after Skosana right away, he would disappear again. Maybe for good this time.

Alet's feet slid around in Boet's boots on the uneven path. She tracked the footprints along the river, up the mountain. Once she got to higher ground, she scanned the valley. There was no sign of the quad bike's headlights. Alet shone the flashlight back onto the path. The road climbed steadily, becoming rocky. She couldn't remember the last time she'd been this wet.

Alet switched the flashlight off to hide her movements as soon as she reached a plateau. The Thokoloshe and his crew would have headed farther up the mountain, monsters crawling around in the dark. There was a small spark of light in the trees ahead, followed by a muted pop and a sudden searing pain in her right shoulder. Alet fell, knocked back by the force of the bullet. She stayed on the ground for a moment, trying to assess the situation. The bullet had missed her vital organs and even though her shoulder hurt like a bitch, she was okay. She had to get out of the open, and quick, before Skosana's aim improved. That meant running toward the shooter and the cover of the trees.

Alet pushed herself off the ground and scrambled over the rocks, her one-hundred-meter sprint fueled by pure adrenaline. Penetrating the treeline, she was immediately engulfed in a dense darkness. She smelled smoke, not sure how anything could be burning in this downpour. She carefully peeled the fabric of her shirt away from her wounded shoulder. It wasn't bleeding too badly, but she couldn't find an exit wound. She reached for her gun, pain surging up her arm. "*Fok.*" Alet let out a stifled cry. Of course they had to shoot her right shoulder, she thought wryly. The guys at STF would have laughed at her, called it a splinter and told her to man up. Bullet wounds bought you bragging rights. Only a bloody man would think this was cool.

Gunshots rang out nearby. Alet crouched down, digging her back into a tree. She couldn't tell where the shooter was firing from. She bit back a wave of panic as she thought of Skosana closing in on her, getting ready for the kill. She switched the 9mm to her left hand. It felt wrong. Pop. This one was much closer. She had to move. She stayed low, her gun out in front of her. She could imagine the six-o'clock news broadcast: Unie police officer wins "most incompetent cop ever" award after walking into a tree.

Alet tried to clear her thoughts, the pain in her shoulder now excruciating. She weaved her way through the trees, pressing her back into each one, waiting, listening, moving again, thankful that her training was taking over. Her feet hit something unexpected and she stumbled, her left hand breaking the fall. Alet felt warm skin under her, a very human smell in her nostrils. Whoever it was wasn't moving. What the hell was going on? Had Skosana accidentally killed one of his own men while he shot at her? Or was he on a spree with nothing to lose, killing everyone that could testify against him? The realization dawned, too late of course, that coming up the mountain after the Thokoloshe may have been a rash, stupid decision. Add it to the list.

A branch cracked right next to her. Alet raised her gun. A blow hit her from the side before she had a chance to pull the trigger. I'm really sick of being a punching bag, she thought as she tried to get out of the attacker's reach. Alet raised her gun again, but a second blow knocked it out of her hand. She screamed, the pain so intense she was sure he had broken her wrist.

His hand was on her throat, a threat of violence rather than the actual thing. "Quiet," said a male voice. Alet started at the familiarity. She hit the man's arm with her uninjured hand with no effect, opening her mouth to call out for help. He pinned her down on the ground. "I said . . ." His fingers tightened. Alet fought for breath, the smell of smoke stronger than before. There was a glow at the edge of her vision, a dull constant hum in the background. Someone burst through the underbrush, yelling. Another flash in the dark. Pop. The hand let go. Pop. Pop. Pop. Random light burst from a gun barrel, as if the shooter didn't know where to aim. Alet's heart threatened to explode, her fear almost paralyzing. She had to get out of there. Another pop. A man screamed, then there was a thump in the underbrush as he fell.

Alet struggled up on all fours and then ran blindly, her right arm limp at her side. She stumbled, collided with nameless obstacles, phantoms tugging at her skin. *Keep moving.* The air grew thick, the smell of smoke nauseating. Her lungs burned, thoughts bombarding her in confused spasms. Why was it so bright all of a sudden? Was she sweating profusely, or was that rain? Everything around her looked the same, a wallpaper repetition of foliage and rocks. She didn't know in which direction she was running. *Keep moving.* When she broke through the trees at last, she came face to face with a wall of flames. The mountain was on fire.

He was there when she turned around, the fire casting menacing shadows on his angular face, his full lips twisted in an ironic smile. "You can't run from me, Alet," he said simply as he came closer. "I will always find you."

Alet looked up at Mike, his eyes eerily pale, the contacts gone, his face shaved clean. "Hallo, Ben," she said.

Wednesday
DECEMBER 8, 2010

The town came into view in the valley below as the sun disappeared in faded pinks behind the mountain. In the houses sheltered under UNIE FOR JESUS, prayers were said, dinners eaten, families already hungover on the excess of the approaching holidays. Adriaan had never been to the town, its only claim to fame some story about a Boer War ghost. Tokkie Mynhardt had kept him up to speed on Alet, said she was doing all right. That was enough for Adriaan. He sighed. Stupid girl. He had made sure she got every opportunity, and then she messed it up because of some half-breed coloured. Perhaps it was good that she now had to get there the hard way.

It was the end for Adriaan. Retirement stared him in the face. But here's to new beginnings, new wife, private consultation work, and not constantly looking over his shoulder. Only one more thing to take care of. Adriaan pondered how everything came together in the end as if guided by an invisible hand. If Alet hadn't messed up so royally, he'd never have reestablished contact with Tokkie Mynhardt. It was Tokkie who sent him those pictures of Alet with the kids on parade. At first glance he'd missed it, but something about the pictures kept drawing his eye to a face in the crowd. He had studied that face closely all these years. Even with dark hair and makeup, he'd known it was her.

The road descended sharply, the rental sedan hugging the curves that led into town. Adriaan drove past the turnoff without slowing. Another five kilometers, then right. Absolute darkness surrounded him once he was on the dirt road, eyes reflecting his headlights through the dust. Another fifteen kilometers, then past the derelict greenhouse and turn into the next lane. Adriaan parked behind two tall trees that obscured his car from the road. As he strapped on his holster, he noticed approaching headlights. The white pickup came to a halt in the lane.

"Mr. Terblanche?" Adriaan extended his hand. The man nodded, barely made eye contact. Adriaan reached into his pocket, retrieving a thick envelope. "What we agreed on." Terblanche stared at it for a moment. "You can count it," Adriaan said.

"No, I . . . Thank you." Terblanche folded the envelope in half and stuffed it into the glove compartment as if it was burning his skin. Awkward silence hung between them. Terblanche ran his hands through his hair. "She won't sell, see? Says she wants the land back when the lease is up."

"You don't have to explain."

"My family's been farming it for almost a hundred years. Now she wants to throw us off because she doesn't approve of . . ." Terblanche pressed his lips together. "What we do here to get a little extra income is none of her business. Times are hard, you know. I have a child on the way." His face had a sweaty sheen to it, his fingers fidgeting with the edges of his green sweatshirt. He ventured a sideways glance at Adriaan. "How did you know to call me?"

That part had been easy. Once Adriaan had found out who the girl was, her connection to the land had led him straight to Terblanche and his financial woes. He smiled reassuringly. "Mr. Terblanche, once we get to your foreman, you should leave. Put this evening out of your mind. You don't know me, okay? You don't mention me or what happened tonight to anyone. It's that simple."

"I just . . ." Terblanche crossed his arms. "I don't know that this is the right way to do this. I mean, Jakob's a good *oke*, just likes the drink too much. He started messing up here, *fokked* up my tractor the other day 'cause he was hungover, but I can't fire him, because of Mrs. Pienaar's agreement with my dad. Nobody likes her, but I can't just—"

Adriaan's smile wavered. "Mr. Terblanche, I don't need the details. I'm taking care of a private matter. It just so happens that it will be of benefit to you too." He fingered the fishing line in his jeans pocket. "Or would you like to hand me back that envelope and forget everything?"

Terblanche's eyes briefly rested on the glove compartment before he got out of the car. "Jakob doesn't live near the others," he said. "He fixed up one of the old places, way up. It's a stiff hike."

Adriaan gestured for Terblanche to go ahead, choosing to ignore the implication of his words. He was in better shape than most *laaities* fresh out of police college these days, prided himself on it. He could teach Terblanche a thing or two if it came down to it, judging by the puffing he heard a short while later. He kept the beam of his flashlight focused on the rocky ground just behind Terblanche's feet, following the man from boulder to boulder in places where the path disappeared. Only once they reached more even ground did he notice how quiet it was up in the mountains. The air was clearer too, the stars brighter than he had ever imagined them. He could see why Jakob would prefer to live here instead of squashed in with the other workers between noise and poverty. There was peace here, nobody to please but yourself, no side to choose but your own. In the distance a troupe of baboons called out to each other. For a moment Adriaan envied the simplicity of the *askari*'s life.

Terblanche stopped short in front of him. "There." He pointed at lighted windows a few yards ahead. Adriaan felt Terblanche's grip on his arm as he moved toward the small hut.

"*Meneer?* It's not right, hey. Let's rather go back."

"Mr. Terblanche!" Adriaan felt rage warm his cheeks, his hands itching for this milksop. He shook himself loose from the man. "Let me make this clear. Our business is done now. Understand? If you do anything to fuck this up, I will make you regret it." Adriaan took the Makarov out of his holster. Terblanche took a step back, his thick lips parting slightly. Adriaan felt a rush of disdain. He'd known men like Terblanche all his life. All of them readily jumping on the bandwagon whenever they thought they could profit, but running to mommy once they realized the party wasn't as *lekker* as they thought it would be. "I said, do you understand?"

Terblanche nodded. He jumped as the door of the hut suddenly opened, light casting a wedge on the ground.

"*Baas?*" Jakob locked eyes with Terblanche. "What are you—"

"Jakob." Adriaan stepped forward.

A high-pitched simpering sound escaped Jakob's lips. He scrambled into the house. Adriaan slammed his body against the door, sending the slender *askari* reeling. Jakob tried to get up, but Adriaan planted a blow with the pistol on the black man's face, fast and hard, forcing him back onto the ground. Adriaan quickly scanned the hut. A mattress lay on the dirt floor, covered in mismatched sheets and a crocheted blanket. Faded photographs were fastened to the wall above the bed with tape. A half-jack of brandy lay on its side next to a pouch of tobacco on the ground.

Adriaan turned to see Terblanche in the doorway, his face pale, his jaw slack with horror. "Time to go now, Mr. Terblanche," he said calmly.

Terblanche hugged the wall for a moment, as if he had trouble standing. Then, realizing that there was no way out, he disappeared into the night like a rabbit. Terblanche might consider going to the police, but Adriaan figured him for too great a coward to go through with it. Just in case, Adriaan decided to give him a call in the morning, to make sure he understood the consequences of speaking out of turn. He shifted his attention to Jakob where he lay curled on the floor, his arms covering his face, refusing to move. Adriaan prodded Jakob with his shoe, kicking the man's back with increasing intensity until Jakob screamed, his breaths coming in short rasps as he scrambled to the mattress, his eyes wild, his mouth contorted in a crazed grimace.

"I'm here to talk, Jakob. That's what you like to do, right? Talk about things you shouldn't."

Jakob compressed his body farther into the corner. "*Nee, Baas.* I didn't talk. I swear. Jakob stayed here. He says nothing."

"But you might decide to be brave one day to impress your Commie buddies, like last time."

"Never, Colonel. I swear."

"How can I trust you, Jakob? After you going to the TRC?"

"I didn't do it. No, sir. Jakob never talked. He knew it was wrong. He knew you'd come."

"How can I know you won't do that again, Jakob? Unless . . ." Adriaan picked up the half-jack of brandy, pretending to consider the matter. "Perhaps there is something you can do for me. Make me forget all of that nonsense."

"Anything, Colonel, please. Just let Jakob be. He is good, he is. Good as gold."

Adriaan opened the bottle. He took a swig before holding it out to Jakob. "Let's have a *dop* together, you and I. Discuss this like men." Adriaan waited, watching Jakob's eyes slowly travel to the bottle.

A noise dragged Tessa out of a deep sleep. Was it that girl again? Alet carried on at all hours, not caring who she disturbed. Tessa regretted taking her on, but she needed the money, now more than ever. She couldn't think why Tilly liked her so much. Tilly. This generation, born free of the blame of what happened, but still having to live with the aftermath, angered and saddened her. Instead of reaching out, they were self-centered, rude, ignorant of the past, only interested in profiting in the present. That her daughter had grown up to take advantage of the poor shamed her deeply. And Jeff . . . she blamed herself for not realizing it sooner, hiding away in this house like an ostrich with her head in the sand. Well she'd be damned if she'd let this carry on. Especially on her land.

Tessa's annoyance at being woken subsided only marginally when she realized that the phone was ringing. She fumbled around for the bedside lamp and glanced at the clock. It was after ten. Who would call this late, unless . . . Tessa hurried to the phone in the kitchen, panicked at the thought that something had happened to Tilly. The girl sped on the roads as if they were her personal racetrack. It was only a matter of time before—

"*Rakgadi?*" The sound of Jacob's voice sobered Tessa. "Sorry, so sorry." His words slurred.

"Jacob? Are you okay?"

"If you don't come it's too late for Jakob. I'm scared, *Rakgadi*." Sobs made Jacob even harder to understand. ". . . hurts bad."

Tessa tried to make sense of his words. "Who is hurting you? Is it Boet Terblanche?" She had long suspected that Boet liked to throw his weight around. If Boet had found out that she planned on putting the farm in Jacob's name, there would be hell to pay. The thought that he might already be assaulting Jacob to get back at her made her furious.

"Too much, too long. It's tickets for Jakob. He says you have to come now, or else."

"You tell Boet Terblanche—"

"Sorry, sorry, Auntie. Time to *chaile*."

"Jacob, wait." A high-pitched dial tone was the only reply.

Adriaan took the burner cell away from Jakob and pressed the disconnect button. "Good boy," he said.

Jakob struggled to his feet, staggering, barely catching himself. Adriaan watched dispassionately as Jakob stumbled out the door, his legs barely able to support his slight frame, threatening to crumple beneath him with every step. Kalo was supposed to have gotten rid of Jakob all those years ago. Adriaan should have done the job himself. He pulled his gun, pointing it at Jakob, just as the *askari* turned the doorknob.

"I didn't say you could go, Jakob."

Jakob turned around, his eyes glazed over, slow to focus on the Makarov in Adriaan's hand. "Is right, *Baas*," he whimpered. "I is just wanting to go check if she come."

Pop. Jakob ducked. He scrambled out the door before Adriaan could pull the trigger a second time. Adriaan cursed as he flung the door open. In front of him lay pitch blackness, the sound of Jakob's footfalls dissipating into the distance. Adriaan trained his Makarov in the direction of the sound and fired. The shot echoed over the valley. Dammit. If he kept this up, someone would notice, and he might lose his chance of getting Tessa Morgan.

Adriaan followed Jakob a short distance up the mountain. Memories of the Zimbabwe bush flashed through his mind as he gave chase through the trees, branches hitting him in the face, blood pumping through his ears as he followed De Beer and the trackers, the enemy on their heels and closing in. "*Bliksem!*" Adriaan's foot caught on a small bush, his rage boiling over as he realized the futility of what he was trying to do. Jakob had the advantage, the knowledge of the terrain. All he was doing was wasting energy. "I'll get you, hear, boy?" Adriaan shouted at the mountain. "We're not done, you and I." He turned away reluctantly, and made his way back to the light in the hut's windows.

A quiet knock rapped at the hut's door half an hour later. "Jacob?"

A wave of electricity rippled through Adriaan's nerve endings as he locked eyes with Tessa, the thing itself much more striking than the picture he had had in his mind. In the photographs Tokkie Mynhardt had e-mailed him, she had been pasted down with makeup, but in her haste, Tessa hadn't bothered with concealment today. Adriaan could see the resemblance she carried to all of the dead girls, the round face and porcelain skin, high cheekbones and delicate nose, but it was the eyes that wiped any doubt from his mind. The other girls had light-colored eyes, but not as ethereal, as silver-pale, as if they belonged to the realm of the dead. He had seen those same eyes staring out from his bitterest enemy and his greatest nightmares.

"At last we meet."

"Where is . . . ?" Tessa was stunned to shocked silence when she noticed the gun. "What? Who are you?"

"You're the one he's been looking for all this time," Adriaan said by way of explanation. "And I've been looking for him."

"Look here, where is Jacob?" Tessa burst through the door, disregarding the threat he posed. She stood in the middle of the empty room, dumbfounded by its emptiness.

"He . . ." Adriaan searched for a way to describe the relationship. ". . . used to work for me." Adriaan was not prepared for the blow as Tessa lunged at him. She was fast, if not strong, her body bulldozing into his, disorienting him for a moment, but he managed to grab on to her. She reached for his face, her nails digging into the soft flesh on his neck as he turned his head to the side, the scratch stinging with sweat. Adriaan dropped his gun while fending her off, clamping his hands around her wrists. She fought him all the way, kicking at him, her knee aiming for his groin. He managed to shove her to the ground and scrambled to retrieve his gun. For a moment he doubted her sanity, but he pointed the gun at her and she backed off, crouching down like an animal.

"There's a good girl." Adriaan backed a few steps away from her in case she tried something again. "Jakob ran away before we could conclude our business, Theresa. But you can find him, can't you?"

"Never." Tessa bared her teeth, a look of disgust on her face.

A sarcastic smile played on Adriaan's lips as he sat down in the rocking chair opposite her. "You have a daughter don't you? Mathilda, I think?"

Tessa's face twisted into a snarl. "You stay away—"

"I'll make this very simple. It's Jakob or your girl. If you don't take me to him, I'll put a bullet in you right now. Zebra House will be my next stop."

"What makes you think I can find him? There are kilometers of land out there."

"I'm not in the mood for games. I know what you are. You and De Beer. I know what you can do, how you see in the dark." At the mention of De Beer, Tessa's body stiffened. Adriaan got up. "So, what will it be?"

Adriaan held on to Tessa's arm, the Makarov pressed into the small of her back as they struggled over the veld. Tessa led him up a winding path bordered by patches of trees and long grass. At places the path narrowed so much that he had to let her go ahead, his gun trained on her, ready to fire. A rustle in the underbrush caught his attention. He heard a low animal growl somewhere nearby and backed away. When he looked back, Tessa was gone.

Adriaan raced up the path, the predator at his back making him jittery. Once he got to higher ground, he crouched down, listening for anything that would betray the girl or the cat. Slow seconds turned into minutes. Furtive movement suddenly stirred the bushes ahead of him. He wasn't sure if he could trust his eyes, but he thought he saw the outline of something human darting across the plateau, barely visible as a cloud swept across the slivered moon. Adriaan raced toward the rocky outcrop, where the figure once again melted into the dark. He had gone a few hundred meters beyond the ridge when he realized that he had lost it.

Adriaan retraced his steps, his breathing labored. He slowly backed down to the bottom of the outcrop, following along its base, dry underbrush crunching under his feet. He pulled his flashlight from his belt and trailed the beam over the rock, aware that he was giving away his position, but it couldn't be helped. Broken roots and branches up the rock face caught his attention. Adriaan's body was not as lithe as it had once been, but his memory was sharp enough to scale the rocks without the aid of the light until he reached a narrow ledge. He inched along, parting branches and foliage until he reached the entrance to an old war lookout protruding from the rock face.

Adriaan's flashlight caught wild silver eyes in its beam. She charged at him, raging, a wild animal, but he was ready for her this time. He grabbed her by the shoulders and drove her into the rock wall. She went limp for a moment from the impact, her skull reverberating with a dull thud. Adriaan forced her to the ground and knelt next to her, his hands around her neck. The girl squirmed and writhed under him. She pulled her legs to her chest and dealt him a deft kick in the stomach. He reeled for a moment, clutching at her. She was gasping for air, struggling to get up. Adriaan beat her to it, pushing her face-down on the ground and straddling her hips. She tried to swat at him, but he put both his knees on her shoulders.

"There is no place for you and your kind here." Adriaan's voice rasped, his breathing as labored as hers. She whined under him. He put his hands around her throat again, but he could not exert enough pressure, his hands pulsing from the strain. She screamed, a rasping sound of despair.

"Shut up." Adriaan slammed his fist into the side of her head, feeling his knuckles bruise as they made contact with her skull. She was dazed for a moment, her movements weak. He took the fishing line from his pocket. Pulling her head back by her hair, he wrapped the line around her neck.

Once he was sure it was over, Adriaan slowly eased his grip, red welts striping his palms. He rolled the small body over. A raw gash ran across her neck where the line had cut into her white flesh. Her dull eyes stared at him, her sweaty face covered in dirt and trash from the lookout's floor. Adriaan carefully dusted it off, as if he might wake her from a slumber. Could it be that these monsters were mortal after all? He touched her a little harder, slapping her cheek to see if she would rise like in some old horror movie, feeling somewhat dissatisfied when she didn't. He hoisted her over his shoulder, her body limp as a slaughtered lamb. He had to move her into the open, put her on display so that the message would be clear. And then De Beer would come for him, there was no doubt in Adriaan's mind. The end was near, and he relished it. At last he would have the chance to finish the enemy.

16

Thursday
DECEMBER 23, 2010

The hazy threat of first light struggled through a veil of distant smoke. The rain had stopped somewhere around midnight, its violent outburst too short-lived to quench the damage that years of drought had inflicted on the area. Alet's lungs felt raw. She touched her shoulder with her left hand. Hot pain flooded to the spot. *"Eina! Moer."* Her voice was raspy, her throat like the Sahara. She rolled to her left side and pushed herself to a sitting position, her body protesting every move. She was light-headed, cold, her joints stiff. She waited a few moments to catch her breath, then propped herself against the wall, surveying her surroundings.

Shapes slowly distinguished themselves in the darkness of the ruin. The room was claustrophobic, low-ceilinged, the window squares too small for an adult to fit through, the thick walls blackened by ancient soot. The dirt floor beneath her was littered by rags, clothes, and a multitude of shoes without mates, as if a family of one-legged people had once lived there. A chair with a broken back stood in the corner, liquor bottles and trash strewn around it. And he was there too, in the shadows. Mike . . . Benjamin. The breaking dawn cast a half mask of light across his pale face, stripped of all disguise. Alet wondered at the resemblance between him and Trudie. The nagging feeling she'd had every time she looked at the old photographs suddenly made sense.

Benjamin had guided Alet around the fire to the west side of the mountain the night before, using her own gun to ensure her cooperation. By the time they reached the other side, fire trucks and emergency blue lights had swarmed the roads below. Alet had tried to break away, run toward them, but Benjamin pinned her down, holding the cocked gun to her head. He forced her back up the mountain. They sheltered in the first old ruin they could find, listening to the sirens and the low humming of the fire helicopter repeating its run between the farm dams and the fire. Benjamin never said a word. Alet could feel his gaze on her in the dark. She was disgusted that she had once thought him attractive. *The Devil hath power to assume a pleasing shape.* She couldn't remember what that was from, but she was tired of waiting for this devil to make his move.

"It's day," Alet announced to get his attention. Tension soured her stomach. "Now what?"

"Alet. So impatient." One corner of Benjamin's mouth lifted in a lopsided grin.

"What the bloody hell is so funny?"

"You, demanding when others would beg for their lives." Benjamin stood up and looked out the window. "You understand so little."

"Enlighten me, then. Start with Trudie."

Benjamin turned around, a strange look on his face. He took a step toward her. "Her name was Tessa," he said tersely, his head low, his posture threatening. For a panicked moment Alet thought that this was it.

"Fine. Tessa," she said. "Look, this mountain is crawling with people. There's no way you're getting out of here."

"Then I have nothing to lose."

"They'll find out what you are."

"Nobody will believe you without Koch, and he . . . Let's just say the doctors weren't terribly hopeful."

"You did that? He figured out what you were, and you . . . you tried to kill him?"

"I have nothing to gain by his death, Alet. Ask yourself: Who had the most to lose from Koch talking to you?"

The man who had attacked her in Koch's office was looking for something in the safe, possibly the book Koch had been writing about her dad's cases. Perhaps whoever did it thought he had incriminating evidence. But Koch hadn't testified at the Truth and Reconciliation hearings, hadn't applied for amnesty when he'd had the chance. If evidence surfaced now that he was covering up murders for death-squad commanders, he'd be prosecuted, especially the way the political landscape was changing in the country. People were unhappy, most of them still living in poverty, and few of the promises made by fat politicians had materialized in the years since apartheid ended. Criticism of the ANC and its leaders was being censored on television, and what the government really needed was a way to remind people of their past victories, of what they'd been rescued from. A careful nudge with a sledgehammer. An old apartheid bad-guy finally getting his comeuppance would do the trick nicely.

"How do I know you weren't behind all of this? You were my dad's commanding officer in Zimbabwe."

"I parted ways with Adriaan Berg long before you were born."

"He investigated the Angel killings."

"He interfered with my work."

"Your work? You mean killing all those women for your perverse pleasure?"

"Pleasure had nothing to do with it."

"Then what?"

"I was chosen." Benjamin hesitated and turned away. "You wouldn't understand God's plan."

"Are you telling me God wanted you to kill blondes?" Alet couldn't keep the incredulity out of her voice. "They're quite a threat, those blondes. Man, I tell you, going around and being all pretty and shit. We can all sleep at night now. Thank you for your service."

"They were abominations."

"Must tell you, Ben, I've heard it all now. Know what I think? I think God is an excellent scapegoat. Hell, I blame Him for stuff all the time. Stupidity, warm beer . . . Haven't quite graduated to murder yet, though. You're way ahead of me on that one."

"Don't you blaspheme—"

"Why don't you just admit the truth, hey? You like killing, and those women were easy targets."

"I didn't have a choice." Benjamin whispered the words, his voice barely audible above the din of the approaching helicopter. "Men cannot presume to know God's plan, to take His work into their own hands. I had to undo the work of my father."

"But isn't that what you're doing with your research? DNA manipulation?"

"Because I questioned, God abandoned me. He took Tessa from me." Sorrow filled Benjamin's eyes, raw and infinite.

"You don't know, do you? Koch tested all your other victims' DNA. Everything we could find, at least. Those girls, they were just regular people. You and Trudie were the only ones who were . . . Well, whatever the hell you are."

"You're l-lying. God revealed them to me."

"You couldn't have known what they were without running DNA, and the technology wasn't around back then."

"I thought it was over. I counted the b-births in the journals. I was s-sure they were all gone."

"Except Tessa."

"We w-were going to b-be t-together."

"But she didn't want you, did she, Benjamin? That's really why you killed the others. In your mind, you were getting back at her." Alet recognized a look of desperation in Benjamin, the same one criminals got when she had them cornered, when they couldn't explain away their guilt anymore. She usually reveled in that moment, but now she doubted herself.

"Tessa was the o-only thing that ever m-mattered."

"Then why the romance job on me? I don't get it. I'm really not your type."

"A-Adriaan. I realized wh-who you w-were." His stuttering was growing worse. Alet knew she had to keep him on the defensive, keep him distracted. She inched toward the door.

"You're going to kill me because of my dad? Stop looking for excuses, Ben! You're a cold-blooded killer. It's because of you that Tessa is dead. You killed her!"

Benjamin let out a yell of frustrated anguish, clasping his hands to his head. Alet dashed for the door. He was on her as soon as her fingers brushed the frame, his hand digging into her injured shoulder. Alet screamed, the pain shooting through her body. She swung around, catching him off-guard, trying to grapple her gun from his belt. Benjamin grabbed her wrist, twisting her arm. Pain blinded her. She fought with everything in her not to pass out. In a sweeping motion Ben lifted her into the air, his body pressing hers against the wall.

"What are you waiting for?" Alet had trouble catching her breath.

"Don't tempt me, Alet. I've had to watch from the shadows all my life. I only have to wait a little longer." Benjamin let her slump to the floor.

Alet thought of all those times it had felt like someone was lurking just outside her peripheral vision. "The night at Mathebe's house, was it you shooting?"

The corner of Benjamin's mouth shifted. "I wouldn't have missed."

"Who, then?"

"Seems you have a talent for making enemies, Alet."

"I do what I can."

"You must have really annoyed your captain's stooge."

"Strijdom?"

"All that talk of going to the Hawks to turn him in? Tut, tut, tut. The walls have ears, you know." Benjamin shook his head. He brought his face close to hers. "Never let the enemy know what you're up to. Didn't your father teach you anything?"

"Why are you doing this, then?" Alet spat the words out.

Benjamin stepped away. "All in good time. First, take me to where Tessa died."

"You should know where that is."

"I don't have time for this." Benjamin raised Alet to her feet in one smooth motion and shoved her through the doorway. Outside, the wind had picked up, carrying smoke and ash toward them.

"You are out of your mind. We're going right toward the fire."

"Do it, Alet, or I'll put a bullet in your skull right here."

As they walked, the landscape transformed into a brittle onyx wasteland. The carcass of a calf lay at the edge of the burn zone, separated from the herd, its body as black as the scorched earth around it. Alet felt her strength ebb with each ascending step. At the sound of an approaching helicopter, Benjamin pulled her behind a boulder, the gun pressed to her side. Alet doubted that anyone was looking for them, and even if someone was, the fire would get priority.

Benjamin pulled her back onto her feet as soon as the helicopter had passed. Sweat pasted soot to his skin, his pale irises a stark contrast against his red eyes. "How far?"

"Half a kilometer, maybe?" Alet pointed at the plateau of the next peak, where the landscape lay untarnished by the fire. "There."

Benjamin nodded. He gestured with the gun, instructing her to lead the way. They descended partway down the peak. The trail dead-ended in a rocky cliff, the path leading down the mountain again.

"This is wrong." Benjamin raised the gun. "Don't lie to me."

"I'm sorry." Alet held her hands up, hysteria threatening in her voice. "I've only done this once before. The path is blocked off by the fire." She felt tired, worn out, her battered body on the edge of betraying her.

"Find another way."

"Here." Alet tapped her forehead. "Shoot me and get it over with. I'm sick of this *kak*."

Benjamin held the gun up. "Move."

"No." Alet closed her eyes, waiting for the gun to go off. A blow burned across her face, the hilt of the gun making contact with her cheekbone. When she opened her eyes, Benjamin towered above her.

"There are things worse than death, Alet. You are going to do this."

"Why should I?"

"Because then you'll know the truth." Benjamin tucked the gun under his belt.

Alet hesitated for a moment. She stood up, not trusting her legs to hold her. He was right. She had to know. Hatred for the man drove each step as she changed direction, going higher, trying to find a way to the other side. They had almost reached the peak when she saw a passage over the rock. It would be treacherous, but it was the only way through.

Alet turned to Benjamin. "We'll have to climb."

"You first."

Alet wiped her palms on her T-shirt. She tested a low foothold in the rock and hoisted herself up, reaching for a notch high up with her uninjured arm. She slipped, just as her fingers reached the crevice.

"This isn't going to work, Alet."

"Wait. I can do it." Alet put her right foot into the indentation again. This time she launched herself with more force, abandoning caution. Her left hand closed firmly around the rocky outcrop, her right hand meeting it, pain tearing her shoulder as she yelled out. She dangled there for a moment before finding the next foothold, using her legs to push herself up. She was aware of Benjamin close behind her. If she slipped and fell, she would crash into him, and both of them would probably fall to their deaths. The thought was tempting. Alet reached the top of the boulder, her breath coming in short, shallow rasps. Benjamin followed as they crossed over to the next peak, then descended sharply to the place where Tessa had died.

The clearing was unchanged from the last time Alet had seen it. Grass swayed in the wind, the uniform yellow marred by blackness. Alet looked up at Benjamin, words unnecessary for him to realize what it meant. He fell to his knees next to it. His arms circled his waist as he doubled over, his shoulders shaking, an unnatural howl escaping his lips. It unnerved Alet. This is wrong, she thought. I was wrong. She looked up as a figure emerged from the ruin at the edge of the clearing.

"*Pa.*"

Adriaan fired a shot, the sound reverberating over the valley. Benjamin moved faster than Alet had ever seen anybody move. He grabbed her, swinging her in front of him as Adriaan pulled the trigger again. The bullet narrowly missed them, the look on her father's face revealing horror at how close he had come to killing her.

"Gunning for your only daughter now?" Benjamin mocked in a hoarse voice, his arm around Alet's neck. Alet felt his heart race in rhythm with her own.

"Let her go, De Beer."

Benjamin's arm stiffened around Alet's throat, his breathing raspy. "She's smart, Adriaan. I bet she's just figured out what you've done."

Adriaan looked at her, the lies falling away, a naked honesty between the two of them for the first time, her father's past, his raw confession of guilt whispered wordlessly to her.

"You killed Trudie, *Pa?*"

"They aren't like us, Alet. Him, the girl. They're dangerous."

"Trudie wasn't a danger to anyone, *Pa.*"

"But he is. I read about that girl in the Cape, the one who got away. Saw what she looked like. I knew he was at it again. That he'd keep going unless he was stopped. Theresa Morgan was the only way to get to him, Alet. Believe me. It had to be done."

"And Jakob, *Pa?* Did you take care of him too?"

Adriaan pursed his lips.

"Tell her the truth, Adriaan. You owe her that much." Benjamin's arm tightened around Alet's neck.

Adriaan nodded slowly. "Tokkie told me he saw one of the old *askaris* in the drunk tank. Jakob was a rubbish. Good for nothing. That *boytjie* should have been taken care of years ago. I almost had him that night, but he got away."

Alet felt a pang when she thought of what Jakob had endured. "Who gave you the right to play God over people's lives like that?"

Adriaan's neck stiffened. "You have no idea what I have had to do to keep this country safe, Alet." He pointed a finger at her. "To keep you safe."

Alet winced at the arrogant conviction of his words. "And Professor Koch too?"

Adriaan shook his head. "I had nothing to do with that."

"You don't expect me to—"

"He was always a terrible driver, easily distracted. Nico would never have testified. We had an understanding. He'd be in it just as deep as I was if he talked. When I heard about the crash, I had to make sure that he left nothing behind. I sent someone."

"The man who attacked me."

"You were supposed to stay away, Alet. I made that clear. This whole mess. You ended up in the middle of it. If you only bloody well listened."

"How did you know about Tessa, Adriaan?" Benjamin's tone was strangely calm. It made Alet nervous.

"You led me to her, De Beer. That day in Triomf. Thanks to you, I had an alias and I had a picture. Never would have put the two together myself. Tokkie Mynhardt did the rest when he posted those photos of the march. Quite a coincidence, I thought, Jakob being in the same town as your girlfriend. So I dug around. Found out who his father was, who she was."

"I told you years ago to walk away or else." Benjamin pressed the gun to Alet's temple. "Unlike you, I keep my promises."

Adriaan held his hands up. "Wait. It's me you really want. Leave her out of it."

"Tessa was everything to me. I want to see the look in your eyes when I destroy the thing most precious to you."

Adriaan pointed his gun at Benjamin. "I will kill you first before I let that happen."

"Really think you can make the shot, Adriaan?" Benjamin let go of Alet and raised the gun without warning, the shot deafening next to her ear. She pushed away from him without thinking, running toward the ruin. Her father was on the ground, a bloodstain spreading on his abdomen, the Makarov still in his hand. He squeezed a round off past her. Alet dove to the ground as Benjamin returned fire, wondering why she wasn't dead. Her dad fell back, his face pale. Alet grabbed the Makarov from his hand and fired blindly in Benjamin's direction. The barrage was met with silence. She scanned the clearing. He wasn't there.

"Stay with me, *Pa*." Alet wrapped her arms around Adriaan and dragged him behind the walls of the ruin, his blood warm on her.

"Alet, I . . ." Adriaan's head lolled. She lowered him against the wall and looked back through the doorway.

Benjamin was out of his hiding place, coming toward them. Alet braced herself against the wall, the Makarov shaking in her left hand. *Get it together, Berg.* She stepped into the doorway and raised the gun. A simple click filled the silence.

"I'm not stupid, Alet. I counted rounds." Benjamin was in front of her, his paleness unreal against the gritty backdrop of the ruin.

No. This is not how this ends. Alet lashed out, the Makarov's butt making contact with his face. Something cracked. Benjamin's hands were on her throat before she had the chance to enjoy the small victory of breaking his nose.

"It's over now," Benjamin said. He pushed her down next to her father. Adriaan made an ineffectual move toward Benjamin. Benjamin kicked him away like a dog. Adriaan stayed down.

Benjamin raised the gun to Alet's head. "Hold on, Adriaan. Don't be in such a hurry to leave us. I want you to see this before you go."

Sound ricocheted, a deafening confusion. Benjamin's pale eyes locked with Alet's, his mouth slightly open. His body crumpled, a marionette without strings, blood spurting onto her from a wound in his neck. Behind him, in the doorway, stood Mathebe, his uniform disheveled, his tie missing, sweat streaming down his face. For a moment they just looked at each other. Alet put her hand in front of her mouth, hysteria suddenly taking over.

Mathebe got down on the floor next to her and held her to him, patting her back rhythmically as if she was a baby. "It is all right, Constable," he repeated in a hushed voice. "It is all over now."

17

"You should be in bed, Constable." Mathebe stood stiffly in the door-way of Alet's hospital room, clutching a plastic shopping bag.

"You should be with your family, Sergeant." Alet sat back down on her bed, dizzy from the effort of standing up. "Besides, I'm really sick of peeing in a pan." She reached for the remote of the small TV in her room and switched off the latest episode of *Generations*. With only the basic stations available, she had become fascinated by the soap opera over the past couple of days. The actors flipped constantly be-tween Afrikaans, English, Xhosa, Sotho, Tswana, Zulu, and a few other languages she couldn't identify. It had a curious effect on her. The black people in the country had had to be multilingual for a long time, transcending barriers out of necessity. It had carried over, even though the born-free generation didn't need to do it to survive any-more. Perhaps that was the way forward for everybody living in this country now, no matter their skin color. They were supposed to be the rainbow nation; perhaps they should all adopt a rainbow tongue. Alet thought about learning Xhosa, like Mathebe, so they could shoot the breeze on patrol. Perhaps in his mother tongue he'd have a sense of humor.

"Christmas pudding." Mathebe held the plastic bag out to her. "Miriam made it."

"Got a spoon?"

Mathebe produced one from the bag, along with a container filled with baked pudding covered in thick custard.

"Tell Miriam I owe her big-time." Alet negotiated the spoon with

449

her left hand. "All I've been getting here are snotty eggs and sand-paper toast. The gunshot didn't get me, but starvation just might."

"How do you feel, Constable?"

"Doctor says I could be out of here by Monday. The shoulder is buggered, but maybe with some physical therapy, who knows, hey?" Alet hoped the cheery front she put on would belie the fact that she didn't believe a word of it. She had trouble moving her right arm. Holding and firing a gun anytime in the near future wasn't going to happen, which meant she'd be stuck behind the service desk.

"I would have brought flowers." Mathebe motioned to the single small bouquet on the nightstand. It was from Theo, delivered with a courteously short visit.

"Flowers die. It's depressing." Alet couldn't hide the embarrass-ment in her voice. "Food is definitely better."

Mathebe shifted uncomfortably in his seat. "Your father—"

"*Ja*, I know. The nurse told me he's in the ICU."

"Would you like to see him? I could go with you."

Alet shook her head. "He's unconscious. Wouldn't matter anyway." She had thought about it almost constantly, lying awake in that hospi-tal bed between doses of pain meds. Someone more educated in these things might have called it avoidance, but Alet knew the word well enough. What she felt was an all-encompassing shame.

"You solved the case, Constable." Mathebe dropped his gaze, his discomfort clear.

"We solved it." Alet smiled at him. "Hey, any news from the Hawks?"

"The captain and Sergeant Strijdom have been suspended, pend-ing the outcome of the investigation."

"They believed you?"

"I offered them proof, which is better." Mathebe cracked a smile. "Dr. Oosthuizen admitted that he drugged Miss Pienaar under pres-sure from the captain, as you suspected."

"Bastard."

"The captain wanted to make sure that Mr. Mens could never talk about his death-squad activities."

"So he finished my father's kill. Made it look like Tilly ran him over. Two flies with one shot and he's in the old man's good graces to boot."

Mathebe nodded. "Miss Pienaar has been cleared, although she is still under investigation for human trafficking. Perhaps with her co-operation, she might receive a lenient sentence."

"What about Skosana?"

"His body was discovered on the Terblanche farm, along with one of his men."

"Benjamin?"

"Yes. He had been following you. Mrs. Frieda Berg stated that he called the house the night before, left a message that your father had to meet him at the place where Mrs. Pienaar had died. He had set his plan in motion and Skosana and his gang were in the way."

"Did Jana . . . ?" Alet felt bad for not asking sooner.

"Mrs. Terblanche gave birth to a son. But she and Mr. Terblanche will both stand trial if the case makes it to court."

"*Ja.* If." Alet knew better than to get her hopes up. The complexity of what had happened suddenly hit home. She put her pudding down, her appetite gone. "My dad knew about Benjamin, all these years, you know."

"Colonel Berg did try to stop him. It would appear that he gave up the Angel Killer case because Mr. De Beer had threatened your life."

"Father of the Year."

"Colonel Berg's prints matched the partial in Mrs. Pienaar's house. I believe he went back to see if he could find something on the where-abouts of Mr. De Beer. He did not realize that Mrs. Pienaar didn't know."

"Trudie died for nothing." A burning sensation flared behind Alet's eyes. Benjamin might have been a killer, but Alet's father, the man she had idolized all her life, was the real monster. "I don't under-stand how all of this happened, Johannes."

"Sometimes when things like these are allowed to fester for a long time, Constable, they cannot help but rise to the surface. If your father did not send you to Unie, to his old contact, he would not have noticed Mrs. Pienaar in those photographs. If he had not killed her on the Terblanche farm, we would not have uncovered what Mr. Wexler had involved the town in."

"My dad thought he was hiding me away. Instead he put me in a snake pit."

"He misjudged you. He did not think that you would go to his old colleague Professor Koch and to Mr. van Niekerk when you could not find the resources to do the job well here." Mathebe looked almost proud of her. "He did not know you very well."

The dam broke, silent tears tracing a path down Alet's cheeks. "Thank you, Johannes. For saving my life."

Mathebe put his hands on hers. "We are partners."

"How did you know where to find me?"

"Mr. Terblanche called me. You were gone by the time I got to the house. There was a dead man in the kitchen, and no note to explain." Mathebe lifted a brow in disapproval. "The fire took everybody's attention, but I noticed your father among the farmers and volunteers. It was strange to me that he was there. I saw him break away from the group. That is when I lost him, but him being on that mountain made me wonder. I went to the place where Mrs. Pienaar was found. It was only a guess. If I had been wrong . . ." He shook his head.

Alet took a deep breath. "Johannes, I want you to know that I will honor my promise. I asked Theo to hand over everything we found on my dad. He will be prosecuted if he pulls through."

Mathebe closed his eyes. "You have fought to give Mrs. Pienaar justice, Constable Berg. For that, you will always have my respect."

Alet tried to hold on to that moment in the months that followed, stuck on desk duty, mandatory psychiatric counseling, and physical therapy twice a week. She only saw Adriaan again at his trial, his testimony stoic, detached, denying horrors that had had her sobbing into the late hours. He never made eye contact as she took the stand to testify against him, his gaze focused in the distance, a self-righteous set to his jaw.

Alet saw her face plastered on the front page of every newspaper in the country, her life dissected by a media frenzy fiercer than a shark attack. She'd become known as the monster's daughter. Some postulated that she betrayed her own blood to get ahead. A publisher approached her with a book deal if she would "tell all," calling her a hero. Alet stopped answering her phone after that.

Booking on her shift one afternoon, Alet noticed that the door to the evidence room had been left open. As she reached for the handle to lock it, she saw April among the shelves, his back to her. She was about to crack a joke, tell him to go home to his new wife, when she realized that he was putting drug evidence into his backpack. Alet walked away without a word, tired of kicking against the stream, so tired, willing to give over, to maybe just once not be at the center of the storm but instead to strive for harmony, even though it meant that she would be betraying everything she had fought for. There was a moment of decision, when anger fell away and no good reason to stay on the force remained, and Alet hesitated too long.

Alet quit the police and moved to Cape Town, where she took a position at a private security firm, doing shifts as a first responder to emergency calls from those who could pay for their safety. The industry was booming, the pay good enough. Once in a while, when the fog lay like a blanket over Table Mountain, she would call in sick and take the cable car to the top, despite the ticket-seller's warnings of poor visibility. She'd wander around in the dense whiteness, the world simply disappearing in a soft haze as the ghosts of the past walked with her. Tessa. Benjamin. Jakob. It was hard to imagine that death could have brought them peace. In time, she knew, people would forget who they were, and who she was. They would even forget about her father and the things done by men like him, as they had forgotten the struggle for their freedom. But Alet knew she would never have that luxury.

Acknowledgments

Thanks to my agent, Markus Hoffmann, and the staff at Regal Literary for your support and hard work in getting this manuscript into the right hands. Thanks to my editor, Mark Krotov, and everyone at Melville House. I owe a great deal to Audrey Niffenegger for her help and guidance, and for telling me to stick to my vision for the book. To my first readers, Mike Bogart, Gary Stephens, Rob Shouse, Jordan Bray, Kevin Kane, Melissa Spor, Nic Bernstein, Lena Kondo, and especially Chris Marnach, who indulged me in many hours of conversation about Alet and Mathebe. Thanks to my husband, Steve, for his unwavering encouragement and support. A big thank-you to Anel and Jan Burger for their hospitality, and for sharing their world with me. And to Dr. Andrew Faull, for generously sharing his work and steering me toward helpful resources. I'm sure I've missed names, and for that my sincerest apologies.

Reading Group Guide

1. How does *The Monster's Daughter* play with and combine established genres? How does this use of genre impact your reading of the novel?

2. Tessa and Benjamin's origins are both tied to Dr. Leath's experiments, but they each experience vastly different childhoods. How is it that two characters with so much in common diverge, developing into entirely opposite people?

3. When Andrew begs Benjamin to leave Tessa, he states that he has "known men like you"(141). What exactly does Andrew mean by this? What qualities does he recognize in Ben and why are they so threatening?

4. Tessa asserts that the marginalization that she and Phillip feel are the same, while her brother insists she could not possibly understand his experiences as a black man. How is Tessa's assumption problematic? Is it possible Phillip is underestimating her? How might their views on the subject evolve throughout the novel? Look closely at pages 114-116.

5. Numerous characters in the book, Tessa and Alet in particular, attempt to start over by resettling in new places. Is it possible to truly start over? Can you actually escape the past or is it destined to permeate the present? Look closely at page 341.

6. After killing a man Benjamin observes, "The more the man struggled, the more alive Benjamin felt. This was personal, a connection that bound them to each other, predator and prey. Jooste had once offered him power. Money, control—all these things were arbitrary compared to the true power of taking a life." How are concepts of power and violence intertwined in *The Monster's Daughter*? How is power equated with violence? In seeking power, are Benjamin and others actually seeking violence?

7. Religion plays a prominent role within the novel. It is used as the justification for war, discrimination, and the actions of individuals. Examine the differing ways in which characters utilize religion. How does Ben in particular construct his identity around religion? Look closely at pages 226, 406–407.

8. Central to the novel is the question of nature vs. nurture. Alet dreads what possible characteristics she has inherited from her father, while Tessa wonders if she can truly save Tilly from following in the ignorant footsteps of her birthparents. Discuss whether the characters that populate the novel are predisposed to certain temperaments, or if they can in fact escape their genetic makeup.

9. Why does Alet decide not to turn in April for stealing drugs from the evidence room? Is this harmony Alet strives for worth "betraying everything she had fought for?" (453)

10. Monsters play an essential role in *The Monster's Daughter*. Who are these monsters? How does the novel define monstrosity, and what does it mean to be given such a label?

About the Author

MICHELLE PRETORIUS was born in Bloemfontein, South Africa. She has written for *Bookslut*, *Word Riot*, and *The Copperfield Review*, among other publications. She received an MFA in Fiction Writing from Columbia College Chicago and is currently a PhD student at Ohio University.